Praise for

'The story is twisty and excit......ng is pacy and there are plenty of gun fights . . . *Silent Predator* is a page-turner and a great way to spend a winter evening, transported to somewhere warm and exotic'

Independent Weekly

'The author evokes a strong sense of place and the plot – fraught with dangers and unexpected twists – unfolds at a satisfying pace'
The Age, Melbourne

'The fluid writing and fascinating descriptions of the Botswana countryside, and its people, will keep most readers happily turning the pages . . . In all, a well-written and highly recommended debut mystery'

Canberra Times

'Good writing, some memorably exciting scenes and some real feeling for its African setting. Park sorts out his heroes and villains with admirable pacing and inventiveness. There's also a lively plot, which is detailed and clever without ever becoming convoluted'
Sydney Morning Herald

Tony Park was born in 1964 and grew up in the western suburbs of Sydney. He has worked as a newspaper reporter in Australia and England, a government press secretary, a public relations consultant, and a freelance writer. He is also a major in the Australian Army Reserve and served six months in Afghanistan in 2002 as the public affairs officer for the Australian ground forces. He and his wife, Nicola, divide their time between their home in Sydney and southern Africa, where they own a tent and a Series III Land Rover.

SILENT
PREDATOR

TONY PARK

Quercus

First published in Australia in 2008 by Pan Macmillan
This paperback edition published in Great Britain in 2010 by

Quercus
21 Bloomsbury Square
London
WC1A 2NS

A CIP catalogue record for this book is available
from the British Library

ISBN 978 0 85738 117 0

10 9 8 7 6 5 4 3 2 1

Printed and bound in Great Britain by Clays Ltd, St Ives plc

For Nicola

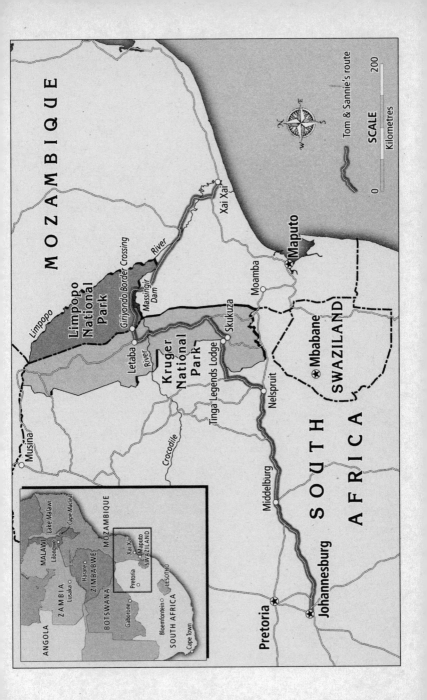

Prologue

Today

Tom Furey groaned.

Each beat of his heart sent a dart of pain to his head as his brain tried to break through the bone of his skull. His tongue was so swollen and dry his first thought was that he might choke. He was aware of a bright light shining on the other side of closed eyelids. He opened his eyes and blinked, the small movement eliciting another moan.

There was an almost mechanical noise beside him, like a motor with a faulty exhaust. Snoring. He turned his head – more suffering – and saw the woman lying on her back, mouth agape, her bare breasts rising and falling. The tangle of sheets was across her lower legs. Like him, she was naked.

Daylight.

'Shit!'

He groped on the side table for his watch and mobile phone. It was six am and the bright African sunlight was streaming in through the sliding glass doors. 'Shit!' he said aloud again. Ignoring the ache behind his eyes he swung out of the king-size bed, grappled his way through the ceiling-to-floor mosquito net and hopped on one leg while he pulled on his shorts. He grabbed the mobile phone and checked it. Not only had the alarm not gone off, it wasn't even set.

Tom buckled his belt and slipped his nine-millimetre Glock 17 into the circular pancake holster above his right hip. He strapped on his watch and checked the time again. Two minutes past six. 'Shit.'

The weight of his pistol was balanced on his left side by an Asp extendable baton, a spare magazine of ammunition and a Surefire torch, all in black leather pouches. He stuffed his remaining two spare magazines in his shorts pocket, along with his Gerber folding knife. Despite the rush he would have felt naked leaving the room without any of his personal kit.

He pulled on a blue polo shirt and left it untucked so that it covered the equipment, then forced his feet into trainers with no socks. Thank god, casual dress was the order of the day.

With nothing more than an angry shake of his head at the sleeping woman, he barged out the door and along the raised walkway of darkly stained wooden logs that wound through the thick thorny bushes behind and between each of the separate luxury suites of the safari lodge. He paused to knock on the door of the unit next to his. 'Bernard?' he called. No answer. Of course there bloody well wouldn't be an answer.

The advisor was ex-Royal Navy. He wouldn't be late for duty. Tom jogged on.

The morning air was still cool, but the sun was already hot on his face as he glanced out across the Sabie River, its smattering of granite boulders glowing pink in the dawn's rays. A hippo grunted, mocking him with its deep belly laugh as his shoes pounded the deck.

He slowed to a walk, to catch his breath and maintain some show of dignity as he entered the sumptuous reception area, where early morning tea and coffee and rusks and fruit were laid on a long table beneath the thatched cathedral-style roof.

'What's going on? You're late.' Inspector Sannie van Rensburg looked at her watch and frowned.

The South African minister was talking to an aide, an empty coffee cup in his hand. He looked at Tom and then beyond him, down the walkway.

Tom motioned her aside with a hand on her elbow. She shrugged off his touch. 'Where's Greeves?' he whispered.

'That's what we want to know. Not only are you late, but he hasn't shown up – neither has his policy advisor.'

He saw the naked disapproval on her face, of him as well as of his tardiness. She must have guessed what had gone on the night before. It was no time to think about what she thought of him. 'He must be on the phone to the UK. I'll go and check on him.'

'I already did that,' she said. 'There was no answer.'

'Why didn't you come and find me?' he asked.

'*Ag,* I've got my own man to look after. I can't be running around after you, Tom.' Her Afrikaans accent, which he'd found appealingly exotic at first, grated on his ears. He strode back down the walkway to the suite of the UK Minister for Defence Procurement. Tom prayed that he was right, that The Honourable Robert Greeves was on the phone to his immediate superior, the Secretary of State for Defence, or a senior bureaucrat on some urgent matter of State, and that was why he hadn't answered the door and was late.

He felt physically sick, but didn't know why. He'd had only one beer the night before. He came to the third suite, took a deep breath to quell the dizziness and steady himself, and knocked. No answer.

'Sir? It's Tom,' he called.

He waited for exactly a minute and knocked again. Nothing. He pulled out his mobile phone and dialled the minister's private number. It was for emergencies only, but Tom could feel his pulse rate rising. Straight through to voicemail. He tried the policy advisor's mobile. It rang out and he heard Bernard Joyce's cultured voice on the message.

Tom went on to Bernard's suite, even though he had already tried it once, and knocked on the door. 'Bernard?' Nothing again. He thumped harder. 'Bernard!'

He jogged down the decking to his own unit, opened the door, strode in and called Greeves's suite. While he waited he saw, through the haze of mosquito netting, the woman still sprawled there. If she was awake she was hiding it. He cursed himself – his weakness. The landline rang out. No answer. 'Shit,' he said. 'Stay cool.' There was no answer in Bernard's

4

suite. They weren't talking on their room phones.

Tom headed back to reception. He ignored the South African policewoman's enquiring look and went to the duty manager, a young white guy called Piet. 'I need the key to Greeves's suite.'

'But, Tom, man, that's highly irregular, can't we just –'

'Now.' The man obeyed this time, unquestioning.

Tom forced a smile for the South African Defence Minister, Patrick Dule, who was having a hard time hiding his impatience. Greeves wasn't the kind to go off with Bernard for an impromptu morning stroll. Tom had learned in a very short time that when a schedule was made he stuck to it, and woe betide anyone who was a minute late.

Tom jogged back to Greeves's suite. Instinctively, he raised his polo shirt, so that the butt of his Glock was exposed, and easier to draw. 'Mr Greeves, sir?' he called again.

He heard footsteps and spun around. It was her. Sannie held up a skeleton key of her own. Great minds, he thought to himself, without mirth. 'Go to number four – Bernard Joyce's suite. There was no answer there, either. Let yourself in.'

She nodded. No time for smart-mouthing any more.

He let himself into the minister's luxurious room. It was identical to his in its safari chic décor and opulence. He took in the signs immediately. The fallen lamp stand, the sheets in disarray, the tangle of mosquito netting on the floor, the bloody palm print on the open sliding door. He drew his pistol. A laptop

5

computer was open, but face down. Greeves's wallet and mobile phone, switched off, on the bedside table.

Tom moved quickly through the rest of the suite, checking the bathroom and toilet. No signs of the man, other than his toiletries and some clothes in the bathroom. He went back outside and saw Sannie running along the boardwalk.

'Joyce,' she panted. 'He's gone. Signs of a struggle. It doesn't look like it was an animal attack.'

Tom shook his head. 'Greeves is gone too. Wallet full of cash and mobile phone are by the bed, so it wasn't money they were after.'

'Oh, dear god,' she said, and it was more prayer than blaspheming.

And Tom Furey needed all the prayers he could get, because he'd just woken to a protection officer's worst nightmare.

1

Eight days earlier

'I need to piss.'

Tom smiled, even though it was too dark in the back of the transit van to see the young constable's face. He sighed and whispered, 'You should have gone before we left.' He'd been waiting for this – as the boy had been fidgeting for the past hour.

'Yes, Dad.'

'Watch it, Harry,' Tom said. He kept his eye on the house, number fourteen, staring at it through the peephole in the side panel of the van. The light was still on in the front room of the nondescript pebble-dashed semi in the quiet Enfield street. He wondered if the neighbours had any idea what was going on behind that green door. They'd be mostly commuters, he reckoned, with safe jobs. Mid-level office workers, secretaries, tradesmen – and they would have a fit if they knew they were living in the same street as a bunch of people smugglers. Someone must have noticed something, though, or they wouldn't be here. Londoners had been jolted out of their apathy after seven-seven, the suicide bombings on the tube and the buses, and curtain twitching sometimes paid off.

'It's only the truth, Tom. You *are* old enough to be my bleedin' father.'

'Perhaps I am. I was in uniform in Islington in the eighties. Your mum ever go to a Bryan Ferry concert?'

'Now you're making me sick.'

At the far end of the cramped space, Steve, the civilian information technology expert, looked over the top of his magazine. Unlike Harry, Steve, whom Harry had quietly dubbed 'the Anorak' by virtue of his job rather than his expensive overcoat, could keep quiet in an op.

Tom Furey sat on a fold-out canvas and tubular metal camp stool, which he had brought with him along with a Thermos of tea, sleeping bag, sandwiches, *The Times* crossword and a paperback novel. He pointed to the last item he'd brought. 'What do you think that empty peanut jar in the corner is for? Or did you think there'd be a chemical toilet in here?' Tom shook his head, but kept his gaze focused on the front door of number fourteen.

'None of this is what I expected,' Harry said. 'It's hardly like on the telly, is it? No electronic monitoring, no bank of TV sets, no infra-red night vision surveillance camera. Certainly no bleedin' chemical toilet. Just a naff old van lined with bloody foam and plywood and a peephole. God save us if this is the front line of the high-tech war on terrorism. And I still need to piss.'

'I got a bladder infection from sharing my piss jar with a bloke during a surveillance op in '92, watching an IRA safe house in Kilburn, and I'm not going to make that mistake again. Like pissing razorblades, it was.'

'Oh dear . . . the IRA. Tell us what else you did in the war, Dad.'

The members of the old Metropolitan Police Special Branch – also known as SO12 – had a wide array of skills which were in demand in the new fight against terrorism, and the reason they were sitting in the van was because the word was that the targets inside number fourteen – Pakistani gentlemen – had possible links to al-Qaeda. As well as prostitutes and illegal workers, their clients were believed to include a bomb maker or two.

Tom had joined the Met twenty-one years earlier, at the age of twenty-two. After his sixteen-week training course at Hendon he'd graduated as a police constable and served his probation in Brixton. Three years later, with the IRA's mainland bombing campaign in full swing, he'd applied to join Special Branch. Being the first on the scene after a bomb had severed an army recruiter in two outside his shopfront had galvanised Tom into taking this next step in his career.

After passing a selection board he'd gone back to Hendon for eleven weeks of training as a detective. As a detective constable he'd done time on B Squad – the Irish squad – and on surveillance on S Squad. Working undercover, often dressed in the foul-smelling rags of a vagrant on the cold streets of London, spending time holed up in abandoned buildings and cold, darkened vans, he'd honed his observation skills and learned patience.

'Give us the peanut jar,' Harry said.

'Quiet.'

After passing his sergeant's exam Tom had reluctantly gone back into uniform – the obligation came with the promotion. He spent time in his new rank at Enfield – another reason why he was once more on the town's streets. He knew the area better than most of the others on this hastily cobbled together operation.

Eventually he'd made his way back to Special Branch, where he believed he belonged and would see out his career. After completing firearms training he'd gone to A Squad, where he became a qualified protection officer. Like anyone else in the job he cringed at the term bodyguard, but that was how a civilian or, worse, a newspaper reporter, would have described him.

There had been innumerable wins for Special Branch against the Irish, but it was some high-profile cases of alleged heavy handedness – including one that was made into a movie – which made the politicians want to rein in the Branch and soften its image. Reorganisations after September 11 and the London bombings of 7 July 2005 had created a new unit to deal with terrorism, but had also removed the structure whereby detectives could transfer easily from squad to squad in the Branch, developing and practising new skills while staying under the same command.

The latest round of restructuring had hived off specialist protection – Tom's specialty – into a new unit,

SO1, under the Special Operations umbrella. Police counter-terrorism operations were now handled by SO15.

Tom Furey had provided protection for a plethora of politicians, a former prime minister, a couple of European monarchs, African dictators, and an Arabian prince or two. Visiting dignitaries were assigned British policemen to guard them when in the UK, and Tom, who had no 'principal' of his own to protect these days, was on a roster of unattached protection officers who waited their turn potentially to take a bullet for a foreign VIP. He liked the work – he met interesting people and occasionally travelled abroad – but if he was honest with himself it was no high-minded calling which kept him in this job. It was the money. With shift allowances he made two to three times what he would as a detective elsewhere in the Met. The downside was that divorces were common in his line of work. He and Alex had been able to cope because they'd spent their entire marriage out of sync when it came to working hours. They'd compensated with some wonderfully luxurious overseas holidays, made possible by their combined wages which were nothing to sneeze at.

Occasionally, when SO15 was stretched thin – such as now – Tom was called on to lend a hand with surveillance or other specialist tasks now out of the remit of a protection officer. The threat level against the UK had recently been upped, as a result of an increased troop presence in Afghanistan, and resources were stretched thin.

Harry, too, was a protection officer, though unlike

11

under the old Special Branch structure he was neither experienced in surveillance nor a qualified detective. He'd only been out of uniform six months. It was a sign of the times.

'Do you expect me to piss my pants, Tom?'

'Shut it,' Tom hissed back at Harry. He spoke softly but clearly and slowly into his radio: 'All call signs, two targets moving. Heading left, towards the high street. Usual clothing. I have eyeball. Four-two, they're heading your way, over.' Tom repeated the direction of movement so there could be no confusion among the other call signs in the area – a mix of police and MI5 intelligence service personnel – about where the two young Pakistani men were heading. Four-two was the code name for an undercover policeman on a motorcycle, Detective Constable Paul Davis in this case, who was currently at the end of the suburban side street, where it met Enfield Road.

Harry was quiet now and Tom could almost smell the sudden burst of adrenaline in the dank confines of the surveillance van.

Three hundred metres away, down the end of the road, around the corner from the off-licence, was a kebab shop. It was the habit of the two targets to walk to the eatery between seven-thirty and eight pm each evening to buy their supper and sit down at the laminate-topped tables in the padded booth seating to eat. With kebabs, Cokes and tea and cigarettes to follow, the meal usually took two hours, according to the other watchers.

Tom spoke into the hand-held radio again. 'Four-two, I've lost eyeball, do you have them, over?'

'Roger. They're on their way to dinner, over. Heading for the shop,' Paul said.

Tom radioed the constable who had driven the van on to the plot – the location of the operation – and told him to come and pick them up. The officer, who had been watching television and drinking numerous cups of tea with an elderly couple who lived ten doors away from the target house, walked up the street. He wore blue tradesman's overalls and carried a canvas tool bag. He climbed into the van without acknowledging the others in the back, started the engine and drove away from the high street, around a bend and out of sight of number fourteen.

'Right, let's go,' Tom said, when the driver switched off the engine.

The back door of the van swung open and Tom, Steve the Anorak and Harry, who seemed to have forgotten his bursting bladder, climbed out.

'Not too fast, now,' Tom said. He looked up and down the street, which was deserted.

Tom wore jeans and a thick black roll-neck jumper, with a duffel coat over the top. It was cold out, a chilly November evening, but the jacket's other purpose was to conceal his weapon. He carried a tool bag, though, like the driver's, it was more for show than anything else. The tools of his trade for this job – his set of lock picks – were in his pocket.

Tom led them back up the street, then along a side path to the semi's back door. Within three minutes they were inside. He didn't need to tell the other two to be quick or quiet, but he reminded Harry, 'You stay here and watch the back. I'll go with our friend.'

The house smelled musty and unloved. He checked the kitchen. Tea bags and a kettle, no plates in the sink or evidence of home cooking. These boys ate out every night and their routine would be their undoing. With more people, more resources, they could have conducted a detailed search of the house, but tonight they had the Anorak, so the computer was their highest priority, and protecting the information technology expert was Tom's.

He took up position in the front room, peering through a crack in the curtains so he could watch the front street for activity.

The computer was in the front room as well, on a cheap flat-pack desk. Apart from the machine and the second-hand office chair in which the Anorak sat, was a tatty velvet couch and a mismatched armchair.

Tom glanced back over his shoulder and saw Steve's pimply young face bathed in a blue glow as he booted up the computer. Fingers encased in latex gloves tapped furiously at the keyboard. He heard a dog bark and the hairs stood up on the back of his neck. 'Everything okay back there?' he radioed Harry.

'Dunno. Something's spooked the dog in the yard behind us. Should I go take a look?'

'No, stay where you are, but keep watch.'

'Fuck,' the Anorak said. 'You should see this.'

'What is it?' Tom asked, his eyes still on the street.

'Porn!'

Tom shook his head. 'Bloody hell. Just get on with it, will you. You know what we're after – emails, names, message traffic. I shouldn't have to tell you your job.'

'No, but, Jesus, you should see this. It's some sick shit, man.'

Tom was about to say something when Paul Davis's voice hissed in his ear. 'This is Four-two. Targets are turning back. Just walked into the shop then came straight back out again. There's an argument going on, by the look of it, and one of them is searching his jacket. Looks like he might have forgotten his wallet. Repeat, they're heading back.'

'Shit,' Tom said. He looked over at Steve, who stared fixedly at the screen. Tom noticed, for the first time, the black leather billfold on the computer table.

'Shut it down, we're going.'

'But this is gold!'

'Leave the fucking porn alone and close down. They're on their way back, so we're moving.'

'No way, man, we can't leave this. I'm taking it with me. This is more than just porn.'

Tom shook his head. This was turning into a monumental fuck-up. 'You know as well as I do we can't nick the computer. Can't you save whatever it is onto a disk or something?'

Steve fumbled in the pocket of his overcoat and fished out a USB jump stick.

'Movement!' Tom heard the word in his earpiece and drew the Glock from his holster with practised ease. He kept a spare magazine of bullets in the right-hand pocket of his jacket so that when he reached for his pistol the added weight helped swing the tail of the duffel out of the way.

'What is it?'

'I thought I saw a man's head, moving along

number twelve's side fence, on the other side,' Harry answered.

'Keep a watch. But get ready to move. The targets are on their way back.'

'Shit.' Harry drew his weapon.

A dog barked and Tom's peripheral vision registered lights being turned on in neighbouring homes. A baby screamed in the house next door, through the communal wall. It was a good reminder there were innocents all around them.

'We're going.' Tom reached out and grabbed Steve by the collar of his coat, but the IT expert brushed his hand away with more strength than he'd expected. 'Leave me alone, Furey! This is bloody important.'

'Shit, there's definitely someone moving on the other side of the back fence,' Harry whispered, his voice barely audible in Tom's earpiece. 'I can see him through the fence palings. What should I do?'

'Move now, out the front door. No arguments,' Tom said to the man behind the computer, then repeated the instructions to Harry.

'Two minutes, that's all I need,' the Anorak pleaded.

Tom swore. He looked out the window, down the street, and saw the two targets walking towards them, a hundred metres away.

Harry came in through the back door. 'Lost sight of the geezer.'

'Tell me this is worth blowing the whole operation over,' Tom said to Steve.

Steve looked up at him, his already sun-deprived face ghostly in the wash of illumination. The man swallowed and Tom watched the overly large Adam's apple bob. 'Yes.'

Tom opened the front door and strode onto the pavement, raising his Glock and cross-bracing his firing hand on top of his left wrist. 'Armed police! Get down on the ground, now!' Harry was beside him, mimicking his stance.

The man on the right reached into the pocket of his vinyl bomber jacket and Tom started to squeeze the trigger. Before he pulled it all the way, however, the man was falling, knocked sideways by an invisible sledgehammer. There was no sound of a shot fired, so it wasn't Harry who had downed him. Silencer.

Tom turned and registered a dark shadow moving by the corner of the house. The falling man had drawn not a gun but a set of keys from his pocket. Tom saw he held a small black plastic remote in his hand, the kind used to activate a car alarm, and presumed he pressed the button as he fell. Before he hit the ground his companion was also knocked over. Tom dropped to one knee and looked left. He registered a running man, dressed in black, a pistol in his hand. Harry shifted his aim and opened his mouth to speak.

Before either of them could order the stranger to stop, the house exploded.

2

A fireman found Steve the Anorak's body after the blaze had been extinguished. Harry sat with his feet in the gutter, his head in his hands. There was the smell of fresh vomit near him.

Tom sat on the bonnet of a police Mondeo, his hands wrapped around a takeaway tea in a Styrofoam cup. The local residents had long since foregone their television sets – in fact, some of them were on TV now, fodder for the reporters who roamed from person to person, looking for the neighbour who could describe the conflagration in the most graphic detail. He tenderly fingered the cut above his left eye. A shard of flying glass from number fourteen's front windows had sliced a furrow parallel to his eyebrow, but the ambulance paramedics had been able to close the wound with adhesive butterfly stitches. Despite the crusted blood down his cheek he would be okay.

'Not much left of our computer wizard,' Chief Inspector David Shuttleworth said, his breath clouding as he strode over. 'Looks like the bomb was planted somewhere in the centre of the front room – perhaps even under the computer desk itself.'

'I don't know what was on that machine, guv, other than some porn, but he died for it.'

'Aye, well, there's no way we'll know now,' Shuttleworth said. He fished a packet of Dunhill from his Barbour jacket and offered Tom a cigarette.

Tom shook his head. 'Given up. Again.'

'Suit yourself.' Shuttleworth paused to light up. 'Cock-up hardly begins to describe this one, Tom. What do you make of the presence of the shooter, as well as the Pakistanis?'

Tom shrugged. 'My guess is that he was watching the house, as were we, and he was sneaking in to take up an ambush position, though I have no idea why.'

'Well, we know the two dead chaps were people smugglers, who were supposedly doing their bit for world Jihad by helping out the odd terrorist with papers and money and the like, but why would our man in black shoot them?'

'Because they knew too much and he couldn't risk them being caught?' Tom sipped his tea.

Shuttleworth nodded and took a long drag on his cigarette. The smoke and frozen breath wreathed his head and shoulders in a shimmering aura, backlit by red and blue flashing lights. 'They're getting better at covering their tracks all the time.'

'The IT guy was just about wetting himself over whatever was on that machine.'

'Why did you not just take the computer or the hard drive?'

Tom looked across at his superior and frowned.

They both knew the answer to that question. The United Kingdom might be at war with Islamic fundamentalist terror groups, but they still had to fight by the rule of law.

Shuttleworth checked his notebook again. 'You say he gave no indication about what he'd found on the hard drive other than . . .'

'Porn. Like I told you. "Some sick shit" was all he said, though I'm betting he didn't stay on just to check out some fuck pictures.'

'Well, we've got two dead suspects, three injured civilians from next door, no computer, no computer expert and a masked assassin on the loose. Not to mention a missing protection officer.'

Tom drained his tea and crushed the cup as the rest of Shuttleworth's comment penetrated the ringing that lingered in his ears from the bomb blast. 'Who's missing?'

'Nick.'

'What happened?'

'He was supposed to be at a political fundraising dinner in the city with Robert Greeves this evening, but he didn't show. Caused a hell of a stink. He dropped Greeves at his home at five, but didn't return to collect him at seven. We've tried his home and mobile phone, but there's no answer. Deidre hasn't heard from him either.'

Tom frowned. Nick Roberts had been a friend once – they had joined the Met at about the same age and had matching careers. Nick's ex-wife, Deidre, had worked as a nurse in the same hospital as Tom's wife Alexandra, and it was really the two women who had been close friends. After Nick and Deidre's divorce, and Alex's death, he and Nick had seen little of each other outside of work. As protection officers, both spent long periods away from home. Those absences had cost Nick his marriage but provided blessed relief for Tom, as the job had helped him a little by taking him away on a regular basis from his lonely home full of memories.

'That's odd. I've never heard of him missing a job.'

'Any problems that you know of?' Chief Inspector Shuttleworth, a Scot, was new to their team, having transferred in on promotion, so he still didn't know all of his officers' idiosyncrasies.

'With Nick? Not that I know of. Likes a drink – who doesn't in our job – but he's never called in sick because of a hangover, if that's what you mean. Seems to have a different bird every few weeks.'

Tom felt uncomfortable singing Nick's praises any more than that. Once, when they were both on the same team protecting a visiting African head of state, a group of a dozen expatriate dissidents had staged a protest outside the London restaurant where the president was dining. Nick had warned one of the demonstrators to back off when he approached the principal too closely. The man, who appeared drunk, had told Nick to fuck off. Nick had punched the man, hard and fast in the stomach, with enough force to drop him. Someone on the team – not Tom – had reported the incident. Tom had expected the protestor to lay a formal complaint, and took the view that if he was called to make a statement he would do so, truthfully. Nick had used unnecessary force. Word got back

21

to the squad's former chief superintendent and Nick had been called into his office to explain his version of events. Fortunately for Nick, the complainant never came forward. There had been speculation around the office that a couple of the president's personal staff had leaned on the witness. Tom had noticed a marked cooling in his relationship with Nick and while he never said anything to Tom's face, Tom suspected that Nick thought it was he who had gone to their governor behind his back.

'Deidre didn't seem too worried when I spoke to her. I know divorce is never pretty, but it was like he could have died and she couldn't have cared less.'

Tom shrugged. 'I can call round his place if you like. We – I mean, I – still have a key. Alex and Deidre used to check in on each other's places when we were on holidays. Water the plants and all. Nick stayed in the family home and Deidre bought a new place.'

Shuttleworth nodded. 'Aye, okay. If you find him in bed with a tart or a hangover, shoot him, please, before the Minister for Defence Procurement catches up with him. It'll be the kindest thing all round.'

Shuttleworth had suggested he see the Met's psychiatrist in the morning for stress counselling, but Tom reckoned a lie-in might be a more therapeutic option. It was going to be a late night.

He waved his thanks to the constable who had driven him to his home in Highgate and walked up the steps to his terrace house. Southwood Lane was pretty posh these days – the habitat of bankers, lawyers, doctors and the like. Though he didn't wear a uniform he was pretty sure most of the people up and down the street knew he was a copper. It was probably why they kept their distance. He'd grown up in the house and lived there most of his life, apart from six years in his early twenties after he'd joined the Met. Tom was an only child whose parents had him late in life and they had passed away, within a year of each other, when he was twenty-eight. He'd been seeing Alex for four years by then and it had seemed logical, in a strange way, that the passing of his folks had been the catalyst for him to ask her to marry him.

Tom fingered the faint scar above his right eyebrow. It was barely noticeable these days, but he saw it, and touched it, every morning when he shaved. His white summer uniform shirt had been drenched in blood from the cut inflicted by a drunk armed with a broken beer bottle the night he'd met Alex, nineteen years ago. She was still an intern and she was so beautiful he couldn't help but ask her out on a date as she stitched him back together. She'd laughed and told him that as far as she knew there were rules against that sort of thing. He persisted. She relented. She was an Essex girl made good and he'd been sure they would grow old together. Her shifts and his unusual hours at home and abroad meant they had never really lived like a normal couple. They joked to friends that they only ever saw each other on birthdays – and never Christmas because they were both working. They'd both planned on retiring early, to make up for all the lost nights.

And here he was. Alone for more than a year now.

Cheated of his life and his wife. He tried not to dwell on it, but everything in the house reminded him of her. How could it not? He left the hall light off as he walked through to the kitchen. Maybe by staying in the dark the memories would dim. He found the key on the hook by the little blackboard where she used to write her shopping lists. It was right where she had left it. Alex was the last person to have touched the key to Nick's home. He stood there in the darkened kitchen and closed his eyes. He held the key in his fist and squeezed it until he felt the pain of the serrated metal edges digging into his palm. He opened his eyes and walked out again, ignoring the four or five letters sitting on the hallway floor.

Tom's old hard top E-type Jag started first time and the V12 purred deeply, like a giant cat welcoming its owner home with a leg rub. Alex had wanted to get a new car, but Tom liked old things – old British things – and with overtime he could even afford to fill the tank once in a while. He could never see himself driving a Renault or something Japanese.

As he drove, settling into a slow lane of traffic, a vision of Alex's wasted body, her eyes so deep in their sockets they looked bruised, popped into his head. He screwed his eyes shut for a second. A horn blasted beside him and he realised he had momentarily drifted out of his lane. He forced himself to concentrate and ignored the young black man's abuse as the boy racer overtook him. 'Get a grip,' he said out loud in the car. The clock on the dashboard said nine pm. He felt like a drink.

Tom let the traffic signs lead him to the A406 and

joined the rolling traffic jam for the leg that would take him around the western side of London to Kingston in the south west, which was where Nick lived, not far from Henry the Eighth's Hampton Court palace. He became conscious of a car beside him, not accelerating or decelerating. He looked across and saw a blonde woman in a BMW Z4 convertible. Pretty, late thirties or well-preserved early forties. She wore a plain white blouse – a businesswoman, he guessed, maybe driving home from work late. She looked across and smiled at him. He smiled back, but mustn't have done a very good job because she planted her foot and whizzed past him. Twenty years ago he might have done the same and chased her through the traffic. Now he just felt guilty as Alex smiled back at him, bravely, despite the tubes draining and filling her poisoned body. He shook his head. They – he – had just passed the one year anniversary of her death. That had been a tough, drunken night.

The drive took him past Richmond Park. Once the hunting estate of kings, it was now a Royal Park, open to all. He negotiated his way off the A307, around Kingston's town centre, and found the quiet street where Nick lived. He'd been there with Alex enough times to remember the way. He pulled up outside the Edwardian semi. He rapped on the door and waited. No reply. He tried again.

He turned the key and opened the door, listening for beeps. He didn't recall there being an alarm in the house and he hoped Nick hadn't decided to install one since his last visit nearly two years ago.

The house was only a few degrees warmer than the

cool night air, so the central heating must have been off. 'Nick?' he called. He walked on thick white carpet down the hallway. He vaguely remembered a darker hue. Deidre had taken Nick's kids to live with her and her boss, an orthopaedic surgeon. Tom recalled thinking that Nick had seemed more angry at her choice of partner than the fact she had left him. Both he and Alex had sensed that the marriage had been on rocky ground for several years.

What did surprise Tom, however, was the new look in the house. The antique sideboards and overstuffed chintz sofas must have been all Deidre, as Tom almost had to blink at the minimalist, virtually all-white décor of the once cluttered lounge room. White leather and chrome retro-modern lounge chairs surrounded a glass-topped coffee table. A wide-screen plasma was hung on the wall and surround-sound speakers had taken the place of Constable prints and poorly exe-cuted landscapes by some relative of Deidre's.

The only colour in the room came from a leopard skin in the centre of the floor. It looked garishly out of place. The kitchen, too, had been transformed from faux-country timber benchtops and wood grain lami-nate door panels into a sleek showpiece of gleaming stainless steel and black granite. 'Nick?' Tom called again, louder.

He walked upstairs and passed one of the kids' rooms, which had been converted into an office with a flat-screen monitor on top of an antique leather-topped desk, the only concession to pre-twenty-first century living Tom had seen so far. The second bedroom contained an array of new-looking gym

equipment – treadmill, exercise bike and a multifunc-
tion piece of kit which looked more like a futuristic
torture device than an exercise machine. Tom jogged
fifteen kilometres every second day of the week, no
matter the weather, and followed his run with a hundred sit-ups and sixty push-ups. He thought gyms
were posy, smelly places populated by people trying
to pick each other up.

The main bedroom was the reverse of the lounge.
Dark blue carpet; a king-size bed with a dark grey
duvet patterned with black Chinese calligraphy;
black satin sheets turned down; a feature wall painted
a colour Alex would have called eggplant, and deep,
dark reds on the other three. Tom turned on the light
and noticed the dimmer switch. He twiddled it and
smiled as he looked up into the new recessed lighting.
On the feature wall was an impressionistic painting
which, despite its blurred lines, was clearly of a naked
woman reclining with her hands between her legs.
Nick, it seemed, had embraced the bachelor lifestyle
with a vengeance and this passion pit was clearly his
operational headquarters. The bedside chest of draw-
ers – made of some kind of black wood – contained
two boxes of condoms and some porn DVDs. The
movies were hetero and hard core by the look of them,
but nothing kinky. Tom slid open a full-length mirrored wardrobe which revealed, in addition to shelves
of neatly folded clothes and a rack of suits, another
wide-screen TV and a player for the disks. There was
also a digital video camera on a tripod. 'You dog,' Tom
said.

What was clear was that Nick was not home and

nor did he appear to have been in the house for some period of time. Tom walked back downstairs to the kitchen, where the telephone was. He had noticed the blinking red light on the answering machine, but had avoided intruding further into his colleague's private life until necessary. It was necessary now. He pushed the button.

The machine beeped and a woman's voice said: 'It's me. I don't know how you got my number, but I'll see you. Tonight. I'm on at the club from six until two.' The tone sounded again. There were no other messages.

She sounded young, though her voice was quite deep, the pronunciation precise, as though the tongue was learned, not native. There was an ethnic accent there – possibly black African. Tom wondered if it was a potential girlfriend. A 'club' could mean a number of things. Being 'on' could refer to anything from working a shift behind a bar to a performance of some sort. He replayed the message. The girl's tone was slightly annoyed. Perhaps Nick had seen her and wanted to get to know her better – hence her concern at him tracking her down. Tom hoped Nick hadn't used police resources to get a woman's phone number, but he wouldn't have been the first to do so.

Tom moved to the refrigerator, intending to check how much food was there and its use-by dates to try to get a better feel for when Nick was last home. Before he opened it, a business card under an *I love Ibiza* magnet caught his eye. He lifted the card, holding it by the edges, for it was glossy and would probably hold a fingerprint quite well. There was a picture of a blonde in skimpy lingerie and high heels holding onto a brass pole and leaning out to one side. *Club Minx* was written underneath. On the back, written in pen, was a name – *Ebony*. A stripper's stage name, perhaps? It gelled, too, with the African accent on the machine.

Tom's mobile phone rang and he fished it out of the pocket of his duffel coat. 'Hello, it's Tom.'

'Any luck? Are you at Nick's place?'

It was Shuttleworth. 'No and yes. There's no sign of him, guv. Doesn't look like he's been here for . . .' Tom opened the fridge door and looked inside. The shelves were bare. In the door was a carton of milk with yesterday's date as the use-by date. '. . . for quite some time. Fridge's empty except for some stale milk. Heating's turned off. Has he been overseas?'

'No, but he was on leave for four days until he went back to Greeves today. The Secretary of State for Defence and junior ministers such as Greeves are being afforded close personal protection at home and abroad now because of the latest al-Qaeda threats. Nick must have gone straight to work from wherever he was spending his break. Then he vanished this evening. Any sign that he may have come home?'

Tom held up the card from the pole-dancing club and wondered. Though they'd once been friends via their wives, he owed no loyalty to Nick, other than what he might feel towards any other member of the team. Still, it didn't do to go insinuating a detective on protection was consorting with sex workers. 'No, but I can pop round to his local and see if anyone there's seen or heard from him.'

'Aye, okay. But don't stay out on the piss until all

hours. I want to see you in my office at eight-thirty tomorrow.'

'What happened to my appointment with the shrink?' And my lie-in, Tom thought.

'That can wait. You seem quite sane to me.'

Tom kicked the fridge door closed and the Ibiza magnet slipped off to the floor. When he knelt to retrieve it, he saw the corner of a small piece of white card sticking out from under the fridge. He picked it up and found it was another business card. It had the name and mobile phone number of a freelance journalist on it. Tom didn't recognise the name. He placed it on top of the fridge after writing the details in his notebook.

Club Minx was in Soho, a part of London Tom didn't care for. He wasn't a prude, and had been to his fair share of strip clubs – or table-dancing clubs as this one billed itself – but the congested, seedy hub depressed him.

The drunken office Johnnys in their suits and loosened ties saw only the smiles and flesh. As a bobby Tom had found teenagers who had overdosed in toilets; toms – whores – who had been beaten by their pimps or sadistic clients; kids from abusive families with nowhere to go and no other source of income than their own bodies; girls from the Far East and the former Soviet republics sold into modern-day slavery. There was nothing terribly sexy about any of that.

By the time he'd driven the Jag back to Highgate and caught the tube into the city it was nearly midnight.

He'd ditched the duffel coat and slipped on a sports coat, so he looked less like a builder and more like an off-duty businessman.

Tom got off the Northern Line at Tottenham Court Road tube station. He showed his warrant card and wished he'd brought a waterproof jacket when he saw the footpath glistening in the reflected glow of streetlights. Raindrops were hitting a muddy puddle which had formed in a gutter dammed by rubbish. He walked down Oxford Street, which was still crowded with tourists and night people, coming or going to and from pubs and clubs. This part of the city was just coming to life.

Soho still clung to its reputation for sin and sleaze, but the truth was that the strip joints, brothels and sex shops were slowly but surely losing ground to bistros, restaurants, trendy bars and cafes. A new wave of busi-nesses, largely fuelled by the pink pound, had also grown up in Old Crompton Street. What remained of Soho's salacious past – at least, what was still visible to passers-by – was hemmed into a warren formed by Berwick, Walker and Peter streets. On Berwick he passed a shop with leather corsets and restraints in the window and ignored the urgings of a tout to come inside and see his fully nude girls.

A grey-haired man in a suit ducked out of an adult bookstore and looked guiltily both ways before dart-ing into the passing throng of people. A group of a dozen lads in their late teens and early twenties sang the chorus of an old Rolling Stones song – badly – as they weaved down the narrow thoroughfare. A tourist couple paused in front of him, blocking the footpath, to check their *London A-Z*. Tom kept his impatience in check.

'Been in a fight?' the bouncer asked him as he descended the stairs from Peter Street.

'Walked into a cupboard door,' Tom said, unconsciously fingering the glass cut above his eye. He'd forgotten about it.

The bouncer looked him up and down and, deciding he wasn't drunk, said, 'All right. Don't think I need to check your ID to see if you're underage.'

The music he heard as he walked past the doorman had a beat he could feel in his chest. Slow, grinding. Music to disrobe to.

'Ten pounds, please,' the girl behind the reception desk said.

Tom wished he had told Shuttleworth about his informal investigation now. There was no way he'd be able to claim entrance to a strip club on his expenses if he wasn't officially working. He didn't want to flash his warrant card to the girl, which would cause a panic among the club's workers and patrons and have them all start disappearing. He'd put money on a few of the girls being illegal immigrants.

'Ta,' the girl said as he handed over his money. She wore a low-cut mini-dress that left little to the imagination.

A man in his fifties, heavy set and bald, stood to one side of the counter. Extra security, Tom assumed. A skinny red-headed girl in a lime green Lycra skirt the width of a hair band and a matching boob tube tottered past on black platform-sole shoes with five-inch heels, leading an overweight man in a suit by the hand. The couple walked past reception, through a door. Tom watched their progress, then glanced back at the girl behind the cash register.

'You been here before?'

'No.'

'Private shows are out the back. Just talk to any of the girls – they'll be more than happy to oblige.'

He nodded and walked into the club. The air was heavy with a cloying mist of disinfectant, cigarette smoke and perspiration, all masked by cheap perfume. A girl dressed in white stay-up stockings and matching bra and pants smiled at him as she brushed by, carrying a tray of drinks.

In the centre of the room was a square podium, joined to the black ceiling by two brass poles. There were seats for maybe twenty people around the stage, though there were only four punters there now, up close, ogling a brunette who was naked except for a brief G-string, black patent leather high heels, nipple rings, and a garter stuffed with notes. She, too, smiled at him as he took a chair opposite the other men.

The girl turned her back to Tom and knelt in front of the men. 'Show us everything,' one of them said, loud enough for Tom to hear over the grinding music. She shook her head and he didn't catch what the girl said, but the man who had spoken got up and returned to his table. His comrade got up soon after and joined him, leaving just two patrons. Tom watched them, beyond the girl's flawless back. They had shaved heads, football shirts and too much bling. If they were crims – and judging by the spider-web tattoo on his neck, at least one of them had done time – they were small-time.

The waitress in bridal white came to Tom and he ordered a Beck's. He also paid thirty quid for some plastic money to stuff in the girl's garter. She was on her knees, but bent backwards until her hair brushed the stage. She was looking at Tom, upside down, and he smiled back at her.

Not getting any joy from the other two men, the girl used the pole to pull herself to her feet and, after climbing and swinging as she slid down again, crawled on all fours to Tom's side of the podium. She grinned and winked when Tom held up a bill. She turned side on to him, so he could slide the money between her garter and her bare thigh. The transaction sealed, she leaned over him, allowing her long hair to fall around his face. Her nose was half an inch from his. She moved her mouth to his ear and blew in it.

'Hello, my name is Ivana,' she whispered.

'Hello, my name's Detective Sergeant.'

The smile vanished from the girl's face as she rocked back on her haunches. Russian, maybe, or Ukrainian, or Latvian, or Lithuanian. It didn't matter. He'd put a hundred quid on her being an illegal immigrant. She looked over her shoulder towards the distant reception counter.

'Don't worry, Ivana, the management doesn't know I'm a copper.' The waitress deposited Tom's beer in front of him.

She closed her legs. 'What do you want?'

'World peace, job satisfaction and a lasting relationship.'

She looked at him, puzzled. 'I have nothing to say to police.'

'Fine then, we can have a chat at the nearest nick, if you prefer. We can stop by your home and you can collect your passport. We'll need to check your identity and residency status.'

'I am not illegal, and I can prove it.'

Tom sipped his beer, then shrugged. 'Says you. I can be back in half an hour with a couple of uniformed officers. That should do wonders for business.'

She looked over her shoulder again. 'I finish dance in a few minutes. We can talk then. But I tell you now, policeman or not, no sex.'

Tom nodded. Ivana returned to the other side of the stage to try to milk a few more quid out of the football hooligans, and Tom found a table in a dark corner of the club.

Ivana finished her dance and stepped down from the stage, to a smattering of token applause from the score or so of other customers sitting at candle-lit tables. She shrugged into an abbreviated vinyl interpretation of a nurse's uniform and walked over to Tom. The waitress returned and Ivana looked pointedly at the other girl, then back to Tom.

'Oh, all right. What'll it be?'

'Double vodka and tonic.'

Tom ordered a second beer and winced when the girl told him the price. He shelled out some notes, wishing again he had done this by the book. The waitress left them.

'If you are police, show me your identification.'

Tom pulled out his wallet and showed his warrant card.

'Furey? It means madness?'

35

'Sometimes.'

'Why don't you tell the owner who you are?' she asked him.

'Where's Ebony tonight?'

The girl leaned back in her chair and sipped her drink. When she put it down, she said, 'What are you, another stalker or something?'

'Another?'

Ivana said nothing.

'Is she working tonight?'

'This is not official business, I think.'

Tom checked his watch. 'Like I said, it can be, very easily.'

Ivana sighed and flicked back from her face a long, straightened strand of jet black hair. 'She called in ill.'

'When was her last shift?'

'Last night. Are you going to stay here all night and spend that tipping money you bought?'

Tom looked at the laminated play money on the table. 'You said, "another stalker"; was there a man bothering her?'

Ivana laughed, and Tom thought how pretty she really was. 'Men bother us every single night, Mr Policeman.'

'You know what I mean.'

'There was a regular customer, a guy who came maybe five, six times in last two weeks – always booked private shows.'

'What did he look like?'

Ivana finished her vodka, slurping as she sucked the dregs through her straw. She smiled sweetly but said nothing.

36

Tom slid over the tipping money and she palmed it off the table.

'Glasses, red hair, freckles. Midtwenties. Short – about five-six. Looks like academician or maybe IT geek.'

Definitely not Nick then. Tom described the other detective.

'That could be any man who comes in here,' Ivana shrugged.

She was right, and Tom knew it. Someone would have to bring back a picture. He wanted to know more about the girl. 'She's black – the girl, Ebony?'

'Now I know why they make you detective.'

'Hah, hah. Where's she from, the West Indies?'

'South Africa.'

That was a bit out of the ordinary. 'Is she an illegal immigrant?'

'Who are you after, her or this big guy with black hair?'

'Has she been acting differently lately?'

'She went home early last night. I assume it was the sickness that kept her away tonight, but I was doing private show when she left, so I did not talk to her.'

'Were any of the other girls on tonight working last night?'

Ivana looked around the club. 'No.'

Tom thought from her studied nonchalance that she was probably lying – perhaps to protect her co-workers. He liked that about her. Honour among strippers. 'There were no other regulars that you know about?'

Ivana shook her head and looked at her watch. 'I am finishing work soon. You like private show?'

Tom smiled at her. 'No, thanks. How long has Ebony been in the UK?'

'About a year, I think.'

'How old is she?'

'Young – but not under-age, if that's what you're thinking. About nineteen, I think. Boss here is very strict on some things. No drugs, no kids.'

Tom wondered if Nick had seen Ebony, and if he had been the reason she had left work early the previous night. He didn't want to draw attention to himself by asking the receptionist.

'You got wife, Mr Policeman?' Ivana asked, intruding into his thoughts.

'No.'

'Girlfriend?'

'That's none of your business.' He drained his beer.

'I thought not. Policemen lousy at relationships. My policeman boyfriend in Russia, he beat me, so I stab him.'

'Bad relationship, indeed. Call me if you remember anything else.' He gave her a card and left the club.

It was nearly two in the morning before he opened the door to his warm but empty home. His face still stung from the cuts and he thought about the explosion again, and the death of the computer guy, Steve. He stripped off and climbed into bed between cool sheets. He looked across at the picture of Alex and smiled at her. He realised it could have just as easily been him caught in the explosion.

Part of him wished it was.

*

'South Africa.'

Tom wasn't fazed as Shuttleworth said the words, neither about the destination nor the lack of notice. He'd been to the Sudan with a foreign secretary and to Morocco with a former PM, but never to southern Africa. He looked out across the Thames, towards the Palace of Westminster. The sky was a dirty grey. Some sunshine wouldn't be bad.

'With Nick missing, I need you to do an advance recce prior to Robert Greeves's visit. Flight leaves this evening, BA from Heathrow to Johannesburg,' the Scotsman said. 'Greeves is a frequent visitor, both for business and pleasure, and on this trip he's doing a bit of both. He's an animal nut – loves the game parks – and he's staying in a luxury lodge he's used before. While he's there he'll be meeting with his South African counterpart, a Mr Dule, to talk about them buying some jet training aircraft from a UK defence contractor.'

'I read something about that.'

'Yes, well, you'll find no shortage of material on the internet to read on your flight.' Shuttleworth pushed two thick folders across his uncluttered desk towards Tom. They were Nick's files on the Minister for Defence Procurement's past visits to Africa. 'Your advance trip is little more than a formality for his visit. He's stayed at the lodge before and you'll be working with the same people from the South African Police Service who've done the last few visits with Nick.'

'What's the lodge called?' Tom asked, not that he would know one safari camp from another.

'Tinga. It's in the Kruger National Park. Five-star luxury, topnotch. Only the best for our Robert.'

'My taxes at work.'

Shuttleworth frowned. 'What did you find at Nick's place last night?'

'Nothing much. A card from a strip club and a message on his phone from some bird called Ebony asking to meet him at a club of some sort, where she would be "on".' Tom had decided to come clean about the only clue to Nick's possible whereabouts; he figured that as he was now picking up his missing colleague's work he owed him no special favours. Also, as he was leaving the country, it was time for someone else to follow up on Nick's disappearance.

'You went to the club.' Shuttleworth didn't even bother framing it as a question, Tom noted, though he saw the disapproval in the by-the-book chief inspector's eyes.

'Yes, but it was pretty much a dead end. There was a stripper named Ebony who worked there, but she'd called in sick. The girl I spoke to didn't recognise Nick's description.'

'Hmm. I'll send Morris and Burnett around to investigate officially. Interesting that she called in sick the same evening that Nick did a bunk.'

'We don't know he's done a runner. Could be something worse.'

'Aye; well, it's damned inconvenient whatever the explanation. Do you know much about his personal life? I remember you said he seems to have a different bird every few weeks.'

Tom shook his head. 'Only heard rumours. I haven't

socialised with him since he split up with his wife. His house looks more like a seventies bachelor pad these days, so it could be he's enjoying single life to the full.'

'Write up your notes and a statement about last night. Once you're done you can get home and pack. It's warm in South Africa this time of year.'

Tom took the files back to one of the hot desk work-stations used by the protection officers and turned on the shared computer. He would have to digest the files now, as they couldn't leave the building. He was flying to South Africa tonight, spending the next day and night in the country, then flying back to the UK the following afternoon. After little more than twenty-four hours to rest up he would then be on Greeves's personal protection team, and getting straight back on another plane to Africa. If there were more resources available he would have simply stayed in-country and waited for the minister and the rest of the team to arrive.

He read a sheaf of email print-outs from the file. The protection for Greeves was very lean, and that was cause for some concern. Not that he could do much about manpower issues. The recently raised security alert meant that even junior ministers such as Greeves were being afforded close personal protection at home and abroad. He didn't have a view yet on how serious a target the man in charge of defence procurement might be, but he was getting a bare-bones service from the Met.

As he read messages Nick had typed to his counterpart in South Africa he wondered again where, when and how his colleague would turn up. He'd half expected, when he let himself into Nick's home, that he would find him dead in the bathroom, his brains splattered on the tiled wall.

That's how he would do it, if he made the decision. Easier to clean the place for the lawyer or doctor or accountant who moved in. Tom was one of a rare breed – a Catholic in the old Special Branch. He kept his religion to himself, not because he was worried about jibes or prejudice, particularly when the enemy were Irishmen of his own faith, but because he no longer really believed. It was ironic, he thought. If what the nuns had taught him as a child were true, then one day he and Alex would be reunited in the afterlife; however, if he took a short cut to get to her by committing suicide he would be damned in hell for committing the sin of taking his own life.

3

'Tea, sir?'

Tom blinked and shook his head to clear his senses. The flight attendant was giving him a smile that almost passed for sincere as she hovered waiting for him to answer.

'Please,' he replied, pulling himself up from the flat business-class bed to a semi-sitting position. Someone had opened the shutter beside him and golden sunlight flooded the cabin of the British Airways 747.

'Did you sleep well?' she asked as she placed the cup on his side table.

'Like the dead,' he said. The late night at the club and early start had been a blessing in disguise, as he had fallen asleep soon after the meal. He'd long gotten over the novelty of travelling business or first class on long-haul flights. He did, however, appreciate the advent of fully flat beds in business.

A short time later the aircraft captain announced the cabin crew would be preparing the cabin for landing. By the time Tom returned from the toilet, where he had run a battery-powered shaver over his chin and combed his tousled grey-flecked hair, his bed had been transformed back to a seat. He leaned over and stared out the window at Africa.

The countryside was greener than he had expected, though the captain announced that rain was forecast at their destination. As well as open grasslands below there were circular farmed fields of some irrigated crop or other. What Tom knew about farming would fit on the back of a London Transport travel card. He knew even less about big game and wildlife. In the parts of Africa he had visited the populace were more at risk from AK 47s than from lions or leopards.

Tom had read his internet print-outs – some general information on South Africa, Tinga Legends Lodge and the Kruger National Park – before falling asleep on the flight. He had a lot to learn about the country he was about to set foot in, but in some respects that didn't matter.

There would be a South African Police Service inspector at the airport to meet and accompany him out to the safari lodge, which he had read was about four hours' drive away. Robert Greeves would actually fly to the park on his visit, but in the meantime SO1 could spend their money better elsewhere than on an internal flight for Tom on this advance visit. He didn't care, as a road trip would give him a better chance to get a feel for what people referred to as the 'new' South Africa.

However, there were things about this job that were already starting to concern him. For a start, he shouldn't have been on his own. A protection team was normally made up of a bare minimum of two members. Another Met policeman, Detective Constable Charlie Sheather, was already in South Africa, but he had leapfrogged ahead to check out the Radisson Hotel in Cape Town, where Greeves would stay after his visit to Tinga. Charlie would do the advance for that leg of the trip, but he and Tom would not be working together until Tom flew to the Cape. It was against standard operating procedures, but the existing staff shortages had suddenly been made worse by Nick's disappearance. Also, Greeves was a junior minister – defence procurement was important but didn't keep the politician in the headlines, unlike the Defence Secretary, who still rated a full team.

There was a distant clunk somewhere back beneath economy class as the wheels were lowered and the flaps extended. Out the window he glimpsed rows of detached houses on small plots of land, some with swimming pools – suburbia. No elephants or zebra. He smiled to himself. Hot air rising from the sun-warmed African landscape produced some 'bumps', as the pilot referred to them, and Tom peered out the window as Africa rose up to greet him.

Tom registered little about Johannesburg International Airport, other than that the terminal was bigger, busier, more modern and more efficient than he had imagined it would be. The few South Africans he had met in London seemed to like nothing better than to berate the new rulers of their former homeland about corruption, increasing crime and a deterioration in services since the advent of majority rule in 1994. Tom wasn't naïve enough to judge a country by its arrivals hall, but it was a reminder that he should leave his prejudices at the entry gate. He was a man who dealt with facts, not anecdotes or rumours. He doubted he would have a chance to form deep or lasting impressions of African and South African democracy from one recce, but he would keep his eyes and ears open.

'Detective Sergeant Furey?'

'That's me.' Tom had looked past the blonde-haired woman in a smart business suit, with nipped-in jacket and skirt. She was about five-nine, four inches shorter than he, though her heels made up most of the difference. Her hair was cut short in a bob but the first thing he really noticed about her, other than her height, was her blue eyes. He knew he was staring at her, but couldn't help it. He forced himself to blink.

She smiled away his awkwardness politely. 'I'm Inspector Susan van Rensburg. People call me Sannie.'

When she extended her hand her grip was firm, the polished bronze skin soft and cool. He detected the Afrikaans accent before she got to her surname. She looked in her midthirties. No wedding band, though there were two rings on her right ring finger, one studded with diamonds. Where he came from, not many female coppers wore lip gloss on the job. 'Tom. Nice to meet you. You got the email about Nick Roberts, then?'

'Yes. Any word of his whereabouts?'

'Nothing yet. You worked with him before?' She led him to the terminal doors, ignoring an African man in a bomber jacket who asked them if they wanted a car. Tom had his travel bag over one shoulder, and he said, 'No thanks,' when a porter offered to carry it for him.

'Yes, I've worked with Nick,' she said, not volunteering any more information, no expression of concern that Tom could trace.

'Are you usually assigned as liaison when Mr Greeves visits?' Tom asked.

'Yes. He's a nice guy. Have you worked with him before?'

Tom shook his head. Interesting that she would volunteer a personal opinion about the minister but not the man she had worked most closely with, and who was now missing.

'Well, I'm ready to go if you are.' Tom carried a second Rohan travel suit, two short-sleeve business shirts, underwear and his toiletries in a carry-on bag, along with a pair of jeans, loafers and shorts and a casual shirt. He followed Sannie out through the arrivals hall. It was warm, though not unpleasantly hot, and shards of blue sky were opening cracks in grey clouds still heavy with rain.

'Here we are,' Sannie said, pressing the button on the key-chain remote. The lights flashed on a Mercedes. Not the latest model, but far from old. She popped the boot and he tossed his bag in and closed it.

'It's just the two of us,' she said. 'We're short-staffed and there's an Organisation of the African Union meeting on in Cape Town today and tomorrow. Still, we don't need anyone else here for the recce as your Mr Greeves has been to Tinga and Kruger many times.'

47

'I know what you mean about being short-handed. We're running a bare-bones operation on this trip. I contacted the British Embassy's security officer and even he's too busy to come out to meet us today.'

Sannie shrugged. 'I've met Giles a few times, but there's nothing a security officer will be able to tell you that I can't. Have you ever been to South Africa?'

'Never. Is the crime problem as bad as the media makes out?' Tom slipped off his coat and climbed into the passenger seat.

Sannie also took off her jacket and hung it over the back of her seat. As she got in she pulled a Z88 nine-millimetre pistol from the holster clipped to a narrow belt at the top of her tailored skirt. She smiled at him and placed the weapon in a slot in the centre console where most people would keep their sunglasses.

'Right,' Tom said. He'd thought it wasn't necessary for him to bring his Glock on the recce – just more paperwork – but now he wasn't so sure.

'It's loaded and racked, by the way. We in the police tell the general public not to try to fight back or use their weapon if they get car-jacked.'

Tom had read that armed car hijacking was a serious problem in Johannesburg and other parts of the country, with robbers often shooting their victims. In the UK the people with guns were usually underworld criminals who tended to use them on each other rather than innocents.

'So what's your plan if we get stopped by a thief?'

'If the car-jacker shoots me before I get him, I want you to kill him, okay?'

'You're serious?'

She smiled as she indicated and accelerated into the traffic outside the terminal.

'Is this a wind-up?' he persisted.

Sannie looked across at him, unsmiling now, and said, 'My husband was a police captain, also in protection. He had worked with Nick Roberts, protecting Greeves. I was still at home on leave, pregnant with my third child. He was off duty, on his way to pick up our son from a friend's place. He was shot at a robot – traffic lights – before he had a chance to go for his gun. It was two years ago. I lost the baby.'

Tom nodded, staring out the windscreen. He was trying to find the right words to express sorrow for her loss, but he knew from his own experience that nothing anyone ever said was right – or made it easier. He looked across and caught her glancing at him before returning her piercing gaze to the road.

'Thanks,' she said.

'For what?'

'For not saying anything.'

It all looked so normal. The industrial suburbs on the border of the airport reminded him of Staines, near Heathrow. He saw as many white faces as black ones as Sannie took an on-ramp onto a six-lane freeway. Signs advertised mobile phones and department stores and a casino. Johannesburg – Africa – might look like other parts of the world, but the pistol lying between them spoke of the violent subtext of life in this part of Africa.

Sannie said nothing more and he watched the way she drove. Aggressively defensive, he would have described it. Watching her rear-view mirror, keeping her distance from the car in front. When the traffic lights – the robot, as she had called it – turned red she stopped five metres from the car in front, so she had room to manoeuvre if someone accosted them.

'You said you had a son?' he said.

'*Ja*, a son and daughter. My boy is nine and my girl is five. My mother lives with us and she looks after them when I'm away.'

Sannie changed lanes and accelerated, pushing the speedometer up to a hundred and twenty kilometres. 'Are you divorced, or do you just take your wedding ring off when you travel, like . . . ?' She glanced across at him.

He looked down at his left index finger. He'd only taken it off six months ago. He'd figured it was time, but he, as had Sannie, noticed there was still a faint tan line and an indentation caused by fifteen years of wear.

'Alex died a year ago. Breast cancer.'

'Oh, man, I'm so sorry. I knew you'd lost someone, but I didn't realise it was your wife.'

'How did you know?'

'Not talking when I told you what happened to my husband and baby. It's the people who haven't known real grief who think words can make it easier. It doesn't really go away, does it?'

'Not that I can tell.' He wanted desperately to change the subject. 'What you were saying before, about taking off a wedding ring when travelling, you said "like". Whose name were you about to add?'

'Forget it,' she said.

'Like Nick?'

'Look, if he's a friend of yours, I'm sorry. And I'm sorry he's missing.'

'But?'

'What?'

'I sensed there was a "but" coming then. Our wives knew each other better than we did. Nick's a colleague, Sannie. I do want to try to work out what happened to him, but I can't say I know him well enough to guess why he went missing – if it was a voluntary thing.'

'Okay, well, I first met Nick about four years ago, when my husband was still alive and when Nick was still married.'

'And?'

'And he tried to hit on me.'

'Really?'

'*Ja.* First trip, in the car on the first drive, just like you and me now. I couldn't believe it. He says to me, "What goes on tour stays on tour." I can tell you, I gave it to him big time.'

'Did he ever try again?'

'Once more, last year, after his marriage is over and my husband's dead and my miscarriage, and he thinks I'm now available. We were in a pub with some other police. My friends were at the bar and we were alone and he says, "Is the time right now, baby?"'

'What did you do?'

'I told him that the time wouldn't be right if we were the only two people left in the world, and then I *klapped* him, good and hard across the face.'

Tom smiled, but he was learning more about Nick and it wasn't good.

'I'm so *gatvol* of men these days.'

'*Gatvol?*' he asked. She had pronounced the 'g' as though she was about to spit at him, so the word, whatever it meant, seemed to match her sentiment.

'Like "I've had enough" in English. But no offence, hey?'

He laughed. 'None taken.'

From a map he'd glanced at, he knew the airport was on the eastern fringe of Johannesburg, and the factories, warehouses, mine slag heaps and outlying gated communities of townhouses hiding behind high whitewashed walls soon gave way to open grasslands and farms. Sannie explained that Johannesburg was on the highveld – at a higher altitude than where they were headed. Kruger was in the lowveld. 'Hotter there. Stickier. I hope you brought your mozzie *muti* with you.'

'Insect repellent?' he checked.

'It's malaria country where we're going, and quite bad this time of year – it's the wet season.'

When they neared the exit for a town called Witbank he noticed his first car-jacking sign. It said, *Warning – hijacking hotspot. Do not stop* beneath a huge exclamation mark.

'What do you do if you break down?' he asked.

'Pray,' said Sannie, 'and aim for the centre body mass.'

In Tom's experience, most people living in supposedly dangerous parts of the world tended to talk down the perceived threat, usually issuing a few common words of warning such as, 'Avoid such-and-such an area at night and you'll be okay,' or, 'It's not as bad as the media makes out'. From what Sannie had told him so far, the reverse seemed to be true in South Africa. People here were under no illusion about their local crime problem.

'A lot of it is organised crime here, and the whites aren't blameless. Also, we have people from all over Africa living in this country. The Zimbabweans who cross the border are dirt poor and some of them turn to theft – same with the Mozambicans. The Nigerians are the worst – they control the drug scene. It was different in the old days, when I first joined the police – back then we had the death penalty.'

And riots in Soweto and police opening fire on civilians, Tom thought, but said nothing. It was her country and he wasn't here to make judgments.

'I know what you're thinking. But we're not all mad racists, you know. I didn't agree with a lot of what happened under apartheid, but we did have the crime problem under control.'

'Depends on who you classed as the criminals.'

She smiled.

Sannie stopped for fuel at a service station just past the Middelburg toll plaza. It was exactly like one of the large complexes he would have encountered on a British motorway. Tom got out to stretch his legs. He yawned, but was feeling okay. There was little time difference between the UK and South Africa and he had slept well on the aircraft. It was good to feel sunshine on his face. Sannie returned with a couple of Cokes and some crisps. 'How far?' he asked.

'*Ag*, shame, man, you sound like my kids. It's about another three hours if we drive fast.'

And drive fast they did. Tom glanced over and saw that the speedometer rarely dipped below a hundred and ten kilometres per hour. The locals had an interesting form of traffic etiquette, where slow vehicles pulled to the left – South Africans drove on the same side of the road as he did in England – to let faster cars pass them. The overtaking vehicle – Sannie in every case – put on its hazard lights as a way of saying thank you, while the car which had just been passed flashed its headlights as if to say, 'You're welcome'. It was like a parallel universe, Tom thought. Similar to England in some ways, but so completely different in others.

The road they were on – the N4 – took them eastwards, towards the border with Mozambique, according to the signs to that country's capital, Maputo. Tom knew Mozambique was a former Portuguese colony, had suffered a long civil war and supposedly had good beaches. Beyond that it was just a name on a map. He thought he would find some books on Africa before he returned with Robert Greeves.

Sannie had the radio tuned to a station called Jacaranda FM, which played easy-listening music, mostly from the eighties and nineties. The announcers and newsreaders switched from English to Afrikaans, sometimes midsentence. 'Do you and your kids speak Afrikaans at home?'

'*Ja*, and English. There are about a dozen official languages in the new South Africa. My kids are learning Xhosa at school. I figure it's good for them to be able to speak the language of the ones who are in charge now.'

'I suppose it's been tough on . . . on people like you, since the Africans took over the country.'

She shrugged. 'First of all, I *am* an African. I just happen to be a white one. Sure, there was a lot of affirmative action after the ANC took over. I suppose I'm lucky that I'm a woman.'

'What do you mean by that?' Tom asked. Traffic had slowed marginally as the road started to descend through a series of sweeping bends.

'In the new South Africa it's all about *empowerment*. Black women have had a hard time, so they're now at the top of the list for good jobs or promotions, followed by black men. Then it's coloureds and Indians and then us white women, followed by white men, who are now at the bottom. It used to be the other way around.'

She didn't seem bitter, he thought, just resigned to making the most of her life. If he was going to judge her, it would be on how she did her job as a police officer, not what she thought of life under black majority rule.

A blurred movement of greyish-green in the grass to the left caught his eye. 'Bloody hell! What was that?'

Sannie glanced over. 'Oh, *bobos*. Baboons – we call them *bobbejaans* in Afrikaans.'

Tom watched the troops of a dozen or so primates. A large one stared back at him and snarled with long yellowed teeth from its dog-like snout. 'But we're not in a national park, are we?'

'No. You'll see *bobos* and monkeys wherever there is still some bush or trees left for them. A lot of this country is taken up with farming, but there are still some wilderness areas.' The toll road split and Sannie explained that while they could go either way to get to Kruger, the right-hand fork would take them via Waterval Boven, down a steep pass where the high-veld ended. 'The countryside's more scenic than on the road via Lydenburg.'

The drive took them along the course of a river which had cut through the rock, forming the pass. Plantation gum trees met their end in a smoking paper mill. Tom saw skinny black workers in baggy overalls, and wondered if the men were ill with HIV-AIDS.

He started feeling drowsy after more than three hours on the road, and Sannie stopped at another garage to buy more Cokes and chips for the two of them. Tom again got out of the car for a stretch and was struck immediately by the change in climate. It was much hotter than Johannesburg and the air felt heavy with moisture. Sannie told him they were approaching Nelspruit, the capital of Mpumalanga province, once known as the Eastern Transvaal. 'The lowveld. We're getting close to the bush now.' She said it with fondness, almost reverence. 'Some people call it the slowveld, because nothing much happens in a hurry. It's the heat.'

In the distance Tom could see a few tall office build-ings, but Sannie turned left before they reached the town proper. They began climbing into some hills.

When they reached the town of White River, all the traffic signals were out. A black policeman was directing traffic with the exaggerated movements of someone doing a robot dance. 'He seems to be enjoy-ing his job,' Tom said.

'*Ja*, but it's no laughing matter. The electricity is out – again. Our power company, Eskom, calls it "load shedding". They switch off entire districts so the whole system doesn't collapse. Supply can't keep up with demand in South Africa, and not enough money's been spent on infrastructure in the last decade.'

Leaving the town they wound through hills forested with plantation trees – pines and Australian blue gums. They crested a high peak and, looking ahead, the forests vanished, replaced by a vista of red dirt and mud-brick shacks of the same hue. There wasn't a tree in sight. 'Townships like this are where a lot of our people still live. The government is building new homes through the regional development program but they can't keep pace with demand. On one hand they're spending tens of thousands of rand to change the names of towns from Afrikaans to African names, and Jan Smuts Airport to OR Tambo, but they can't put a decent roof over their own people's heads or keep the country's electricity supply working.'

Tom heard the bitterness in her voice. Most of the houses had rusting tin roofs. Some looked as though they were made entirely of homemade mud bricks and old packing crates. He smelled wood smoke through the aircon's inlet and guessed it was the trees which had once stood on these hills. Toddlers walked barefoot, their lower legs spattered with red mud. A skeletal woman carried a baby on her back, wrapped in a piece of stained cloth tied around her midriff. Sannie kept her speed up and ignored the malevolent stares of a group of teenage boys dressed like

American ghetto dwellers, brightly coloured boxer shorts protruding above low-slung jeans. Plenty of bling. Would-be gangsters.

'We don't want to break down here,' she said. They passed a turnoff to the Kruger Park's Numbi Gate, but Sannie said they were headed further north, to an entrance closer to the park's internal police station. 'I just wanted to show you how some people live, so you can maybe understand the crime problem a little better.'

Tom nodded. Something Sannie had said before, about African women, reminded him of his brief informal investigation into Nick's disappearance. 'Did you ever notice Nick taking an interest in black African women?'

Sannie sniffed. 'That man would take an interest in a cobra if you held its head. Why do you ask?'

'I think one of the last people to have seen him was a South African woman.'

'A hooker?'

'You really don't like him, do you?'

'How can you guess?' Sannie asked, giving him a deadpan look.

'Actually, she was what we might in polite circles call an exotic dancer.'

'A stripper? Sounds like him. He and a couple of the male cops went to a table-dancing club in Pretoria one time. My colleagues told me Nick was particularly interested in the one girl, and she was black.'

'I wonder if it could be the same one,' Tom said, thinking out loud.

'Could just be that he was into any girl who would

talk to him – even if he had to stick money in her garter, you know.'

They had passed back into rural countryside, lush farms which covered the mountains in different shades of emerald in the afternoon sun. Tom noted banana farms and tropical fruits such as avocados and mangoes for sale on the side of the road. Fertile country. 'I grew up near here, on a banana farm,' Sannie said as they passed through a small but chaotic town – a *'dorp'* she called it – named Hazyview. 'I was a real bush baby. My family took my brothers and me into the Kruger Park every school holiday and many weekends. But I never got sick of it.'

Workers heading home thronged the sidewalks, and pick-ups laden with farm produce and fertilizer queued at the robots in a mini peak-hour traffic jam. Loud hip-hop blared from giant ghetto-blasters parked outside an electrical goods store. A gaggle of schoolgirls in starched uniforms giggled at something.

'Did you stay at a lodge like the one we're heading for? From what I've read it's very expensive.'

She chuckled. 'You've got a lot to learn, my friend. Kruger gets about three million visitors a year, and most of those are local families. You can stay in national parks rest camps which have camping sites and self-contained rondavels – huts. You don't need to stay at one of the *larney* places. There's something for everyone, although when I was a little kid the park was for whites only. It's good now, though, to see more black families visiting. I take my kids camping there a few times a year.'

*

They continued driving and Sannie checked her watch. The kids would be out of school soon, and when she could she would call her mother to make sure they had got to her place safely and talk to them for a bit. Tom appeared deep in thought, and she guessed he was still mulling over what had happened to his police colleague. As much as she disliked Nick, a tiny part of her still felt bad that a detective who, despite all his faults, was always punctual and professional – at least around the man he was protecting – had suddenly disappeared. She felt a pang of guilt that she had secretly wished him ill. She hoped he would turn up drunk or stoned in the bed of some African stripper. The bollocking – to borrow an English word – that he would receive would be long overdue and might teach him a lesson. She had never seen Nick use drugs, though when they were off duty she had noticed him easily matching Pol and Kobus, the other members of her team, drink for drink, and they were major soaks.

She had been mildly offended the night in Pretoria that the three of them had announced in the pub that they were going to the strip club. Not because they were leaving her, but because they hadn't even asked her if she wanted to go too. She'd never been to such a place, not even as part of her job, and she was curious to see what went on.

Sannie took the turning to the Paul Kruger Gate, a major entrance point to the national park. She really did love coming to this place. Whether in the old South Africa or the new, the park was a Garden of Eden, a natural oasis where one could forget the day-to-day problems and challenges of life and immerse oneself in the restful, inspiring tranquillity of the bush. Even though she was here on a work assignment, she felt the stress melt from her body and her grip on the steering wheel relax as she crossed the Sabie River. She pulled up a hundred metres short of the thatched gatehouse and unloaded and cleared her Z88. She noticed Tom watching her out of the corner of his eye. She handled her weapon confidently and safely and was an expert shot, regularly outshooting all of her male colleagues on the firing range. She put the pistol back in its holster and smiled at him.

'Won't you need that for lions and tigers?'

'No tigers in Africa, I'm afraid. No, this place is about as safe as it gets in South Africa – as long as you stay in your car.'

Tom grimaced and she laughed at him. He was a good-looking guy. Solidly built. He had a full head of hair and blue eyes, which she liked the look of, and a strong jaw. Unlike some of the other detectives she worked with, this one obviously kept himself fit. There was no sign of a beer belly hanging over his trouser belt.

Sannie had only come close to sleeping with one man since Christo's death, and that had been one time only. It was a disaster. She had been drinking at the squad's Christmas party – in fact, she had been so drunk that she had decided not to drive home. She was about to call her mother when her boss, Captain Henk Wessels, had offered to give her a lift. He lived not far from her home in suburban Kempton Park – only a couple of streets away.

At the time it had been a little more than a year

since Christo had been shot and she had been so preoccupied with the kids – helping them to stay focused at school and to deal with their grief – that she hadn't even thought about having another relationship. When Wessels stopped outside her home he had leaned over from the driver's seat to give her a goodnight kiss.

It was not entirely appropriate for a senior officer to do something like that to a subordinate but, what the hell, she had thought, it was Christmas and it had been a damned good party, and he had taken her home. As she leaned over to offer her cheek he struck, fast and predatory, like a mamba, and planted a kiss on her lips. She leaned back, surprised, and not sure if it had been a mistake of timing or positioning. Henk was not an unattractive man. He had left his wife and four children for a girl of twenty-five, who was only a little more than half his age. It had been a bad situation, made worse for the captain when the younger girl ditched him after seven months. Sannie thought he was seeing a nurse these days, though the two were not living together. He smiled at her. He was a bad man.

And that, she had realised, was exactly what she needed right then. The thought came to her with the clarity that only seven brandy and Cokes could bring. They kissed and clawed at each other like a pair of teenagers after the matric dance. 'Not here,' she whispered.

'My place,' Wessels panted.

Sannie felt lascivious, wanton, desperate for the feel of a man again. She had her hand in the captain's pants as he drove, dangerously fast, back to his empty house.

The drive there should have been enough to warn her that the night was not going to improve. Henk had been unable to rise to the occasion, and no amount of her ministrations had helped, not in the car, or in his shabbily furnished, untidy house. He had eventually admitted defeat and dropped her home. Exhausted, drunk, frustrated, embarrassed and dreadfully sad, she had cried herself to sleep. Mixed with her hangover the next morning was a crushing feeling that she had been unfaithful to Christo. She tried, in vain, to tell herself she should get on with her life, perhaps even go looking for another husband, but her feelings of guilt won out. She wondered later if she would have felt differently if they'd had sex.

'Is that the welcoming committee?' Tom Furey asked.

'What? Oh, sorry. I was just thinking of something I need to tell my mom about the kids. Yes, that's Captain Tshabalala from Skukuza. That's the park's main camp and there's a police post there. He'll escort us in so we don't need to worry about entrance fees and park permits and whatnot.'

The captain was a rotund, smiling man in his mid-forties with whom Sannie had worked often over the years. She liked him, even though he was exactly the sort of person she would have been trying to arrest pre-1994 when Nelson Mandela had led the country to majority rule. Isaac Tshabalala had trained in the former Soviet Union as a member of Umkhonto we Sizwe – the spear of the nation – the military arm of the African National Congress. Thankfully, South Africa had made the transition to true democracy without Isaac's training in explosives and sabotage needing to be put to the test.

'Welcome to the Kruger National Park,' Isaac said to Tom as he shook hands. '*Kunjani*, Sannie. How are you?'

'Fine, sir, and you?'

Isaac ushered them into the gate office and spoke rapidly, in the language of the Shangaan people, to the young woman behind the desk. Sannie understood every word. She had learned it from her nanny as a child and practised with the children of the farm labourers. Her mother had not approved and had smacked her bottom on more than one occasion for talking in the language of the majority of inhabitants of their part of the old Eastern Transvaal. Her father had winked at her whenever the punishment was delivered, which took some sting out of the blows. Isaac was now telling the woman they were all police officers, even the pretty but too skinny blonde one. The receptionist put a hand to her mouth to cover her laugh. Sannie had never let on to the captain that she spoke his language and she kept a straight face, knowing an African language was a handy card to have up one's sleeve and one to be played judiciously.

Captain Tshabalala drove ahead in his ageing Toyota Venture people-mover. 'Look, on the right . . . some giraffe,' Sannie said to Tom matter-of-factly.

'Where? Boy, you've got good eyesight. Blimey, that's incredible. Look at them just wandering around without a care. That's just . . .'

He was lost for words, literally, and she smiled as she noticed him craning his head back to continue staring at the animals as she drove on behind their escort. She wished she could remember the first time she had seen a giraffe. The awesome, addictive terror of her first close-up sighting of a lion, when she was five, was something which would stay with her for-ever. It was one of her earliest childhood memories. The Africa bug had just bitten Tom Furey for the first time. The more incredible things one saw – lion kills, a leopard stalking an impala, bull elephants fight-ing – the more one needed to keep coming back. Tom's new principal, Robert Greeves, was clearly a hopeless addict. She remembered him saying once that he had been to Africa, either on business or pleasure or both, annually for the past fifteen years.

'Damn, my camera's in my bag.' Tom sounded disappointed.

'Don't worry, there'll be plenty more giraffe for you to see later – and everything else.'

Tshabalala led them to the Skukuza police post where, over coffee, he explained for Tom's benefit the local chain of command and areas of responsibil-ity. Basically he and his officers, who were limited in numbers and resources, would be available to provide initial uniformed back-up if any incident during the visit required it. Political relations between South Africa and the UK were good, so there was no threat of any demonstration or protest – not that such actions would even be feasible within the confines of a national park where, for the most part, animals rather than people held sway. Isaac explained that should

Greeves be taken ill, or injured in any way, there was a doctor on call twenty-four hours a day at Skukuza, and Nelspruit hospital was forty-five minutes away.

'Really, I can't think of anything that could go wrong, other than the minister falling ill, or being eaten by a lion on a game drive.' The burly captain's whole body shook and Sannie swore she felt the floor vibrating under her high heels as he laughed at his own joke.

Tom, she saw, smiled politely, then asked questions about police radio communications, emergency frequencies, phone numbers, and crime figures for the national park and its surrounds. He was very professional, but Sannie expected nothing less of the Englishman. As she had reflected earlier, even that sleaze Nick Roberts was good at his job. Being a protection officer – dropping in and out of other people's turf – required diplomacy, and Tom had it.

Their briefing session over, Sannie and Tom left the captain and went back to her car. 'The lodge is only about ten minutes from here.'

'Do you share his confidence about the risk assessment here in the park?' Tom asked as she unlocked the Mercedes by remote. The horn gave a little beep and the hazard lights flashed as the alarm was disabled.

'I lock my car, even when I know there's about a one in a million chance of it being broken into or stolen outside a police post in the middle of a national park.'

Tom opened the car door. 'That's why we're here.'

4

'**M**r Speaker, will the Minister for Defence Procurement elaborate on remarks he made to defence contractors recently in which he indicated the government in fact has no real intention to further scale back troop numbers in Iraq? Further, will the minister come clean on the government's timetable for withdrawal?' The opposition backbencher grinned, and sat as the guffaws rose from his side of the House of Commons in the Palace of Westminster just as the groans and jeers from the government benches mocked him.

Robert Greeves buttoned his suit jacket as he stood and approached the despatch box and coldly eyed the members of Her Majesty's loyal opposition, though how loyal this cretinous mob of political featherweights were was debatable. 'Mr Speaker, once more for the slow learners . . .'

He paused as the peals of forced laughter erupted from the government benches. When the theatrics had subsided, he continued. 'Mr Speaker, this would be a laughably dim question if the subject were not so desperately serious. We sit here in parliament today, safely surrounded by armed police, security staff, metal detectors, cameras and an array of protective systems. Out in the deserts of Southern Iraq, and on the streets of Basra and Baghdad and many other towns and villages of that poor benighted country, there are British men and women in harm's way. Men and women who face the dangers of improvised explosive devices – bombs to you and me – rocket-propelled grenades and bullets.'

'So why don't you bring them home?' an opposition member jeered.

Greeves knew better than to take the bait and get into a slanging match. He paused and stared at the member of parliament opposite who had asked the question. His silence was effective and infectious. The whole house was quiet, waiting for his deep, measured voice to continue.

Although a relatively young fifty-two, he was one of the longest serving members of parliament, having been elected at the age of just twenty-six. He had never aspired to the prime ministership, though countless hacks and plenty amid his own Party had speculated or urged that he should. He had been a member of parliament longer than the current prime ministerial incumbent, and he had helped put the man there. Robert Greeves was not a king but a king-maker. His satisfaction was in steering his Party towards government – and that goal had been achieved after years in the wilderness of opposition – and helping to place a succession of talented, driven, intelligent people in the top job, for as long as his Party held power. For himself, all he wanted was a challenging cabinet position where he could make a difference. Leaders came and went, and when they left the highest elected office in the land, that was generally the end of their political career. Greeves wanted to be in politics until he died. It was his life. It was his calling. And he was very, very good at it.

'However, Mr Speaker, I address the house today not on the subject of the fine men and women of our own army and Royal Air Force who serve in Iraq, nor our equally upstanding seamen in the still troubled waters of the north Arabian Gulf. I speak of the men of the fledgling Iraqi defence force and the Iraqi police force.

'It is these men who risk assassination, hatred and intimidation not only of themselves on a daily basis but also of their families, by daring to do the right thing and don the uniform of their newly independent, newly democratic country.

'How can we say, "We, like you, don't believe that foreign insurgents should be allowed to kill your women and children indiscriminately with car bombs, but we've had enough now and it's all over to you"?'

'It's not our war!' called another opposition member.

'Tell that to victims of the seven-seven London bombings!' Greeves shot back at the interjector. Damn, he said to himself. He had risen to the challenge and this prompted a fusillade of catcalls from both sides. He did get emotional, however, when discussing terrorism and the global fight against it.

Skilled politician and orator though he was, he was only human. When relative calm followed the banging of the speaker's order, he continued.

'Mr Speaker, we cannot leave the Iraqi recruits to their own devices just yet. I cannot say whether they will be ready to do the job next week, next month or next year. The war they fight is the same one Britain fights against the rise of cruel Islamic fundamentalists who bring shame on their people and their faith. I would like to use this opportunity to bring members up to date on the events of two days ago at Enfield.'

Greeves gave a rundown on the explosion at the house in Enfield, without going into detail about the operation to hack into the occupants' computer. His praise of the young man killed in the blast was heartfelt, though he released neither the name nor the occupation of 'one of the security service's best and brightest young people'. He silently also congratulated himself on turning a question about the government's frankly nonexistent exit strategy in Iraq into a reminder of the threat of terror attacks on the homeland.

'Mr Speaker, the two suspects killed at the scene of this bombing were, it would appear, slain by one of their own. It can only be surmised that these two men, of Pakistani origin, carried information about a terrorist network or an impending attack that was so vital their co-conspirator could not risk them being arrested and questioned. This, too, explains why the terrorists blew up their own lair, thereby denying our security services access to whatever materials or information may have been stored there.

'This is a reminder to us all that the foes our young

Iraqi friends face – side by side with their comrades from the British armed forces – are the same as those at work in our own backyard. It is a reminder to us all to be vigilant, determined, strong and courageous in the face of adversity. It is a reminder, Mr Speaker, to be British, and proud of it!'

The roars of support from the government benches drowned out the opposition and Greeves turned to his colleagues, many of whom nodded genuine wishes of congratulations.

His press secretary intercepted him as he left the chamber. 'Choice,' said Helen MacDonald, using a favourite adjective from her New Zealand upbringing. A year earlier Greeves had poached her from a tabloid, where she had put in ten years' service as a political reporter since leaving the *New Zealand Herald*. Helen had often been stinging in her criticisms of the Party and its governance of the country, and that had been one of the reasons he had hired her. In part, taking her on board was removing a thorn in their side. However, he also wanted to ensure there was at least one member of his staff who was not a self-serving political apparatchik, merely biding their time until a safe seat could be found for them. A press secretary needed to be independent – ideally, apolitical – honest, and not afraid to deliver criticism. 'You overdid it a bit at the end. I could almost hear "Land of Hope and Glory" coming out your bum.'

He laughed. He'd chosen Helen well. 'As ever, you flatter me too much, Helen. What's up?' He knew she would not have come looking for him simply to give her critique of his performance in question time.

'What is it with you and Africa?' she asked as they walked together along a corridor.

'You might be from New Zealand but that doesn't mean I don't think you're smart. You know very well I'm going to South Africa to push the sale of some jet training aircraft to their defence force.'

'No, that's not what I mean. A couple of the journos have asked me from time to time why you spend your holidays there as well as jumping on any junket heading for the dark continent. The people that make those planes don't need you to help peddle their wares.'

'It was forthrightness I wanted when I hired you, Helen, not impertinence.'

She let the jibe wash over her. Their feisty banter was no greater than usual. 'I've got one who wants to do a profile piece on you – the real Robert Greeves and all that crap. He's particularly interested in your apparent love affair with Africa – how it started.'

'Not interested,' he said, opening a leather-bound folder and checking his next appointments as they continued to walk. 'Give him the usual line from my bio that I first went to Zambia as a young geologist and developed a great affinity for Africa, its people and its amazing wildlife – you know the drill.'

'It's a shame, though. A nice warm and fuzzy profile with you establishing some strong green credentials could help you in the future.'

'I'm quite happy as Minister for Defence Procurement, thank you, Helen. In case you didn't catch all of my reply to that question, there is a war on, you know. It's my duty to concentrate on this portfolio. Where are you lunching?'

'Sorry, I'm meeting a contact.'

'Always working, eh, Helen? It's not good for you.'

Helen MacDonald left the Houses of Parliament via St Stephen's gate, grateful as ever for a breath of fresh air and a cigarette. As she smoked she weaved to avoid a throng of Spanish tourists armed with digital cameras.

It was grey – as it was most days in London. It was all very well for Robert to tell her all work and no play made Helen a dull girl. He'd be swanning off to Africa soon enough. He was taking Bernard, his defence industries policy advisor, with him. It was obvious there would be no photo opportunities on this trip. A break from Robert would be good for her, in any case, and she might use it to sound out her old contacts in newspapers about a return to journalism.

Unlike many of her former colleagues she didn't see taking a job as a press secretary as selling out. True, the money was better than she'd earned as a reporter, but that wasn't her main motivation for crossing over. She'd always been interested in politics and politicians – what made them tick – and if she returned to newspapers she'd be a better journalist for her time in Westminster. She knew all the tricks of political spin-doctoring now – she'd put them into practice at some time or another. No flak would pull the wool over her eyes ever again.

Arriving from New Zealand as a twenty-five-year-old reporter she had been surprised at first at the minute scrutiny in the UK press of politicians' private lives, particularly in the tabloids. In her country, and in Australia where she had worked for a year on an extended holiday, rumours abounded about the sexual proclivities of members of parliament, and about affairs within the corridors of power, but these rarely made it into the public domain. If they did, the story usually involved a political leader rather than a mere minister or member of paliament, and it was generally revealed by a fellow parliamentarian as part of a wider smear campaign. In England, however, it seemed that who a politician slept with – and how he or she did it – was equally important as their policies or views on world affairs.

She had also wondered why such a high proportion of senior politicians seemed to be committing adultery. That was, at least, until she fell for Robert Greeves. He was a handsome man undoubtedly, and witty and smart and driven, and still idealistic after all this time in politics. But more than that, he was a powerful man. On his word men and women went to war, alliances with other nations were forged and broken, multibillion-pound contracts signed, the fate of a nation decided. And his grey eyes were gorgeous.

'Stop it,' she said out loud, flicking her cigarette butt onto the pavement in front of her and grinding it out without breaking step.

Helen had accompanied him on a trip, not to Africa, but to Germany, for a conference of NATO defence ministers. She had felt her feelings for him grow over the three months leading up to the meeting. She had felt infatuation, followed by denial as she told herself it was morally wrong to be attracted to a married man. There were no signs that he was unhappy at home.

Still, despite her attempts to subdue her feelings, she wanted him.

A suited businessman walking towards her smiled and tried to make eye contact. Damn him, she said to herself. Not the suit, whom she ignored, but her boss. At thirty-seven she could still turn heads – and get the eye from strangers on the street. She worked out six days a week, and watched what she ate – not easy in the confines of parliament where booze and food and lack of opportunity for exercise were daily threats to one's shape. Narrow waist, good legs, pretty face, pert bum.

In Berlin Robert had called Helen to his hotel suite late in the evening. It was eleven o' clock, after the official dinner, and he wanted help reworking his speech. She had been seated with a group of journalists at a back table and, thinking her work was done for the day, had demolished the better part of two bottles of wine by herself.

When she knocked and he opened the door he was in his black dinner suit trousers and white shirt, the sleeves rolled up and top two buttons undone. She caught a glimpse of a thicket of grey chest hair and wanted to put her hand inside to stroke it. 'Thanks awfully, Helen. I'm sorry to call you up so late, but I want to get this right. I've got a bottle on the go if you'd like a glass.' He had nodded to the white wine in a dewy silver ice bucket. His bed looked enormous.

They had sat side by side on the sofa and gone through the speech. At the end he had been particularly effusive in his thanks for her help. They verbally sparred so often that words of praise had seemed out of place. She knew that he appreciated her work and her counsel, and that had always been enough for her.

'I really mean it, Helen. Sometimes I don't know how I'd get on without you,' he'd said.

She'd looked deep into his steel grey eyes. What was going on? Could it be that he felt the same way about her as she did about him? Before she knew what she was doing she had laid her hand on his thigh. 'My pleasure,' she'd said, in a voice lower than usual, as if the words were being spoken by another – someone out of her body. Later she would blame it all on the wine. She had leaned closer to him, eyes half closed, waiting for him to make the next move. For the kiss which would surely come.

He had recoiled, like she was a bloody snake or something. He'd been polite about it, with his smooth words, but she had clearly misread all the signals. Perhaps, she wondered for the thousandth time as she approached St Stephen's pub, opposite the Palace of Westminster, he really had been tempted and had simply had a last-minute attack of guilt. Perhaps, of course, she was a complete fool ever to have thought he would cheat on his wife.

'Helen, I meant what I said,' he had explained as he stood and moved away from the sofa, 'but I love my wife and children. It wouldn't be right for anything to happen between us – in this way.'

Damn him, she thought as she felt the pub's warm fug engulf her and saw the reporter sitting in the corner, waving to her. The only thing wrong with her bloody boss was that he was too good for politics.

5

Tom found the idea of driving in an African game reserve and passing families in cars towing caravans quite odd. It didn't gel with what he'd seen in wildlife documentaries on satellite television. Sannie turned off the tar road – which in itself had been another surprise – onto a dirt track.

The African bush was a mix of drab grey-green stunted trees interspersed with bright new shoots of grass. The seasons were on the turn, and the sky was clouding again. It was hot – like being in the Far East, almost. The foliage was thicker than he had expected, and so far he hadn't seen a single grassy savannah. As well as not meeting his preconceptions, South Africa was throwing plenty of challenges at him from a protection officer's point of view. If the bush was this thick around the lodge it would be easy for someone with the right skills to get in close. It was the same as telling people back in England to keep their trees and hedges trimmed in their yards, so as not to provide too much cover for burglars. The difference here, of course, was that the villains would have to get past two-hundred-kilogram cats out patrolling the garden.

After leaving the police post at Skukuza they had crossed on low-level bridges the Sabie and Sand rivers. Sannie had slowed the Mercedes and he'd had close-up sightings of the huge bewhiskered snouts, piggy eyes and swivelling ears of hippos. A big-horned, scarred buffalo had watched them as it chewed a mouthful of grass. Tom tried to keep his cool, but it was undeniably exciting being this close to wildlife. He found himself wishing that Alex was with him to share the experience and this realisation dampened his excitement.

They followed the signs to Tinga Legends Lodge and at the end of the dirt track came to a rather ornate-looking dark wooden gate topped with curled wrought iron and set between two white posts. Without the press of an intercom or a buzzer, the gate opened automatically. Cameras or sensors, Tom thought.

The Merc's tyres crunched along a gravelled drive-way which took them around a landscaped circle to an imposing thatch-roofed building as tall as a two-storey house. A woman in a loose-fitting white blouse and tight khaki pants and boots stepped off the wide porch. Her face was framed by long, straight jet black hair and she wore a necklace of what looked like small gold nuggets. She appeared to be about thirty. Attractive. A pretty young African girl with her hair twisted into tiny spikes stood behind the white woman, holding a silver platter.

'Beware of Carla,' Sannie said. 'She's the closest

you'll get to a man-eater on this trip.' They walked towards her.

'Hello, welcome to Tinga, I'm Carla Sykes. You must be Tom?'

Tom shook her hand and then accepted a cold towel from the platter borne by the African girl, who Carla introduced as Given.

'Sannie, how lovely to see you once again,' Carla said. Tom thought her smile looked a little less sincere this time.

Sannie just nodded. 'You too, Carla.'

'Precious will organise one of the guys to bring your bags and move your car. Same drill as usual, Sannie. What can I get you to drink?'

Tom was dying for a beer, but said, 'Ginger ale would be fine, please.' Sannie ordered a mineral water and Carla relayed the orders to an African man standing behind an enormous dark wood bar off to their right.

Carla led them through the airy reception area. Sannie's heels clicked pleasingly on the polished caramel-coloured floor, whose hard surface was softened here and there by Turkish rugs. Overstuffed leather lounges and chairs faced a huge fireplace, the mantel of which was topped with a black-and-white photo of a reclining leopard. In contrast to the outside, the lodge's reception was cool and shaded, the light coming from soft bulbs set in antique wall fittings and an overhead chandelier. The barman emerged from behind his fortress-like bar and brought their drinks on a platter. Tom glanced at the cream-coloured walls. As well as more monochrome photos there were antique prints of animals. The place was a mix of colonial indulgence and modern ethnic African chic. Elsewhere this might not have worked – been too over the top – but the place felt smooth and sophisticated and welcoming all at once.

If the reception area was grand, it was understated compared with the spectacular natural view at the other end of the open hall. Carla stepped onto the patio overlooking a wide river studded with pinkish-coloured boulders and stands of lush green reeds. Something which sounded like a five-hundred kilo-gram goose on steroids honked from out there.

'Hippo. You'll have to get used to them, I'm afraid, Tom. This way.' She touched his arm to steer him down a set of wide stairs to an octagonal-shaped stained timber deck with a giant tree in the centre. Off to the right was a grassy terrace set with a swimming pool, and below the deck was another open area with a smaller platform, jutting out over the river itself.

Carla motioned them to take wooden seats around a table in the shade of the tree, again touching Tom. She gestured to the branches above them. 'This is a jackalberry tree. Tinga is set on the site of an old National Parks Board camp called *Jakkalsbessie*, which is Afrikaans for jackalberry. It was a very exclu-sive place – a favourite of the ruling elite during the apartheid years. Because it's so close to the Kruger air strip, which is just up the road, the bigwigs could fly in from Pretoria and Jo'burg and have their meetings and a little fun in seclusion.'

'Where does the current name come from?' Tom asked.

'Tinga is an abbreviation of a Shangaan word, *Tingala*, which means "many lions". The "Legends" part is based on the camp's history. There are plenty of stories about secret meetings that used to go on here. It's said that some of the African national parks staff here were actually undercover ANC operatives, who used to eavesdrop on the government's dastardly business. Not that Mr Greeves will need to fear spies these days!'

'I know you've been through all this before, Carla, and it must seem like a bit of a chore, but . . .' Tom began.

'It's perfectly fine, Tom. I understand how things need to be done, and the value of an advance visit. We get plenty of overseas dignitaries staying here – and a few of our own, including our president – so I'm used to dealing with people such as yourself. Besides, I can't think of a better way to spend an afternoon than in the company of a handsome policeman. You must tell me later about all the people you've been a bodyguard for.'

Tom smiled politely and noticed Sannie rolling her eyes.

'By the way,' Carla asked, 'how is Nick? Is he ill? I got your email saying you'd be carrying out the advance and assumed he wasn't well.'

'Actually, he didn't report for work the other day. We're trying to locate him.'

'Oh, shame,' Carla said. 'That doesn't sound good. He always struck me as particularly . . . conscientious.'

Tom glanced at Sannie and saw she was making a show of looking away out over the Sabie River.

'Were you in contact with Nick at all in the last week or so, in the lead-up to this visit?' Tom asked.

'Err, well . . . I mean, there was the official notification of the meeting between the two ministers, which came through two weeks ago from the British Embassy, and the bookings for the rooms and conference room . . .'

Tom said nothing. Something about Carla's tone of voice and Sannie's attitude and earlier remark told him Carla had had more than official contact with Nick. He knew that the best way to get someone talking was to keep quiet and let the other person fill the void.

'Perhaps one or two other follow-up messages,' Carla said, looking down and brushing the front of her pale linen pants with her palms. 'There was nothing odd, if that's what you mean.'

'Odd?' Tom said.

'Well, Nick sounded fine in his emails. He liked Africa and working with Robert, and was looking forward to coming back again and seeing . . .'

'Seeing?' Sannie prompted.

Tom smiled inwardly. He didn't mind that she had interrupted his questioning; he would have said exactly the same thing. Carla couldn't stop talking once she started. Her accent was softer than Sannie's and Tom guessed from her name being Sykes, which he assumed was her maiden name as she wore no wedding ring, she was a South African of British descent, as opposed to an Afrikaner.

'Seeing all the fabulous game we have here on the concession,' Carla said to Sannie, punctuating the sentence with pursed lips.

'Thank you, Carla, I'm sorry to put you on the spot like that, but we're trying to put together a picture of Nick's movements and contacts over the days leading up to his not reporting for work. Any bit of information might help.'

'Well, if I think of anything, I'll pop by later,' she said, smiling again at Tom. 'Now, if there's nothing else you need to discuss, I'll show you to your rooms. Your afternoon game drive is at four, in just over an hour. I presume you want to go on it?'

'The minister's itinerary includes an afternoon drive, so I'd like to see the route we'll be taking,' Tom said.

'Don't forget your camera – for research purposes only, of course,' Carla laughed. She appeared to be grateful the talk had switched from the topic of her and Nick back to preparations for the visit.

Their suites were separate dwellings, strung out along the Sabie River. The rooms were linked by a walkway made of timber logs, set about a metre above the ground. While the bush had been cleared in front of each suite to allow uninterrupted views of the river, the trees and other vegetation between and behind the individual units appeared to be natural.

'What about wild animals coming into the grounds?' Tom asked Carla on the way to his room.

'We've got low-level electric fences around the accommodation which deter rather than prevent the game moving to and from the river. Our guests like the feeling of being in the wild and everyone is escorted to and from their suite after dark by a security guard.'

'So animals such as lions could feasibly jump over the fences?' Tom asked, doing his best to sound unperturbed.

'We've got a resident leopard that manages to wander around at will. I think he walks under the fence. You might get to see him if you're lucky,' Carla said brightly.

'Right.'

Inside the suite he could see why Tinga charged what it did. This was as luxurious as he imagined an African safari lodge could be. The room was arranged in a linear layout with the separate lounge, bedroom and bathroom all facing the river through large plate-glass windows. Sliding doors opened from the lounge onto a private deck with table, chairs, sun beds and a personal plunge pool. Tom knelt and dipped a finger in. It was heated. Of course.

Back inside there was airconditioning, a sound system, widescreen television and a DVD player, and a phone and computer connection. The bathroom boasted a deep tub on a raised platform, for game viewing while washing, and a shower big enough for two.

'I'll leave you to settle in,' Carla said.

She was a beautiful, sexy, apparently single woman. Why wouldn't she and Nick have become involved? Tom wondered. It wasn't a particularly professional thing to do, although Nick wouldn't have been the first protection officer to get lucky on an away trip. Tom thought that he'd have to report back to Shuttleworth and maybe get Carla to print out hard copies of Nick's emails. If Nick had been telling her he was looking forward to getting back to South Africa to see her, that was a good indicator he had no plans to skive off from a free trip here.

Tom dumped his bags and then, using the key Carla had given him, went next door to the room which would be used by Greeves. This part of the recce was second nature to him.

He walked through the room first, making sure the layout and orientation were the same as his. He checked the locks on the entry door and the sliding door out onto the private deck, testing them, making sure they could be secured from inside. He'd get a list from Carla later of how many duplicate keys and master keys the lodge held, and who had access to them. Walking out onto the deck he looked to see if any of the other suites overlooked this one. As he had expected, privacy was part of the package at Tinga, which was good, but it also meant Tom couldn't keep an eye on the exterior of Greeves's suite. The bush was as thick around this room as it was around all the others – and that was a minus.

The lack of other team members continued to niggle at Tom. There were ways around this, though. The police at Skukuza didn't have the manpower to provide night duty uniform cover, so Tom intended bringing a passive alarm system back with him from the UK. He would set up infra-red sensors on the deck and outside Greeves's door, so that if the beams were broken Tom would get a warning signal in his room. The risk wouldn't normally warrant the extra security, but in this case technology could help make up for the lack of round-the-clock coverage.

Tom checked the room's landline was working, and noted the internet connection as well. He would check out the private dining room in which Greeves and his South African counterpart would take their meals when he went up for his own, after the game drive. He'd also put Carla on notice that he'd need a list of restaurant staff, cleaners and other people who had access to the areas the officials would visit. He wanted dates of birth and other details of new employees. He'd give the list to Sannie to run through the South African criminal records system.

Satisfied for the time being, Tom locked the door to Greeves's room and went back to his own. He changed out of his business shirt, jacket and chinos into a pair of dark blue shorts and a white T-shirt, and swapped his brogues for a pair of trainers and white socks. Feeling himself starting to tire after the flight and long drive, he grabbed a can of Coke out of the well-stocked mini-bar. There was a knock at the door.

'Shame, man, you can't go into the bush dressed like that!' Sannie said. She was wearing green shorts – which were very short – rubber sandals with Velcro straps decorated with some sort of geometric African pattern, and a sleeveless khaki button-up shirt which hung over her holster.

'Why not?' he asked, mildly offended.

'We'll be getting out of the vehicle at some point. I'm not having some bloody elephant charge that snow-white target you're wearing! Stay here, I'll be back.'

Miffed, Tom turned on the television and watched some people in a soap opera talking Afrikaans. He understood not a word. Then there was another knock on the door.

'Here,' Sannie said. 'Your new best friend Carla said this should fit your "big broad shoulders". *Jissis*, but that woman is transparent.'

She walked into the suite while he pulled off his white T-shirt and donned a khaki golfing shirt with a Tinga lion's-head logo on the left breast. 'You think there was something going on between her and Nick?' Tom asked.

Sannie laughed. '*Think?* I *know*. I caught her coming out of his suite one night on an advance visit. She's hot for cops, that girl.'

'What do you think?' Tom said, showing off the new shirt.

'At least we won't be killed by an elephant. Let's go.'

Tea, filter coffee and a selection of cakes and homemade biscuits were laid out in the reception area when Sannie and Tom returned. An American family, parents and three children, was busy clearing the spread. At Sannie's suggestion she and Tom skipped afternoon tea and headed outside to where two Toyota Land Cruisers were parked. Carla introduced them to their guide, whose name was Duncan Nyari. 'It means buffalo,' he said. 'Nyari, that is.'

The vehicles were open on all sides but each had a canvas roof supported by a metal framework. In the back were three rows of tiered seats covered in green rip-stop canvas. Duncan gave them a briefing which came down to a few key rules: don't stand up, as the movement would alarm any animals they were watching; keep the noise down; and don't get out of the vehicle unless told to.

'You are working for Mr Robert Greeves?' Duncan asked Tom as he and Sannie climbed into the seat immediately behind the driver's.

'Yes.'

'He is a good man. He loves Africa and its animals, and the people too. He has provided some textbooks for my eldest son for his university studies – even though I did not ask him for these. He is a good friend.'

Tom nodded, silently impressed. Greeves had a reputation as a hard arse in politics – some in the media called him 'Iron Bob' – so it was interesting to hear he had a human side as well. 'Will we follow the same route today that you'll be taking Mr Greeves and Mr Dule during the visit?'

Duncan shrugged. 'Generally we go where we think the animals are – we get calls on the radio from our vehicles and talk to other guides and people on the road. However, we will stay in the area of our concession for the most part for the ministers' visit, so you won't have too much contact with the other park users.'

'Going where the animals are sounds fine. Unpredictability's good.' In Tom's line of work the most dangerous periods were when people were entering and leaving buildings – homes, offices, even the heavily guarded Houses of Parliament – at set times. The things which couldn't be changed provided opportunities to potential assassins.

As they drove out of Tinga's electronic gates Duncan explained that Tinga was one of a number of private concessions within the Kruger National Park. The concessions had been awarded several years earlier as a means of raising revenue for the National Parks Board. The old Jakkalsbessie camp had been partially destroyed by catastrophic floods which hit the park in February 2000 and, rather than rebuild it, the government had decided to lease the site and a parcel of land to a private operator for exclusive game drives. Tinga's concession encompassed a block between the parallel-running Sabie and Sand rivers – prime game-viewing country with year-round water. The lodge's vehicles were also free to roam the public roads in the national park, which were open to holiday-makers from South Africa and abroad. However, inside their own concession they were able to drive off road into the bush – something strictly forbidden in the rest of the park.

Sannie produced a map book of the Kruger Park, the pages of which were illustrated with drawings of wild animals, birds and reptiles, and descriptions of their behaviour. Tom followed their progress as they turned onto a sealed road and crossed the Sand River via a single-lane low-level bridge. Duncan pulled into a passing bay to let a car towing a caravan pass. 'Hippo,' he said, pointing to their right.

Tom put down the map book and grabbed the camera from his day pack. 'They say the hippo kills more people than any other animal in Africa, but I don't believe this,' Duncan said.

'What does then?' Tom asked, switching on the digital camera.

'Mosquitos,' Sannie said.

'True,' said Duncan. 'Snakes kill about a hundred and twenty thousand people around the world every year, plenty of them in Africa. Myself, I think the crocodile kills more than the hippo. The deaths take place in the remotest parts of Africa, particularly along the Zambezi River, but you never hear about these on the radio or television. However, when someone gets killed by a hippo, that's news.'

Tom was disappointed. The hippo had submerged again.

'Never mind, there'll be other hippos, I can assure you,' Sannie said as Duncan pulled back out into the bridge's main lane.

On the other side of the river they drove up the steep bank, but before reaching the crest Duncan turned right onto a dirt track. By the side of the road was a stone cairn with a sign featuring a red circle with a white bar through it. It said *No entry* in English, and *Geen toegang* in Afrikaans.

'This is the entrance to our concession. No other vehicles can come in here except ours. Once we get to this part of the park your ministers will be safe from prying eyes,' Duncan smiled.

Tom was glad to leave the sealed road; this felt more like it, more as he'd imagined a drive in the African bush would be. There still was no sign of open savannah or thousands of migrating wildebeest – he knew these images were from Kenya and Tanzania, in any case – but there was a sense of tranquillity mixed with a spookiness about the thick bush on either side of the vehicle. Most of the trees seemed to be studded with thorns. It looked inhospitable in there.

In his early twenties Tom had served in the Territorial Army with the 10th Battalion of the Parachute Regiment for four years. He'd quite enjoyed spending weekends as a part-time soldier in the outdoors, but the freezing, barren hills of Wales and an exercise in the forests of Bavaria had given him few skills that would translate to the African bush.

Duncan slowed the vehicle almost to a crawl and looked down at the dirt.

'*Ingwe*,' he said, almost to himself.

'Leopard,' Sannie translated. 'How long ago, Duncan?'

'Not long – maybe an hour or less. There is nothing marking the tracks – no ant footprints, no leaves blown in them. I know this one. He is a big male.'

'I thought leopards were nocturnal,' Tom ventured.

'No,' Sannie said. 'They're active day and night – opportunistic hunters and very adaptable. Here in Kruger some of them have become quite used to the presence of vehicles and actually use them to help them hunt. They use the noise of the engines to cover the sound of their movements as they stalk impala.'

'You seem to know your stuff.'

'Duncan's the real expert. He's probably forgotten more than I'll ever know.'

'I like guiding for people who know the bush,' Duncan said modestly. 'It makes me work harder. This leopard is following the river now, keeping to cover. We might come across him later.'

Tom found the drive informative and also relaxing as Duncan stopped every now and then to point out a colourful bush bird, a small herd of braying zebra, a pair of giraffe, and a shy bushbuck, which had a milk chocolate coat painted with delicate white stripes and spots. He'd almost filled his camera's flash card when Duncan said, 'Shush! No talking now.'

Tom and Sannie had been discussing the likelihood of media interest in the minister's visit. Tom had explained that Greeves's press secretary, Helen MacDonald, had emailed him advising that the Westminster press gallery had no particular interest in the sale of jet trainers to South Africa, although some defence correspondents would follow up the story and one journalist from a London tabloid had asked if there would be a photo opportunity of Greeves viewing game in the Kruger Park. Helen had said there would not, but warned Tom in her message that the reporter had been quite miffed that there would be no official photos released. There was the remote possibility he would hire a South African stringer to try to get a shot. Sannie had doubted the Johannesburg media would intrude on the visit to Tinga. 'Compared with your lot, our media are positively well behaved,' she'd said just as Duncan urged them to silence.

'There, see the ear?' Duncan whispered.

'Got him,' Sannie said.

'I can't see a bloody thing,' Tom confessed.

'Don't look *at* the bush, look *through* it,' Sannie replied.

She leaned closer to him, pointing across his chest to his side of the vehicle. He smelled her perfume. It was like roses. 'Where?' he said.

'There, just past the blackened tree. Rhino.'

He saw its bulk. The dull grey hide was the perfect colour for blending into the dry, dusty growth. Its front horn looked as long as his forearm and hand. Its huge head was lowered, and now that the vehicle's engine was off and they were all silent, he could hear the almost mechanical sound of its grazing, *grunch, grunch, grunch*, as it cropped the brittle yellow grass. The rhino's big trumpet-like ears twitched and swivelled like antennae.

'This is a white rhino. He cannot see very well, but his hearing is good,' Duncan explained.

The massive prehistoric beast seemed placid enough to Tom, almost like a giant horned cow. 'Are they dangerous?'

'Like most animals, only if you by surprise get too close to them. Sometimes when we walk I will clap my hands, to make a noise to let him know that we are near. We don't like them getting a surprise. The other ones, the black rhino, are more dangerous. They are aggressive and will sometimes charge if they are having a bad day.'

Tom stifled a laugh.

Eventually, the rhinoceros ambled away further into the thorn thickets, its hide impervious to the scratches, and Duncan started the Land Cruiser. The sun was accelerating towards the horizon and getting redder by the second as it entered the band of dust that seemed to hover above the drying bushveld. Duncan pulled off the dirt track onto a grassy clearing, overlooking a stretch of river.

'Sundowners,' Sannie announced. 'My favourite time of the day.'

Duncan slid a trestle table from brackets at the rear of the Land Cruiser, politely declining Tom's offer of help. He opened the tailgate and slid out a cool box and a hamper with glasses, plates of snacks and, to Tom's surprise, a white tablecloth.

Sannie asked for a gin and tonic and Tom decided that the working day had come to an end. He took a can of Castle Lager from the ice. It opened with a satisfying pop. 'The sounds of the African night,' Sannie said as she sipped her G and T.

Duncan opened a can of Coke and the three of them stood in companionable silence for a few minutes, watching the sun slide behind the darkening bush. Birds cried and frogs began their evening chorus. Somewhere down in the river hippos honked in unison. Then came a noise that Tom struggled to identify. It sounded like a very loud, very deep wheezing. *Ugh . . . ugh . . . ugh.*

'*Ngala*,' Duncan said.

'Lion?'

'You're right,' Sannie said. 'Most people expect a big roar, like the MGM lion in the movies, but it's more mournful; softer, even – unless, of course, they're right outside your tent, then it's bloody terrifying!'

'You get lions around your tent here, in Kruger, when you camp?' Tom asked.

'No. Here it's all electric fences. We went camping in Zimbabwe a few times, before it got bad up there, and in some of their parks there are no fences around the camps. We had lions walking through the camp ground. I nearly wet myself.'

'Just you and the kids? That's very brave.'

'No. Me, my husband and the kids.'

'Oh, I'm sorry, Sannie,' Tom said.

She shrugged. 'It's funny, but it's at times like this, when everything is so nice and peaceful and calm, that I miss him the most. I can deal with problems at work, and the rubbish from the kids when they play up. I have to, being a single mom now, but it's when everything seems to be perfect that I realise I don't have anyone to share things with. Sorry. I don't mean to sound so depressing.'

'No, it's okay. I was just thinking the same thing. How much Alex would have liked it here. We'd talked about going on a safari holiday for years.' He realised how much harder the grieving process must be for Sannie, having to bring up her kids and be strong for them. He admired her not just for carrying on in the circumstances but for being so honest. She wasn't afraid to talk about her grief, something he usually found hard to do.

'It can't be easy for you,' she said.

'We had our future planned. It was as if we put the first half of our married life on hold, with the idea that we'd make up for it during holidays and after an early retirement . . . My turn to apologise now. I don't usually talk this much about Alex.'

She laid a hand on his forearm, briefly. 'It's not often I can find someone who'll listen. I'm sure policemen are the same in England as they are in South Africa. We bottle up a lot of bad stuff and make out it doesn't affect us.'

She smiled and Tom nodded. It was so hard not just to stand there gazing into her eyes. He felt a growing connection to her that was comforting, exciting and a bit scary all at once.

'Where was your favourite holiday destination?' she asked.

He was grateful she spoke again; he was starting to feel as self-conscious as a teenager. 'A little Greek island, just off the coast of Turkey, called Lipsi. Beautiful, unspoiled, and far from the tourist crowds. A bit like here, I suppose.'

'Oh, don't be too sure about that. You should see Kruger in the school holidays – it's like Jozi peak hour sometimes on the roads here.'

'More drinks?' Duncan said. They both said yes, though Tom was a little disappointed that Duncan had interrupted their conversation.

Unlike in England, darkness descended in Africa with the suddenness of a curtain closing. It was pitch black, the night moonless, as they drove back to the lodge. As well as having his headlights on, Duncan held a spotlight in one hand as he drove. He swivelled it continuously left and right, searching for the eyes of night creatures, which he explained would glow like reflectors in the bright beam.

He stopped and Tom peered into the inky bush. 'In the tree – the big one,' Duncan hissed.

Tom followed the shaft of light up the pale trunk and saw the cat. The leopard crouched on a branch. Gripped in its vicelike jaws was a fawn-coloured antelope – the cat had it by the throat.

'He has killed that impala by suffocation,' Duncan explained in a matter-of-fact tone while Tom's heart pounded in his chest. He was awestruck, silent.

Duncan started the truck's engine again and turned off the road, moving at walking pace closer and closer to the tree. The leopard stared malevolently down at them, its eyes glowing like yellow beacons. Duncan shifted the light slightly to one side of the animal, so it was still visible but not shining directly into its eyes.

'He can carry between two and three times his own body weight in his jaws. He needs to climb into a tree to eat his prey, otherwise lions and hyenas will steal it from him. This is the big male whose tracks we saw this afternoon on the road.'

'Amazing,' Tom whispered.

'You're very lucky,' Sannie said. 'Some people go their whole life without seeing a leopard.'

The cat walked backwards up the branch and hung the antelope's carcass in a fork, wedging it there securely. He bit into its rump, his spotted face immediately stained red.

'They kill by suffocation so that the prey does not make a noise and attract the other predators. The silent predator,' Duncan said.

Tom lathered his body under the strong, stinging hot shower spray, washing away the African dust that had coated his skin. Despite the short time he'd spent in the afternoon sun, he noticed his arms and legs were already pinking up.

He reached across the ledge and grabbed his Castle. He'd liberated one from the mini-bar to drink while showering, which seemed an appropriately decadent thing to do in the five-star safari hideaway. He smiled as the cold lager ran down his throat in delicious contrast to the water on his body. It had, he thought, been a great day. Business travel for him usually meant moving from one hotel room to another. In the down time there were hotel restaurants and bars which were indistinguishable save for the language of the bar staff. The venues he'd had to advance were more often than not hotel conference rooms or function centres, or perhaps a school or a hospital – other favourite haunts of high-profile politicians. Never had he had an experience on a protection job as he'd had this afternoon. He could see the attraction now of protecting someone like Robert Greeves – even without the two beautiful women he'd also come into contact with.

Tom thought about Sannie and how vulnerable she'd seemed in the moment she'd mentioned going on holiday with her husband and kids. It was amazing that they'd both been thinking virtually the same thing at the same time. He sensed she was still brittle and shook his head at Nick's insensitivity. Still, he could see how a ladies' man like him would certainly consider it worth a try.

Carla Sykes had been all ears for Tom's leopard story when Duncan had dropped them at the entrance to Tinga. He imagined she must hear guests talking about amazing game sightings every working day of her life, but she had seemed genuinely to be hanging on his words. She had laid a hand on his forearm and said, 'You do realise how very, very lucky you've been tonight, Tom. I wonder how we'll be able to top that experience?'

Flirty, no doubt. It was little wonder she and Nick had hit it off.

He dried and changed into chinos, brogues and a fresh shirt. He checked his watch. Seven-thirty. He opened the door of the suite.

'Good evening, sir,' said the uniformed African security guard and saluted him. The man held a torch as long as a night stick, and carried the real thing through a ring on his belt.

'Evening,' Tom said. He was impressed at the man's punctuality. He'd followed the lodge's rules and arranged for the guard to be at his accommodation at this time. As Carla had briefed him earlier, after dark the lodge encouraged guests only to move to and from the main building with a security escort. They obviously took the threat of encounters with nocturnal wildlife seriously. He didn't know if Robert Greeves would expect an escort, but Tom felt a whole lot happier knowing there were people who knew the local scene available to perform this task. What would he, an Englishman in Africa, do if he and Greeves were bailed up by a leopard on the walkway? Draw his Glock and shoot it? He smiled at the thought and followed the man.

Sannie was already in the dining room, at a table for two, reading a paperback novel and sipping a glass of white wine. She had changed into jeans and a loose-fitting peasant top, and wore a necklace comprising a shell flanked by chunky wooden beads. She looked relaxed and fresh, and smiled at him when he walked in.

'Sorry about the book,' she said, putting it away

in her handbag. 'Too much time waiting around by myself in this job.'

'I know exactly what you mean.'

'I've already ordered wine, do you want some?'

He nodded and over a drink they talked through the remaining details of the joint ministerial visit – timings, routes, vehicles, communications, and recapped the emergency plan. After discussing business and over a meal of marinated kudu steaks – a bigger type of antelope than the leopard's meal they had seen earlier, Sannie explained – she talked about her kids and asked him why he and Alex had never had any.

'It didn't start out as a conscious decision. It was the job at first, for both of us. She was a doctor – an intern when I met her – and we were both working crazy hours. When I went to what was then known as Special Branch, a lot of my work was undercover or on surveillance, back when the IRA was our main threat. We got used to going abroad for our holidays – spending our wages on ourselves – so I suppose we both eventually agreed children wouldn't really fit us.'

'Do you regret it now, now she's gone?'

He shrugged. 'I would have liked to have had a reminder of her, I suppose, but I don't know if that's a good enough reason to have children.'

'It was for me.' Sannie frowned then sipped more wine to hide her sorrow.

He wanted to reach out and hold her hand at that moment, but he didn't. He knew his attraction to her was growing by the minute, but there were plenty of reasons not to follow his instincts. Firstly, he told himself, it was unprofessional. He told himself, too, that he should still be feeling guilty, even though Alex had been gone more than a year. Thirdly – and if he was honest, most importantly – he didn't want to do anything too soon which could jeopardise what might just be growing between them. He didn't want her to think he was using their shared experiences as a pick-up routine.

After dinner Carla joined them for drinks. She had flitted from table to table during the evening meal, ensuring all was fine with the food and the service. The Americans had turned out to be demanding, asking for 'plain grilled shrimp' rather than the sesame-coated pan-fried prawns each the size of a small lobster which were offered on the menu. Two German couples had also arrived while Tom and Sannie had been on their game drive.

'Meals for Mr Greeves and Mr Dule will be served in a private room,' Carla explained as she sat down with a glass of wine in hand. She downed it quickly, Tom noted.

With the last of the guests escorted to their rooms, it seemed Carla wanted to make up for lost time. She ordered two more drinks before Tom had finished his cleansing post-dinner lager. Carla was full of questions about London and mentioned that several of her friends had left South Africa for the UK to escape what she called the abominable crime problem.

'Of course, if I had a big strong detective to look after me and protect me from car-jackers I'd happily stay in South Africa,' she cooed.

'I'm sorry, but I'm quite tired this evening; please excuse me. Goodnight and see you in the morning,' Sannie said.

Tom was sorry, too, to see her leave. He'd enjoyed her company all afternoon and evening and felt that Carla was intruding on something. Also, her crack about having a policeman to look after her was not only overtly flirtatious, but insensitive if she knew who Sannie's husband was and how he had died.

'It's after eleven,' he said, looking at his watch.

'Party pooper,' Carla chided him, giving him a light punch on the arm. It wasn't the first time she had touched him during their conversation. With each drink she leaned a little closer.

Tom could read the signs – he wasn't blind. Carla was pretty, flirtatious, sexy and getting increasingly drunk. He played a straight bat and said, 'We've got an early start tomorrow, so I really should get some shut-eye.'

'The security guard's just seeing the girls back to their quarters. I'll escort you – if you trust me to ward off any dangerous game, that is.'

He wouldn't trust Carla behind the wheel of a car right now, and he had no idea how she would see off a lion if she couldn't walk a straight line, but he shrugged and said, 'Of course I trust you.'

Carla took a torch and walked ahead of him. He couldn't help but notice the pleasing way her pants clung to her firm bottom.

'Here we are, home sweet home. Nice and safe from the predators.' She leaned against the wall beside the doorframe as he opened the door.

'Night, Carla. Thanks for everything.'

'Night,' she said, and he thought he saw the trace of a pout crease her lips.

Tom turned on the lights inside and slipped off his shoes. With only an hour's time difference from the UK he wasn't jetlagged and, despite the impression he'd given Carla, he wasn't all that tired. The game drive had been a buzz and he still hadn't come down from it. While he was tossing up whether to have a final beer or not, there was a knock at the door.

Carla stood there, a wicked grin curling the corners of her mouth. 'I didn't ask you if you wanted your bed turned down, sir.'

She put her palm on his chest and pushed him into the room.

6

'You look a little bleary-eyed. Did you stay up late jolling?' Sannie asked, looking up from her book and a plate of bacon and eggs.

'If you mean partying, no. I got to bed soon after you,' Tom said.

When the waitress came, Tom said he was famished and ordered a full cooked breakfast. Sannie asked nothing about Carla's movements during the night and he volunteered the same as she finished her breakfast and he tucked into his.

The drive back to Johannesburg was uneventful and their conversation sporadic and mundane. Sannie thought he was being particularly guarded today, and wondered if he had something to feel guilty about. Carla had been all over him after dinner and had made Sannie feel like a third wheel. The line about having a policeman boyfriend to protect her from car-jackers had been the final straw. She recalled once telling the woman what had happened to her husband. Perhaps Carla had forgotten in her drunkenness.

Sannie was feeling a little guarded herself. She had talked too much about Christo. Perhaps it was the fact that Tom had also lost his partner that encouraged her to open up more than she normally would have. Perhaps it was just as well that Carla had intruded after dinner – who knows what else they would have gotten around to discussing and where it would have led. She certainly wasn't the kind of woman who slept with a man the first day she got to know him, but she had recognised her own feelings of physical and emotional attraction to Tom. He was a good-looking guy, smart, sensitive and almost childlike in his awe at his first visit to the bush. She liked that about him the most. Also, he was still in pain, as she was, and maybe her maternal instincts were taking over, making her want to look after him.

Stupid, she thought. She had two kids already and didn't need another dependent – or a one-night stand or a boyfriend who lived half a world away. When the time was right for her to be with another man she would know it. It had been wrong with Wessels and it definitely would not have been right with Tom last night. Her cell phone rang.

'Hello?' Sannie listened to the woman on the other end of the line. 'Oh no!' She shook her head. She told the caller in Afrikaans she would be there as soon as possible.

'Everything all right?' Tom asked.

'That was my kids' school. My boy fell in the playground and has cut his head. They've put some Band-Aids on him but they think he should see a doctor. My mom's in Pretoria visiting my aunt.'

'Well, don't mind me. I've still got a few hours to kill before the flight.'

'I'm sorry, Tom, but thanks. It won't be far out of our way. Maybe I can pick him up, then drop you at the airport on the way to the doctor.'

'Get your boy seen to first. I've got nothing better to do in the meantime. If worse comes to worst I can call a taxi later.'

She thanked him again and put her foot down. Bugger the speed traps, she thought. If her boy needed stitches he might be suffering a concussion as well. It was good of Tom not to make a big deal about getting to the airport. He asked if she had a car charger for a cell phone – his was the same make as hers – and she told him it was in the glove compartment. He set it in the console next to her Z88 pistol as she drove at breakneck speed to the school.

Sannie turned off the N12 on the R21 exit, barely checking her speed. It was late morning so the traffic wasn't too bad. Though she was trying to be calm for Tom's benefit she was dreadfully worried about Christo, who had been named after his father. With her job and its irregular hours she felt guilty sometimes that she did not see enough of him and Ilana. Her mother picked them up from school most days and was with them three or four nights a week. What could she do? She had to put food on the table and that was enough of a struggle on her basic wage, even with the overtime she earned protecting dignitaries at nights and weekends. She didn't want to go back into uniform, or into homicide or any other detective branch for that matter. She loved what she did and, as usual, told herself she would just have to live with the guilt.

When she arrived at the primary school in Kempton Park, Christo's teacher, Mrs De Villiers, was there to meet her. Sannie holstered her weapon and told Tom he should wait in the car, but he said he would come with her. That was a nice gesture, but Sannie could see the enquiring look in Mrs De Villiers's eyes when she was introduced to Tom. 'Tom's a work colleague, on assignment here from the UK,' she explained, putting paid to any rumours before they circulated around the school staffroom and the other mothers.

'Hello, you've been in the wars, eh?' Tom said to Christo when they found him lying on a bed in the sick room. Christo looked down, shy in front of the stranger.

Sannie hugged him then held him at arm's length to inspect the cut under the Band-Aids. His dark thick hair – a legacy from his father and yet another constant reminder of him for Sannie – was matted with dried blood and the gash looked quite nasty. 'Are you okay, my boy? How do you feel?' she asked him in Afrikaans.

'Fine, Mom,' he replied.

'Ag, you're so brave. Still, we have to get you to the doctor to make sure everything is fine.' Sannie switched to English. 'This is Mr Furey, Christo. He works with Mommy. He's from England.'

'Hello,' Christo said, holding out his hand, which Tom shook. Sannie was proud of his manners. 'Do you play rugby in England?'

Tom laughed. 'Not me. I used to play football – soccer.'

'That's funny,' Christo said. 'Do you know Kaizer Chiefs?'

Then Sannie laughed, and said to Tom, who was shaking his head, 'Soccer's mostly played by the black Africans in this country. That's why he's interested in you playing it. Come, let's go.'

Mrs De Villiers returned a few minutes later with little Ilana, whose hair colour and cut, nose and mouth were all carbon copies of her mother's. 'Christo fell over, Mommy. Who's this man?' she asked in Afrikaans.

Sannie repeated the explanations and introduced Tom, but Ilana maintained a shyness act in front of the British policeman. Sannie said goodbye to Mrs De Villiers and bundled the kids into the back of the car.

The doctor's surgery was in a small shopping centre, surrounded by a fence of spike-topped metal poles and patrolled by security guards, low-key by Johannesburg standards. Tom went into the waiting room with Sannie and sat with the kids while she spoke to the receptionist. Fortunately the doctor would be able to see them quickly, after his current patient. She thanked the woman and went back to her family. Ilana, she noticed, was showing Tom a picture of a lion in an old copy of *National Geographic*. Tom asked her what sort of noise it made, and the five year old let out a mighty roar that caused an old lady sitting across from them to burst into laughter. The kids seemed at ease around Tom already and Christo was asking him if he had any scars.

'I'm so sorry to drag you through all this,' Sannie said to him.

'Like I said, I've got nowhere else to go and nothing to do until my flight. Would the kids like an ice cream? I saw a shop next door.'

The two small faces turned to her, nodding their approval. They hadn't had lunch so normally she wouldn't have agreed, but with Christo injured and the kids so settled in his company it couldn't hurt. 'You don't have to, Tom, but I'm sure it would cement the friendship.'

Tom left them. A cell phone started ringing in her handbag, but the ring tone was unfamiliar. It was Tom's. In her state of concern over Christo she'd instinctively scooped up Tom's phone from the Merc's console, as she never left her phone open to view in a car park, even one with security. She looked over her shoulder out the window of the surgery and saw Tom had disappeared into the ice-cream shop. She could let the call go through to voicemail, but it could be something important. She answered.

'Tom Furey's phone.'

'Hello? Oh, Sannie, is that *you*?'

'*Ja.*' It was a woman's voice. Just as she recognised it, the caller continued.

'It's Carla. Are you two still together?'

'I'm taking him to the airport.'

'Oh, cool. Look, would you be a dear, please, Sannie, and ask him if he saw one of my gold earrings this morning? I've looked everywhere and the maids can't find it. The only other place it could have come out was Tom's suite. It might have got mixed up with some of his *kitundu* when he was packing this morning.'

'Sure, no problem. I'll pass the message on,' Sannie said and hung up. She felt queasy. Perhaps it was the smell of the doctor's surgery. Perhaps not.

Tom sat in the BA lounge at OR Tambo International Airport, sipping a bloody mary he'd just fixed himself from the self-service bar. The lounge was in tranquil contrast to the bustling departure terminal upstairs.

He'd realised straightaway that Sannie's change in attitude towards him was due to the message Carla had left. He'd tried, twice, to tell her what happened, but Sannie had shut down the explanation before he'd had time to get it out.

'I told you, Tom, it's got nothing to do with me. We're all adults here. What you do in your off time is your business.'

She was right, of course, and he was a bit pissed off that her tone suggested he'd done something wrong when, in fact, he hadn't. It was a shame, though, that their time had ended coolly, just when he thought he was getting to know her better. While he hadn't pushed things over dinner, he wanted her to like him – and not just in the professional sense as two colleagues who would still have to work together closely. The kids had surprised him, as well – how much he enjoyed the brief time he spent with them. Ilana had pretended to read to him from a magazine while they waited for Christo to get his head stitched, and the boy had proudly showed off his sutured wound to Tom when he and Sannie had at last emerged from the doctor's room. He felt a sense of loss now, as though he'd let something precious slip through his fingers.

The *Daily Mail* he was flicking through must have come in on the morning's flight as it already had a small piece about the explosion in Enfield. The Home Secretary was reported as saying: 'Security service officers had this house under surveillance because its occupants were suspected of having links to a terrorist organisation.'

Tom frowned. That was a bit of an oversimplification. The house was occupied by suspected people smugglers who had *possibly* provided refuge to terrorist suspects. The fact that Steve had found pornography on the computer also led Tom to suspect the illegal immigrants who moved through the house were bound for the sex trade. Still, he knew politicians liked to simplify things and the 'T' word was always good for a headline. He thought again about the computer expert who had lost his life. What a bloody waste. They'd probably never know what it was that he had been so excited about.

One thing there was no doubting, the occupants had to have been hiding something very sensitive in the house – presumably on their computer – to blow it up. He wondered if they were, as the government was speculating, in the process of planning another 'spectacular' in the league of the Twin Towers or the London Underground bombing.

He checked his watch and called Shuttleworth's direct number from his mobile phone. When the chief inspector answered, Tom gave him a brief rundown on the advance recce in South Africa and assured him everything was in order at this end.

'We've still had no word from Nick,' Shuttleworth said.

'How about the strip club, guv?'

'Nothing there, either. That girl, Ebony – real name Precious Mary Tambo – appears to have done a bunk. She's an illegal and they've had no further word from her. We've got a home address, though. Frank and Bill are going around to check it later today. Nick's ex hasn't heard from him, either.'

'I'll type up a report when I get back, but from here it seems our Nick was getting his end away when he could while he was in Africa. Also frequented a table-dancing club in Pretoria and seemed to prefer African girls.'

'Hmmm. I don't like any of this, Tom.'

Tom agreed. Had Nick got himself into some kind of trouble? Drugs? Gambling? Seeing a stripper wasn't grounds for dismissal from the force, but it was possibly an indicator that he was involved in something on the fringes of the law. Had Nick been seduced or coerced into helping the African woman? Police officers didn't just disappear.

The flight to London Heathrow was called and Tom drained his bloody mary. He was looking forward to reaching home and getting a good night's rest before his first full day with Robert Greeves.

As he got up he noticed a glossy coffee table book standing on a bookshelf. It was about the wildlife of the Kruger National Park. He remembered the excitement of the close encounter with the silent predator – the leopard – in the darkness. Despite his misgivings about the job, he was looking forward to coming back to Africa in a couple of days' time.

If this was a normal job, he would have been staying in Africa. Another protection officer would have escorted Greeves on his flight and Tom would have met them at the airport. But these were not normal times, as the increased threat alert and Nick's disappearance had proved. It meant they were cutting corners and Tom felt his initial niggling concerns growing.

7

Tom straightened his tie and knocked on the dark blue door set in the white stone facade of the Belgravia townhouse. The place was worth a fortune, though he was not surprised by the size or location of Robert Greeves's London residence. He knew from his briefing that the assistant minister was extremely wealthy, in addition to being a successful politician.

Greeves's family was old money and, unlike many of their breed, they knew how to make a quid as well as spend it. Greeves's wife, Janet, also came from a well-off family, although hers had made their money in trade, running a nation-wide chain of supermarkets. She came from a long line of party faithful and Tom had read that she had served on the executive.

A girl in her late teens opened the door. She had a pierced nose, a studded leather collar around her neck, jet black hair and a long black dress on. 'Dad!' she yelled. 'I think it's your bodyguard.'

'Protection officer, ma'am,' Tom said. The girl rolled

her eyes and turned without a word of greeting and walked down a corridor. Tom smiled. It seemed the picture-perfect political family had at least one gothic sheep.

Greeves appeared, shrugging on his suit jacket and stuffing a piece of toast into his mouth. 'I want you in by eleven, Samantha,' he called back through his breakfast. 'Even though I'm not going to be in the country, I'll call you.'

Tom looked over his shoulder to make sure all was well on the street and saw Greeves's official driver, Ray Butler, in the car with the engine running. Greeves had a briefcase and overnight bag in the hallway, ready to go. Tom made no move to pick up the bags, and he'd instructed Ray to stay in the ministerial vehicle.

Sally, the other protection officer who worked with Nick on Greeves's UK team, was standing next to her BMW five series, its exhaust curling around her legs as the chilly morning breeze caught it. She nodded to Tom. Sally was acting as close protection officer, while Tom was the PPO – principal protection officer. In Nick's absence he was also the team leader.

'Hello. Robert Greeves,' the minister said politely, though completely unnecessarily. 'Don't mind my daughter. She can be almost civil when you get to know her well. She's at college, stays here in the London house when she's not out clubbing. My wife Janet's at our country place in Buckinghamshire.'

'Detective Sergeant Tom Furey, sir.' Tom shook the minister's hand. It was the strong grip and eye contact, Tom thought, of a man who had spent a large proportion of the past twenty years shaking people's hands for a living.

'You and I should have a word, Tom, about how things are going to work between us. It's a busy day, as usual. Where's Ray?'

'In the car's the best place for him, sir. With the engine running.'

Greeves looked at him for a second, then down at his bags, before picking them up. Tom wasn't fazed. If Nick did things differently – let the chauffeur act like a bellboy – then that was his business. Tom moved to one side as Greeves walked out past him. Tom pulled the house door closed, then said into the microphone of his radio, 'Moving now, Sal.'

'Okay, Tom.'

Tom moved ahead of Greeves, opening the back door of the dark blue Jaguar saloon. Greeves tossed his bags in ahead of him and climbed in. Tom closed the door. He'd once been protecting a newly promoted minister who'd insisted that he should sit in the front seat, next to the driver, and that Tom should sit in the back. Also, he'd told Tom he didn't want his protection officer opening the door for him, like a footman. Tom had politely but firmly explained that the reason he acted as he did was not out of courtesy. 'I control the door, sir,' he'd said. 'I don't get in until I know you're secure and the street is clear, and you don't get out, sir, until I know it's clear outside.'

Tom took another look up and down the street. 'Clear, Tom,' Sally said into his earpiece. When they were talking on the back-to-back channel, for interpersonal communication, it was first names. Tom looked back and saw she was waiting outside her car until he was in the front of the Jag. She was good, even if Nick had let things slide. The Jag indicated and pulled away from the kerb, with Sally following in the BMW.

Tom scanned the road ahead, looking for anything unusual – cars or vans double parked, people on the street who took an interest in them.

'Funny business about Nick,' Greeves said from the back seat.

'Yes, sir,' Tom said, without looking back at the minister. 'We've got detectives out looking for him and following up leads.' Tom checked the wing mirror and saw Sally was close behind them.

'I'm starting to become concerned about his welfare, Tom. Nick seemed a bit of a lad in his spare time, but he was never a second late for a job, and that counts a hell of a lot to me. What he got up to in his own time was his own business, but I'm alarmed at hearing reports of investigations in strip clubs and so forth.'

Tom was surprised that Greeves had that much detail on the investigation, although he certainly had the clout and the motive to keep himself informed. A threat to his protection officer could mean a risk to Greeves himself, if someone was trying to get at Nick or compromise him in some way. Greeves had enemies the world over, as well as plenty at home.

'Nick and I got on,' Greeves went on, 'because he was good at his job and he was always ahead of the game. I know of your background – it's similar to Nick's – and I'm sure you'll do just as good a job.'

'Yes, sir,' Tom said dutifully. It was the sort of

welcome he'd expected. Robert Greeves might be well known, rich and powerful, but he was just a man to Tom, flesh and blood who could fall to a bullet or a bomb or any number of other threats as easily as anyone else in the street. It was simply Tom's job to see that it didn't happen on his shift.

'What did you think of Africa?'

That took Tom by surprise. 'Very nice, sir.'

'A man of few words, I see, but well chosen. Are you hooked by her?'

'Her, sir?'

'Africa.'

Tom thought of the drinks under a setting red sun, hearing the lion calling in the distance, seeing the leopard and its prey. He thought of Sannie van Rensburg, even though they'd parted on frosty terms. 'Could be, sir,' he said.

'Well, if poor old Nick doesn't show himself soon this won't be the last time you get to go to the dark continent.'

Tom pulled the printout of the day's schedule from the inside pocket of his suit coat and glanced down at it. As Greeves said, it was a typically busy day for a minister, even though parliament had risen the previous day. Their first appointment, where they were headed now, was a fundraising breakfast in the city, aimed at garnering and shoring up donations for the coming election campaign. After that was a last-minute briefing from the defence company vying to sell aircraft to the South Africans, followed by a media conference at the company's offices with its chairman; a visit to an HIV-AIDS clinic in Islington – a cheque presentation of some sort; afternoon tea with selected constituents in the Westminster office at Portcullis House; and then, finally, off to Heathrow for the evening flight to Johannesburg. Tom's bag was in the boot of the police car. He wouldn't see home again for another five days. He'd call Charlie Sheather in Cape Town to make sure things were ready there. It was another reminder that this was a shoestring operation. Sally couldn't come to Africa because she was due leave and had a daughter about to go into hospital to have her tonsils out.

The breakfast function was Tom's first opportunity to see Greeves address an audience in the flesh. Tom had sat through hundreds, maybe thousands of these types of speeches while protecting various politicians over the years. He considered himself a cynic when it came to politics, believing there was little to differentiate either of the main parties. He would have classed himself a left-leaning conservative, and that meant he might as well close his eyes and use a pin to pick the people he voted for. It was rare that someone could hold his attention in a speech, especially as part of Tom's job was to keep a weather eye on the audience, catering staff and anyone else in the room *other* than the person doing the talking. This crowd were invitees who had paid five hundred quid a head to listen to Robert Greeves. They were blue pinstripe to the core. While Tom didn't drop his guard he did keep an ear open to the words coming from the man behind the lectern. He wanted to learn as much about Greeves as he could during the day.

'Does it really matter,' Greeves was saying, leaning forward, elbows on the lectern in a bid to get closer to his suited audience, 'if there were weapons of mass destruction in Iraq – chemicals, poison gas bombs, Scuds full of nerve agents, et cetera, et cetera?'

Greeves waited during the seconds of hushed silence. Tom half felt like chirping up and saying, 'Yes, it bloody well does matter, since the government sent us into a war based on a dossier of fiction and half-truths.'

Greeves seemed almost to be looking right at Tom when he said, 'There *was*, in fact, one WMD in that country that we know of for sure. Saddam Hussein. Is it right for Britain or the United States to sit back and do nothing while a man gases his own people, assassinates dissidents by the score; while his sons torture, rape and massacre at their whim? No, ladies and gentlemen, it was not right to deal with Iraq in the way we did. It was not right to stop at the gates of Baghdad in 1991; it was not right to abandon the marsh Arabs when they rose against Saddam after that war; and it was not right to say, "Leave him to his own devices, eventually one day his people will wake up and get rid of him. It's not our fight."'

Tom had heard the argument before – and it continued to smack of bandaid policy to him. This government was still trying to convince the people that it had been right to get involved in Iraq, even if it wasn't for the reasons originally put forward. Tom hadn't become a convert, but he was impressed by the way Greeves was putting his case forward. He went on, as he had done in parliament the day before, to personalise the conflict, to make it about standing up for the people of Iraq – presumably the majority – who were sick of the bombings, the fighting, the executions.

Metropolitan police protection officers had been to Iraq and Afghanistan, accompanying the Prime Minister, Defence Secretary and the Foreign Secretary. Tom hadn't been picked for these teams as he had yet to renew his qualification on the Heckler & Koch sub machinegun – the weapon he would have carried on such an assignment. He'd go if he was told to but, unlike some of the younger officers, he wasn't volunteering.

Greeves alluded again to the bomb blast in Enfield and Tom couldn't help but listen in now; he had felt the heat of the blast, seen the charred remains of the computer expert wheeled out.

'We'll probably never know what the terrorists were planning when that brave member of the security services lost his life in that house, but what we *do* know, ladies and gentlemen, is that Britain remains at war with the forces of evil. All of us, not just our tireless security services, need to remain vigilant, committed and resolute in our determination that Britain *will not* yield to terror; that we *will* support and agitate for democracy in places around the world where decent people can only dream of such a concept, and that we *will* remember all those who put their lives on the line every day for people like you and people like me.'

The applause was as close as Tom had seen to thunderous in many years. He, too, found himself on his feet, not wanting to be seen as the only person sitting, but also oddly moved by the speech, especially the last line. A young banker at his table, his face still spotty, who had introduced himself to Tom and therefore knew that he was Greeves's protection officer, nodded to him and mouthed, 'Well done.' Tom felt embarrassed.

'He's good,' Sally said. 'Too bad he can't get his bleedin' children to behave as well as this mob,' she added as an aside.

Sally left first, as Greeves moved from table to table, shaking hands with the Party faithful. Tom stayed just behind him, at his shoulder.

'Vehicles ready. All clear outside.'

'Thanks, Sal,' he replied into his radio. 'Moving now.'

Greeves read *The Times* in the backseat on the drive to the aircraft manufacturer's headquarters in a business park in Ealing. Tom and Sally repeated their routine on arrival. They waited in an anteroom in the office tower while Greeves had his meeting with the company's executives. Tom knew the contract was important, not only for local jobs, but for Britain's standing in the international defence and aviation industry – hence the minister's personal lobbying in South Africa.

The press conference was held in a purpose-built room on the ground floor. Tom moved in with Greeves and positioned himself off to one side of the podium, where the minister sat with the chief executive officer and chairman of the board. The company's PR people said all of the reporters in the conference were known to the firm and their identities had been double-checked. From what Tom knew of the media and its workings, this conference was poorly attended – only half-a-dozen reporters and he recognised none of them. No one from TV or radio, and none of the usual Westminster gallery hacks were present. These were defence correspondents, most of them from industry magazines.

The company's chairman, an ex-Royal Air Force air commodore, gave a long-winded introduction about the merits of the jet trainer on offer to South Africa and Greeves followed with a succinct spiel about the importance of creating British jobs and maintaining good relations with Africa's most stable democracy.

The questions were a mix of technical probing about the jet's reported avionics flaws and points of clarification regarding revenues, jobs and the possibility of more sales on the African continent if the South Africans came on board. When the conference was nearly over, one reporter, a young man with red hair and glasses, said, 'Mr Greeves, why is it that you've made fourteen visits to southern Africa in the last four years?'

Greeves looked slightly off balance as he reached for the glass of water on the table in front of him. Tom noted that two of the other reporters looked askance at their colleague, as if they, too, were surprised he had asked something out of the ordinary. Clearly these defence journalists were a different breed.

'Africa's important to Britain,' Greeves began, quickly regaining his composure. 'We have, of course, strong historical links to many of the countries on the continent and, if you read the papers,' this brought a chuckle from a few of the other members of the press, 'there are also many serious, pressing issues which require the attention and input of this government.'

'Why so often for pleasure, as well as business?' the young man persisted.

'Who is he?' Tom whispered to the company's media relations director, who was hovering off to the side of the podium.

'Michael Fisher, the *World*.'

If the media was an 'estate', as the Americans put it, then the *World* was the gardener's snot rag. It was tits and arse and barely legal page-three girls. What, Tom wondered, were they doing here?

'Where I spend my holidays is my business. Now, as I was saying before, the important points to remember about this contract are that it's good for Britain – four hundred jobs in the factory in the north; good for South Africa – they get a modern, safe, state-of-the-art aircraft at a very good price; and it's good for British industry and technology. Ladies and gentlemen, thank you.'

Greeves had shut down the media conference expertly. Tom was impressed. Tom spotted the reporter, Michael Fisher, springing from his chair as Greeves left the conference room. Tom slid in behind the man he was protecting. He didn't say a word or lay a finger on Fisher, but the man quickly got the message that he would get no closer to the minister. The PR woman moved in to corral the journalists as the officials walked through a security door back into the bowels of the building.

'I'm sorry, Robert, if that upstart caused you any concern,' the company chairman said as Tom followed them. It seemed the RAF man knew Greeves personally.

'No problem at all, Hugh. The opposition ran a line a few months ago about "taxpayer-funded safaris". The *World* bit and even had a cartoon of me in a pith helmet,' Greeves laughed. 'I do love Africa, but that's not why I travel there for business, and I'm keen to shut those sorts of questions down as quickly as possible. I do not want the people of Britain thinking I'm using my position to get free air miles.'

'Of course not,' the chairman said. 'I'll put out a statement today, if you like, saying that you refused to allow us to pick up the bill for your accommodation at the safari lodge.'

'Thanks, but I don't think that's a good idea,' Greeves said.

'Why not, it's true. I can also mention the company – at your suggestion – sponsoring an AIDS education program and providing funding for a workplace clinic for the workers we will employ in South Africa if we get the deal.'

'All good stuff,' Greeves agreed, 'but I want to downplay this visit. When you win the contract, go large with it in the north – that's where it's the most important. I want to see your factory expanding, Hugh. I'm not the story here, your men and women on the factory floor are.'

Tom thought he sounded like he actually meant it.

The visit to the HIV-AIDS clinic in Islington was a low-key affair. The job was over in half an hour and consisted of Greeves meeting the director, his staff and a couple of outpatients.

Tom had expected there to be media present, perhaps even one of those naff big cheques for Greeves to hand over as part of a naff photo opportunity. There was neither. Tom had thought it odd, in any case, that a defence minister would be handing over funding for something which was clearly a health ministry responsibility.

As they drove through London to Westminster, Greeves finished annotating the last of a stack of briefing notes he had pulled from his briefcase. Tom saw his chance to raise the concerns he had about the lack of protection officers. 'Sir, I'd like to bring some additional security equipment with us to South Africa – a passive alarm system which I'd set up on the door and balcony of your suite at Tinga.'

'Are you asking me or telling me, Tom?'

'It's not intrusive, sir, and I wouldn't be monitoring you, only the access to your room. It's my recommendation, sir, given that we're one man down on the team.'

'Very well.' Greeves signed another file and closed his bag.

Their car pulled into the security parking area beneath Portcullis House, the multistorey labyrinth of parliamentary offices opposite the Palace of Westminster but joined to it by underground passageways.

During the afternoon tea in the anteroom of Greeves's offices, Tom introduced himself to Helen MacDonald, the press secretary. Tom was curious about why the minister was presenting a cheque to a healthcare organisation which was clearly outside his portfolio.

'It's his own money,' Helen said, sipping a cup of tea while Greeves entertained some housewives, local businessmen and a gaggle of grey-haired grannies.

'Really?' Tom was surprised. 'How much?'

'He wouldn't want me to say, even if I knew – but you can bet it'd be at least five figures, from what I know of his past donations to charity. He's a true philanthropist, is our Robert.'

Tom nodded, impressed. He knew Greeves was rich, but he didn't know that he was generous as well. 'Why didn't he get some publicity for it? Help raise awareness of AIDS and all that?'

'I used to try to get him to let me tell the media, but it's a firm rule of his never to publicise his personal donations.'

'I suppose he doesn't want to be hit up by every other charity in the country,' Tom speculated.

Helen shook her head. 'No. You know, I think he does it in private because it's the right thing to do. He's not like any other politician I've ever come across, in that respect. Not cynical – at least, not in that way.'

Tom told Helen about the questioning from the journalist, Fisher. 'Nothing to worry about,' she said. 'They're flogging a dead horse, but do try to keep him out the way of photographers in South Africa. The *World*'s gunning for him for some reason.'

There was nothing Tom could do to stop anyone taking a picture of Robert Greeves in a public place, especially in another country, other than try to alter their routes to avoid the paparazzi. To try to outrun them could be fatal – as had been the case with Princess Diana – and to manhandle reporters and photographers who weren't actually physically threatening someone was considered to be assault. Still, Tom held his tongue and simply nodded to Helen. He was sure she knew the limitations he worked under.

Tom travelled armed with his Glock, Asp, knife and ammunition as they passed through Heathrow escorted by two uniformed police – one with a Heckler & Koch – and a security officer from British Airways special services. Once through immigration he, Greeves and the minister's policy advisor, Bernard Joyce, parked themselves in the first-class lounge for the hour before departure.

The flight was uneventful and Tom slept well in the first-class seat behind Greeves, though he couldn't drink alcohol.

At Johannesburg they were first off the aircraft, and the British Ambassador to South Africa was waiting on the air bridge, along with the South African Minister for Defence, Patrick Dule. Sannie was there, protecting the minister, and she nodded a curt hello to Tom. They were led by airport staff and security to a VIP lounge, where their passports were stamped by immigration officers and the two ministers had coffee with the British ambassador, who would not be accompanying them to Kruger.

South African soldiers in dress uniform, incongruously armed with umbrellas, were waiting downstairs outside the terminal to cover the official party for the couple of metres to two cars parked waiting in the torrential rain. They were driven across the taxiways to a South African Air Force Boeing business jet VIP transport aircraft, which was waiting on the Tarmac with its engines already turning. This time they would be flying to the Kruger National Park. Tom sat at the back of the aircraft, but was still three seats away from Sannie, so he couldn't converse with her.

There was no one from the company which manufactured the jet trainers travelling with Greeves; this was ostensibly a political visit and, while Greeves would talk up the merits of the UK bid and its benefits to the British economy, he would also be discussing other defence issues with Dule.

Dule was an affable, urbane, rotund man in a tailored designer suit with a crisp white shirt, burgundy silk tie and matching handkerchief in his pocket. Tom remembered Sannie's bitterness about the poverty in which so many South Africans still lived. Majority rule hadn't brought fresh water and decent housing to all, but it had made some well fed and well off, Tom reflected.

Tom had been unable to put Sannie out of his mind completely these past couple of days. He'd also been unable to shake the feeling that something good had passed him by, and he wanted at least to make amends with her, if not pick up where he thought they had left off. She looked cool and sexy in her lightweight cream business suit. He had tried a smile on her as she took her seat on the aircraft, but she ignored him. It was annoying. For some reason he felt compelled to tell her that he had not slept with Carla Sykes. It was none of Sannie's business, but he sensed she thought less of him because of what Carla had said.

Carla had some cheek, he mused, telling Sannie she believed she had left an earring in his suite at Tinga. Perhaps it was because she *had* been with Nick – and somehow he felt he was intruding on something – or perhaps it was just her over-the-top personality, but he didn't feel she should be the first woman he slept with after Alex's death. He had felt the stirrings of physical arousal when they had been drinking together and Carla had laid her hand on his thigh, but he had put the inevitable thoughts out of his head. He'd never had sex while away on a job; he'd been faithful to Alex during their marriage, and since then the opportunity had never arisen.

He'd politely fobbed off Carla, saying he was tired from his flight and his game drive. Undeterred, she had said, 'Well, that's one cup of coffee you owe me when you come back with your VIP.' He'd turned her around and gently ushered her out of his room.

He wondered, as the aircraft took off, if Carla would still be interested in him when they returned. She had said, as she'd left, 'I can't promise not to try again.'

'Mint?' Bernard Joyce, Greeves's defence policy advisor, asked him from across the narrow aisle. 'Helps me unblock my ears when we take off and land.'

'No thanks,' Tom said.

Helen MacDonald had told him: 'You'll like being away with Bernard. He's a scream. Camp as a row of tents, and sharp as a tack. He's ex-Royal Navy – youngest second-in-command of a nuclear submarine ever.'

'I hate Africa,' Bernard said, leaning across. 'Bloody dust and heat, and all those wild animals.'

'I saw a leopard on my first visit, just a few days ago,' Tom said.

'Bully for you. Completely unnatural, if you ask me, driving around with no doors and windows, three feet away from lions and hyenas and the like.'

'As opposed to cruising around half a mile under the water?'

'Ah,' Joyce said, raising an eyebrow, 'I imagine our big-mouthed Kiwi spin doctor has been giving you the gossip on everyone?'

'It's all been good so far,' Tom assured him.

'I'm sure it has. We're an odd bunch, we loyal foot-soldiers of Robert Greeves, but he's a great man, Tom, don't doubt it.'

He nodded. He was starting to think so himself.

Three of Tinga's open-sided Land Cruisers were waiting at the Skukuza airstrip.

Once the official airport for the Kruger National Park, the Skukuza runway, which was inside the park's borders, had been reserved for private charter aircraft since the building of a new regional international airport near Nelspruit about forty kilometres to the south.

'Welcome, Minister Dule, Minister Greeves,' Carla Sykes said. She looked sophisticated and attractive, despite the shimmering heat haze rising from the Tar-mac. Tom reminded himself to concentrate on the job.

At Dule's urging, Greeves posed for a photograph of the two of them, with three air force flight attend-ants, in front of the Boeing.

'Oh, I found my earring by the way,' Carla said both to Sannie and Tom as they all waited for the picture to be taken. 'It wasn't in Tom's room after all, it was in the library!'

Sannie van Rensburg wondered who Carla had been fucking in the library. She was still angry at herself and her petty jealousy of the woman, and she tried to concentrate on the broad back and bald black head of Patrick Dule. She was in the back row of seats of the Land Cruiser carrying the two dignitaries, while Tom sat in front, next to Duncan Nyari.

There was something about Carla that grated on her – many things, in fact – but it was hard to fathom why she felt as strongly as she did about the woman. So she slept around, big deal, but it didn't seem appropriate, she thought, for a woman in her position to flaunt herself in front of guests, particularly when they were there on business, as Tom Furey had been.

She chided herself again. Hadn't she almost slept with her workplace superior? How professional was that? Anyway, all these thoughts only served to remind her that business and pleasure most definitely did not mix. It was good to be back in the bush again so soon. The sights and smells and general feeling of wellbeing she got from the Kruger Park almost made up for the fact that she would be missing her kids by nightfall. Little Christo had recovered from his head wound and was back at school. He'd asked if she would be seeing Tom, the Englishman who played football. 'I want to show him my scar,' he'd said.

Tom glanced back at her. She looked away, scanning the bush for wildlife and other lurking dangers.

Three of Tinga's staff were waiting for the vehicles. Two carried platters filled with cool drinks; the third, a tray stacked with cold hand towels. Carla leapt from the Land Cruiser she had shared with the ministers' staffers and started organising other employees to escort everyone to their rooms. The politicians were looked after first. The South African minister's policy advisor was an Indian woman called Indira. Sannie found her brusque and bossy, unlike the minister, who was actually quite charming.

'Sannie, won't you please take my bag to my room. I have to go and check the meeting room for the minister,' Indira said to her.

'I'm sure the staff can do that,' Sannie replied. She wasn't the minister's bag carrier, and she certainly wasn't Indira's lackey either.

'Hello there,' Tom said, walking up to the two women. 'Sannie, have you let Captain Tshabalala know that we've arrived?'

'Of course,' she said, knowing she sounded irritated and seeing that he picked up on her feelings. She had overreacted, but he was telling her how to do her job now. She guessed that Tom was simply trying to ensure everything was being done by the book, and he couldn't have known that Indira had just irked her as well. 'Yes, Tom,' she said, her tone softer now. 'I've made the call.'

'Good,' he said. 'I'll take a stroll along the boardwalks on either side of the lodges.'

'I'll check out the conference room. The meeting's

not due to start for half an hour – it'll give the politicians time to freshen up.'

He nodded, looked at her as though there was something else he wanted to say, but she guessed the presence of Indira, who was squawking into her cell phone beside her, stopped him. He left and she went off to the conference room, leaving the bags with Indira, who gave her a pained look, which Sannie ignored.

Sannie watched Tom walk away. She regretted snapping at him and wanted to tell him what Christo had said. Perhaps she would try to be a bit more civil to him later on. They might have time to chat while their principals were locked in their meeting and working lunch.

A maid was placing jugs of juice and iced water in the private room, but otherwise it was empty. Sannie walked out onto the deck and surveyed the bush around the lodge's function area. There were no animals in sight, and no sign of spoor or flattened grass to indicate anything or anyone had been circling the room in the last couple of days. It was all clear.

When Sannie returned to the central reception area she saw Tom walking back from the far end of the boardwalk, but he was not alone. Carla was walking by his side – very close, as the walkway was quite narrow. She laughed, too loudly, at something he had just said and the cackle sounded to Sannie like a hyena's call. Carla put her hand on Tom's arm and any charitable thoughts Sannie had had disappeared.

'Can't wait to get the VIPs sorted,' Carla said in an exaggerated stage whisper to Sannie as they approached her, 'then we can all settle down to some lunch and gossip.'

8

Lunch at Tinga was every bit as good as Tom's last meal at the lodge. This time they had kabeljou, a South African fish grilled and served with golden chips. A simple meal but very tasty.

It started with him and Sannie sitting down together to discuss arrangements for the afternoon, and ended with Carla joining them and taking over the conversation. He could see now that Sannie quite clearly couldn't stand the woman.

Indira and Bernard popped in and out of the meeting at different times to make or take calls on their mobile phones, but for Tom and Sannie most of the afternoon was spent waiting. Carla left them to check on the guides for the afternoon game drive, but by that stage Sannie had already drifted away to read her novel, and Tom felt as though he'd missed another opportunity to talk to her. He went back to his room to change out of his suit into casual clothes for the afternoon drive.

They boarded the Land Cruisers at four pm sharp.

Both VIPs seemed cheery and friendly to each other, so Tom guessed the afternoon's lunch and meetings had been positive.

There were only two vehicles out on the drive. Indira and Bernard sat behind their respective ministers in the lead Cruiser, while Tom, Sannie and Duncan were in the second.

'Nothing happened, you know, between Carla and me last time,' Tom said quickly, getting it all out before she had a chance to interrupt.

Sannie looked at him. 'It doesn't matter, Tom. I told you before, I don't care.'

He waited for her to say more, to fill the void, but she was a police officer too. She knew when to shut up. Stalemate.

On the private dirt road leading out from Tinga, they passed small herds of impala and waterbuck, and three kudu. The kudus' delicate features, big ears and doe-like eyes made them look the most innocent of creatures, Tom thought. Sannie remained silent and Tom, disappointed, told himself she was not going to crack.

'Christo wants to show you his scar.' She looked straight ahead, dutifully noting the zebra that Duncan had just pointed out.

Tom smiled. 'Greeves suggested on the flight over that if I came with him again, if Nick . . . well, you know, that I take some leave and spend a few days over here after his next visit. Perhaps I could drop in and say hi to the kids.'

'That might be nice.'

He could see she was gripping the bar in front of

their seat, even though the dirt road was well graded and there were no bumps. Slowly, he told himself. This is a big move for her. 'Perhaps dinner.'

'That also might be nice. Tom . . .'

'Yes?'

'Just friends, okay?'

'Fine by me.'

'Here comes the tar road.'

He focused his mind back on the job, though he felt a flutter of happiness for the first time in a long time. Instead of feeling as though he was being unfaithful, he thought Alex would have liked Sannie. They were both bright, articulate women who, unlike him, were good at expressing their feelings. Tom was sure that Alex, who had a passion for wildlife conservation, would have loved the African bush as much as Sannie did. Tom looked around as they turned onto the Tarmac. There was one car behind them, a white Corolla, pulled over on the side of the road. He saw the reflection of late afternoon sunshine on a camera lens. It was pointed their way, not into the bush. 'We've got company,' Tom said, reaching into the pocket of his shorts for a notebook and pen.

The car pulled into the road and accelerated rapidly, trying to catch them. 'Duncan, how far to the turnoff to the concession?' Tom asked as he scribbled down the licence plate number of the Corolla.

'A kilometre.'

'Get on your radio and tell the lead truck to put his foot down.'

'It's a fifty kilometre an hour limit in the park on tar roads.'

'Then tell him to wind it up to fifty. Now.'

Duncan complied and Tom felt the breeze on his face stiffen as they accelerated. Tom looked around. The car was closing on them, and the driver had put on his right indicator.

'Move right, Duncan, as if you're going to overtake the lead vehicle. I don't want this guy passing us before the turnoff.'

The four passengers in the lead vehicle all turned around at the sound of the Corolla's horn, and Greeves looked puzzled at the sight of Tom and Sannie's Cruiser driving on the wrong side of the road.

The Corolla driver steered with his left hand and held his camera, fitted with a telephoto lens as long as Tom's forearm, out the window. The tricky manoeuvre caused the man to swerve, then overcorrect, losing speed in the process.

'Maniac.' Tom was pleased to see Greeves's head snap around to the front, so he wasn't facing the photographer.

'Turnoff's coming up, Tom.' Duncan started to drift back onto the left-hand side of the road, then suddenly said something in his own language, which sounded to Tom like swearing.

Tom looked left and saw the photographer accelerating hard to overtake them on the near side. 'Careful.' Tom wanted to keep the photographer at bay, but certainly didn't want to cause a traffic accident in the process.

The lead vehicle swung right, just as the Corolla pulled level with Duncan's Land Cruiser. Duncan turned the wheel hard and they were off the sealed onto the dirt. The Corolla braked twenty metres up the road and started to reverse. Tom looked back as the driver started to turn onto the track and then saw the *No entry* sign. Tom smiled.

The lead vehicle rounded a bend, and when they were out of sight of the main road, the truck carrying the VIPs pulled over. Duncan acknowledged a radio call and pulled up beside the other Land Cruiser.

'Looked like our friend was from the press,' Greeves called to Tom over the idling engines.

'Yes, sir,' Tom said, unsure what Greeves would make of his actions. He had been a bit heavy-handed.

'Well done, Tom, and nice driving, Duncan. Thank you.'

All in all, Tom thought, it was turning out to be a good afternoon.

They stopped at the same small riverside clearing where Duncan had taken Sannie and Tom previously. The two officers were on duty now, so alcohol was out of the question. She smiled at him over her glass of mineral water, then returned to her conversation with Indira. Tom was standing opposite Sannie in the circle of dignitaries and flunkies, intermittently scanning the clearing and surrounding bush. He noticed Carla walking towards him.

Carla had been at the drinks spot ahead of the main party, having travelled there in a third Land Cruiser, along with a barman and two maids who had already set up trestle tables covered in starched white tablecloths. The girls were ready with silver platters of biltong, *droëwors*, chips and nuts when the other trucks arrived. Carla had changed into a green safari skirt which ended six inches above her knees.

'Excuse me, Tom, I've got something to show you. It arrived by email while you were on your drive,' she said, holding up two sheets of paper. Tom excused himself from the circle.

'It's very important,' Carla added.

'News about Nick?'

'No, not quite.' She led him to the end of the line of parked Land Cruisers. Darkness was falling rapidly and Tom wanted to make sure he could still see Greeves. They stopped on the far side of the lead vehicle and Tom took the papers from Carla. He noticed she was smiling.

The first page was a blank fax cover sheet with the Tinga letterhead. He looked at her quizzically.

'Read the next one.'

He smiled and shook his head. On the second page she had written, in a bold girlish hand: *I'm going to fuck you tonight, after dinner*.

He laughed, but felt her take his hand. This was silly; though, he had to admit, slightly arousing. He felt himself begin to stir. Carla looked up and down the line of trucks and drew his hand to the hem of her skirt.

'Stop,' he tried, but he let her move his hand. She used it to raise the fabric. He felt her. Bare skin. The folds, the heat, the wetness. God, it had been so long.

Carla stood on tiptoes, letting go of his hand. He knew he should move it, but it was an intensely erotic moment, made even more so by the risk of getting caught. 'No,' he said, finally removing his hand. He thought of Sannie, the way he had finally broken through her resolve and convinced her nothing had gone on between him and Carla.

She ground her lips against his, trying to open his mouth with her tongue. Tom broke the kiss and turned at the sound of a footfall.

'Time to go,' Sannie said, emerging from between the second and third Land Cruisers.

Sannie sat on the bench seat behind Tom for the trip back to Tinga. She ignored his pathetic attempts to explain away exactly what she had seen. Fondling that bloody woman and kissing her while the man he was supposed to be protecting was not ten metres away.

'What were you thinking? You're a protection officer!' It was the only thing she said to him for the whole drive.

'I told you, she made the move on me. I told her to stop it, and I *always* had Greeves in sight.'

She ignored him. To think she had almost let him into her life and, worst of all, had almost let him into her children's lives.

Sannie had meant what she said to Tom earlier, about taking it slowly and just being friends for now, but she had allowed herself the briefest fantasy about what he might look like out of his shirt. His skin was pale – typically English – but his face and arms were showing the beginnings of an African tan. With his dark hair and thick eyebrows she guessed he had some Celtic blood in him. She felt stupid now, not only for allowing herself to have feelings for the man, but for the way she felt betrayed by someone she had no legitimate claim on.

Tom tried to apologise again when they all met in the reception area for pre-dinner drinks, to convince Sannie he'd done nothing wrong. He failed, spectacularly. She turned on her high heels and walked away from him.

'Lovers' tiff?' Bernard sauntered over with a gin and tonic in his hand.

'Misunderstanding.'

'I'd go for the raven-haired one, if I were you. Better dress sense and I think she'd go off.'

Tom smiled and shook his head. He, Bernard, Indira, Carla and Sannie were seated together for dinner, while the two politicians dined at another table with three senior officials from the Kruger National Park and one of the lodge's owners.

Sannie took the seat opposite Tom, but an elaborate silver candelabra made face-to-face conversation with her impossible, even if she had wanted to talk to him. Instead, Sannie chatted to Indira, whom Tom knew she disliked intensely, and Bernard, who managed to make her laugh a couple of times over dinner.

Carla was seated next to him, and he was sure he caught Sannie giving him the evil eye at the precise moment that Carla was squeezing his thigh under the table.

Greeves stood, clinking his glass with his fork, and made a short speech of thanks for the hospitality shown to them all by the staff at Tinga, and the South African government and National Parks Board. Dule responded, alluding to the 'positive talks' the pair had had on a range of issues.

After coffee, Greeves and Dule excused themselves at the same time. Carla winked at Tom, but he ignored her, as both he and Sannie followed the lodge security guards who were allocated to escort Greeves and Dule back to their rooms.

'Thanks, Tom.' Greeves opened the door to his suite. 'Good work eluding that photographer today. Go get yourself a nightcap and I'll see you at six in the morning. Don't be late.'

'Night, sir.'

Sannie was walking towards him, having just seen her principal safely off. 'If you let me buy you a drink I'll explain to you that this was all a mistake. There's nothing going on between me and Carla.'

'Then why was she stroking your cock during dinner? Goodnight, Tom.' She made his name sound like a four-letter word as she left with her guard.

'Bloody women,' Tom said to himself. He could have gone back to his suite then. Should have. 'Take me back to the lodge,' he said to the security man instead.

Bernard and Indira had turned in, but Carla was behind the bar. She waved him over, then bent down, out of sight. By the time he reached her she had a frosted glass of lager waiting on the polished counter.

'I shouldn't,' he said.

'Go on. One won't kill you.' She poured herself a glass of wine.

Tom picked up the now dewy glass and took a long drink. She was right, one wouldn't kill him. 'You were pretty outrageous today, out in the bush.'

'You haven't seen anything yet.' The security guard was hovering nearby, near the reception area. 'Thanks, George,' she called. 'You can leave for the night. I'll see Mr Furey back to his room.'

They walked to his suite and, when they stopped outside, he kissed her. A beautiful woman wanted him to make love to her. Sannie didn't want to speak to him. He felt light headed, but put it down to dehydration, and maybe her perfume.

He needed Carla, right now, but when they got inside she excused herself and went to the bathroom. He felt dizzy, and had trouble parting the mosquito net. He cursed and sat heavily on the turned-down bed. He put a hand to his eyes. No. This wasn't right.

When she returned she was naked, her hairless body gleaming gold in the soft light of the bedside lamp. The protest died on his lips as she lowered herself to her knees and undid the buckle of his belt.

9

Today

The *Kruger Park Times* was a small newspaper which served the national park and the private game reserves and local communities bordering Kruger.

Shelley du Toit was six months out of varsity and counted herself lucky getting a journalism job anywhere in the country. A white city girl, she was no expert on the bush and had only visited the lowveld a few times on school holidays. Shelley was determined to make up for lost time, however, and had gladly relocated to the other end of South Africa to get her first job as a reporter.

She was determined to become an expert not only on her country's wildlife, game reserves and South Africa's flagship national park, but also to practise the skills she had been taught at Rhodes University. Shelley was interested in hard news, as well as the usual puff pieces about fundraising activities, school sports and regurgitated press releases that filled any local newspaper. She had made it a priority, soon after getting the job and moving to the tiny *dorp* of Hoedspruit, to get to know Kruger's police chief, Isaac Tshabalala.

Isaac, naturally, wanted to paint a picture of Kruger as a crime-free paradise, which was kept that way by the vigilance of his hard-working officers and, of course, himself. He wanted stories carrying regular reminders about the road rules in the park, and announcements of holiday blitzes on speeding and unroadworthy vehicles. That was all well and good, and Shelley was happy to oblige, but she had recently heard about a scam where park supplies – everything from toilet paper and soap, to sheets and towels – were being smuggled out and sold to middlemen in neighbouring communities. It was a black market in government property. A real-life, honest-to-goodness hard news story. Perhaps the first step on the road to her dream to work as an investigative reporter on a daily newspaper, initially in South Africa, and later abroad.

She had asked to see Isaac, to put some hard questions to him about theft of park supplies, and he had offered to pick her up early from Orpen Gate, the nearest entry to the park to Hoedspruit. He was going to check on the operation of some state-of-the-art speed cameras and told Shelley he would be happy to answer her questions on the condition she brought her camera with her and did a story on the new enforcement cameras. It sounded like a fair deal to Shelley.

'How *concerned* are you, Isaac, about this wholesale

theft of government property?' she asked him. In journalism school she'd been taught how to ask open questions, ones that couldn't be answered with a simple 'yes' or 'no', and to load her queries with emotive words that made for good copy.

Isaac Tshabalala had been talking to reporters for many, many years. 'Shelley, the South African Police Service takes any reports of the loss of property extremely seriously and investigates all such matters to the full. Now, as I was saying to you on the phone yesterday, our new speed cameras provide a valuable tool in the fight against dangerous driving in the Kruger Park.'

Shelley frowned. He was going to be a tough nut to crack, but she liked Isaac and would play along with his lame speed camera story for the moment to keep him happy. 'How many people were charged with speeding in the park last year?'

'Well, there were –' Isaac's mobile phone played a rap tune.

Shelley smiled. The guy was old enough to be her father.

'Talking on your phone while driving is also illegal, unless you have hands-free. I just had mine installed,' Isaac said as he pushed the green button to take the call. 'Captain Tshabalala.'

'Isaac, hi, it's Sannie van Rensburg. We've got a big problem.'

Shelley sat up straight in the passenger seat of Isaac's Toyota Venture.

Isaac looked across at her, his face creased with a flash of panic as he swerved off the sealed road onto the dirt verge. He reached out for the phone, but appeared to be unfamiliar with the locking device which held it in its new hands-free cradle. The woman on the other end of the line said, 'Isaac, are you there? Greeves is missing. And an aide – it looks like they've been kid –'

Isaac wrestled the phone free at last. 'Sannie, I've got a reporter with me. Say that again. I might have to call you back.'

Even with the phone pressed to Isaac's ear, Shelley heard the woman on the other end of the line swear in Afrikaans.

'Oh, dear god, Tom,' Sannie said, and it was more prayer than blaspheming. They were in Greeves's room.

'I've just called Captain Tshabalala,' she went on. 'He's sending some uniformed officers here.'

Tom nodded. He would have to contact London. It was a call he had hoped he'd never have to make in his career but, as much as he dreaded it, he knew speed was of the essence. He dialled the number he'd saved for just such an emergency.

'Reserve room, DC Hyland,' a male voice said on the other end of the line in New Scotland Yard. The night duty officer yawned.

'This is DS Tom Furey, providing close personal protection to the Minister for Defence Procurement, Robert Greeves, in South Africa. We have a situation here. The minister is missing.'

'Do what?'

Tom repeated himself and the man seemed to become fully alert. The night duty officer worked in the reserve room of the Counter Terrorist Unit. Tom wasn't calling him because he suspected this was a terrorist action – not yet, at least – but because this number was manned twenty-four hours a day. The duty officer would now consult the night duty binder, a list of names and numbers of everyone who needed to know about an incident such as this. The man would be busy for some time. Tom gave him the details he had, left his cell phone number, then hung up. Next he called his immediate superior, at home.

'You're calling early,' Shuttleworth said.

Tom repeated the facts.

'Good god almighty. Are the South Africans on the job?'

'Uniforms are on their way, and the detectives will be called next, I expect.'

'What are you going to do next?'

'I'm going to bloody well find him.'

'Keep your cool, Tom. If a crime's been committed in South Africa you've no jurisdiction. We'll need you there, in contact, as our link man. I'll be on the next available flight. There'll be two detectives coming with me, to start our investigation. Jesus Christ, Tom.'

There was no way Tom was going to sit on his hands and play receptionist. 'Okay. I'll sit tight,' he lied. He ended the call.

Sannie walked back into the living area of the suite from the bathroom where she had been making calls on her mobile phone. 'Tshabalala's on his way, but he's up near Orpen, so he'll be a couple of hours. He's got two officers at Skukuza, and they're closing up and heading here now-now.'

Tom had learned already that repeating the word 'now' meant immediately in Africa. Two officers. 'What about detectives?'

'According to the plan, Tshabalala will be mobilising a team from Nelspruit – the nearest big town.'

'Good.'

'I thought you had Greeves's room alarmed?' Sannie said.

Tom nodded. 'It didn't go off. I checked the laptop that controls the passive alarm, but it hasn't registered a thing, and I didn't hear it in the night – obviously. I don't know how they got around it.'

'Um, there's something else, Tom.'

'What?'

Sannie told him about the reporter in the car with Isaac, and the fact that she had overheard at least part of Sannie's message.

'Jesus. I was hoping we could keep a lid on this for a little while longer. What's the chance that Isaac can keep the reporter quiet?'

'If you were a twenty-two-year-old journalist straight out of varsity and you found out a foreign government minister had been kidnapped in your backyard, would you sit on the story?'

The obvious answer meant Tom had no time to lose. 'I'm going after them.'

'You're *what*?'

Tom walked out of Greeves's room onto the walkway. Sannie followed him, opening her mouth to protest.

'Hey, what's all the commotion?' Carla, her hair in disarray and buttoning her safari shirt, walked out of Tom's suite. She was barefoot and her green skirt was askew, a rear pocket facing the front.

Sannie shook her head in disgust. 'You tell her,' she said to Tom. 'I've got more calls to make and you, Tom, are going nowhere. This is now a South African Police Service matter and *I* have jurisdiction until a more senior officer arrives. Get yourself cleaned up, Carla. There's bloody work to be done.'

Tom turned and walked back through reception, past the South African minister and his advisor, out front to where the Land Cruisers were still parked in preparation for the morning game drive.

'Duncan, get your rifle; we're walking!' On the dashboard of Duncan's Cruiser was a Czech-made Brno hunting rifle, which the guide carried in case he took his tourists for a game walk in the Tinga concession.

'What?'

'I'll explain as we walk.' And Tom did. 'Ignore them,' he said as they moved through reception. It seemed everyone had a cell phone pressed to his or her ear and all were talking at the same time.

Tom led Duncan back into Greeves's unit and then to Joyce's, explaining what had happened. Duncan climbed over the balcony railing outside Bernard's suite and dropped the metre to the long grass below. He started moving in an arc, around the front of the suite, to the far side of Greeves's and then back to a central spot between the two. 'This way,' he said.

Tom jumped down into the grass. He would have liked to have changed into trousers and a stouter pair of shoes, but shorts would have to do as there was no time to waste.

Duncan pointed back towards Bernard's suite. 'That man put up more of a fight. Is he the young one?'

'Yes,' Tom said. It figured. Joyce was ex-navy, physically fit and well built. Over dinner last night, he'd lamented the lack of a gym, saying he visited his local in Westminster daily when in London. Greeves didn't carry any excess weight, but as a politician his life consisted of being driven from one free meal to another. It was not surprising the older man had been easier to subdue. Tom was already impressed with Duncan's skills.

'Six men moving through the bush, here. Two plus one, and two plus one,' he said, pointing to each unit, and Tom understood what he was saying. Two pairs of assailants had made the abductions. Duncan moved now, head down, walking bent at the waist, looking for flattened grass. He broke off a yellowish stalk and held it up. Tom saw the dried brown stain. He didn't need to be told it was blood. Greeves, it seemed, had been injured somehow in his room. There were no bloodstains in Bernard's room. 'One man, the younger one, I think, is being dragged now. See here, his heel marks in the dirt. They have made him unconscious, I think.'

Tom tried to imagine the kidnappings. Perhaps the assailants knocked on their doors, masquerading as Tinga staff; perhaps they were in the victims' rooms already, waiting. All staff would have to be interviewed later, as a matter of course. If it was an inside job they'd soon be able to spot the accomplice or accomplices through some rigorous interviews. 'How old are these tracks?'

Duncan paused and dropped to one knee, brushing some stalks of grass aside. 'A mouse has crossed the path, here, and a small cat, a genet or wild cat, has stopped to sniff the blood on this grass. The blood is dry. The grass that was flattened has recovered. These tracks may be three or four hours old.'

Duncan led him under the boardwalk, then over one of the knee-high electric fences. 'They stopped here, to lift the two men over the live wire.'

That made sense, Tom thought. They couldn't have risked Greeves making a noise, or maybe coming to, if the fence zapped him, although presumably by this stage in the escape he would have been gagged. Tom picked at a branch studded with thorns, which had snagged on his shorts. His arms were already latticed with scratches from the short walk.

'Four men lay here. Look, you can see where the grass is flattened.' Tom looked to where Duncan was pointing at what must have been the lying-up point prior to the attack. The attackers had waited here, in deep bush behind the elevated walkway, at the base of a thickly leafed tree. They could look up, through the foliage, and out over the boardwalk, but anyone on the walkway would have been hard-pressed spotting them, especially in the dark. 'Look.'

Tom was about to move on, when Duncan held up a box of matches to the morning light. Tom wished he hadn't touched it, as it might contain a DNA trace or even partial fingerprint. Still, the niceties were already out the window on this investigation. Time was all important. It was careless of one of the men to leave behind evidence, let alone to be smoking while waiting to get the jump on someone.

'Mozambican,' Duncan said, handing the matchbox to Tom. The label was yellow and carried the words *Pala Pala, Fosforeira De Mocambique* above a picture of a curved-horned sable antelope on the front. Tom turned it over. On the back was a map of Mozambique, and a drawing of a compass.

'Can you buy these in South Africa?'

Duncan shook his head. 'I've never seen them.'

The Kruger Park occupied a long, narrow swathe of land running north–south along the border between South Africa and Mozambique. Were the kidnappers from the former Portuguese colony, and was that where they had taken Greeves and Joyce? Dropping the matchbox and possibly smoking while waiting told him the men were not professional. Another piece of the puzzle and a small point in their favour, but only if they moved quickly.

Duncan led him along the wooden fence that separated the accommodation units from the staff quarters, which were housed in the buildings of the old national parks camp which had survived the floods in 2000. From there, once they passed the last hut on the extreme left, the trail hooked back around to the entrance road, over another low-level electric fence. Tom cursed. The concept of letting animals move to and from the river through the lodge's grounds had created an opening for the kidnappers.

Tom was sweating by the time they made it to the dirt track. Duncan moved fast, and the rising sun burned the top of Tom's hatless head and stung his bare arms, which were also becoming scratched by thorny branches. He guessed they were about three hundred metres from the Tinga entrance gates – far enough for a vehicle to have been started up without attracting anyone's attention. 'Did they have a vehicle parked here?'

Duncan circled the area where the footprints met the road, holding up a hand, silently telling Tom to stay back from the track. He retraced his steps, careful to stay in his own footprints. He knelt on the edge of the road and beckoned Tom over. He was smiling broadly as he nodded to himself.

'What is it?'

'Oil.'

'So?' Tom had already deduced the kidnappers had rendezvoused with a vehicle.

Duncan dipped a finger in the liquid and, just as he did, Tom registered the significance of what he was seeing. 'It hasn't sunk into the dirt yet!'

'Even better,' Duncan said, his eyes echoing Tom's excited look. 'Feel.'

Tom reached out and touched Duncan's fingers. 'It's still bloody warm!' It was the best news he'd had since waking. The vehicle had been there a very short time ago. 'Follow the tracks to the tar road, Duncan. I'll call for some help.'

Tom had his mobile phone out as he jogged down the dirt road towards the entrance gate. He scrolled through his address list and called Sannie's mobile number.

'Van Rensburg.'

'Sannie, meet me at the entrance gate – now. We've found the tracks of the getaway vehicle. They only left half an hour or so ago.' He didn't stay on the line long enough for her to object.

She was frowning when he met her at the gate. 'Tom, I've called the detectives at Nelspruit. They'll be here soon.'

'Christ, Sannie, we can't wait. They must have hidden in the bush waiting for sun-up, though I don't know why.'

'I do,' she said. 'Private citizens can't drive in the park after dark. If they were seen by a ranger they would have attracted attention to themselves immediately. More likely they hid up in the bush nearby and, when the kidnappers had your guys, radioed for a pick-up. The rest camp gates open at five-thirty and Skukuza's close by. Tinga's game drives don't get onto the public roads until about six-thirty.'

Tom checked his watch. It was six-twenty. 'So what you're saying is they could have left some time in the last forty-five minutes or so and not aroused suspicion?'

She shrugged. 'It's possible.'

'Then we've got to act *now*.'

She looked back over her shoulder towards the lodge. He could understand her conflicted loyalties. On one hand she, like him, would want to get on the trail of the abductors as soon as possible, but at the same time her prime job was to protect the South African defence minister. Also, she had to wait at Tinga for Isaac Tshabalala to arrive, as well as the detectives from Nelspruit. 'Tom, you've got no jurisdiction here.'

'I've also lost the two men I was supposed to be protecting. There's nothing more I can do here, Sannie. Can't you see?' He told her about the number of men, and the discovery of the Mozambican matchbox. He handed it to her.

Duncan trotted down the road towards them, his rifle held loose in his right hand. His tight, short green shorts, cut high above the knee, and his brown ankle boots emphasised his well-developed thigh and calf muscles. He was barely perspiring, while Tom was wiping his brow with the back of his shirt sleeve. 'They went left onto the tar road, heading north-east. That's all I can tell you about the vehicle right now. I can't track it on the sealed road. Also, I had another look at the point where they met the vehicle. There were two spots of oil. The front drops were from the engine – it was black sump oil, very thin. The rear stains were gear oil, from the diff.'

Tom nodded. 'An old vehicle, you think?'

Duncan nodded too. 'There was one more set of footprints – the driver. There were drag marks and footprints at the back of the vehicle, and footprints only on the sides of the vehicle where they got in.'

Tom was already building a mental picture of the getaway car. 'That's five suspects, plus the two victims. Drag marks at the back, you say? That means Joyce might still be unconscious. Were they loading him into the rear of a vehicle?'

'Yes, a *bakkie*, I think.'

'A what?'

Sannie interjected, 'What you would call a pick-up or a utility vehicle. Sounds like a double cab. Two men in the front, two or three in the back. Maybe one guy in the load-carrying area to keep a gun on the two victims.'

'That makes more sense. The rear area could be enclosed with a canopy, probably with tinted windows. That narrows down the possible range of vehicles.'

Sannie shook her head. 'A double-cab *bakkie* with a canopy on the back, old enough to be dripping oil from the engine and the rear diff? Tom, that describes about every second vehicle in South Africa!'

'It's something, damn it. Not every holiday car in this park is going to have five or six men crammed into it.'

Sannie was already on the phone to Isaac, giving a description of the likely vehicle and number of occupants, along with a suggestion – she couldn't issue orders – that the description be radioed to all police officers in the park and all entry and exit gates. 'There are security guards at every gate,' she explained to Tom after hanging up. 'They check vehicles on the way out for plant and animal products that people might have illegally picked up.'

'I need a map.'

'There's one in the Cruiser. I'll go and get the vehicle,' Duncan said, sprinting off.

Sannie looked as though things were rapidly moving out of her control, but she was not quick enough to stop Duncan. It was incredibly frustrating for Tom to think that he had possibly missed Greeves and Joyce by mere minutes. 'I've got to get rolling, Sannie. There's mobile phone reception in most of this part of the park – you told me that – so you can keep in touch with me and I can keep in touch with London. If I *do* catch them – and that'll be a miracle – I'll call for back-up.'

'Okay.' Sannie pinched the bridge of her nose with her fingers and closed her eyes for two seconds. She took a deep breath. 'You know it's the wrong thing to do in this situation, but it also makes the most sense.'

Duncan pulled up and jumped from the Land Cruiser but left the engine idling. He opened his Kruger map book to the pages that showed the south-west corner of the park and laid it on the vehicle's bonnet.

Sannie pointed to Tinga Legends Lodge, just north of Skukuza, near the border of the park in a section that bubbled out to the west, like the toe of a long boot. Otherwise, the park was roughly a long, narrow rectangle stretching north along the Mozambican border. She traced the route out from the lodge to the tar road, which was shown in red on the map. 'Okay. They're heading north-east, possibly towards Mozambique, though we're basing that on a discarded matchbox. From here there are two official border crossings within a day's drive. They could head south-east,' Sannie's finger moved off the map at the bottom right-hand corner, 'and leave the park via the Crocodile Bridge Gate and cross into Mozambique at Komatipoort. That's the main crossing for people travelling from South Africa and very busy.'

'Would that make it harder or easier to smuggle through two guys bound and gagged in the back of your vehicle?' Tom said.

'Harder. The customs guys are thorough on the

other side. They hate South African holiday-makers taking their own drinks and groceries into Mozambique instead of buying locally, so they always check the boot looking to make you pay duty on something. The other crossing is up here,' she flipped over a couple of pages of the map book and traced a route to the north-east, 'about midway up the park, through the new Giriyondo border post. This one was created to allow access into the new transfrontier national park which has been set up opposite Kruger. It's quieter and the customs guys might be more relaxed, but I can't imagine kidnappers risking using the official crossings.'

'Could they just drive through the bush?'

'Not drive all the way, but maybe walk.'

Tom was surprised as Sannie briefly described how many Mozambicans illegally crossed into South Africa via the wilds of the Kruger Park, in search of work and a new life. 'Some are killed by lions and other game on the way, but enough of them think it's worth the risk.'

'So they could cross anywhere, if they abandoned their vehicle?'

'Sure,' Sannie agreed, 'but there aren't many roads on the Mozambican side and they wouldn't want to be on foot with two prisoners for several days.'

Duncan leaned in to study the map. 'I know this area. My parents were from Mozambique originally. The nearest towns on the other side are Machatunine, Macaene and Mapulanguene.'

Sannie peered closer at the map. 'There's a tar road south of Kruger's Satara rest camp that ends very close to the border, near the Singita private lodge – the old N'wanetsi National Park camp. That last village you mentioned is not far across the border from there.'

'Mapulanguene,' Duncan repeated, nodding. 'No more than twenty kilometres.'

'*Ja*. The N'wanetsi River cuts through the Lebombo Mountains there, but it's overlooked by Singita and a public national park picnic site, isn't it?'

Tom looked at the map to where they were pointing. 'What about this dirt road, just to the north?' The parallel route, called the S100, was a little south of Satara camp.

Duncan rubbed his chin. 'Yes. Perhaps they could take the dirt road, cross the border into the bush, and cut down to the N'wanetsi, out of sight of the tourists.'

Tom asked Sannie if she could task police or national parks patrols to cover the three points in the park where there were roads and villages within striking distance on the other side of the border in Mozambique.

'I'll do what I can, Tom. It's the closest thing we've got to a plan. Of course, if we're wrong about the Mozambican connection, we could be heading in the wrong direction.'

'Right now, I just want to be heading somewhere.'

'Tom, be careful. These men must know the bush, particularly if their plan is to set off on foot through the park. They'll be armed, and that area is lion country.'

'I'll look after him,' Duncan said, climbing into the Land Cruiser as Tom got into the passenger seat.

'You should probably be staying here, Duncan, but I didn't see a thing.'

'Let's go,' Tom said.

'Tom, wait.' Sannie placed a hand on the sill of the vehicle's cut-down door. 'Good luck.'

Sannie walked back down the driveway to Tinga's reception area. Carla was in the foyer. 'I need somewhere to set up a command post. It needs to be private, have telephone access, a TV with DSTV, and somewhere to set up a computer.'

Carla had found time to do her hair and makeup. 'The function centre's booked for a seminar all day today. It's one of the banks from Jo'burg. I can't put them anywhere else, and the delegates are taking up all our spare rooms tonight. Why don't you use Tom's room? He's going to want to be in on the action whenever he gets back from wherever he's gone.'

'Okay. I'm going there now to set up. Call me when Captain Tshabalala arrives.'

'Yes, ma'am,' Carla said, giving her a mock salute.

Sannie was in no mood for humour, or Carla. She strode down the walkway and let herself into Tom's room. When she got there, she couldn't ignore the rumpled bed, or the smell of perfume. She grimaced. As sorry as she felt for Tom, she was still annoyed at him for trying to smooth-talk her all day and then bedding that tramp Carla without a second thought. She left the front door ajar and slid open the glass sliding doors to get a draught going through the room to expel the odours.

Sannie helped herself to a Coke from Tom's mini-bar, sat down at the polished wooden writing bureau and pulled her notebook out of her handbag. She started writing a timeline of everything that had gone on since she left for bed last night, through to Tom's late arrival not long ago. She also noted Duncan's preliminary findings about the number of suspects, his assessment of the type of vehicle used, and the gang's apparent modus operandi.

She wondered about motive. With the exception of some bombings a few years back which had been linked to local Muslims, South Africa had so far been free of terrorism linked to Islamic extremists. However, there were sizable Muslim communities in Mozambique and South Africa. Their origins dated back to Arab traders who plied the coast of Africa, trading everything from spices to slaves. In the past she had worked as a liaison to American secret service teams protecting a former president on a visit to South Africa, so she had sat in on security briefings which alleged there were al-Qaeda support cells and affiliated groups already established – though probably 'sleeping' – in southern Africa. Greeves was not a high-profile minister, but he had made recent statements in parliament, reported even in South Africa, about Britain's ongoing commitments in Iraq and Afghanistan.

Terrorism aside, the other possible motive was good old-fashioned money. Sannie knew from Tom, and Nick before him, that Greeves was a very wealthy man. Perhaps the kidnappers were criminals after a ransom. The complicating factor in this theory, of course, was that Bernard Joyce had also been abducted.

Sannie wished she could have gone with Tom; he was right – at least he was doing something. Having made her notes and called all the appropriate people, she felt next to useless now, sitting in Tom's empty suite. She got up to go to the toilet.

As she moved through the bathroom, the morning sun slanting in from the window bounced off something on the vanity benchtop. She stopped and looked down on it. It was a small, square travel mirror. She bent closer. Running down the centre of the glass was a thin line of white powder. Sannie sucked in a deep breath.

'Sannie?' She heard the deep voice of Isaac Tshabalala and remembered leaving the door open.

She emerged from the bathroom.

'Is it as bad as I think it is, Sannie?' Isaac asked.

'Have a look at this, Captain. If possible, I think it just got a whole lot worse for someone.'

10

Tom Furey wasn't praying. He was swearing.

In front of him, despite the early hour and the fact that they were in the middle of the African bush, was a traffic jam. In London the cause might have been a car accident, but here it was a lion. Three lions, in fact. And it was gridlock.

Ahead of them was a line of four cars, parked bumper to bumper, waiting their turn to get onto a bridge across a mostly dry river. On the structure itself four cars were parked side by side, effectively blocking it. The canvas canopy over the open-sided Tinga Land Cruiser was high enough for Tom to stand up in the passenger seat, to get a better view of the mess ahead. He caught a glimpse of a big, shaggy mane as one of the trio of lions raised its head from the tar. It lay down again, out of sight.

'The lions like the warmth of the tarred roads in the early morning. They'll sleep there until they eventually get sick of the cars, or the sun gets too hot for them. Then they will move into the shade of the trees,' Duncan explained.

'How long will that take?'

The guide shrugged. 'Five minutes, an hour?'

'We don't have that much time.'

Up ahead a horn sounded a short, sharp blast. Tempers were rising along with the sun. The bush on either side of them was painted a warm orange-gold by the morning rays, the grassy flood plain dotted with stunted ilala palms. It would have been beautiful, if not for the traffic jam and the fact that two men's lives were hanging in the balance. The source of consternation, from what Tom could see, was a tour vehicle, a minibus towing a luggage trailer, which had pulled up sideways, blocking the bridge on the far side. Even if the drivers in the queue on their side of the river had their fill of lion photo opportunities and wanted to move on to allow the next in line a chance to see the cats, they were prevented from doing so. Tom watched through Duncan's binoculars as the driver of the tour van gave someone the finger. 'This is fucking ridiculous.' He leaned over and honked the Land Cruiser's horn. This brought a flurry of sympathetic hoots and catcalls from some of the other drivers, but both the tour bus and the lions remained stationary.

'What will the lions do if they see a man on foot?' Tom asked.

Duncan looked over at him. 'You are not serious?'

'Tell me.'

Duncan scratched his chin. 'Well, one of two things. They will either run away or they will attack and kill that man.'

Tom drew his Glock and opened the passenger

door. Duncan reached out to grab him, but was too slow. 'Tom! Don't be an idiot, man!'

Tom walked along the left-hand side of the first line of vehicles. Duncan started his engine and squeezed past them, driving on the dirt verge, directly behind Tom. 'Get back in,' he shouted.

People were starting to look back now and a child called out something in Afrikaans. Tom imagined it was something like 'Look at that stupid bloody man about to be eaten'. A woman screamed and ducked behind the sill of her car door when she saw his gun. 'Get back in your bloody vehicle,' an elderly man yelled at him. Tom ignored him as he closed on the bridge. Duncan drove as close as he could to him, but there was no way the Land Cruiser could get onto the bridge itself.

Tom could see the lions now, but they were lying facing the other way, towards the tour van. The guide driving the bus saw him now and pointed, alerting his tourists to the madman approaching. Tom saw four lenses swing in unison to face him. 'Police!' he yelled. 'Back off that bridge, now!'

The driver stared at him, hardly believing what he was seeing. The lions raised their heads as one at the sound of his voice. One stood and uttered a throaty, bass growl that sent a chill up Tom's back.

'Get in,' a woman said to him, leaning back and opening the rear door of her BMW. Tom sidled up to the car but did not take up the invitation.

He held his gun up, pointed in the air. 'Back up, now!' The tour operator driver finally saw sense and started his engine. As he tried to reverse, however, he jack-knifed his trailer and had to engage first gear to move forward again. All three lions were on their paws now, growling and facing outwards in different directions. The van's erratic movements were spooking them, but the cats, like the other drivers on the bridge, were trapped. 'Move it!'

The lion that had spotted Tom caught sight of him again. Cornered, it had only one option. It bounded between two cars and started running directly at Tom. Women screamed and cameras whirred as the lion closed the gap, charging for the kill. Tom had moved to the front of the BMW better to communicate with the van driver, but now he saw the flash of tawny fur streaking towards him. 'Get in!' the woman behind him yelled again. He needed no further prompting. He took three paces back and dived, headfirst, onto the rear passenger seat. The woman was trying to close the door but his foot was in the way. He yelped as he felt the door crush against his ankle but, turning around to look back over his shoulder, he saw it was not the woman who was closing the door any more. She was bent double in the front seat, screaming maniacally. The lion was standing on its hind legs, roaring. The pressure on the door was coming from two massive paws, and the leathery pads, each the size of a dinner plate, were pressed against the car door's window. The beast's foul breath fogged the glass. Its deep, wheezy growls rocked the car almost as much as its massive weight as it fought to get inside the vehicle.

Tom lay on the back seat and racked his Glock, chambering a bullet as he let the slide fly forward. He reached out and pressed the electric window button in front of him, on the door opposite the lion. 'What the hell do you think you're doing, you fucking idiot?' the woman's husband said from the driver's seat. He had been in shocked silence so far. As the window slid down, Tom felt the pressure relieved on the car. The lion hadn't left, it had just got smarter.

He saw the hooked claws protruding, each as long as one of his fingers, as the lion hooked one huge paw into the gap in the partially open door. He was going to open it. Tom pulled his foot free at last and thrust his right hand out of the window. He squeezed the trigger four times. Children cried and parents hollered. The lion withdrew its paw at the deafening sounds of the gunshots, and turned and ran back over the bridge in pursuit of his two brothers.

The tour van had finally turned around and was speeding away. Like a champagne bottle uncorked, the road was now clear and cars spewed across the bridge, eager to put as much distance as they could between themselves and the madman with the gun as quickly as possible. Inside the BMW the woman who had probably saved Tom's life was a sobbing wreck. 'Get out of my fucking car now, you stupid *rooinek*,' her husband spat at Tom.

Duncan pulled up beside them in the Land Cruiser, shaking his head. 'Well, you cleared the bridge,' he said.

'Sorry,' was all Tom could think to say to the couple in the car. He climbed out and leapt back into the front passenger seat of the game-viewing vehicle.

Tom noted the sign on the bridge as they raced across the Sweni River. He checked the map as

Duncan drove. People honked their annoyance at them as Duncan overtook car after car, not caring any longer that he was going almost twice the fifty kilometre per hour speed limit. They had already covered roughly sixty kilometres from Skukuza, but still had more than twenty to go, on dirt, once they reached the S100 road, just south of Satara camp. If the men they were pursuing were sticking to the speed limit, in order not to draw undue attention to themselves, then Tom was hopeful they would catch them before they abandoned their vehicle. Assuming, of course, they were on the right road and had correctly figured the kidnappers' plan.

'Can't you go any faster?' They had turned onto the dirt road now and Duncan had slowed the Land Cruiser to about sixty kilometres per hour – still twenty above the maximum for gravel.

'If we hit a buck or an elephant you'll be going nowhere.' Duncan returned his concentration to the road. Tom held the bar on the front dashboard for support as they roller-coastered through a drainage culvert. All four wheels left the road as they hit a hump where a grader had turned off.

They left a cloud of red dust in their wake, which blanketed a pair of cars and their occupants, who had stopped to photograph a trio of giraffe. The long-limbed animals, scared by the roar of the Cruiser's speeding diesel engine, cantered away, looking as though they might trip at any moment.

Tom was still looking backwards when Duncan braked hard, and he was thrown into the dashboard, his right shoulder connecting with it painfully. 'What?'

He looked up to see a family of warthog, a big male, his female and three tiny piglets, galloping away, their tails pointed up like antennae as they ran. Duncan accelerated again and ground through the gears until they were back up to their safe maximum speed.

'*Bakkie* ahead,' Duncan called. It was the fifth such vehicle they had seen. This one had its brand, Isuzu, written in bold, raised black letters across the tailgate. Tom noted that the enclosed rear canopy was heavily tinted. He slid his pistol from its holster and held it loose in his lap.

'Take them,' Tom said. Duncan pressed his foot to the firewall.

Tom saw a face in the driver's wing mirror as Duncan brought them alongside the right rear corner of the pick-up. It was an African and he was watching them intently. He saw the rear passenger window of the twin cab start to come down. Tom raised his pistol so that it was level with the dashboard, but still out of the sight of any occupant of the other vehicle.

A man's face peered out, but only for an instant. His complexion was dark, swarthy, but not black. If Tom had to guess he would say Arab. 'Get ready to ram them if I tell you.' Duncan's face was grim, but he simply nodded.

Duncan slowed marginally as they prepared to draw alongside. At that moment, Tom heard a whining protest of changing gears and the other vehicle shot forward, accelerating. 'Faster!'

Duncan changed down quickly but the *bakkie* was pulling away from them. Tom had only a split second to make his decision. They could simply be local men who might resent some rich tourist from a private game lodge and his guide trying to overtake them at speeds in excess of the legal limit. Or they could be Robert Greeves's kidnappers.

He raised his hand and aimed at the right rear tyre of the other vehicle. As he squeezed, Duncan hit a deep rut and had to wrestle with the wheel to keep them straight. Tom's shot went wide. If the driver of the other vehicle heard the shot he did not heed it as a warning and continued to accelerate. Tom coughed as they drove through the dust plume churned up by the Isuzu. It would be hard to get a clear shot through the red-brown mist of grit and he was worried about accidentally killing one of the people they were trying to save.

Any doubt Tom had about the identity of the other vehicle disappeared when the tinted rear window of the *bakkie*'s canopy suddenly flew up. Tom lifted his arm instinctively, but then ducked as he saw a man wearing a black ski mask pointing a short-barrelled version of an AK 47 at them. Duncan saw the threat too and swerved wildly as the assault rifle opened up on them. The rough ride made it hard for the gun-man to aim and the bullets sailed high. Tom glanced up and saw two holes had been punched through the canvas sun canopy.

Tom felt no satisfaction that they had taken the right route, nor that they had found the criminals' vehicle. They were outnumbered and outgunned. He didn't imagine that was the only automatic weapon in the *bakkie*. He couldn't shoot back – he was certain that the man with the AK was guarding Greeves and

172

Bernard, who would be lying in the back of the truck's cargo area. All they could do was keep them in sight.

'Keep on them but don't get too close,' he said to Duncan, who was doing his best to do just that.

Tom fished his mobile phone from his pocket and held it up so he could see the screen. 'No signal. Shit. We're on our own, Duncan.'

'Not quite.' As he drove one-handed, Duncan snatched up the handset of his two-way radio and started talking rapidly in Shangaan. Tom listened in as he kept his eyes on the vehicle ahead, visible now and then through a swirling dust cloud. A series of acknowledgement messages came through in African dialect. He also heard some radio chatter in Afrikaans when Duncan turned up the volume. 'We might get some support if we're not too late.'

'We can use it. Can you get Tinga on that thing?'

'We're too far away now, but I can try to relay a message.' After some more talking on the radio, Duncan was able to pass a message back to Tinga giving their location and confirming that they were in sight of the missing persons.

As they bounced and skidded through tight turns and a dry river crossing, a message came back from Tinga. Duncan translated it. Sannie was relaying through another guide that the police were on their way, but there would be no air support, as the parks board's helicopter, normally based in Kruger, was in Johannesburg for an engine overhaul. They were trying to get military air support from the nearby air base at Hoedspruit. 'Still on our own,' Tom said bitterly.

'This road ends soon, in a T-junction. They can go

left or right or, if your theory is right, they'll ditch their *bakkie* and continue on foot.'

'Well, let's hope we've foiled that part of their plan. I'm assuming you can take this thing through the bush?'

'You better believe it, man.' Duncan slapped the dashboard fondly. 'They're slowing. What do you want me to do?'

'Hang back.'

Tom's command was too late. The *bakkie* in front of them skidded to a halt. Even though Duncan hit his brakes as well, the distance between them closed rapidly as a result of the lead vehicle's sudden stop. 'Get down!' Tom yelled as he saw the gunman in the back taking deliberate aim. One of the rear doors of the twin-cab passenger compartment opened and another man in a ski mask climbed out. He carried a cut-down Russian assault rifle identical to the other man's.

The two AK 47s fired on automatic and Tom felt the impact of slugs slamming into their engine. The front of the Land Cruiser sagged and Tom knew the tyres had been hit. Steam hissed from their punctured radiator and Tom heard the Isuzu's engine start up again. He raised his head and saw the trailing dust cloud once again. 'Grab your rifle.'

Tom got out of the stricken four-by-four and started running up the dirt road. He knew the track would end soon, and even if the other vehicle went off road, its momentum would be slowed by the bush, perhaps to walking pace if the trees were as thick ahead as they were to each side of him. He looked back and saw Duncan trotting behind him, working the bolt of his heavy hunting rifle and chambering a round as he ran. He felt a momentary pang of guilt at putting the safari guide in danger. He was a civilian and this was not his fight. Tom had no business ordering him into harm's way, and he told him as much when he drew alongside.

'Mr Greeves and Mr Joyce were clients. Their safety is as much my responsibility as yours, so be quiet and save your breath for the fight.'

Duncan raised a hand and moved off the graded road into the long golden grass and thickets of thorn-studded trees on their right. Tom followed the guide, who had reduced his pace. They heard the Isuzu's diesel engine ahead, but it had slowed to a laboured growl. Duncan paused and dropped to one knee, and Tom followed suit. Ahead of him through the bush, he could see the intersection.

Duncan cocked his head to one side. 'They have gone on ahead, driving through the bush. They will not move fast. Listen.'

From their left, Tom heard another vehicle's engine, though this one was screaming at a high pitch. He squinted into the morning sun and saw a dark green Land Rover closing on them, a dust cloud in tow. The vehicle stopped at the intersection, and Tom and Duncan emerged to greet it.

'Howzit, my *boet*,' the Afrikaner driving the Land Rover said to Duncan as they shook hands, African style, linking their hands by the thumbs halfway through the traditional European greeting. The man was grey-haired and his face, tanned to the colour of mahogany, was lined with deep furrows, worn by age and a lifetime in the unrelenting African sun, and his beard was stained yellow by tobacco smoke. He conversed rapidly with Duncan in Shangaan. In the rear of his Land Rover, which, like Duncan's Cruiser, had no sides or solid roof, just a canvas awning above, were two plainly confused tourists, a young couple.

'Duncan's explained what's going on?' Tom asked the man.

'*Ja*. I'm Willie. He tells me you want to take my Land Rover off road into that bush, to follow those other *okes*.'

'That's right,' Tom said. 'We don't have time to waste. Radio your position and get someone else to come collect you and your clients.'

'Hold on, *bru*. You don't tell me what to do, and no one, not even Duncan, gets to drive my vehicle. I've told him to stay here. I'll drive you.'

Duncan looked at Tom and shrugged. The white man went on, 'I was a recce commando in our war in Angola. If those *okes* are as bad as Duncan's made them out to be, you need someone like me more than someone like him.' Willie took his own rifle from its cradle on the Land Rover's dashboard and inserted its bolt and then chambered a bullet as long as Tom's middle finger. 'Now then, folks, my colleague Duncan here is going to look after you while this gentleman and I go look for some *tsotsis* in the bush.'

Before the confused tourists could ask too many questions, Tom was sitting in the passenger seat beside Willie. The big Afrikaner engaged low-range four-wheel drive and the boxlike truck lurched down a drainage ditch and into the bush. Ahead of them the trail carved by the Isuzu was plainly visible. 'This should be fun.' Willie veered off to the right.

'What are you doing?'

'They'll be watching their backs, expecting us to follow their tracks. Look around you – this is a valley. They're only going in one direction, and that's east, towards Mozambique. I'm going to try to outflank them. This beast of mine will go harder and faster through the bundu than theirs will – take my word for it.'

The ride was almost sickening as the Land Rover lurched up and over fallen logs, bounced through hidden holes and plunged in and out of ditches and sandy watercourses. Thorn-covered branches whipped past them, shredding the canvas canopy and Tom's exposed arms in the process. If Willie felt the stings of the vicious barbs he said not a word. Tom saw his crazed grin and knew the man was completely and utterly in his element.

'After Angola I served with the parks board for a while. I know this country better than most,' Willie said above the protesting whine of the engine. 'There's a town on the Mozambique side, not far from here. The road starts there and leads all the way to the coast.'

'So I've been told.'

Willie nodded. 'We're also about to hit a fire trail, which, hopefully, your bad guys don't know about. It's not on any publicly available map.'

On cue, they crashed through a screen of low bushes, flattening the saplings in the process, and landed on a cleared dirt track. It was rutted and rock-studded, but after their carving ride through virgin bushland it felt like a four-lane motorway to Tom. Willie disengaged low range and floored the accelerator. A tiny antelope – a steenbok, according to the Afrikaner – darted across their path and bounded deeper into the bush.

The track took them down a natural ridgeline above a re-entrant to the Olifants River valley, which both Tom and Willie had reasoned would be the escaping vehicle's most logical path into Mozambique. On a downhill stretch, Willie cut the engine and coasted in neutral. 'Listen now.'

Above their vehicle's noises they heard the Isuzu's engine, still groaning slowly as the *bakkie* ground its way through the uncleared country. Willie turned the steering wheel and let his vehicle plough into some thornbushes. 'Ambush time,' he grinned.

Tom climbed down, ignoring the barbs that raked him and snagged his already torn shirt. He followed Willie through the bush. Every few paces the bigger man stopped to listen. He raised his nose at one point. 'We're downwind, I can smell their exhaust smoke – it's blowing past them, faster than they're moving.'

They picked their site well, in among a cluster of granite boulders, looking down over a dry tributary. 'They'll be following that game trail, I reckon,' Willie said, pointing to a well-worn path about a metre wide, which wound through the bush on the floor of the shallow valley. 'They'll have to slow to cross. That's when we'll flatten them.'

'Aim for the driver and the passengers in the cab.

Don't fire on the canopy and the load area. That's where the hostages are.'

Willie nodded, resting his hunting rifle on the smooth surface of a boulder.

Tom had had three magazines of seventeen rounds each at the start of the day, and now he was missing six bullets from two of them. Up to five men in that vehicle were armed. For now, he and Willie had surprise on their side but that was about the only factor in their favour. What worried Tom was a gut feeling that if the men thought they were at risk of being captured they would shoot Greeves and Joyce. He was out of options, though, and the noise of the truck was getting closer. The blue bonnet of the four-wheel drive came into sight. Tom used a two-handed grip to steady his pistol.

'We shoot to kill, hey?' Willie whispered.

Tom nodded.

Willie's first shot killed the driver of the Isuzu instantly. The .458 calibre round was designed to stop a charging bull elephant and it took the top of the man's skull clean off, spraying the other four occupants and the interior of the twin-cab with his blood and brains. The *bakkie* slewed off to the left and rammed into a leadwood tree. Its engine continued chugging, but it was going nowhere.

Tom fired two aimed shots into the rear of the cab, but couldn't see if he had hit anyone because their first salvo was already being answered, more than in kind. The man sitting behind the driver had rested his AK 47 on the open sill of the window and was firing blindly on full automatic. Most of his rounds were sailing high, but a few knocked chips of pink granite off the rocks behind which Tom and Willie were hiding, close enough to make them duck.

When Tom risked looking over the rock again he saw all the vehicle's doors bar the driver's were open, as was the rear window and tailgate.

Willie gave a primal war cry and, chambering another round as he stood, climbed over his protective rock and scrambled down the valley floor. An African man, without a mask to hide his face, was kneeling and changing the magazine of his AK. Tom ran after the crazed Afrikaner and raised his arm and fired two shots. The second round hit the African with the assault rifle in the chest, knocking him backwards.

More fire came their way, and Willie slowed to take cover behind a stout tree trunk. Tom pushed on ahead, now uncaring about the risk to himself, the blood lust and anger seizing control of his emotions and swamping them. Something burned across the skin of his upper right thigh, and he stumbled and fell. When he looked up he saw two hooded figures being dragged from the rear of the *bakkie* and thrust forward, past the nose of the crashed vehicle. Tom tried to stand, found he could, and then braced himself against a tree to take aim again. A man was shouting something in a strange language, possibly Arabic, at Greeves and Joyce, who were being prodded along by another, who used his rifle as a combination prod and club.

Willie's weapon boomed again but the noise of the single shot was soon drowned out by two AKs firing on automatic. Tom was forced to kneel again as leaves and twigs rained down on him and bullets whizzed past him on both sides. He heard other rounds thud into the tree, which protected him. He had to regain the initiative, he told himself. He stepped from behind the tree and started to run. He was only twenty metres from the disabled Isuzu and that would be his next firing position.

As he ran and stumbled along – now more than aware of the pain in his thigh and the blood soaking his shorts – one of the masked gunmen stepped from behind a tree. It seemed the other two had vanished, with the captives, down the dry watercourse. The man fired, one handed, across Tom's front and he heard a cry of pain from the direction he'd last seen Willie.

In the gunman's other hand was a cylinder about the size of a can of soft drink, but painted green. The man knelt, dropped his rifle and yanked the pin from the grenade.

Tom heard Willie shout a warning, as his own brain registered what was going on.

Tom flung himself flat and heard the blast, which was not as loud as he recalled from his military days. He looked up and his vision was seared by a flash of blinding white light from within the Isuzu.

'White phos!' Willie called.

Tom blinked, seeing stars, and felt a wave of stifling radiant heat rolling across him. He rolled away from the Isuzu and crawled blindly through the grass as the vehicle's fuel tank erupted. All around him, the bush seemed to be burning. When he managed to sit up he saw the white phosphorus was burning fiercely and brightly, and had ignited a fire that was spreading fast along the valley floor. The pall of smoke from the blazing vehicle, and the spot fires created everywhere the incendiary material had landed, had covered the terrorists' withdrawal.

Tom raised his pistol as he heard movement through the dry grass beside him.

'Don't shoot,' Willie said, staggering into view. He clutched his left shoulder. Blood oozed through his fingers, coating his right forearm. 'Wind's against us. This fire's going to be on top of us any second.'

Tom shook his head. 'I've got to keep going. I'll try to get around the fire. How's your shoulder?'

'*Ag,* I've had worse. I'll live.' Then the big man's face seemed to lose all its colour and he passed out.

'Shit,' Tom said. Ash and burning embers were already swirling around him as he knelt and heaved Willie across his shoulders in a fireman's lift. His thigh still stung from the wound he had received, but he had checked and found the bullet had grazed a shallow furrow across his skin rather than penetrating skin or muscle. That was about it, he reckoned, for his quota of good luck so far today.

He staggered under the weight of the safari guide and felt Willie's blood, hot and sticky, soaking his shirt. He should have bandaged the wound, but if he didn't get moving they would both be burned alive. The smoke was strong in his nose and he noticed movement in the dry yellow grass on either side of him. Rats and lizards, and God alone knew what else, were fleeing the encroaching blaze. Birds swooped and rolled around him, catching insects flushed ahead of the fire. He could feel the heat on his back and forced his legs to work harder.

Tom followed through the bush the path of destruction left by the Isuzu *bakkie*. Another explosion behind told him what he had suspected, that Willie's Land Rover would be engulfed by the flames. He glanced back and saw a black-and-orange pyre rising above the bushfire. Tom hoped that Sannie had been able to organise some air support – that would be their only hope now of keeping up with the gang.

He grunted, pausing for a second to readjust Willie's body across his aching shoulders. As he looked down he saw the grass around his feet was burning. He coughed as smoke entered his lungs. Forcing himself to keep moving he set off again. Somewhere in the distance he heard an elephant trumpet. Wild animals were the least of his worries now.

Tom risked another glance back and saw a tall tree ablaze. Still moving, but not watching the ground, he stumbled as his foot went into some creature's hole and he pitched face forwards into the grass. Willie's bulk crushed him, knocking the air from his lungs. When he tried to get them working again he sucked in smoke and ash and retched. He was pinned under the Afrikaner and felt a furnace-like blast of hot air singe the hairs on the back of his legs. He tried to get the man off his back, but strength seemed to have left him. Now, he thought, was a good time to die.

Without warning, the pressing weight was off him. Light-headed from the smoke, his eyes watering, he was vaguely aware of someone calling his name. A black hand was in front of his face, fingers outstretched. He reached for it.

'On your feet, Tom. Come on,' Duncan said. He

yanked on Tom's hand, rolling him over and dragging him to his feet.

Duncan knelt and grabbed Willie under the arms. The white man, his shirt now drenched in his own blood, came to and groaned. Tom stood and got under one of Willie's arms while Duncan supported the other. Tom felt slapping on his back and looked across at Duncan, whose eyes were wide with horror.

'Your shirt was on fire, man! This is too close!'

They ran, with Willie's help, as a lofty leadwood tree crashed down behind them, sending a shower of sparks and ash into the air.

Three other safari vehicles from different lodges were waiting for them at the T-junction. Tom and Duncan laid Willie in the back of a Land Rover, along a green canvas-covered bench seat. Tom had grabbed his first-aid kit before leaving Tinga, and Duncan handed it to him. Tom ripped open a dressing and did his best to patch up the man who had done so much in such a short time.

'The terrs . . . ?' Willie coughed and winced as he tried to sit up.

'Lie down, mate. We have to get you to a doctor.' Tom looked back at the burning African bush as Duncan climbed in next to the guide behind the wheel and told the man to head to Tinga.

11

Sannie had her mobile phone to one ear, on hold to the air force base at Hoedspruit, and was talking to the Nelspruit detectives' office on the landline when Tom walked in.

His exposed skin was blackened by soot and dirt and his shirt looked like it had been tortured with a lighted cigarette – there were burn holes everywhere. His shorts and left leg were encrusted with dried blood. He pulled his shirt off over his head as he entered, saying nothing to her.

'I'll call you back in ten,' she said to the detectives' civilian administrative assistant. She kept the mobile phone near her ear as she followed him to the bathroom.

'We bloody lost them,' Tom said. 'We were so fucking close, Sannie, I could see them. They're alive, though one of them – Greeves, I think – looked injured. He was limping badly. We got two of the bastards, though the fire will have destroyed the bodies.'

She had spoken to Tom as he'd driven back to

Tinga, as soon as he had entered mobile phone range. He had passed on descriptions of the gang, so she already knew most of what he was saying. She heard the shower running.

'What are you doing, Tom?'

'What does it sound like? I'm getting cleaned up, changed and I'm going after them again.'

Sannie turned at the sound of the door to the suite opening. Isaac Tshabalala walked in, accompanied by a policeman in grey-blue fatigues. 'They just told me that he's back. Where is he?'

Tom walked out of the bathroom, a towel around his waist. 'He's here. What's happening? Have you been able to organise some air support yet? They're probably still on foot.'

Tshabalala moved his right hand to the butt of his holstered pistol. 'Detective Sergeant Furey, the progress of this investigation is no longer your concern and –'

'Like hell it's not my concern. I need a vehicle to get to the nearest border post.'

'You're going nowhere. Hand over your pistol, handcuffs, and any other weapons and ammunition you're carrying.' Tshabalala motioned for the uniformed officer to move forward and the man stepped towards Tom.

'What's this about?'

'We found the coke, Tom,' Sannie said.

She saw the puzzlement on his face. 'Coca-Cola?'

'The cocaine, in the bathroom,' the African officer said.

Tom laughed. 'Do what? I've never used illegal

186

drugs in my life. What the hell's going on here? Get out of my way.'

Tshabalala put a hand on his pistol. 'Your gun and handcuffs. Now. You're going to be charged with possession of an illegal narcotic, Furey. The suspected drugs Inspector Van Rensburg discovered in your bathroom go part of the way to explaining why you were late reporting for duty this morning, and how you managed to let the man you were supposedly guarding get taken from under your nose.'

'Carla,' he said, looking straight at Sannie. She felt uncomfortable and couldn't meet his gaze. 'It's hers. She was acting wild last night. Ask her.'

The same thought had crossed her mind as soon as she'd entered the room. However, she'd immediately remembered that it had been Carla herself who had suggested setting up the command post in Tom's room. She explained this to Tom, and the rationale that the woman would not be stupid enough to set herself up for arrest.

'No, she's only bloody set me up, is all,' Tom said. 'This'd be funny if it weren't so daft. Where is she?'

'Gone to Tinga's other lodge, Narina. She'll be back in an hour or so,' Sannie said.

'I've been taking complaints all morning about your little escapade through the park,' Tshabalala said. 'Menacing people with a firearm, breaking every national park rule.' Spittle flew from Isaac's mouth as his anger mounted. 'You have no jurisdiction in this country and you cannot commandeer vehicles and men to do the job you should have done in the first place. This is not your little colonial fiefdom! Arrest him!'

Sannie felt as though an injustice was being done, but the evidence all pointed to Tom and, no matter how much she sympathised with the Englishman, everything Isaac Tshabalala had just said was correct. She heard a voice on her mobile phone.

'*Ja*,' she said, listening to the air force captain on the other end.

Tom was staring angrily at Isaac as the uniformed officer retrieved Tom's pistol, magazines and Asp collapsible baton.

Sannie ended the call. 'That was Hoedspruit. They say they can't send a helicopter into Mozambican airspace until they get permission from the defence minister's office or higher. I spoke to Indira ten minutes ago and she said Dule was waiting for a call back from his counterpart over the border.'

'Christ, you people couldn't organise sex in a brothel,' Tom said.

'Who do you mean by *you people*?' Tshabalala said.

Sannie shared Isaac's sense of offence. Tom was in no position to be criticising the South African authorities. After all, *he* was the one who had lost Robert Greeves.

'Cuff him,' Isaac said to the policeman. 'Sannie, keep an eye on the prisoner. I'm going to speak to Minister Dule, and then Ndlovu and I,' he gestured to the uniformed officer, 'are going to Skukuza to wait for the Nelspruit detectives to arrive and brief them. Call me if there are any new developments at this end.'

'Yes, sir.'

*

'Unlock these things, Sannie.' He sat on the bed and held his hands out to her.

'You know I can't, Tom.'

'Carla's not coming back. You know that, don't you?' He brushed the hair back from his face with his manacled hands.

She felt a cold tingle of dread creeping up her spine. When Carla had come to the room and said she had to go to Narina to deal with a guest's complaint, Sannie had been on two telephones. She had simply nodded.

'She's part of this. Can't you see it? She set me up to take the fall and slow down the pursuit. It's why she came on to me so strong, probably why she was sleeping with Nick Roberts. She used him to get information about this visit and took me out of the game last night. I haven't been late for a job in my life and I didn't drink enough to wake up feeling as bad as I did this morning. She must have slipped something in my beer last night. I bloody passed out after one drink. Either the alarm covering the entryways to Greeves's room went off and I slept through it, or she nobbled it. For whatever motive, Carla's part of this set-up. Give her a tug.'

'What?'

'Run a criminal check on her – see what comes up. Talk to her family and friends, maybe she's found Allah late in life. She wouldn't be the first European woman to get sucked into a foreign terrorist network. Maybe it's all about money. I don't bloody know.'

Sannie realised that she and Isaac had been blinded by the drugs and Carla's deception, which now seemed heavy-handed. She believed Tom: he wasn't the sort of man who would take drugs – and if he was, he wouldn't have been stupid enough to leave them lying about. And Sannie wouldn't put anything past Carla.

'She suggested you use my room for the command post in order to lead you to the drugs. And how stupid would I be to leave a line of coke unused in the bathroom? You've got to help me, Sannie.'

She turned her back on him and paced across the thick Persian rug on the floor of the suite and stood, arms folded, staring out over the Sabie River. An elephant sucked up a trunkful of muddy water and showered itself with black goo. She, like Tom, knew that minutes counted at this point in a pursuit, and that valuable time was being sacrificed to the dictates of petty bureaucracy. Men's lives were at risk while they waited for diplomats to get out of bed and return phone calls.

'I've got to get to Mozambique, Sannie.'

'Isaac's just arrested you, man. If I set you free now I'm breaking the law. I'll be branded a racist for going against a black superior and siding with you – whether you're right or wrong. That'll be it for me and the police service. I'll end up working security at a Pick 'n' Pay.'

'Two men will die if we don't move now.'

She shook her head. Damn him. He was right, and probably right about Carla Sykes as well. Tom had made a mistake by falling for the woman's advances and Sannie had been almost as guilty in falling for her set-up.

Sannie strode across to the writing desk and took out a Tinga pen and some stationery. She sat down

190

and started writing. 'Go to the mini-bar, get a bottle of soft drink, empty it out, rinse it and piss in it,' she said, not looking back at him.

'What?'

'I'm writing a note for Tshabalala. I don't want to explain this over the phone. I'm telling him I watched you give a urine sample and that he should get it analysed and get Carla Sykes thoroughly checked at the same time. If the urine sample comes up negative for drugs you'll be partly vindicated. If it comes out positive, I'll bring you back to Skukuza and he can lock you up. In the meantime, I'm taking custody of you and doing what he told me to do – keeping an eye on you. I'll be sidelined off this investigation as soon as the detectives from Nelspruit get here, so I won't be missed.'

Tom opened the mini-bar and tipped the contents of a bottle of soda water down the bathroom sink. As he unzipped his shorts, his hands still cuffed, he called out to her from the toilet. 'You said you won't be missed. Where are you going?'

'Mozambique.'

12

Helen MacDonald sat at her desk in her office in Westminster and tried again to get the words right for the holding statement. She wiped away a tear with the back of her hand.

The phone rang.

'Hello, I'm calling from South Africa. My name is Pauline le Roux, from Radio 702. I'm glad to get through to you at last, Helen. Look, we've had a call from a reporter in the east of the country near our Kruger Park and she says that Robert Greeves has gone missing. I need you to confirm that, please, and tell me all the details you have so far.'

'Have you gone to air with this yet?'

'No, and no one else has either. So it's true?'

'I don't suppose there's anything I can say to you that will stop you from running this story for twenty-four hours, is there?' It was worth a try, Helen thought morosely.

'I'll take that as a yes, then. And no, you're right, there's nothing you can say that would stop me running this story. If you want to go on air, I'll take you now.'

'I'll send you a statement in half an hour.' Helen hung up. She had neither confirmed nor denied that Robert was missing. She'd bought herself enough time to finish her statement, but the news was out now. She called the Prime Minister's office.

Forty-five minutes later, at midday South African time, Eugene Coetzee, freelance photographer, tuned the radio in his Corolla sedan to 702 to listen to the news. There had been some funny goings-on around Tinga that morning.

Eugene guessed his quarry, the English politician Robert Greeves, would be going on an early morning game drive from Tinga. Having missed getting the shot the previous afternoon, he was determined to ambush the minister this time.

Eugene had booked himself into a rondavel at Skukuza camp the night before – he was sure the British newspaper he was stringing for would cover the expense of a self-contained hut – and set the alarm on his cell phone to wake him at five. He'd recovered quickly from the several Klipdrift and Cokes he'd had the night before and been in the head of the queue of cars waiting at the camp gates when they had opened at five-thirty.

He knew Tinga's schedules. It had only taken a phone call a few days ago, with him pretending to be interested in staying at the lodge, to find out how many drives they offered per day and their departure times.

He knew the official guests wouldn't leave the lodge before six-fifteen, and they first had to drive along the private road that linked Tinga Legends Lodge with the main sealed road. Eugene was waiting on the corner, parked on the dirt verge, at six-fifteen sharp. But no game vehicles had come.

He had wondered if they had deliberately changed the schedule after his bid to get a picture of Greeves yesterday. In all his twenty years as a member of the paparazzi, Eugene had never encountered a politician so shy – mostly they lived for getting their pictures in the newspaper. He had no idea why the *World* was so interested in this guy, and didn't particularly care. But Eugene loved a challenge, and this was shaping up to be a battle of wills.

Not long after six-thirty, he heard the growl of a Land Cruiser and started his own engine as the Tinga game-viewing vehicle came into sight. Oddly, there were only two people in it – an African guide driving and a white man sitting next to him, the one who had been sitting in the rear of the vehicle that had cut him off and prevented him from getting his shot yesterday. The pair accelerated rapidly, quickly reaching a speed that looked dangerously close to illegal, and they pulled away from Eugene's Corolla.

He smiled. Such an obvious decoy. Did they expect him to follow them? Perhaps he was supposed to think that Greeves's game viewer, with Minister Dule on board, had left earlier and they were speeding out now to catch up with them. Eugene switched off his engine and waited. And waited.

He listened to the radio news at seven – nothing

of much interest on the bulletin – and then decided to turn on his radio scanner, which was tuned to the police and national parks frequencies. Immediately he picked up some agitated chatter. A Tinga game viewer had been reported speeding. Isaac Tshabalala, the old man in charge of the cops in Kruger, was heading from Orpen down to somewhere in the south of the park. Something funny was going on.

Throughout the rest of the morning he had watched an odd assortment of vehicles coming and going from Tinga. Cop cars, an unmarked detective vehicle – at least, a detective was what the beefy white man behind the wheel had looked like. Then, a short while ago, the pair from the Tinga vehicle – the guide and the man he assumed was Greeves's bodyguard – had returned, but in a different game viewer. They were hunched over something or someone in one of the back seats.

The midday news brought some clarity and sent a jolt of adrenaline coursing through his veins. Robert Greeves was missing from the luxury game lodge, presumed kidnapped. Dule was unharmed. And he, Eugene Coetzee, was the only photographer on the scene – for now, anyway.

An ambulance screamed past him and Eugene started his engine again. He accelerated into the vehicle's dust cloud as it raced down the private access road to Tinga. Eugene was a member of the press following a story – the gloves were off now. He stayed close to the ambulance and tailgated it through the unmanned electric gates that led to the luxury lodge.

*

195

Major Jonathan Fraser stood on the Tarmac at RAF Lyneham in Wiltshire. The busy military air transport hub was based in the otherwise peaceful green chequerboard of West Country farmland, a short drive at high speed from the Special Air Service's home at Hereford, near the Welsh border. He watched as the last of six black Land Rover Discovery vehicles rolled up the rear cargo ramp into the waiting C-17.

The big fat grey aircraft's jet engines whined at an idling speed. The members of Fraser's SAS troop filed across the apron to the ramp to await their turn to walk on board. The noon day sun was barely making its presence felt through the whited-out autumn sky.

Fraser wore civilian clothes – blue blazer, tan trousers, oxford button-down collar – they didn't move about in uniform when on counter-terrorist operations lest they draw any more attention to themselves than a convoy of black four-wheel drives would otherwise have done. The Director of Special Forces, a major general, had been driven straight to Wiltshire from a meeting with the Prime Minister.

'You know the odds aren't good, Johnno?' The major general had been commanding officer of the regiment when Jonathan had been one of his young troop leaders. No one else would get away with calling him that.

It had been Jonathan's feeling for many years that while the SAS were highly trained in hostage rescue, they were making a mistake common to most fighting forces throughout history – they were training to fight their last big battle. The DSF was right. There was little chance that they would find Greeves alive and, if they did, the terrorists would be well prepared to execute both of their hostages and a good number of the assault force as soon as the direct assault began. The hostage situation at Beslan, in Russia, where Chechens had held a whole school captive, was, in Jonathan's view, solely an exercise in targeting Russia's special forces troops. He believed it had never been the intention of the captors to release any of the children under any circumstances, and that the whole operation was geared towards generating terror – in its purest form – and wiping out a good number of trained counter-terrorist soldiers in the process. Britain was still fighting the war on terror with the gloves on. The Yanks were marginally better at it. If they identified three or four al-Qaeda types driving through the desert in someone else's country they wiped them off the face of the earth with a hellfire missile fired from an unmanned drone. Pre-emptive strikes – that was the way to go, in Jonathan's view. Get the bastards before they did their dirty deeds, not afterwards. Sadly, Greeves's execution may have already been filmed for release to the satellite television networks. 'Yes, sir. Even if we find Greeves and his man they'll probably kill them before we get near them.'

'Exactly. Still, they came damn close to catching the culprits this morning. Some poor oaf of a plod who lost Greeves in the first place almost redeemed himself.'

'"Almost" doesn't really cut it in our game, does it, sir?' He'd read the preliminary intelligence reports and, while he knew little about the copper who had been Greeves's replacement bodyguard, he had noted with interest that two of the terrorists had been killed in a fire fight in the African bush that morning, while he'd been driving to Lyneham. Perhaps there would be a scent for Jonathan and his hounds to follow after all.

'You've got the boats as well?'

'Mozambique does have two and a half thousand kilometres of coastline, sir, so if that's where they are, the boats could come in handy.'

'You always were a cheeky sod.'

'Yes, sir.'

The boats were rubber Zodiacs, packed deflated into containers which could be pushed out the back of the C-17 and then reinflated via compressed air cylinders by the troopers who would follow the load out of the aircraft. They could be dropped kilometres offshore, unseen by the enemy, and motor in for an assault. As well as the cargo aircraft taking them to South Africa, Fraser would have air support from the South African National Defence Force in the form of three Oryx helicopters

'Of course, if you do pull it off, you'll write yourself into the history books.'

'It's just another job, sir.'

'That's the spirit, Johnno. Remember, though, it's Africa, and someone else's country, won't you?'

'Yes, sir.'

'One other piece of good news for you, before you leave. Our cousins across the Atlantic have offered what support they can. They'll retask a satellite to give us imagery if you get an idea of where they've holed up. Also, there's an American carrier in the Indian

Ocean at the moment. I've asked for an aircraft with FLIR and they've offered an FA-18. It'll be at the South African base at Hoedspruit by the time you get there, OPCON to you.'

That was the best news he'd had so far on this job. Being given operational control of a fast jet equipped with a Forward Looking Infra-red camera from another country's navy was a good indicator of the magnitude of the operation and the faith his superiors were placing in him. If the terrorists were traced to a fixed base, the jet could fly over at altitude but use its radar to pick up heat signatures of people inside. The aircraft would also be carrying enough bombs and rockets and guns to win a small war.

'PM's most upset by this brazen attack, Johnno, as you can imagine. He's intimated to me that if we're too late, if Greeves and his flunky are dead, and you still get eyes on the target, then we don't want to be messing around with arrests and show trials and whatnot.' The major general raised his eyebrows. 'So feel free to use your aeroplane to maximum effect. The Yanks won't mind a bit.'

'Understood. Better go, sir. Don't want to miss my flight.'

13

Sannie had organised for Duncan to drive her to Skukuza rest camp in another Tinga vehicle. Once there, she used her personal credit card to hire a car from the Avis office at the camp's main reception building.

The only car available was a tiny, bright blue Volkswagen Citi-Golf Chico, a two-door hatchback with a 1.3 litre engine. It was hardly a vehicle to take overland into Mozambique, but she neglected to tell the woman behind the counter that was where she was headed. She wondered, as she signed the paperwork, if she would have any trouble getting the vehicle across the border, since she didn't own it. No, she told herself. In Africa, a police identification, backed up by some cold, hard cash, could get one past most barriers.

Sitting behind the steering wheel she paused and again asked herself the most obvious question. Why am I doing this? She tried to distil her reasoning, but reason wasn't her strong suit at the moment. Gut instinct? Tom was morally right to pursue the abductors as quickly and efficiently as possible, despite the legal impediments. But there was more. It shouldn't be a factor, but she wanted to be with him, helping him. It wasn't good policing, adrenaline or glory that drove her. Indeed, this might be the end of her career. She shook her head.

It didn't matter. There was no time to waste. Around her, in the car park outside Kruger's headquarters, tourists came and went as though nothing was wrong. For South African families Kruger was a haven from the day-to-day worries of crime and the increasingly tough grind of making a living. This terrible thing that had happened to Robert Greeves would be bad news for the park when it hit the media. She drove out the main gates and turned left at the four-way stop.

Back at Tinga Legends Lodge she noticed a white Corolla parked outside the entry hall. As she stepped out of the Chico a man in a photographic vest also stepped out and started taking her picture, his expensive camera clicking as fast as an automatic weapon. Instinctively, she put a hand to her face. 'Who the hell are you?'

'Eugene Coetzee, Independent News Agency,' he said, still firing away as he walked backwards, in front of her.

'Get out of my way or I'll arrest you.'

'Ah, so you're police. Can you confirm it's terrorists who have kidnapped Robert Greeves?'

Duncan was standing inside reception. Sannie gestured to the photographer with a thumb. 'Who let him in here?' The guide shrugged. 'Well, get Carla to get him off the premises. Is she back from Narina yet?'

'No.'

Damn it, Sannie thought. She should never have let Carla leave the lodge. There were too many things to do at once. 'When she comes back – *if* she comes back, tell her Captain Tshabalala needs to talk to her. It's very important.'

Tom was showered and changed into long pants and a blue cotton shirt when she reached his room. He was already packed. She warned him about the press photographer hanging around reception. He nodded and told her that an ambulance had come and gone, taking the Afrikaner safari guide to the hospital at Nelspruit. 'He deserves a medal.'

'Well, there'll be no medals for us if we don't get your man back. Only jail time, more like it. Let's go.'

The photographer was still in reception when they strode through. Tom paused, standing in front of the man as he snapped off picture after picture. Sannie sighed. They really didn't have time for this.

'You're the bodyguard, aren't you?' Coetzee said over the whir of his digital SLR camera. 'How does it feel to have lost the man you were protecting?'

'How does it feel? Something like how it's going to feel when the doctor tries to extract that lens from where I'm about to shove it. Who are you working for?'

'Eugene Coetzee, Independent News Agency. And you are?'

'No, I mean who are you stringing for, Eugene. Don't tell me you just hang around trying to get pictures of British politicians for the hell of it.'

Coetzee shrugged, as if there was no point in trying

to hide who was paying his bills. 'One of your English tabloids, the *World*. Journalist there by the name of Michael –'

'– Fisher?'

'Yes, that's the guy. Do you know him?'

Tom shook his head. 'Bye.'

'Hey, I was the one who was supposed to be asking the questions.'

As they got into the Chico Sannie ignored the photographer, despite the fact that he kept his lens pressed to the driver's window, walking alongside them as she reversed, turned and then drove up Tinga's driveway. In her rear-view mirror she saw Duncan laying a hand on Coetzee's shoulder. 'What was all that about?'

Tom shrugged. 'Nothing. I don't know. Greeves was being hounded by that reporter, Fisher, before we left London.

'Is Greeves in trouble back in England?'

'No, far from it. From what I've seen of him so far he's a clean skin – no faults that I've read about. A few eyebrows raised about the number of overseas trips he takes, particularly to Africa, but that's about it.'

'Perhaps that's why your tabloids are taking an interest in him – trying to find some dirt on a clean politician is their style, from what I know of them.'

'Yeah. Impressive vehicle, by the way. Are we seriously going to be driving through the jungles of Mozambique in this?'

'Don't be smart. It was all they had. We'll probably strike some bad roads, but a lot of money's being spent in that country trying to fix things up. Shame – they were just starting to get themselves sorted out after the end of the civil war in 1992 when a cyclone came along in 2000 and flattened a whole heap of bridges and coastal resorts. Still, the country's bouncing back again.'

Sannie had called her mother on the drive from Skukuza to Tinga and told her what had happened – it was all over the news now. She would collect her grandchildren and they would stay at her place until Sannie returned, though she was unable to say exactly when that would be. Her mother had seemed annoyed down the phone line, though Sannie knew she was really just worried about her safety. So she wasn't the only one.

They followed the same route Tom and Duncan had taken earlier in the morning in pursuit of the terrorists. Sannie stuck to the main sealed road to make better time, though she refused to go faster than fifty kilometres per hour. 'We want to get there in one piece, Tom,' she had protested. 'It's no good if we hit something.'

The countryside became more open and drier the further north they headed on the H1-3 towards Satara camp. This was lion country, with open, rolling grasslands that provided good grazing for plains game such as zebra and wildebeest.

'Why, Sannie?'

'Why what?' she replied as she slowed to negotiate her way through a traffic jam of cars and game-viewing vehicles – though not as bad as the one Tom had forced his way through on the bridge. As they passed, a man in a Kombi said, 'There's a leopard somewhere in the bush in there,' but Sannie and Tom had no time to stop.

'Why are you helping me?'

'I have asked myself the same question many times already. It's a combination of reasons, I suppose. I feel like our system was not good enough this morning, that we've let you down. Also, I can imagine myself in your situation. I know that you shouldn't be doing any of this, and neither should I, but I can't just sit around and hope it all works out for the best. We're following the best lead available – someone has to.'

She thought about Carla and the smell of her perfume in his room. She continued to be angry at him, on a personal level, and there would be no going back to what might have been, but she still felt for him professionally.

They drove in silence, passing a herd of about two hundred buffalo, and Sannie explained to him that if they were encountered on foot, the huge black bovines were among the most dangerous and unpredictable animals in Africa.

It was a hundred and sixty kilometres from Skukuza to Letaba camp and another thirty-four beyond that to the Giriyondo border post and the crossing into Mozambique. At the rate they were driving, it would be close to four pm by the time they crossed and she was worried about driving the tiny car along the bush roads on the other side of the border at night.

He studied a map of Mozambique as she drove. He had found a southern African road atlas in the Tinga Legends library while she had gone to collect the rental car and he traced the route they had discussed.

'If they're terrorists, what do they want, what do they need?'

They had only a rough plan of where they would head at this stage – basically eastwards, to the coast, as soon as possible after they crossed the border. Sannie chewed her lower lip. 'Privacy. Somewhere to hide.'

'Sure,' he said. 'But that could be a remote camp in the middle of the Mozambican bush, or in a city where strangers wouldn't stick out.'

'They need a getaway, in case we find them again.'

'Right.' Tom moved his finger through the green swathes of wilderness on the map. 'But if you're about to be surrounded by police and you're in the middle of the bush, then your only way out is on foot or by four-wheel drive.'

'We're assuming they picked up another vehicle across the border, but they won't want to use it for long. Travelling those back roads they will have been noticed, and if there are police roadblocks they'll be remembered.'

'So they'll want to ditch the vehicle soon and maybe get a new one, possibly steal one, but if they've got the money and connections for special forces weapons and white phosphorus hand grenades, then they can also afford to buy a couple of cars and have them pre-positioned.'

'Which is easier to do in a larger town,' she said, following on from where his reasoning was taking them, inexorably towards the coast.

His finger, she saw out of the corner of her eye as she geared down and waited for a herd of a dozen elephant to cross the tar road, had reached the blue waters of the Indian Ocean. 'Where you also have a means of escape via the sea, through an established port or marina, and an airstrip if your budget extends to an aircraft.'

'Xai Xai?' she said. Following a straight line from where the gang had illegally crossed the border, the coastal town of Xai Xai – she pronounced it 'Shy-Shy' – fitted the criteria they had set for the terrorist group's hideout. She wondered, however, if they had come to that conclusion simply because it gave them somewhere to go. 'Or anywhere else on the two and a half thousand kilometre coastline.'

'Yeah,' he sighed.

The little Volkswagen town car had no airconditioning and Tom's saturated shirt was plastered to his back. He was as relieved as Sannie to get out and stretch his legs when they entered Kruger Park's Letaba rest camp.

He'd noted on the map of the park that the camp was nestled on the banks of a river of the same name. The foliage inside the perimeter was lush and green, typical of what he'd noticed along the other permanent rivers in the park. It was a welcome change from the dry, dusty browns they'd been driving through all afternoon.

While Sannie filled the Chico's petrol tank she gave him directions to the camp shop, along with instructions to use his debit card to draw out some rand from the cash teller machine he would find at the store. As he walked he mused yet again how different from his expectations Africa was turning out to be. Here was a continent where people died by the million from malaria because they didn't have mosquito nets, yet a game reserve had a cash teller machine in the middle of the bush. Bizarre.

On his way he was surprised to see delicate brown antelope wandering between the permanent safari tents and huts that made up the camp's fixed accommodation. After withdrawing the equivalent of three hundred British pounds – the most his bank would let him take out in foreign currency in one transaction – he went into the shop. It was well stocked with frozen meat, soft drinks and alcohol, souvenirs, curios and all the little camping bits and pieces that a holidaying family might forget to pack. He grabbed a basket and selected a collapsible cooler bag, some cans of soft drink, a five-litre plastic bottle of drinking water, a six-pack of Castle beer, two frozen steaks, a bag of ice cubes, some potatoes, a cooking pan, salt and pepper, margarine and some canned peaches. It wouldn't be a feast, but Sannie had told him to buy food for at least one night. He was paying by credit card when Sannie entered.

'Got everything?'

'Hardly seems like enough for a safari into the wilds of Africa.'

Sannie checked her watch. 'Let's go. Better move if we want to make the crossing before the border closes at four. Also, this will probably be the last place you can get cell phone coverage for quite a while.'

As she drove out the camp gate, Tom took a deep breath and dialled Shuttleworth's phone. When the

Scot answered he told Tom he was at Gatwick, waiting for his flight to Johannesburg. 'Where should I meet you tomorrow morning?' his boss asked him.

'I'll be in Mozambique.'

'*What?*' Shuttleworth was not a man given to emotional outbursts, so Tom wasn't ready for the tirade that followed. He was told, in no uncertain terms, and with expletives used in lieu of punctuation, to get his arse back to Tinga Lodge immediately. Tom held the phone away from his ear and rolled his eyes theatrically. Sannie smiled back at him.

'There's no point in going back to Tinga,' Tom said to Shuttleworth.

'What the hell do you mean, *no point?*' Shuttleworth yelled.

Sannie whispered to him, asking if he wanted her to pull over so he could finish the conversation. She had turned right at a four-way stop outside the camp and was now driving down a steep hill to the wide, mostly sandy expanse of the Letaba River.

Tom shook his head. 'I've typed up my notes and printed them out on the Tinga computer. It's all there waiting for you. I'm crossing the border tonight and I'll try to pick up their trail tomorrow. We probably haven't got a hope in hell, but there's nothing for me to do at Tinga except sit around and wait to lose my job officially. The South Africans already tried to arrest me this morning.' Tom smiled at Sannie, again holding the phone away so they could both hear Shuttleworth yelling until the phone signal dropped out.

'Now we're really on our own,' she said.

*

Away from the park's traffic Sannie pushed the accelerator pedal harder and the hatchback juddered along a corrugated-dirt, ochre-coloured road flanked by dry yellow grasslands towards the Giriyondo border post, which sat on a navigable hill on the pass through the Lebombo mountain range.

The mountains, which to Tom's eye weren't much more than a string of low, hazy blue hills, marked the natural and actual border between South Africa and Mozambique.

Bristling with lightning rods, radio antennae and satellite television dishes, Giriyondo border post was a relatively new addition to the Kruger National Park, set up to provide access to an old hunting reserve on the Mozambican side which had been incorporated into the new Greater Limpopo Transfrontier National Park.

The new park had been designed to re-establish traditional animal migration routes and to help impoverished Mozambique cash in on some of the tourist dollars that came South Africa's way via Kruger. It was still in its infancy, but already proving popular with local and foreign visitors looking for a different bush experience, or a short cut from Kruger to Mozambique's beaches. The reserve's wildlife, Sannie explained as she drove through the post's gates and parked outside a new tan-coloured thatched building, had been decimated by poaching during Mozambique's civil war. They were unlikely to see as many animals as they had in Kruger once they crossed the border.

The South African authorities were trying to

restock the park, particularly with elephant, whose numbers had grown in Kruger since the government buckled to international pressure and ended the practice of culling. 'The bunny-huggers overseas stopped us culling our elephants, so now there are too many of them in the park, and they're causing damage to the environment. The parks guys moved some across the border, but elephants are smart and they knew that Mozambique was a dangerous place. Many of them simply walked back across the border into South Africa.'

They got out and closed the car doors and Tom braced himself for a test of African bureaucracy. Once inside, however, Sannie switched continuously from Afrikaans to the local dialect, and soon had the immigration and customs officers on the South African side smiling and charmed. She used her police credentials to satisfy the national parks staff member on duty that they did not need exit permits as they were travelling on official business.

Things slowed, however, after they walked next door to an identical building, across a white line on the ground which marked the crossing from South Africa to Mozambique.

'*Bom Dia,*' the blue-uniformed immigration official smiled as they entered, though his pleasant demeanour disappeared once they submitted their passports and completed entry forms.

'No visa?' he said to Tom, passing back his passport across the counter.

'I need one?' he asked Sannie. She spoke to the man in Tsonga Shangaan, the Mozambican version of the tribal language, and he raised his eyebrows at her knowledge of it.

'He says South Africans are granted visas here, at the border, but you'll need to go to the high commission in Nelspruit or the embassy in Pretoria to get yours.'

Tom felt his face flush as the anger surged up inside him. 'What the fuck does he mean by that? They're hundreds of kilometres away. Tell him there's a man's life at stake and –'

She put a hand on his arm and he looked down at it. The touch calmed him. 'Shush,' she chided. 'I told you before, the best way to deal with bureaucracy in this part of the world is to remain calm and be patient and you've blown that already.'

'Yes, but –'

'Yes, but leave it to me.'

The official sat back, crossed his arms in front of his chest and continued to shake his head as he spoke. Sannie switched her attention to the customs official, sitting next to the immigration man, who had been taking an active interest in the conversation.

The immigration officer and his colleague conversed with each other, switching from Tsonga Shangaan to Portuguese. Tom figured they wanted to keep that conversation private from Sannie. She looked over her shoulder at him and winked. 'It's okay,' she mouthed.

'Come,' the immigration officer said, standing and beckoning Tom.

Tom looked at Sannie for an explanation. 'Whatever he asks for, just pay him. We don't have time to bargain, and the law's on their side,' she said.

It was the height of irony, Tom thought as he followed the immigration man into an adjoining private interview room, that the poster on the wall read, *Mozambique says no to corruption*.

Inside he sat down at a desk opposite the man, who took out a blank entry form and wrote on the back *R1000*. 'Bloody hell,' Tom said out loud, reluctantly reaching for his wallet. The amount was close to a hundred pounds. He counted out the notes and threw them down on the table. The immigration man looked left and right, though the room was empty except for the two of them, then slid the money off the tabletop and into his pocket.

Sannie nodded grimly to him when he emerged. 'The customs guy will want his cut as well.'

She was right. Outside the airconditioned building the man made a show of checking the car's interior and boot, saying he was looking for alcohol and groceries. The customs officer then demanded a further five hundred rand in import duties, though he didn't specify on what the taxes were to be levied. Sannie nodded to Tom's pants pocket and he peeled off more of the blue hundred-rand notes.

Tom swallowed his indignation and paid the bribe, thankful at last to be waved through the gate. 'Do you want me to drive?' he asked.

'I'm happy to keep going until we hit the tar road. I learned to drive on dirt roads in Africa, Tom. I'd be lost in the traffic in London, though.'

Tom studied a map given to them when they paid their entry fee to the national park, which on the Mozambican side was called the Parque Nacional

Do Limpopo. The park's emblem was the curved-horn sable antelope, the same animal Tom had seen on the box of matches left behind by one of Greeves's abductors.

'We're not likely to run into any speed traps here in the bush, nor many animals,' she said when she noticed him glancing at the speedometer. 'I want to get as close as we can to the coast before nightfall. The road's better there.'

She hovered on eighty, pausing only to gear down expertly a couple of times when the Volkswagen's path was momentarily slewed by some deep sand. The car skipped along the ridges of the corrugations on the harder surfaced tracks and the suspension absorbed the worst of the ride when they bounced along a section which was cobbled with round rocks each the size of a softball. Once or twice Tom winced as the underneath of the Chico scraped over an earthen mound or rock, but Sannie maintained the relentless pace, taking each curve like a seasoned rally driver.

The vegetation was different on the Mozambican side and Sannie confirmed Tom's suspicion that the trees were more mature and bush thicker because of the lack of browsing and grazing animals. In the first hour of driving he saw only two impalas and a single steenbok, a delicate little brick-coloured antelope which took off at the sound of their approach. Animals of the four-footed variety were the least of his concerns now.

Sannie slowed as they entered the village of Macavene, a widely dispersed string of mud huts with thatched-reed roofs. There was the ruin of an old farmhouse, Portuguese they presumed, but no one was living in the gutted building now. A cluster of children gathered around them, staring in silence. Sannie asked for directions and a young man pointed to the left fork of a road as the route to Massingir Dam, their next waypoint.

The road deteriorated rapidly after they left the village and Sannie was forced to drive most of the badly rutted and eroded track in second and third gear. She muttered curses in Afrikaans as she scraped her way along and took the little car up the side of a washed-out section of road so that they were riding at an alarming angle for a hundred metres. At one point Tom instinctively reached out to brace himself against the dashboard when it felt as though they might roll. She laughed at his face and it relieved the tension of the pursuit for a precious minute.

When they arrived at the manned gate marking the border of the Limpopo Park, there was a car ahead of them, a shiny new Corolla, which turned out to be a rental car driven by two middle-aged brothers from Tasmania in Australia. Tom shook his head after chatting briefly to them. It seemed he and Sannie weren't the only crazy people braving the unknown in Mozambique.

Massingir was an impressive man-made addition to the African landscape, an earthen dam five kilometres long and topped with new concrete, a roadway and modern spillways. It blocked the Olifants River, and the land immediately downstream of the wall was green and fertile, a stark contrast with the uniform khaki of the bush on either side of the watercourse.

Tom saw fishermen in canoes hugging the lake shore as they set out for the evening's work. The trees on the banks were taking on the soft golden hues he had come to associate with the onset of Africa's brief twilight.

He suddenly felt guilty, for taking Sannie away from her children and having her share the risks in a bid to make up for his mistakes. 'You know, I couldn't do this without you,' he said.

'I know. It's why I'm here.'

She let Tom take the wheel after they crossed the dam and encouraged him to push the car up to a hundred and twenty. The road was narrow – just enough room for two cars to pass – and while the tar was studded with gravel it was smooth enough to allow him to reach the maximum speed limit. The bush encroached to the very verge of the surface and he realised that if a goat or a cow – or even a person – emerged from the trees on either side he would have virtually no chance of stopping in time. He gripped the wheel harder and pushed the accelerator until the engine was screaming, before changing up a gear.

Just when he was beginning to think all of Africa was covered with thorny bushes and stunted acacias, the road they were on ended in a T-junction and the countryside changed. Turning right on to a wider, smooth-tarred road they passed into wide open flat land of treeless flood plains. Here the road was raised, on a kind of levee bank. A long, straight irrigation or drainage canal ran parallel, on the left, complete with locks similar to those found on English canals. To the right of the road was a railway line.

'Good farming country,' Sannie said. 'I remember the fruit and vegetables here were some of the best I've ever had. The greenest lettuces, the reddest tomatoes you'll ever see.'

Here and there the seemingly endless verdant farmlands were dotted with white houses with red roofs that looked like terracotta tiles. It was only later when they passed closer to one such farmhouse that Tom saw the roof was actually corrugated asbestos painted to look like tiling. It was a little piece of imitation Portugal, erected by long-gone colonists who must have pined for the far-off homeland they were feeding with the rich soil of Africa and the sweat of her people.

In the small towns they whizzed through were more signs of the old rulers' influence: signs in Portuguese, Catholic cathedrals, stout concrete buildings of the colonial administration, and clusters of merchants' villas with a distinct Mediterranean flavour. Some of the houses were freshly painted in pale pastels – more faux Europe – while others bore the bullet holes and black scorch marks of the post-colonial orgy of violence.

They passed a small mosque with a stunted, pointed minaret which was more a gesture to Islam than a tower from which to call the faithful to prayer. It made Tom think about the men they were pursuing. He was assuming they were Islamic fundamentalist terrorists, though he had no proof of their motive, cause or identity at this stage, beyond one man's facial features. As he reminded himself to keep an open mind, the enormity of the task – the probable futility of their race across a foreign country with no support, no back-up – hit him like a bullet in the chest.

On the edge of the canal beside the road, life went on. Women in bright wraps washed themselves and their babies in soapy plastic washing bowls; small boys dived off bridges; men fished with long reed poles with fishing line tied to the ends. They passed a man in a suit and a cowboy hat riding a bicycle, and a new Land Cruiser driven by a fat, waving Portuguese farmer.

'Some of the old farmers from the colonial days are returning, and there are white Zimbabwean farmers here too. They were kicked off their own land by their government, which was once allied to the ruling party here in Mozambique. That's Africa for you,' Sannie said.

Tom shook his head.

'What is it?' Sannie asked. 'You're looking grim.'

'You don't need to be here, Sannie.'

'Yes I do.'

They were silent for a few seconds as they both considered the implications of that, but Tom finally broke their reverie.

'We don't have a chance in hell, do we?'

'Probably not.' She took a sip from a can of Coke and handed it to him. 'But there's nothing else we can do.'

14

B ernard Joyce had spent the better part of eight years at sea. He had lived for the wide expanses of empty ocean, even though he was under it for most of the time. Now he prayed that he would see the water again.

He knew they were by the coast. He could smell it. The dank odour of salt water damp was as much a part of a multimillion-pound nuclear submarine as it would have been on one of Nelson's ships of the line or an Arab trading dhow. And though he knew nothing at all about African birds, seagulls made the same irritating squawk the world over.

His world was one of darkness and pain. He lay on a cold concrete floor, his face covered with a rough hessian sack tied about his throat with string. His hands were cuffed behind his back with plastic cable ties and his fingers were numb. His shoulders ached from the position he had been kept in since the abduction in the cool dark pre-dawn at Tinga.

Time was a hard thing to measure when kept in

darkness, but the coarse weave of his hood had let in daylight when he and Greeves had been bundled into the back of the truck, and for parts of their nightmarish journey. He had been elated to hear gunfire, then terrified as the hot bullet casings rained down on him, burning his bare arms, as their captor fired on whomever was pursuing them. Would they be killed before their rescuers got to them? He imagined their abductors – who had so far said virtually nothing – were terrorists rather than petty criminals, and that they would ensure their hostages died if it looked as though they might be caught. But there had been no evidence of a pursuing force since the gun battle in the bush, which had ended with explosions and fire.

Bernard's feet throbbed with unceasing pain. He had been barefoot, undressed for bed except for a pair of boxer shorts, when they had come for him. They had let themselves into the room – an inside job, for sure – and the needle's jab had silenced him before he could fight back, though he had managed to call out first. He'd awoken in the bush and panicked at the feel of the tape over his mouth. He'd always suffered sinus problems and needed consciously to force himself to breathe as deeply and slowly as possible through his nose.

His feet had been punctured and torn bloody in the first few steps through the bush, and made worse, later, when he had been dragged from the back of the vehicle and made to run as the bullets flew around him. They had marched him and Greeves hard and fast through the bush, each step compounding Bernard's agony. Several times he'd tripped and fallen and had either been dragged upright by his cuffed hands – an excruciatingly painful experience – or kicked in the ribs until he forced himself to his feet. 'If you keep trying to delay us,' a man had whispered in English to him, though with an oddly Latino accent, 'we will simply kill you. It's not you we need, and you know it.' They had seen through his ploy immediately. He'd thought that by causing himself to fall more times than he did by accident, he might slow their progress and thus allow their pursuers to gain ground. 'No one is coming now,' the man had said with an air of certainty.

An hour later, perhaps two, Bernard had arrived, bleeding, panting, dehydrated, bruised from the captors' boots, at another dusty roadside. There he and Greeves had been pushed and dragged into the rear of a pick-up. The road they travelled, at high speed, was badly corrugated. Dust entered the cab and found its way through the hessian weave to clog his nostrils and throat, and he was slammed into the unforgiving metal floor of the cargo compartment with every tortuous bump and pothole. Twice they had slowed to a stop and heard voices. Each time, Bernard had felt a blanket drawn over his body, the heat adding to his fears of suffocation, and felt the hard cylindrical metal imprint of a rifle barrel pressed against his temple under the covering. Police checkpoints? he wondered. It was difficult to hear what language was spoken, enclosed as he was in the back of the truck and smothered, but it wasn't English and it didn't sound like an African dialect. Portuguese? That was the language of Mozambique.

When they arrived at their destination he had smelled the sea. The air was cool on his bare arms and legs and it was a relief just to stop moving, and to stand there for a second or two and stretch his aching, battered limbs. The relief was short-lived. They had come for him once and said nothing. Two of them had dragged him across the slippery, polished concrete floor to another room, lain him on the bare squeaking wire frame of a bed, cable tied his ankles to the tubular metal foot of the bed, and laid into the soles of his already tortured feet with a cane. The tears had flooded the inside of his hood, though the tape had muffled his screams. They didn't ask him a single question – didn't speak a syllable.

He'd had the lecture on resistance to interrogation as part of his training as a naval officer deployed overseas on sensitive operations. He knew the techniques the men were employing, but that didn't make them any easier to bear. He was being disorientated, kept in the dark in a state of sensory deprivation. He was being kept off balance – he knew nothing of what they wanted from him, so he couldn't develop a means of misleading them. He had already learned to associate the sounds of footsteps with pain. He had been humiliated already – he had pissed himself out of sheer necessity. When the footsteps came again he'd try hard not to void his bowels in fear, but he couldn't trust himself not to.

He heard the scream, and it made his whole body start.

Again. An animal noise, but coming from a man. From Robert Greeves.

'Never!' Greeves yelled.

Bernard had heard dull thuds and another scream – even more high-pitched than the last. There had been muffled voices, sometimes raised, followed by defiant profanity, yelled by his urbane, educated political master. The bastards. More wailing.

The noise of water being poured, an open palm slapping flesh. Had Robert passed out? Were they trying to revive him? Then silence.

Bernard's heart pounded as he heard the footsteps. Doors opening and slamming shut. Footsteps getting louder. God help me, he prayed silently.

Two of them entered and grabbed him under the armpits. They dragged him – he couldn't have walked if they'd let him – the tops of his toes burning from the friction on the polished floor, and lifted him onto a wooden chair.

Bernard blinked as the hood came off, his eyes seared by the unaccustomed light. The tape stung as it was quickly ripped off his mouth, but that was the least of his pains. He was at a desk, a man sitting opposite him, smiling. The face was dark – handsome, even – with a thick black moustache, Saddam style. A cigarette was smouldering in a tin ashtray, next to a small electronic device which looked like a portable DVD player. The room was otherwise unfurnished, the walls whitewashed but grubby. The windows were set in metal frames, but the light came from a bare overhead bulb; paper or plastic had been taped over the glass panes.

'Leave us,' the man said in English to the other two. Bernard blinked and looked over his shoulder at his captors. One wore jeans, the other three-quarter length cargo pants. Their shirts were plain cotton, one blue, one white. Both had ski masks on, but from their hands, and the ankles of the one in the shorter trousers, he could see they were black Africans. The men, who each had a mini version of an AK 47 slung over his shoulder, departed without a word.

'Hello, Bernard.'

Joyce said nothing. From his brief training he recalled that he should give only what was known as the 'big four', and nothing more. The big four were name, rank, date of birth and service number. As he was no longer a serving naval officer, he decided to limit it to two – name and date of birth. For now, though, he said nothing.

'Cigarette?'

He was about to say he didn't smoke, then realised that would be breaking the first rule. 'My name is Bernard Joyce and I was born on the sixteenth of November, nineteen seventy-four.'

The man laughed, and the noise echoed off the bare walls. 'I don't care, Bernard. And that's the truth.' He picked up the cigarette and drew deeply on it, blowing the smoke towards the ceiling. 'Filthy habit, I know.'

'My name is Bernard Joyce and I was born on the sixteenth of November, nineteen seventy –'

The man held up a hand. 'I need nothing from you, Bernard. I don't need to know about your job as policy advisor to Robert Greeves. I don't need to know about the Royal Navy's nuclear submarines, and I don't need to know about your future plans for troop deployments to Iraq, Afghanistan, or anywhere else for that matter. I don't even need to know that you are homosexual, save for the fact that it is a useful detail – a good way of breaking a man down is to anally rape him, but perhaps that wouldn't work on you. In fact, Bernard Joyce, born nineteen seventy-four, I don't really need you at all.'

Bernard shifted in the chair. He felt sick to his stomach. The man wouldn't have revealed his face if he had any intention at all of letting him live.

'So here is my dilemma. What do I do with you, and can you be of any further use to me? You see, Bernard, you were insurance. In the unlikely event that Robert Greeves was killed in the abduction phase, you were to be my back-up hostage. But Robert, for the time being, is very much alive, if not too well at the moment.' He smiled at his own cruel joke. 'So you, my friend, are redundant.'

Bernard felt like he was going to shit himself. He wondered if this talk would end with a bullet in his head, or a slower, more barbarous fate. He needed to stay alive if he was to fulfil his duty as a former officer – to try to escape. He was as good as dead already, so he would not go peacefully.

'What thoughts, I wonder, are going through your head now?' The man waved the lighted cigarette in the air, as though punctuating his words with a question mark. 'Will you become my Scheherazade, talking and talking now to keep yourself alive, trying to think of something to say that will keep me from killing you? Or will you try to escape, risk your life on a futile gesture, but go out fighting, as the Americans would say?'

225

Bernard said nothing. The man leaned across the table and flipped open the screen of the portable disc player. 'There are many ways to fight a war, Bernard, as I'm sure you know. My people, the people oppressed by the Israelis, the British, the Americans and their puppets in Pakistan and the House of Saud, do not have nuclear submarines or jet fighters or B-52 bombers. My people are good at making the most of what they have. This little device – and the video camera in the next room – are what military people call force multipliers. Do you know what that means?'

Bernard did, but he was sticking, for the time being, with his say-nothing strategy.

The man sighed. 'It means that I can inflict disproportionate damage on my opponent by using a tool which will enhance my meagre military resources. The media, Bernard, is a force multiplier, and one that my people are very good at using. As good as your submarines and jets and bombs are, your people are hopelessly inept at using the world's press, radio and television to your advantage.'

If the conversation were being held over drinks in the Naval and Military Club, Bernard would probably agree with the man.

'Now, Bernard, allow me to multiply the power of my words with some home videos.'

Bernard took a deep breath, then closed his eyes.

'Open them, Bernard, or I'll get one of my men to slice your eyelids off.'

Bernard blinked, looked at him again and swallowed. There was no smile on his face, just a deadpan look that said he had every intention of carrying out his last threat and would think no more of it than if he had just stepped on an ant. He leaned over and turned the player so than Bernard could see the small screen.

The screaming started as soon as the image appeared. Robert Greeves was lying naked on a steel bed, the same type that Bernard had been tied to when they had beaten the soles of his feet, except that the masked man was not beating Robert. The camera had been placed at an obscene angle, facing between Greeves's legs, at about bed level. Greeves shrieked then raised his head. The man with the ski mask moved from between the politician's legs and Bernard could see a hand-cranked generator on the floor, which the man knelt behind. Wires ran from the dynamo to clips which were attached to Robert's testicles. The man started to crank and Bernard winced and screwed his eyes shut again at the terrible, piercing scream.

'Never!' Greeves screamed on the recording. Bernard realised it was a recording of the torture session he had heard earlier.

'Why? You are asking yourself why we are doing that,' the man said as he pressed stop. Bernard looked at him with pure loathing, fantasising at that moment about freeing himself and killing the man. 'Do you think I want him to cower on camera, to plead with his leader, with the British people, to release the inmates from Guantanamo Bay, or pull out your mercenary troops from Iraq?'

Bernard had assumed the message would be something like that.

'Well, between you and me, Bernard, I don't want him to say anything. And no, in case you're thinking my friends and I are mere criminals, no, this is not about obtaining a monetary ransom.' He stubbed his cigarette out in the ashtray.

Bernard was genuinely confused now.

'I'll explain then, if you won't guess. If things go as I plan, I won't be inflicting much more pain at all on your master. I *want* Robert Greeves to be brave when I film him and release the video to the Western world via a friendly television network. I *don't* want him crying and betraying his ideals by begging for the detainees to be released or the troops pulled out of Iraq. I don't want the people of Britain to think of him as weak, because then, secretly, many of them won't care if he is beheaded on TV. However, someone has to deliver the message . . .'

Bernard felt the bile rising in his throat and swallowed hard.

'Having a spare hostage – you, Bernard – allows me more air time, as simple as that. I can show a video to the world of my men standing behind Robert Greeves, the sword resting on his shoulder, and one of us can make our demands, in Arabic, and that will play for two or three days in a row. If, however, I release a second video, this time with someone pleading for Greeves's life – saying, perhaps, that the men who are holding you hostage have threatened to cut off one of Greeves's fingers and toes each day that the UK government delays making a decision, then the effect will be enhanced, don't you agree?'

Bernard stared into those cold, calculating eyes and

a tiny part of him marvelled at the fact that a human being could be so resolute, so cruel, so pitiless.

'I'm not going to torture you, though, Bernard, to make you talk on camera for me. And, remember, I don't need Robert to say a word in the video. So, here's how we'll do it.' The man turned to face the door, the better to project his voice, and yelled a command in Arabic.

From the next room came the sound of screaming again, and Bernard knew it was Greeves.

'Enough!' Bernard said.

The man called another command, and had to yell very loudly this time to be heard over the shrieks of pain. 'You know, if this works out well, you may be released, Bernard. If, in the unlikely event that the Prime Minister does pull your forces out of Iraq and some innocents are released from the American prison, I will keep my word and release you and Robert. If, however, you cause me any problems, or attempt to escape, then I can promise you an extremely painful death. Let me show you another small movie to make my point.' He pushed play again.

Bernard looked down at the screen. There was a man stripped naked, tied to a chair. He writhed in agony, his whole body shaking, straining against the restraints, but he was gagged, so only guttural groans filled the soundtrack. Twin streaks of blood ran down his face, from where his eyes had been.

'Amazing how hard it is to recognise someone without their eyes, don't you think? Force yourself to take a closer look, though. This video, by the way, was shot somewhere in London, not here in Africa. Just a few days ago. That's the only clue I'm giving you.

Despite the horror, Bernard blinked and refocused. The hair, the shape of the nose, even though it, too, was bloodied, the strong jaw. 'Nick . . .'

'Well done. One hundred per cent correct. Detective Sergeant Nick Roberts, as the police might say, was assisting us with our investigations into your itinerary and Robert Greeves's security arrangements. We were planning on killing him quickly, but he tried to escape, so I removed his eyes, one at a time.'

The video continued and Bernard saw the black cylindrical barrel of a silenced pistol held to the side of Nick's head. He heard the whimpering. The gun fired, its report just a tiny cough, but the effect was instantaneous. Bernard watched for an instant, long enough to see the eyeless head thrown sideways, the blood spattering the wall beside him.

Tears rolled down Bernard's cheeks. 'What do you want me to say?'

15

'Chokwe's just ahead,' Sannie said, looking up from the map and rubbing her eyes. The sun was nearly touching the horizon.

It had been a long, tiring day, but rest was the last thing on Tom Furey's mind. Chokwe was an important waypoint on their journey. If their theory that the terrorists were heading for the Indian Ocean was correct, then the little farming town was where the dirt road the criminals would have taken after crossing the border met the main sealed road to the coast. It would be the point where Tom and Sannie's path would at last cross the abductors'.

From here on, their plan was to question the police at every roadblock and station they came across. Sannie was prepared to use her language skills, her charm and their stock of South African rand to get answers. Tom suspected the last weapon at her disposal would be the most persuasive. She had warned him already that while the police in Mozambique were generally polite and friendly, they always had their hand out,

231

and worked off lists of petty rules and regulations all designed to convince unsuspecting tourists to pay a fine.

The road into Chokwe was flanked by market stalls, mostly housed in corrugated-tin sheds. The vendors, who were now in the process of shutting up shop, offered an eclectic mix of goods, including tyres, coffins, plastic buckets, television antennae, lettuces, bicycles and clothing. A minibus taxi in front of them put on its brakes, forcing Tom to stamp on his pedal and swear. As he indicated and passed the bus, which had stopped for a fare, he saw the words *Talk to my lawyer* painted on the back window. He smiled, despite his annoyance.

As with the smaller towns they had passed through, Chokwe was a mix of decaying colonial elegance and chaotic, noisy African life. Music boomed from ghetto-blasters, and impatient drivers leaned on their horns. The milling of people on foot, on bicycles on the road and its verges, had forced Tom to slow down, so he was surprised when a rotund policeman in blue trousers and a white shirt waddled out into the middle of the thoroughfare and flagged him down.

'How fast were you going?' Sannie asked.

Tom checked the speedometer. 'No more than fifty-five.'

'Speeding. Licence,' said the policeman, who was leaning on Tom's windowsill, catching his breath.

'Rubbish,' Tom said.

'Calm and patient, remember?' Sannie said under her breath. She smiled at the policeman and greeted him in Tsonga Shangaan, immediately disarming him.

'What does he say?' Tom interrupted their burgeoning conversation.

'He says you were doing sixty-two.'

'Tell him to go fuck himself.'

Sannie kept a straight face and whispered, 'Careful, he might know *that* much English.' Tom smiled again and nodded like an imbecile at the policeman. Sannie talked at length with the man, never raising her voice and, eventually, pulled her South African Police Service credentials from her handbag. Tom saw the look on the man's face change, possibly to one of worry. It was hard to tell. She fired a series of questions at him, and the African scratched his chin as he talked, and gesticulated with a thumb over his shoulder, towards the coast.

Sannie's eyes widened. 'Tom! He says everyone's looking for two or three men in a *bakkie* with a tinted canopy on the back, heading for the coast.'

'What else?' Tom wiped away the rivulets of sweat that were stinging his eyes. It was hotter and much more humid the closer they travelled to the coast. Sannie spoke to the man again.

'He says they've just had a radio call from Maputo, via their station in Xai Xai, to be on the look-out for up to three men in a Toyota HiLux, suspected of carrying two kidnap victims in the back.'

For the moment Tom shared her enthusiasm. At least they weren't the only ones on the trail of the suspects. He wondered where the new intelligence had come from and suddenly wished he could call Shuttleworth – or anyone on the team, for that matter. However, there was no signal showing on his mobile phone.

The policeman looked past them anxiously. There were already three other cars – two overloaded pick-ups and the minibus taxi Tom had very nearly rammed – that had been pulled over for speeding by another officer and were queued up behind their Volkswagen. 'Well, has he seen them?'

Sannie spoke to the man again. 'He says he only came on duty two hours ago and there's been no vehicle matching that description so far on his shift. I've got the name of his colleague, though, who was working this afternoon. He's at the main station at Xai Xai.'

'That's something.' The policeman waved them on, without them having to pay a bribe or a fine, obviously thinking there were easier targets behind them. They pulled over after leaving Chokwe and Sannie took a turn behind the wheel. She was a godsend, Tom thought. He knew he would have been completely out of his depth if he had crossed the border alone.

Twice they found themselves behind Toyota pick-ups and Tom slipped his pistol from his holster and held it ready between his thighs as Sannie, knuckles white on the steering wheel, accelerated and brought the Chico up beside the four-by-fours, which towered menacingly above the little car. One was driven by a Portuguese woman who had four children on board with her; the other's occupants were an elderly African man and a woman of similar vintage, presumably his wife. Tom was frustrated, but also relieved as either truck could have sent their little car flying off the road into the bush with a gentle nudge.

They came to a T-junction where the road from

Chokwe met the EN1, the main north-south road along the coast of Mozambique. 'Well, here we are. Right or left? Right goes to Maputo, the capital; left goes all the way to Tanzania eventually.'

Tom glanced at the map again, touching the red line that marked the road, as if some unseen force would guide him. 'It gets quieter, less populated as you go north, right?'

Sannie nodded. 'Though a gang of kidnappers could very easily lose themselves in the slums of Maputo.'

Tom closed his eyes. 'North,' he said. Sannie turned left.

They made good time heading up the coast, with Sannie winding the Chico up to a hundred and twenty between towns where they were forced to slow to sixty again, both to avoid speed traps and to ask more local policeman if they had seen the fugitive vehicle. There were no confirmed sightings and Tom felt seeds of dread germinating in his gut.

They crossed a broad flood plain on a raised road and then a suspension bridge to enter the town of Xai Xai. It must have been quite pleasant in its day, Tom thought. There was more of the architecture he had already come to associate with the country – white-washed Portuguese-style villas with red roofs and rendered buildings painted in pastel hues, but, unlike the other settlements they had passed through, Xai Xai was a holiday town. There were a couple of white concrete hotels, neither of which Tom would have fancied staying in, and a grassy park with a band-stand. It could have been any holiday town on the

Mediterranean coast. Outside a cafe, two Portuguese men sat with four much younger African women in western clothes, one of whom was breastfeeding a coffee-coloured baby. A boy in board shorts and an American basketball shirt held up the largest prawn Tom had ever seen as they coasted past him.

'River crayfish,' Sannie said of the creature, which looked nearly as long as the lad's forearm. Music pumped from a bar and it seemed the beat was almost loud enough to cause their car's windows to vibrate as Sannie stopped to let a minibus disgorge passengers ahead of her.

It was hot and muggy here on the coast and Tom could smell the cloying scent of salt water above the diesel exhausts and the oily smoke of chicken grilling over sizzling charcoal. Youngsters ran alongside their South African registered car, waving bags of cashews and yet more prawns. 'Howzit, my *boet*,' one yelled at him and Sannie smiled and shook her head as she translated the Afrikaans slang for 'Hello, my brother'.

'This was once a nice place, but it's too busy now. We stayed here not long after the country was opened again to South Africans, but I'm afraid my people have spoiled this part of the coast. These days you can buy cashews and prawns cheaper in South Africa than you can from these guys.'

Sannie had sourced directions to the main police station from the last speed trap they had stopped at and she turned off the main road through the centre of town and parked under a tree outside a building that looked as solid as a block house. The pockmarks in the wall told Tom that the police station had been well built to withstand gunfire and the civil war had proved the point.

Inside, Sannie asked the female police officer on duty at the front desk for Capitao Alfredo – she didn't have his second name. The woman looked at her blankly for a few seconds, then turned and walked into a back room. Sannie looked at Tom and he shrugged.

'Ah, good evening,' said a thin man in blue uniform trousers and a starched white shirt, wiping his hands on a paper serviette as he emerged from the back room. 'I am Capitao Alfredo Manuel.' He wiped himself again, this time on the front of his trousers, and then shook hands with Tom and Sannie, who introduced themselves by name and rank. 'My colleagues from South Africa and England. I have heard you would be coming.'

Sannie complimented the captain on his English and he explained that, ironically, he had learned the language in Russia, where he had trained as a soldier for Frelimo, the rebel force which had subsequently become the government in Mozambique. 'I also speak Russian, of course, and German. I was a teacher before joining the struggle.'

'Thank you for agreeing to help us, Captain,' Tom said.

'Not at all. The pleasure is all mine. It is not every day that we get reports of a senior politician being abducted by terrorists.'

He led them around the charge counter down the corridor to another room, which was his office. Tom and Sannie took bare metal chairs in front of a large antique wooden desk. Capitao Alfredo sat in a leather office chair. 'Cigarette?'

They declined, but Alfredo lit up a Benson & Hedges anyway. Behind him on the wall was a map of Mozambique and a second one, which Tom couldn't see clearly but guessed was of the local area. There were coloured pins stuck at intervals on what looked like the main north–south road. On the desk was an open Styrofoam takeaway food container with the bones of a half-chicken in it. Tom smelled chilli and fat. 'You have heard that one of my officers saw a suspicious vehicle that matches the description of the one you are seeking?'

'Yes, Captain . . .' Sannie said.

'Please, call me Alfredo.'

Sannie smiled. She was a white Afrikaner and he was a black African, but Tom thought the captain's eyes were pure Latino when he looked at the attractive blonde. He also thought he saw a trace of a blush on Sannie's cheeks. 'Well, Alfredo, yes, we have heard that you are looking for the same Toyota HiLux we are pursuing and that one of your officers may have seen the vehicle in question.'

Tom was impressed at how she was winging it. The truth was that they only now knew they were looking for a Toyota because one of Alfredo's men had told them that was the vehicle they had been warned to look out for. Tom and Sannie were still behind in the game, but this was their chance to catch up and, hopefully, get ahead.

Alfredo stood and turned to the maps behind him. '*Sim*,' he nodded. 'In fact, more than one of my people have seen it. After the bulletin came through, one of my men at Chisanno recalled seeing a HiLux with a tinted rear cab pass by him. He recalled it as unusual because the other windows on the double cab were untinted. He saw the *bakkie* about one o'clock this afternoon. You can talk with him if you wish. I have had him called to the station in case. I thought this may be the vehicle and warned all of my officers to be extra vigilant.'

He gave them a long, thoughtful look, as though giving them time to appreciate how efficient he had been in his policing. Perhaps, Tom thought, he was waiting for praise for having done his job. Just get on with it, he willed the man.

'And then?' Sannie prompted.

Tom looked at his watch.

Alfredo turned back to the map and planted a bony finger on a dot. 'Here. Near Chongoene, about thirteen kilometres north-east of Xai Xai, later in the afternoon a HiLux with a tinted rear cab but untinted front cab ignored a direction by one of my officers to stop.'

'Why did he flag it down? Did he recognise it as the suspect vehicle?' Tom asked.

Alfredo turned back to him and shook his head. 'Regrettably, no. The officers' radio was unfortunately not working, but the vehicle was speeding. Sixty-five in a sixty zone.'

Tom thought the captain had talked about the crime as though it was one step removed from murder. 'They didn't pursue it?'

Alfredo shook his head again. 'This is a poor

country, Detective Sergeant Furey. Not all of my officers have cars or motorcycles. They had no way of pursuing the Toyota, but the officer used his cell phone to call the next checkpoint, at Chidenguele. The officers there said the description matched that of the suspect vehicle you have *lost*.'

The emphasis did not escape Tom, and he remained silent.

'And that checkpoint notified you?' Sannie ventured, looking for a way to defuse the confrontation before it began.

Alfredo smiled at her efforts. 'Yes, Sannie. I ordered the police in the speed traps to set up roadblocks and check every *bakkie* passing through that area.'

She nodded. It was good policing and a swift reaction.

'However,' Alfredo continued, taking his seat again and, as though he had just got back from running after the truck himself, mopping his brow with one of the serviettes that had come with the takeaway chicken, 'the vehicle never reached Chidenguele.'

'You're sure?' Tom said, almost instantly regretting the words.

'I am sure, Detective Sergeant.'

'Hard to miss it with a static roadblock in place,' Sannie said, as much in reproof of Tom for doubting the Mozambican officer's word as in support of Alfredo. 'May I?' She stood and walked around the enormous desk so she could study the map more closely. Alfredo swivelled in his chair and looked up at her.

'As you will see,' he said, 'there is a side road they could have taken, away from the coast.'

240

'Or they could be somewhere here.' Sannie circled the stretch between Chongoene and Chidenguele. 'About forty-five kilometres of coastline.'

'Didn't you say this is one of the busiest parts of Mozambique?' Tom observed. 'We were thinking they might prefer somewhere more remote, perhaps further north.'

Alfredo started to speak, but Sannie beat him to it. 'The established coastal resorts, such as Xai Xai and Bilene, further south, are busy, but this part of the coast is still very empty, if I'm not mistaken, Capitao?'

Alfredo nodded. '*Sim*, Sannie. There are only a few resorts, but they are mostly quite inaccessible. One needs a four-wheel drive to get into them because of the coastal sand dunes in this area.'

Sannie looked back at Tom. 'Remote, inaccessible to most vehicles, on the coast . . .'

'Perfect,' Tom agreed. 'And still only a couple of hours' drive from Maputo if they need to fly anywhere or disappear into a city.'

'Some of the beaches – mostly those near the resorts – are protected by natural reefs, so you could bring a small boat in or out as well,' she said.

'Captain,' Tom said, trying his best to sound humble and beseeching, 'what assets do you have at your disposal to search this part of the coastline?'

'Naturally, I will devote what resources I can to this task,' Alfredo said. 'It is, of course, of great importance to the British government and I would hope that they would be grateful for the assistance of our poor police force.' He spread his hands wide, over the desk, palms upwards.

Tom half wondered if he was expected to pay a bribe at this point. He forced the uncharitable thought from his mind. 'Vehicles?' he said.

'I have four cars and two motorcycles, though only one four-wheel drive – my own Land Cruiser – which we will, of course, use to investigate any leads that my officers turn up.'

This hardly filled Tom with confidence. 'Boats?'

'Alas,' Alfredo said, shrugging his shoulders, 'there are some inflatable boats, donated to the police by the government of Portugal, at the *praia*, but they all have punctures.'

'The *praia*? What's that, the beach?'

Sannie nodded. 'The *Praia do Xai Xai*, the town's beach, is about ten kilometres from here.'

'I will have my officers contact all of the accessible villages and resorts on this stretch of the coast first thing tomorrow morning,' Alfredo said, standing as if to signal their meeting was over. 'If we receive word of the stolen vehicle I will be ready to depart, at a moment's notice, in my Land Cruiser. I will keep four men here with me, armed with AK 47s, to act as the reaction force.'

'Thank you, Capitao. We are very grateful to you for staying back to meet us, and for your kind offer of assistance in the morning. We will be here first thing to monitor the search.' Sannie stood and nodded to Tom to do the same. Her look told him to keep his mouth shut.

Tom turned on her as they walked outside into the sticky, salty night air. 'What the fuck is all this mañana bullshit? We're wasting time.'

242

'Easy, easy.' She placed a hand on his arm, as she had done at the border. 'Look at the realities of policing in Africa, Tom. This guy's got no boats, no helicopter, one four-by-four and a few bicycles. You saw the station – it's empty except for him and the woman on duty. All of his officers will be off in their villages by now. The police here spend most of the time standing by the side of the roads with speed cameras, or on roadblocks hassling tourists. You're not going to get a SWAT team rappelling out of the sky, no matter how much you want it.'

'I've got to get on a phone and tell the people back in the UK. They might even have people on the ground by now, in South Africa or here. At least we've got the vehicle confined to a limited geographic area.'

'Exactly.' She removed her hand from his arm. 'I'll do the same with my people and until we can get some back-up over here, I'm afraid there's not very much more we can do until Alfredo gets his people on the job tomorrow morning.'

Tom walked away from her towards the Volkswagen, his fists clenching and unclenching as he went. He felt like hitting something, running somewhere, getting in the car and charging up and down the coast road in pursuit of a vehicle they had only a vague description of. It was all so maddeningly frustrating. All the long day he'd been just a step behind the abductors. They were close, but close wasn't good enough in this game. He turned and saw Sannie standing there, giving him space to vent. 'It's not about me, Sannie. I want you to know –'

'I know, Tom,' she said sympathetically.

'I'm probably finished as a protection officer no matter how this pans out. I cocked up royally and I deserve all I'll get, but there are two men's lives at stake here. I can't just sit on a beach and do nothing.'

'It's why I'm here as well. God knows, I've probably screwed my career up too.' She tried to force a laugh, but it was hollow and they both knew it – her words were too close to the truth. 'But we'll do more harm than good charging around blindly, and you know it. Say we did find the vehicle by ourselves and went in there, guns blazing . . .'

'They outnumber and outgun us,' he conceded.

'If we make a mess of it, the first thing they'll do is kill the hostages. You know that, Tom. This is the time for others – the military, whoever – to make a plan to rescue them. But we can still look for them. Tomorrow. Carefully.'

He sighed and slumped against the car. 'Christ, I'm hungry – and thirsty. But I keep thinking how bad things must be for Bernard and Greeves.'

'They know you're on their trail, Tom. You nearly caught them in Kruger. That will keep your men alive. That will give them hope.'

'So where to next? A hotel?'

Sannie shook her head. 'African towns aren't generally renowned for the choice of accommodation. I don't like the look of anywhere I've seen so far. Hotels in small towns often double as brothels.'

'So where, then?'

'The beach is about ten kilometres from here. There's a municipal camping ground that has some small chalets. We stayed there a few years ago. It's not luxury, but it should be okay.'

Tom shrugged. He was, as he had been from the moment he touched down in Africa, out of his depth and totally reliant on her. It wasn't a bad feeling – not nearly as bad as the frustration he felt now that it appeared they would be spinning their wheels for twelve hours until morning. 'Lead on.'

Sannie drove, and after the main road took them up a hill, out of the centre of town, she turned right at a sign with a beach umbrella on it that said *Praia do Xai Xai*. There were no streetlights, and only pinpricks of illumination showed in the dark from lanterns in villagers' homes. The Volkswagen careened up and down a roller-coaster of hills which were under cultivation with bananas, and other crops that Tom couldn't make out. Unlike the townships he'd passed through on the way into Kruger, the villagers here seemed to have left plenty of mature trees growing amid their homes, either for shade or to help stabilise the sandy hills they lived on.

The road to the beach ended in a roundabout on top of a cliff and Sannie swung left onto a side road that deteriorated rapidly from potholed tar to dirt as they wound down towards the Indian Ocean. The wind was up and Tom could see white horses pinpricking the dark sea through the gloom. He smelled salt air through the open window and, despite the breeze, it was still warm outside. As they drove down the hill he saw holiday homes that looked like they had come out of a 1970s timeshare brochure. There were curving verandahs, angular geometric designs, and lots of whitewash. Some of the villas still looked run-down, though many, he noticed, had been spruced up with a coat of pastel paint and had well-tended gardens. One particularly nice place, re-done in an ochre coloured render, had its own security guard out front in a blue beret and military-style uniform.

Sannie momentarily seemed to have lost her bearings at the bottom of the hill. 'Sorry, should have turned left, not right,' she said, executing a three-point turn. In front of them was a multistorey white concrete hotel, but no lights were shining in its rooms. Tom looked back as Sannie changed directions and caught a glimpse of the hotel's facade. It was completely gutted. The rooms were empty – all the glass panes and, presumably, all the contents, were gone. In its way, the hotel reminded Tom of Egyptian temples in the Valley of the Kings, or the ruined city of Petra, in Jordan, which he'd visited while protecting a former foreign secretary. The hotel was yet another relic of a disappeared people. He wondered if someone would reopen the hotel one day, though from what Sannie had said, the tourism boom had bypassed sleepy, run-down Xai Xai in favour of nicer beachfront real estate further north.

At the gates of *Campismo do Xai Xai*, an elderly African security guard greeted and led them through the camping ground, which was set back from the beach below a line of low dunes topped with trees and hedges. Tom noted a security fence amid the shrubbery, but also saw it had been trampled in places. There were neon lights in several trees around the small camping area, though about one in two seemed to be broken.

There were only two parties of campers – a couple in a caravan towed by a Mazda pick-up which looked like it had seen better days, and an old Toyota Cressida parked next to a two-man tent. It hardly looked like a playground of the rich and famous.

Sannie spoke to the caretaker when they pulled over and he unlocked the door of a small blue bungalow, the walls and roof of which looked as though they were made of asbestos sheeting. He switched on the light and a single naked light bulb revealed a double bed at the front of the room and a kitchenette. They walked in and, behind a curtain at the rear, found an alcove with two single beds.

'I was worried there for a moment.' Sannie nodded at the double bed. 'You were almost spending the night in the car. You get one of the singles. I hope you don't snore.'

The hut smelled mouldy and damp, and Tom heard mosquitos buzzing around his ears. When he asked Sannie the price he thought it seemed exorbitant for what it was, but neither of them was in the mood to haggle. 'We'll take it,' he said to the caretaker, and Sannie translated.

He checked his watch as they walked back out to the car to unpack their meagre supplies and belongings. 'Let's listen to the news again.' It was close to nine pm and Tom pulled out the battery-operated portable shortwave radio from his bag. He always took it with him on overseas trips and they had tuned in at regular intervals to the BBC World Service. While the news of Greeves's abduction still rated highly, it had been usurped as the lead item by a report of a scandal involving footballers' salaries. Typical, Tom thought. The pips sounded the hour.

'I'll get us a drink,' Sannie said, opening the rear hatch of the Chico.

'Thanks, I could use one.'

'*An African-based terrorist group has claimed responsibility for the abduction of British defence procurement minister Robert Greeves and an as yet unnamed staff member and released a video in which they threaten to behead . . .*'

'Coke?'

'Shush.' Tom beckoned her closer. The reception was bad so they both leaned in to hear the report.

'*Mr Greeves is seen in the video, head shaved, dressed in orange overalls, kneeling in front of three men wearing camouflage uniforms and carrying automatic weapons. One of the alleged terrorists holds a long-bladed sword resting on the minister's shoulders and says, in Arabic: "This war criminal, Robert Greeves, will be beheaded in forty-eight hours unless the British Prime Minister agrees to withdraw all of his country's troops from Iraq and Afghanistan." The low-resolution video clip was reportedly emailed today to an Arabic language satellite television news channel and has been airing for the last hour. The abductors say they are members of a so-far unknown group called Islamic African Dawn. Mr Greeves, who says nothing in the video, disappeared from a luxury game lodge in South Africa yesterday morning following talks with . . .*'

Tom straightened in the car seat as the announcer recapped the story. 'They must have sent it this afternoon, while we were out looking for them. That means they've stopped – holed up somewhere.'

Sannie nodded. 'So they couldn't have gone much further than where Alfredo's men last saw them. The newsreader said "low-resolution video". They could be sending it via a satellite modem, or even from a phone. If it's a phone-camera they'll need to be in an area with mobile reception.'

Tom nodded. 'At least he's still alive – and they're giving the government forty-eight hours. No news of Bernard, though.'

Sannie leaned against the car, arms folded, her mind processing the new information. 'They might want to use him in a separate video, to keep the media interested in the story. You know TV – they can only show the same footage so many times before people lose interest.'

'Let's hope so, for his sake. I'd like to see that video.'

'Over there,' Sannie said, pointing to the caravan.

'What about it?' Tom asked.

'Come with me.'

As they approached the caravan they saw an over-weight white man sitting in the annex area. His camp chair looked like it might buckle under him. He drank from a big yellow can of Laurentina beer while his diminutive wife mixed something in a bowl at a fold-out table. Sannie walked towards them and Tom followed. As they closed on the couple, Tom saw flickering light reflected in their faces and heard people talking in Afrikaans. The couple, though, were silent.

Sannie pointed to the rear of the caravan and it

dawned on Tom what he was seeing. A portable satellite dish, about the size of a large wok, stood on
a white metal pole which was anchored to a spare
wheel, sitting on the sandy ground. A cable led into
the annex and, although Tom still couldn't see the
screen, he realised the couple were watching satellite
television – hundreds of kilometres from home, on a
stretch of beach in Mozambique.

'*Ja*, we love our TV,' Sannie said. 'Some of these
people wouldn't leave home if they thought it would
mean missing their soap operas or their rugby
games on the weekend.' She greeted the couple in
Afrikaans.

The man looked up from the screen, a slightly
annoyed look on his meaty face. '*Ja?*'

'We need to see your TV, please. Can you please
change it to BBC World or one of the other news
channels.'

'My wife's watching her soap opera,' he said
dismissively.

'This is important. We're police officers – I'm
Inspector Susan van Rensburg.'

The fat man laughed. 'What, you come to check my
TV licence? This is Mozambique, not South Africa.'

Tom walked in front of the screen. 'The lady said it
was important.'

The man started to stand, but then saw the look on
Tom's face. 'We need to see the news.'

'You can't just –' But the man's wife had changed
channels with the remote and his protest was silenced
when the image of Greeves, kneeling under the exe-
cutioner's threatening blade, filled the screen. Tom

and Sannie crowded into the annex for a closer look. 'You're after these *skurke*?'

Sannie nodded, watching the video in silence.

'Sorry, hey. Good luck. But I think this guy's for the chop,' the man said as the news item finished.

Tom had seen the three armed men in the grainy video clip and knew that while he and Willie had hurt them, reducing their number by two, the big man was probably right. There was nothing they could do right now, except wait.

'I'll pray for him,' the thin lady said.

'Can't hurt,' Tom said. He felt Sannie take his hand, and looked across at her, at the unexpected gesture. He saw that her eyes were downcast and that her other hand was in one of the big man's and his, in turn, was joined with his wife's. Tom felt a lump suddenly come to his throat at the gesture from these strangers; and at the sight of Sannie – beautiful, smart, determined, brave Sannie, who was risking her career for him – praying.

Tom took the elderly woman's hand to complete the circle.

He bowed his head and said, softly, 'Please.'

16

Even though it was midnight, it was still hot under the aircraft hangar's tin roof at Hoedspruit air base, close to the western border of the Kruger National Park. The black fire-proof jumpsuit that Jonathan Fraser wore didn't make him any cooler, but he would stay dressed like this, ready to don the rest of his gear, until the situation was resolved one way or another.

His men didn't need to be told what to do – they were all professionals. Weapons were being unpacked from carrying cases; the M4 assault rifles and Heckler & Koch MP5 submachine guns stripped and cleaned; pistols checked and magazines loaded with ammunition. Demolitions experts rigged charges of varying strength to blow in everything from a wood door to a welded steel security gate. Until they knew where the civilians were being held, and what sort of stronghold the terrorists were using, all they could do was try to prepare for any eventuality. SAS troopers cross-trained as combat medics unpacked and repacked their first-aid kits, checking that their controlled stores of morphine and bags of IV fluid had survived the trip.

Outside, the aircraft at Fraser's disposal were bathed in floodlights and watched over by a black African airman with an Alsatian guard dog. The British C-17 looking as elegant as a pregnant walrus; three sturdy Atlas Oryx helicopters – upgraded South African versions of the French Aérospatiale Puma – resting like a rank of stationary cavalry mounts; and the US Navy FA-18 Hornet, as sleek, grey and deadly as a shark.

A South African colonel had hastily been put in nominal command of the multinational operation, but Major Jonathan Fraser was under no illusions who would be calling the shots if and when someone set eyes on Greeves and Joyce: him. For now, though, all he could do, apart from clean his own weapons and check and recheck his personal gear – body armour, radio, stun grenades, tear gas – was wait and study maps and aerial pictures of the wide stretch of coastline where the policeman who had gotten them all into this *believed* the hostages were being held.

Fraser's signallers had in record time done a sterling job of getting their satellite communications system up and running inside the hangar. As well as secure phone and email links back to the UK, he had a broadband internet connection. Until they could get access to direct feeds from a rerouted CIA satellite – which the Americans had promised – he was making do with images from the civilian equivalent, Google Earth, to start getting a feel for the coastline north of Xai Xai.

The police chief inspector, Shuttleworth, had arrived

an hour ago, picked up from the local airport by a South African National Defence Force driver. His connecting flight from Johannesburg had been delayed. Fraser had no idea why the man was here – the UK police element of this operation was irrelevant. If their man had done his job in the first place, none of them would be here now. 'Morning, Chief Inspector.'

Shuttleworth sipped from a plastic water bottle and checked his watch. 'So it is, Major.' He had discarded his suit coat, and large damp patches stained the underarms of his shirt. He looked pale and close to expiry.

'Jonathan, please. And nice to see a fellow Scot on the job.' Fraser prided himself on his diplomacy. It was the same on exercises. There were always egos to stroke before the regiment was eventually called in to finish the job, once the police had realised they were out of their depth. 'You've spoken to your man Furey?'

'Aye.' Shuttleworth had been in the air when Furey had tried to call him with an update of the progress across the border in Mozambique, but the Met's switchboard in London had put him through to the COBRA situation room in Downing Street and they had given him Jonathan Fraser's secure satellite phone number at Hoedspruit. Tom had passed his information on to the SAS commander, and Shuttleworth, playing catch-up after his delayed flight, had just made Tom talk him through the same information again. 'The Mozambicans did a good job today, identifying the suspect vehicle – assuming it was the right one – and they'll be ready to start their search at first light.'

Fraser had to stop himself from laughing. Talk

about shutting the gate after the horse had bolted. As usual, the military was one step ahead of the civil police, and not afraid to take decisive action. It was the South African defence force which had provided the description of the likely getaway vehicle to the Mozambicans. Several hours after the kidnappings had taken place, the South African military had still not been given permission to cross the border in pursuit of the terrorists. To his credit, though, the colonel in charge of the operation, an African chap who had once been a senior cadre in the ANC's military arm, had ordered one of the Oryx helicopters carrying a stick of South African recce commandos across the border to try to pick up the trail of the fugitives.

Fraser had been impressed by the man. Not only by his risk-taking decisive action, but because the colonel had had the foresight to order the commandos to Hoedspruit as soon as he was appointed. They wouldn't be assaulting any terrorist strongholds in Mozambique – South Africa wouldn't risk offending its neighbour if things went pear-shaped – but they were an excellent resource to have on tap during the pursuit phase. There were six of them, all intimidating-looking fellows. The whites reminded Fraser of Springbok forwards; while the blacks could have played Zulu warriors. The British SAS prided itself on its ability to sneak into a place undetected and slit a few throats or rescue a hostage or two, but this bunch of recce commando ruffians looked like they would ram in the doors of a hideout with their foreheads and lay waste to everything and everyone in their path.

One of their key skills was a knowledge of tracking

in the African bush. That afternoon, while Fraser and his men had been flying to South Africa from England, the recce commandos had crossed the border and found the spot where the fugitives had picked up their second getaway vehicle. The recces were able to identify the likely make of the vehicle – another four-wheel drive pick-up – from its tyre treads. The bad news was that, as with the first truck the gang had used, it was an all too common model. On his arrival the team had briefed him and Fraser passed the information on to Shuttleworth.

'This man Furey, bit of a maverick, is he? Likes taking off on his own?'

Shuttleworth looked Fraser in the eye. 'He's one of the best protection officers I have. Taking off across the border was, of course, completely unauthorised, but he's been on the heels of these terrorists ever since the abductions occurred.'

'Hmm.' Fraser was yet to be impressed by the man's capabilities. Protection officers, to his mind, should take a bullet protecting their man, not chase him across international borders.

'Aye, and he was taking down IRA bombing cells with the Branch when you were in short pants, Jonathan. Don't forget that if you have to face these buggers down there'll be two less of them because of Tom Furey's work this morning.'

And they wouldn't be here at all if it weren't for one of the Met's best men, Fraser said to himself as he returned to the computer and his detailed maps of the Mozambican coast.

17

Bernard Joyce awoke to the sound of the door opening. Outside he could hear frogs croaking. Night-time; though it was perpetually dark under the stifling hood.

He smelled someone else in the room. A hand moved to his throat and he recoiled in terror, but a voice said, 'Still.' He forced himself to relax – he would show no more fear in front of these men – and felt the fingers untying the knotted string which held the hessian sack secure.

Bernard snorted warm, sticky, salty night air, which was still deliciously cooler and fresher than his own breath in the hood. He blinked, for even though the room was dim, lit only by a light somewhere out in the hallway, the door to the cell was open and he could smell the outdoors. The man had the black hands of an African and wore a ski mask. Bernard was sure he was one of the two who had come for him to take him to his meeting with the Arab. But this time the man was alone. Before he had dozed off, though he had no idea

257

how long he had been asleep, he remembered hearing a car's engine starting. Had the others gone on some errand? His mind raced. There had been little time to establish a routine, and no doubt they wanted to keep him off balance. His captor's weapon was slung, pointing down as he removed Bernard's hood.

The little luxuries continued as the man ripped off the fresh duct tape that had been applied to Bernard's mouth after his earlier interview. Bernard didn't begrudge the pain of the tape being removed, as it allowed him to suck in more air. He felt some calm return to him now that he didn't have to rely on his feeble nasal passages muffled inside a hood in order to stay alive, and could almost feel his brain starting to function better.

The man pulled a knife from a leather scabbard at his belt. Bernard tried to control his fear and the man bent forward. Again, 'Still,' was all he said. He reached behind Bernard and slid the cold, narrow blade between Bernard's bound wrists. He didn't flinch, though he was terrified the man might cut him by mistake. With barely a flick of the wrist Bernard felt the thick cable ties snap. His gratitude at being able to feel his hands again was swamped by the immediate rush of pain that flowed with the returning blood to his fingers.

'Rub them.'

Bernard did as he was told, massaging his wrists, seeing and feeling the raw skin where the plastic had drawn blood because of its tightness. Still holding the knife, the man reached behind his back and pulled a pair of metal police handcuffs from his belt. He held them in front of Bernard. 'Put these on – hands in front.'

Bernard was disappointed, but anything would be better than the plastic ties, and to have his hands in front would at least relieve the ceaseless pain in his shoulders from having his wrists bound behind his back. He reluctantly locked the open cuffs on each wrist, but kept them loose enough so that they weren't contacting his skin. The man reached down and checked them, closing each manacle another notch for good measure, though Bernard still had full circulation to his fingers and his hands were already feeling better. The man dropped to one knee and slashed the tie binding Bernard's ankles. As with his wrists, the relief was mixed with fresh pain and the blood flow seemed to reignite the aches in the tortured soles of his feet.

'Stand.'

More pain, but again it was good to get his circulation moving. The man returned his knife to its pouch and unslung his shortened AK 47. He pointed it at Bernard's belly and inclined his head towards the open door. 'Move.' Bernard hobbled, the pain in his feet increasing with each step. The man prodded the stubby barrel hard into his spine and he shuffled into the corridor. 'Right.'

Bernard looked around him, risking what punishment might come. He was in a hallway. He had been hooded the last time he was taken from his room. He noticed cream-painted wooden doors on either side of the one he had just come from. Looking up he saw a high cathedral-like thatched roof. The floor was concrete and, like the one in his room, polished to a dull sheen with some kind of wax that made it quite slippery. A hallway window was covered in black plastic and sticky tape, just like the one in his room. At the end of the corridor, in front of him, was another cream-coloured door, with a key in the lock. Glancing back, until another shove made him face forward again, he saw a wooden door at the other end of the corridor. The walls were plastered and whitewashed.

The man in the mask motioned him to the door at the end of the hallway, then reached around him and turned the key in the lock. The door opened on to a bathroom, with a combination bath and shower, and a toilet. The enamel on the bath was chipped and stained and the place smelled of mould and old urine, but Bernard had forgotten just how wonderful such simple facilities could be. He had pissed himself, but so far managed to avoid voiding his bowels. He stank and he ached and he almost thanked his captor when he said, 'Wash.' Bernard noticed there was water in the bottom of the tub and, looking at the floor, he saw a pile of grey-black hair sitting on three spread sheets of newsprint. On a shelf off to one side was a set of hair clippers, plugged into a power point on the wall. As a weapon, they would be useless. He wondered if the hair on the floor was Robert's and if his would be added to the pile next. Presumably the hair was on the newspaper so it could be bundled and disposed of. The thought chilled him.

The man stood in the doorway as Bernard, his hands still manacled in front of him, stripped off his stained boxer shorts. In addition to the bruises on his body and the cuts and welts on his feet, his pale skin was covered in mosquito bites. Out of modesty, he turned away from the terrorist and ran the taps. He felt hot water coming out of the shower head. Sitting on the toilet he stared at the man, who smiled behind his mask at the Englishmen's attempt at showing some defiance despite his embarrassment. Facing back towards the corridor, Bernard now saw a simple wooden chair behind the door. On it was a pair of folded orange overalls. His mind flashed back to videos he'd seen of the captives of Arab terrorists in Iraq. Often the victims wore the same type of garb, that reflected the uniforms worn by the detainees in Guantanamo Bay. Was he being cleaned up for his television performance? Quite possibly. If he could get to the chair he could use that as a weapon. However, the man stood blocking the doorway, his right hand on the pistol grip of the assault rifle, his finger curled through the trigger guard. His eyes followed every move Bernard made.

Naked, he stepped under the shower and attacked his filthy body with the bar of soap. There was a small window of frosted glass set high up on the wall beside him and if he'd stood on his toes he might have been able to see out. It was only opened a few centimetres and he sensed that if he tried to look out or open it wider he would be clubbed down. The man seemed to read his mind for, when Bernard glanced back over his shoulder at him, he shook his head. Bernard nodded his acquiescence. He lathered his hair with the soap and washed himself from head to toe again.

As he rinsed, Bernard caught a strong whiff of

smoke. He looked back again at the guard and saw that he, too, had his nose in the air, and was sniffing. A gust of sea air brought a curling wisp into the bathroom, along with some black flakes of ash which disintegrated as soon as they landed on Bernard's wet skin. Bernard stepped back from the window.

'Enough! Out!' The man brandished his AK and Bernard stepped out of the bathtub, dripping on the polished concrete floor. 'Sit.' Bernard followed the barrel's direction and sat on the floor, knees drawn up, in the corner next to the commode.

The terrorist stepped into the bathtub, took another menacing glance at Bernard and quickly raised himself on his toes and looked out the bathroom window. He swore in the Latin language Bernard had heard spoken before – probably Portuguese. 'Stay,' he barked at Bernard, then turned and walked out, slamming the bathroom door behind him and turning the key in the lock.

Bernard leapt to his feet and got back into the bathtub. He opened the tiny window a few more centimetres and peered out. The darkness outside was lit by flames. Next to the dwelling he was in was a small separate circular cottage with white walls and a thatched roof which was rapidly being engulfed by fire. Bernard could feel the growing heat on his face. No one else was outside and he heard a door open somewhere else in the house. The masked terrorist, his rifle now slung over his back, ran outside to a tap hidden in a flowerbed of bougainvilleas, and uncoiled a garden hose.

Bernard scrambled out of the bath, nearly slipping

in his haste, and pulled on his dirty boxer shorts. He put his eye to the keyhole and smiled for the first time since his abduction. He saw nothing – the key was still in the lock. He looked around him for something to stick in the keyhole. The flushing mechanism on the toilet had long since broken off the top of the cistern and a piece of wire now protruded through the hole in the top of the porcelain cover. He pulled the top off the cistern and unhooked the wire. Next, he tipped Robert's hair from a sheet of newspaper and slid the paper under the door and poked the wire into the keyhole. 'Come on, come on,' he whispered as he jiggled. The key fell with a clatter and he held his breath. Hopefully it hadn't bounced off the newspaper. He pulled the sheet to him. 'Yes!' he exclaimed as the key slid under the door. Picking it up in his cuffed hands he almost dropped it in his anxiety. He turned the key in the lock and the door opened.

Bernard quickly grabbed a towel and dried his feet, leaving a pink stain. He didn't want to leave footprints on the polished floor of the house and make it easer for his captor to trace his movements, but his soles still oozed blood. So be it. He moved quickly down the hallway. 'Robert?' There was no answer from the first door. He moved past the room where he had been imprisoned and stopped by the next. 'Robert, it's Bernard. Are you in there?' In answer came murmuring from the other side and the noise of metal rattling on metal.

Bernard tried the bathroom door key in the lock and, to his surprise, it worked. This was hardly state-of-the-art security, but the terrorists were also relying on their prisoners being bound and gagged most of the time. Robert lay on his back, dressed only in underpants, on the bare springs of an iron-framed bed, his wrists and ankles handcuffed to the frame. Bernard moved to him and untied the hessian hood, then peeled off the duct tape from the politician's mouth. His head had been shaved close to bald, the skin of his scalp showing purest white against his tanned face.

'Thank god,' Robert Greeves said, working his jaw. 'What's happening?'

'Fire outside. Looks like there's only one man guarding us.' Bernard tugged on Greeves's handcuffs then ran his hand along the bed frame.

Greeves turned his head to follow Bernard's hands. 'It's solid – same as the one I was on when they, when they . . .'

'It's all right. I'll get you out of here somehow.'

'How?'

Bernard's panic was mounting. Greeves was right. He was cuffed to a solidly welded frame. Without a key, or bolt cutters to sever the handcuffs' chain, Greeves was trapped. They couldn't even remove the bed's head and foot as these, too, had been welded to the spring base. 'Oh, shit.'

'Bernard, listen to me.' Bernard ran a hand through his hair in frustration and looked down at Greeves. His eyes took in the man's injuries. Blue-black bruising about his chest and abdomen, bloodied feet – like his – and dried blood all down his left leg from below the knee. It looked as though they had cut him there. Greeves's eyes were bright, though. Defiant. 'Bernard, get out. Now!'

'No, Robert, I can't leave you, I –'

'Listen to me. This is an order, Bernard. You know you can't get me out of here and you probably only have a few minutes before the guard comes back. You *must* get away and find help. If he's alone he won't be able to move me until the others come back. Did you hear the vehicle leave earlier?'

Bernard nodded. 'But, Robert –'

'Shut up, man. The quicker you go, the better chance I've got.'

'I'll overpower him, get his gun and shoot the chain off your cuffs.' Bernard turned to move.

'No! Stay here and listen to me, damn it. He's got an assault rifle. If you botch it, then we're both dead. The best chance you have is to get away and get help, Bernard. I'm more valuable to them alive than dead. Go now, before it's too late. With luck you can organise a rescue while this chap's still on his own.'

Bernard looked back at the door, expecting the guard to return any second. He smelled the smoke, which was stronger now, though he heard the spray of the hose. He took Greeves's chained right hand in his and squeezed tight. 'You're right, damn it. God be with you, Robert.'

'I've got you, haven't I? That's all I need.' He forced a smile, then it vanished from his face. 'If, well . . . just tell Janet and the kids I love them. And tell the PM these bastards can go fuck themselves.' Bernard smiled down at him, feeling the first tears prick the corners of his eyes. 'I'm sure Helen will massage that into something more palatable and patriotic for the media, but you get the general idea.'

'I do.'

'Then go. Hurry. Get help.'

Reluctantly, Bernard replaced the duct tape and hood, and closed and locked the door. If they didn't know he had been in Robert's room, perhaps they would go easier on the minister. He paused in the hallway near the covered window and unpicked some tape holding plastic sheeting over the glass. He peered outside and saw the terrorist had nearly extinguished the blazing thatch. He was continually glancing back towards the main building, no doubt worried about what Bernard was getting up to. If he could find a weapon, he thought again, he could kill the bastard, get his gun, and free Robert. The idea of abandoning him cut him to the core. Bernard heard the sound of a motor vehicle's engine, and the courtyard and garden outside were suddenly bathed in white light from the headlamps.

'Shit.' The pick-up had returned. Bernard ran down the hall and tried the door at the far end. It was open. He looked in and saw what must have once been the villa's lounge room, with a kitchen off to one side. Instead of furniture, though, was the equipment needed for making a video – a camera on a tripod, lights on a frame, a white sheet with green Arabic writing stuck to one wall as a backdrop. There was also a laptop computer on a desk and a satellite phone, with a separate antenna plugged into it.

Bastards. If nothing else, he'd slow down their propaganda effort and cut their communications. He looked around for something heavy and found a stout metal carry case. He put the laptop on the floor and pounded it with a corner of the heavy box. After doing so twice more, the thing looked wrecked. He unplugged the satellite phone and heard raised voices outside. He would have smashed the camera as well but he had to move. The men were arguing, accusations flying.

Clutching the phone, Bernard let himself out the kitchen door, into the warm, black tropical night, taking deep, greedy breaths of sea air as he ran down a sandy track.

There was no moon, which was good for him. Around him was only blackness – no other lights except the glare from the truck's headlights and the sparks from the nearly extinguished fire being sucked high into the sky. He kept moving away from the house, allowing his eyes to become accustomed to the night. He paused and sniffed again, his nose and the wind guiding him to the sea. He turned and ran for it, like a turtle scurrying across the sands to find refuge from its predators. His feet squeaked on fine sand that glowed white despite the absence of natural or artificial light. Bernard's progress slowed as he climbed a tall dune, his aching feet slipping in the soft sand.

When he reached the summit, which was thickly vegetated on either side of the pathway, he saw the Indian Ocean. The water was calm, telling him that there was a reef out there somewhere, protecting the beach from waves. The tide was high and the waters lapped to within ten metres of the base of the dune he was standing on. He ploughed down the hill, slipping and rolling the last few metres before dragging his aching body upright again. His tracks would easily be visible in the soft sand near the high-water mark, so he sprinted straight to the water. The warm salt water stung the raw wounds on his feet, but he knew it was doing him good. The terrorists would find his tracks to the water, but would not know whether he had turned left to the north, or right to the south. If nothing else this small ruse would split their forces. Water splashed up to his chest as he ran, knees high, legs pistoning as he drew on hidden reserves of strength, fuelled by pure adrenaline. If it came to it, he would swim out to sea, though he didn't want to lose the satellite phone if he could help it. As he jogged he fiddled with it, eventually finding an on switch.

His mind raced as he tried to remember a phone number – any one – to call. He didn't know what the local number for emergency services was, or how to dial it from a satellite phone. Although he had an IQ bordering on genius level, Bernard now could not for the life of him recall the switchboard number of Greeves's office, or of the Houses of Parliament. 'Bloody stupid,' he panted. Then he thought of Helen. How could he forget her extension – 6969. It was a running joke throughout Westminster, but one the New Zealander took in good humour. At least he knew how to dial out of a foreign country, remembering the code for England – 44 – and the first few digits of their work telephone number. Would Helen be there at this time of night? He bloody well hoped their predicament was keeping the poor girl at work all hours.

He pushed send and, after some strange pips and beeps, was rewarded with a ring tone.

'Helen MacDonald.' She sounded weary.

'It's Bernard!'

'Bernard? My god! Where are you – where's Robert? Is he . . .'

Quickly he stilled her questions and explained, still moving through the shallow water at a trot. He could give her no information about his whereabouts other than that he was on a beach and guessed he was in Mozambique. 'What's your number?'

'I have no bloody idea. Give me someone else to call . . .'

'Who?'

He tried to focus. He would need someone local, who could relay messages to whomever was coordinating any search and rescue operation. 'Tom Furey. Give me his cell phone number now and I'll key it in while we talk. I've got no idea how long the battery will last on this thing. Stay at your desk, Helen, and I'll call you as soon as I find someone to tell me where the hell I am.'

'I'm going nowhere.'

He told her to get a pen and paper, then gave her a quick briefing about the number of men who had kidnapped them, their weaponry and a rough layout of the house where Greeves was still held prisoner.

'Okay, got all that,' she said when he paused for breath again. 'There's an SAS team in South Africa waiting to move as soon as they get the word. Blast, but I don't have their numbers. Furey ended up in Mozambique somewhere – and caused a hell of a fuss in the process. By the time you call back after phoning him, I'll have all the contact details you need. Are you all right, Bernard?'

His feet felt like raw meat and his whole body throbbed in pain, but he was alive and doing something. 'I'm fine. It's Robert we have to worry about.'

Tom sat at the tiny dining table in the camp-ground chalet and pored over their simplistic tourist map of Mozambique. He slapped at a mosquito that had landed on his neck.

Sannie saw the stress in Tom's knotted shoulders. Despite the killer insects, he was shirtless in the evening heat. She set a can of cold Coke down on the table beside him and he opened it without taking his eyes off the map.

'That was nice of you before,' he said, sipping the drink.

'What was?'

'When you prayed with the old couple.'

'I'm not overly religious, but my mom takes the kids to church and Sunday school. I go when I'm not working.'

She thought he was probably referring to the way in which she had taken his hand, but there was nothing intimate or sexual in the gesture. It was the way her mother prayed when they ate their meals together as an extended family, though, with her dad and her husband gone, it never really felt as though the circle of hands was fully joined. It had been nice, though, to hold Tom's hand, if only for a minute. It was as if she was sharing some of his burden, letting some of his pain and angst flow into her. From the look of him she thought he could do with a neck and shoulder massage as well, but she didn't want to risk touching him. 'At least we know whose side Carla was on now,' she said, changing the subject.

In Xai Xai both of their cell phones could get reception and Tom had spoken to the commander of the hostage recovery force, an SAS major, and his superior, Shuttleworth, a short time ago. Although for security reasons they were careful about how they described the rescue force in their telephone conversation, he had told her after he got off the phone that the special forces team was at Hoedspruit in case the terrorists' location was pinpointed. Shuttleworth had also relayed from Isaac Tshabalala, for both their benefits, that Carla Sykes had boarded a flight to Maputo, Mozambique after leaving Tinga.

'I know the police here have been alerted, but she was probably a long way from Maputo by the time they got the word. You know, Sannie, it was all a bit hazy for me the other night, but nothing –'

'Tom, this isn't the time or the place. I can accept that Carla probably drugged you, but the fact is that you let her come to your room voluntarily and, whether anything happened or not, there was intent. As I told you after the first time, what you do in your own time doesn't concern me. The fact that it looks like Carla was working for the terrorists changes nothing.'

He started to say something else, but she knew the look on her face was enough to silence him. It worked on her kids and it used to work on Christo as well. He had laughed about it often enough. Besides, she didn't want to go over old ground with Tom now. Part of what she said was true – what concerned her was that, drugged or not, he had not resisted Carla. However, she realised that what he did on his own time actually *did* concern her. Her feelings for him were growing stronger – she couldn't deny it. She admired his doggedness, and whether it was the tension, the excitement, the adrenaline of the pursuit or just his physical presence, right now she felt more alive by his side than she had since Christo's death. Her husband would have liked Tom, she decided, and was pleased she could think of the two men without feeling that she was betraying her husband.

Her heart went out to Tom, too, seeing him sitting there, staring at the map as though it would suddenly yield some previously unthought-of solution. As with any police investigation, what they needed was a break – some vital clue to fall into their laps – and there was little use driving endlessly up and down the Mozambican coastline while they waited for it, even though that would give them something to do in the morning.

Sannie rested her chin in the palm of her hand as she sat at the table, looking at Tom. She was angry at herself, but there was nothing she could do to stifle the realisation that she hadn't only crossed the border with him because she empathised with his living through the worst scenario a protection officer could face. She was also there because she cared about and wanted to be with him.

When Sannie had checked her messages she found she had two missed calls from Isaac Tshabalala. She had taken a call from her boss. Wessels had told her that she was officially reprimanded for ignoring the

Skukuza police commander's orders and she could expect a slap on the wrist from him for crossing the border with a foreigner suspected of drug possession on an unofficial investigation. Unofficially, he wished her luck, told her to come home as soon as she could, and to make sure she kept herself safe. 'Think of your kids, Sannie. Don't let that Englishman put you in danger.'

His warning was and wasn't fair. She did owe it to her children not to take unnecessary risks – and this assignment certainly fell into that category – but she resented the fact that Wessels had all but accused her of being a bad mother. He was kind, and a good boss, but, as far as romance went, there would never be anything again between her and Henk.

Tom's phone rang again. He answered it, listened for a few seconds, and when he jumped up knocked over both of their drinks, spilling them all over the maps.

18

Tom swore again as the Volkswagen's front wheels clanged in and out of a pothole as wide as the car's axle.

'Careful!' Sannie reached out and braced herself on the dashboard with one hand.

He barely checked his speed, keeping the needle close to the one hundred and twenty mark. They raced along the darkened EN1 north of Xai Xai and Tom kept a close eye on the odometer, counting off the kilometres as they neared the thirty-five mark.

When he'd gotten off the phone with Bernard he'd taken down precise directions from the Afrikaner owner about how to get to the beach resort. He'd told Bernard to wait there – once he'd ascertained the man's injuries weren't life-threatening – rather than try calling a Mozambican ambulance or the local police. He wanted Bernard Joyce back under his protection as soon as possible and Sannie was a hundred per cent in agreement.

Tom braked hard as a truck loomed large in his

windscreen. The vehicle was travelling with no lights. He cursed and swerved around it, his foot flat to the floor.

Tom recapped his brief conversation with Bernard as he shifted back down to fourth and revved the underpowered engine into the red before ramming the gearstick viciously into fifth. Bernard had already spoken to Greeves's office – to Helen, the press secretary – and she had passed on Tom's mobile phone number to him. Bernard's next call, when Helen found the number, was to the SAS commander in South Africa. Tom hadn't wasted time, or Bernard's satellite phone battery, when they spoke. Bernard had been jogging along the coastline somewhere in Mozambique, his breath heavy from the exertion, and Tom had listened in silence as he explained that Greeves was alive, and the circumstances of his lucky escape.

'I couldn't overpower them, Tom. There were too many of them in the end and Robert told me to go . . . It wasn't my choice . . .'

Tom cut him off, seeing where Bernard was heading. 'You did the right thing, and Greeves was right sending you to get help, and we're on our way but you have to give us an indication of where you are. I'll stay online with you or you can call me back.'

At that point Bernard had reported that he could see lights in the sand dunes ahead and to the left of him. Tom waited breathlessly as Bernard laboured up a path through the dunes. 'It's a bloody pub!'

Dressed only in stained boxer shorts, his feet caked in sand and blood, and his eyes wild with relief and lingering terror, he'd stumbled into a beachside bar attached to a small coastal resort. Tom heard the amazed response – loud talking in Afrikaans – as Bernard burst in on the owner, who was tending bar, and a half-dozen fishermen on holiday. There had been a pause as explanations were given and Tom heard one of the men saying they had just been watching a news item on CNN about the abductions.

Bernard had passed the phone to the bartender, whose English was passable but halting, so Tom had transferred the phone to Sannie, who spoke rapidly in Afrikaans as Tom bundled their gear into the back of the Chico. It turned out the resort was less than forty kilometres from Xai Xai and while the owner had been about to close the bar – in order to send the drunken fishermen to bed – he would certainly wait for their arrival. Not only that, but he would have to meet them on the road into his encampment as the last kilometre was through deep sand.

'This is it,' Sannie said, spotting a property development sign and another marking the end of the *Distrito do Xai Xai*, which the resort owner had described. Tom swung hard and skidded into a right turn onto the unmarked sandy track. It seemed the lodge's owner was happy to promote himself by word of mouth only as there was no sign to his property, which was called Paradise Cove.

'The police would never have come down here looking for them,' Tom said.

Sannie nodded in agreement. Their luck had been in, though neither of them dared predict what the kidnappers would do with Greeves now that they knew their hideout had been compromised. Tom's very real

276

fear was that even though Bernard had escaped less than an hour ago, his abductors might have already shut up shop and be on their way to a new location.

They had called in at Xai Xai police station, but the female officer on the night shift, who had been dozing at the front desk, spoke no English or Tsonga Shangaan. Sannie and Tom had said Capitao Alfredo's name over and over again and pantomimed using the telephone, but the female officer had steadfastly refused even to try to understand them. 'Fuck it,' Tom had said at last, unwilling to waste a second more. They were on their own again.

The first six kilometres from the main road were on a sandy but firm track through gently undulating dunes which were well stabilised with grass and small trees. With his window down, Tom caught the sound of cattle lowing in the distance. They passed a coastal lake, the light from the now risen moon reflecting off its mirrored surface and illuminating a raft of water-lilies. At another time he might have slowed to admire the countryside.

'Right fork here,' Sannie ordered, but Tom had already seen the sign to Paradise Cove. 'Another kilometre and then he should be there waiting to meet us.'

Lights flashed ahead of them and Tom slowed. There was a cluster of three mud huts with thatched-reed roofs, a sleepy-looking African man and a white man. The white man stood next to a rusting red Nissan Safari four-wheel drive, whose headlights were turned on. Squinting, Tom could make out another figure in the front of the vehicle. The passenger door opened and Tom saw Bernard Joyce step out, holding a hand up to his eyes. Tom switched off his own lights and coasted to a stop.

Bernard hobbled three steps towards Tom as he got out of the Volkswagen and put his arms around him and hugged him.

'My god, Tom. I never thought I'd see another Englishman again.' Tom felt the sting of hot tears on his cheek. They were Bernard's, not his, though he felt a lump rise in his throat. Bernard was wearing a pair of garish board shorts and a golfing shirt with the name of the resort embroidered on the left breast.

'Sarel Bezuidenhout,' the big white man said as Tom eased himself away from Bernard. They shook hands and Tom introduced Sannie to Sarel.

'Was that you chasing us in the bush, in the gunfight?' Bernard asked Tom.

Tom nodded.

'Bloody good show, Tom. Too bad the bastards got away, but I can't tell you how good that felt, to know someone was coming after us. Did you get any of them?'

'Two,' Tom confirmed.

'Arseholes. Have you got a spare pistol with you?' Bernard looked to Tom and then Sannie.

'I've got a two-two in the bar for monkeys and a nine-mil for the human thieves,' Sarel said in heavily accented English. 'I come with you.'

Sannie held up a hand. 'Look, this is not my decision to make, but I think we at least need a plan.'

Tom agreed and suggested they all get inside. He had already spoken to Shuttleworth on the drive to the coastal lodge and had been told in no uncertain terms that he was expressly forbidden from launching any ad hoc rescue mission.

He had, however, told Shuttleworth that he was going to find the terrorists' lair and get 'eyes-on' the target to confirm they were still there; his superior had not argued with this commonsense suggestion. 'Just don't go charging in there by yourself. You know the terrorists will kill Greeves as soon as they think someone is coming in.'

On the short drive in the old four-by-four down one steep sand dune and up another, Bernard filled Tom in on his discussions with the coordinator of the rescue mission, Major Jonathan Fraser.

'Turns out I know him,' Bernard said. 'I worked with him and his chaps when he was a captain a couple of years ago, before I left the navy. Landed him on a coast somewhere in the Middle East. Good man. A hard bastard.'

Bernard had hand-drawn a map of the layout of the house where he had been imprisoned and faxed it from Sarel's bar to the operations base at Hoedspruit. Bernard said that from his description of the surrounding area and the distance he had run – he'd had the presence of mind to count his paces as he ran through the water – Sarel had been able to identify the property.

'It's the only old house in the area for five kilometres. Used to belong to a Portuguese cattle farmer in the old days. It's been empty since I came here three years ago. Good place for a hideout. Only accessible by four-by-four for three kays in – that's why no one has developed it as a resort.'

Tom nodded.

'Fraser's calling back in thirty minutes with an outline plan. He said that if you were here, he wanted you in on the conversation,' Bernard said to Tom.

Sarel navigated the Nissan around a tight bend and up yet another dune until they arrived outside his timber-clad bar. They all followed the owner up a flight of steps that creaked and groaned under his enormous weight. There was a verandah out front overlooking the inky, calm Indian Ocean. Inside, the bar smelled warm and musty, the building still holding some of the day's heat. Sarel switched on the lights and turned on the ceiling fans. He also pressed a button on a remote control and a television high on a wall in the corner furthest from the bar came to life.

'How long would it take us to get to the old farmhouse to check it out?' Tom asked Sarel.

The Afrikaner scratched his beard. 'Thirty minutes if you walk along the beach, ten if we take the quad bikes. Tide is going out now, so we can make it on the bikes.'

'And from the beach?'

'Another ten minutes' walk.'

'Sannie,' Tom said, 'you stay here with Bernard and wait for Fraser's call. Tell him I've gone to check the place out. The best plan in the world is no good if they've already left the house.'

Sannie looked doubtful. 'Perhaps I should come with you.'

'They've got a US Navy FA-18 on its way to do a reconnaissance flight,' Bernard said. 'Fraser reckoned it would be overhead within forty minutes of his last call, which was fifteen minutes ago.'

Tom checked his watch. 'High tech stuff is okay, but someone needs to get in on the ground and suss things out.'

'Then let me come too,' Bernard said.

Tom looked down at the bloody scuff marks on the timber floor of the bar. 'Stay here and rest, Bernard. You'll need to be here to talk Fraser through the lay-out of the house again. He'll want to know it inside out and back to front, and he'll have more questions for you.'

Bernard looked down at the floor. Tom could seen he was emotionally and physically spent, though he, like Tom, obviously felt he couldn't rest until Greeves was safe.

'I'll be back in less than an hour. After that there'll be a role for all of us in this rescue. Sarel, I've no right to ask you for your help, but . . .'

The Afrikaner reached under his wide wood-topped bar and pulled out a nine-millimetre automatic pistol. It looked like a toy in his huge hands as he pulled back the slide and chambered a round. 'We go now,' he said, stuffing the weapon in the waistband of his shorts.

'Tom,' Sannie said as he turned to leave.

'Yes?'

'Be careful.'

The exhaustion and feelings of hopelessness that had started to cripple him in the stultifying heat of the camping ground at Xai Xai had disappeared, replaced with a continuous transfusion of pure adrenaline. Tom revved the throttle of the four-wheel-drive quad bike and followed Sarel down the steep incline of the sand dune.

The still-wet sand left in the wake of the receding tide felt as solid as concrete when they turned onto it and Tom gunned the bike to catch up with Sarel, whose curly hair looked even wilder as he accelerated.

So as not to alarm the occupants with the sound of engines so late in the night, they would leave the bikes a couple of hundred metres from the base of the dune where the track led to the old farmhouse. Sarel pulled his quad into the moon shadow cast by a tall dune and Tom parked behind him.

'It's about one kay from here. We go this way,' he whispered, pointing upwards.

'No, I go that way,' Tom said, shaking his head. 'Just give me the directions.'

Sarel looked as though he was about to argue, but Tom told him, 'If you hear gunfire, get back and tell the others. Take Sannie back to the main road and tell her to set up a roadblock. If you want to use your gun then, be my guest, as I'll already be dead.'

Sarel smiled. 'Walk up the track for two hundred metres and you'll see the farmhouse on the top of the next dune back from the ocean.'

Tom climbed the sandy pathway. He kept to one side, close to the cover of the low bushes that covered the dune.

Near the top of the dune he found a little-used side track leading off to one side and decided to take that rather than sticking to the main route. His luck was in. The detour took him to the top but allowed him to stay in cover. He thought the path must have once been a shortcut used by farm workers or fishermen. He crouched when he saw a light.

As his eyes adjusted he made out the angular form of the old Portuguese farmhouse. The light in one of the windows was weak. At first he thought it was from a lantern, but as he crept closer he saw that a curtain had been drawn across the window and the light was shining through it. A shadow flickered on the fabric, as someone passed between the source and the drape. Tom dropped to one knee again and nestled into some bushes.

His spirits soared – they were still in there. But then a piercing scream made him catch his breath. It was a shriek of pain the likes of which he'd never heard before, despite all the fights he'd seen and been involved in as a copper. 'Bastards,' he whispered. They were torturing Greeves. Perhaps they were trying to find out if Bernard had spoken to him before he left.

Tom risked moving a little closer and his every instinct told him to rush the place now, kick the bloody door in and nail the swine who were abusing a defenceless human being. He took a deep breath and forced his pulse rate down. Shuttleworth had not only given him a direct order, he'd been right about it.

From behind the trunk of a tree that stood nearly as tall as he was, Tom saw moonlight playing off the windscreen of a Toyota pick-up that had a canopy covering its rear compartment. The vehicle description had been spot on. He considered moving in and disabling the pick-up, but checking his watch told him he needed to be getting back with the updated information asap. He comforted himself with Sarel's advice that it was four kilometres of hard driving through sand in and out of the farmhouse. The US Navy jet would be overhead soon, and if they got word that the abductors were leaving, Tom and Sannie could head them off before they reached the main road. He winced as he heard another screech from inside, then quickly retraced his steps back over the dune and down to the water's edge.

'They're still there,' he said to Sarel. 'Let's move.'

Tom sat his mobile phone on the bar and pressed the loudspeaker button so that by crowding around the device he, Bernard, Sannie and Sarel could all hear Major Jonathan Fraser's voice tinnily coming through.

Fraser was dialling in from Hoedspruit, and the Defence Secretary and other senior military officers and bureaucrats were on the secure link-up from the Cabinet Office briefing rooms in Downing Street. Nicknamed COBRA, this was the government's emergency response nerve centre.

Despite the presence of his superiors on the conference call, the major was running the virtual meeting. 'Well done for getting eyes-on, Tom, but the FA-18 has already confirmed the same information – in a bit more detail.'

Tom tried to ignore Fraser's condescending tone and held his tongue as the SAS man continued.

'The Hornet's FLIR – that's Forward Looking Infra-red camera to the civilians among us – picked up the heat signatures of four people in the house. One was stationary in a room – presumably, Mr Greeves still chained to his bed – and three X-rays moving about the house, quite briskly, according to the pilot.'

Sannie mouthed the word 'X-rays'.

'Bad guys,' Tom whispered in explanation.

The major continued, 'My concern is that they may be preparing to leave the house. This calls for a fast direct action. As we speak, the C-17's engines are warming up and my men are enplaning. We will be in the air within minutes of the end of this briefing, so listen in and keep any further questions until the end.'

19

The plan, such as it was, had more holes in it than a poster of Saddam Hussein on the day after the invasion of Baghdad. Jonathan Fraser had been in the smoking, shell-shocked city that day and had seen a tyrant fall. He'd also been back twice to a war that seemingly had no end. He knew that the best of intentions, the finest of plans, sometimes backfired.

The other old military adage, Fraser recalled as he listened to the pilots of the C-17 chatting through the cans – the headphones he wore in the spare seat on the cockpit deck – was that no plan survived the first shot or the first ten minutes.

Despite his ingrained pessimism, something he proudly attributed to his Scottish heritage, the plan was as sound as anyone could have hoped for in the circumstances.

'Dagger, this is Gunsmoke,' came a Texan drawl through the headset. Lieutenant Junior Grade Pete 'Frenchy' Dubois was straight out of central casting,

Fraser thought. The young American FA-18 pilot had a spiky gelled crew-cut and the chiselled looks of a Hollywood movie star.

'Gunsmoke, this is Dagger, over,' Fraser replied, keying his radio switch. Fraser had transferred control of the operation from Hoedspruit to the C-17 as soon as they were airborne. They were now orbiting at fifteen thousand feet over the Indian Ocean, just off the town of Xai Xai on the Mozambican coast, waiting for the last of the assets at Fraser's disposal to get into position.

'Dagger, I confirm target is still in position, no change. One soul down and hogtied, the other three moving around like they're on speed, over.'

Fraser smiled to himself. The American's laconic patter barely concealed his excitement. Fraser, too, was keyed. If he pulled this one off, it would be the biggest coup in the regiment's long list of honours since Princes Gate, when counter-terrorist troopers had stormed the Iranian Embassy in London and liberated the hostages held there. Much of the SAS's wartime and peacetime operations was so secret that few members of the British public knew of the elite force's exploits – at least, in between sensationalist tell-all books by disaffected former members – but if this op was a success there would be media coverage and analysis of it for months to come. As much as he usually voiced contempt for former soldiers who wrote books about their time in the SAS, Fraser thought he might try his own hand at writing after this one. He hadn't joined the army for the money but he had a weather eye on retirement. He might get the CO's slot if they saved Greeves's life, but if he didn't a million quid in publishing royalties and newspaper extracts would be a good consolation prize. 'Roger, Gunsmoke.'

'Cheetah six, this is Dagger, send locstat, over,' Fraser said into the radio.

The slowest elements, though potentially the most vital, were his South African National Defence Force Oryx helicopters. There were three of them inbound from across the border and Fraser wanted to know exactly where they were. On board two of them were a dozen of his men, in two teams of six. Each team included a pair of snipers. These teams would be his blocking force. They would rappel from the helicopters a kilometre in from the main sealed road, the EN1, and take up blocking positions in the sand dunes to the west of the target farmhouse. If the terrorists were indeed packing up – his greatest fear at the moment – then the soldiers on those helicopters would stop them from escaping and do their best to free Greeves. If it came to that, Fraser was pessimistic about their chances. His snipers might be able to take out the driver of the getaway vehicle and the front passenger, but that still potentially left one other trigger man who might very well have a pistol at Greeves's temple. One bullet was all it took to turn historic success into abject failure. The only small consolation was that once those helicopters disgorged his men onto the sand, no X-rays were getting out of Mozambique alive.

'Dagger, this is Cheetah six,' came the South African-accented reply. 'We've made good time and are five minutes from the DZ. Your men are keen – already on their ropes, over.'

'Roger, Cheetah six. Good work. Let me know when they're on the ground.'

Fraser checked his diver's watch and allowed himself a small smile. It was almost time for him to leave the C-17. He beckoned to Warrant Officer Class Two Peter 'Chalky' White, the squadron sergeant major, and held up both hands to indicate ten minutes' warning. Fraser switched channels and said to the C-17's crew, 'We go in ten, gentlemen.'

He felt the aircraft start to bank. It was a rush, the amount of power at his fingertips, a high Fraser was sure no drug could match. Single malt whisky was the only mind-altering substance he allowed himself, and by god, he would be giving it a nudge when they were back in South Africa later in the day. No matter what happened next.

'Dagger, this is zero-alpha, over,' said a Welsh voice through the headphones.

'Go, Taff.' Sergeant Hugh Carlisle was one of his signalmen and well known to him after Kosovo, Iraq and Afghanistan, hence the informality in Fraser's reply. The pug-nosed, tattooed veteran was manning an array of radios, satellite phones and cell phones back at Hoedspruit. Taffy Carlisle was keeping their military and political masters in the UK informed about the progress of the operation, and providing a relay of communications from the two police officers on the beach in Mozambique, who were using the sat-phone Bernard Joyce had stolen from the X-rays.

'Plod's in position, Dagger. Vehicle on the beach is ready to turn its headlights on when you need it.

Uncle Tom Cobbly and all in London want to know what's happening.'

Fraser smiled again. Some at regimental HQ would frown on his decision to accompany the assault teams, rather than stay back and direct the operation from Hoedspruit, but he knew that once the shooting started he wanted to be there. If he failed he would be crucified as an irresponsible glory hound. It was, he reckoned, worth the risk. 'Roger, Taff. Keep up the good work.' If it did all go to shit in the next hour the policeman on the ground would take the biggest fall. He was the one who lost his man in the first place.

'Dagger, this is Cheetah six. Your boys need a new stamp in their passports. They are on the ground. Repeat, all are on the ground, safe, over.'

Fraser acknowledged the South African's call. The two helicopters which had carried the troops in would now rendezvous with the third, which was groaning under the weight of several two-hundred-litre drums of aviation gas and a portable pump. The three birds would land on a village soccer pitch ten kilometres from the target and refuel. No doubt they'd be fending off some curious bystanders. At the end of the operation – whichever way it went – the helicopters were their ride back to South Africa. The whole assault team plus Greeves and Joyce and the police officers wouldn't fit on the three birds, so there would be more than one wave. 'Roger, Cheetah. See you in a little while.'

Fraser switched to the C-17's internal frequency and confirmed with the pilot of the massive jet transport that they were over the drop zone.

'Circling now,' the RAF squadron leader confirmed. 'Ready when you are, Jonathan.'

'Well, I'd best be getting ready then. See you back in sunny South Africa.'

The pilots waved to him as he took off his headphones and the navigator reached over to shake his hand. 'Good luck,' the man roared over the whine of the aircraft's engines. Fraser did his best to smile, and climbed down the stairs from the cockpit into the belly of the flying whale.

Around him was a sea of busy yet ordered activity. His men checked each other's free-fall parachute rigs, oxygen masks and altimeters, and the weapons and diving fins that were secured beneath their parachute straps. Chalky White hefted his boss's parachute rig and Fraser slid his arms into the harness. White continued to help him rig up with his weapon – an MP-5 – life vest, oxygen, flippers and helmet.

The cargo hold was illuminated by red lights set in the high ceiling, which bathed the men and their cargo in an alien spaceship glow. The men looked like automatons as they shuffled towards the tail of their mother ship.

Tied down to the floor, near the hinge of the giant ramp which would open shortly, were three Zodiac inflatable boats, deflated and packed into separate containers each about the size of a large washing machine. A parachute sat atop each of the PLFs, which stood for 'parachute load follow'. Fraser and his men would do just that, follow each of the deflated boats to the ocean below once the RAF loadmasters on board the C-17 had dispatched them over the ramp. Once in the water the boats would be reinflated with bottles of compressed air, and Fraser and the other seventeen men in the main assault force would get the outboards fired up and race in towards the beach, three kilometres from the landing point. The C-17, Fraser knew, was now flying at twelve thousand feet, out of sight and virtually out of hearing of anyone on the ground. If the terrorists did happen to hear the faint, far-off whine of jet engines they would mistake the bird for a passenger aircraft. There was no chance of anyone on shore seeing the men or the compact boats exiting.

'Five minutes,' one of the loadmasters yelled, holding up an open hand and waving it in front of all the SAS men he could see. Those who saw him passed on the signal, but the sudden draught of air and the switching on of red jump lights on either side of the lowering ramp told them all it was nearly time.

Fraser loved parachuting – which helped in his line of business, as he had made over five hundred jumps – but for once it was excitement and the fear of what awaited on the ground that preoccupied him, not the ride down. Chalky gave him a thumbs-up, as if to reassure him all would be fine. Fraser nodded and returned the gesture.

The boats rolled over the edge of the ramp. 'Green on. GO!'

Tom and Sannie huddled at the base of the sand dune which marked the start of the trail up to the farmhouse. They had followed Fraser's instructions and were not overlooking the target, as Tom would have preferred. He was anxious to be up there now, keeping an eye on the dwelling and its occupants.

'You know he's right,' Sannie whispered, not for the first time. 'If we were seen now, that could be disastrous for your Mr Greeves. Also, Fraser's right to be concerned about his own men. If one of his snipers with their night-sights saw you pop your head over the top of a sandhill he might pot you.'

Tom nodded. She was right, of course. Fraser was right, of course. But that didn't make him feel any better. For all they knew, the terrorists could be getting ready to cut their losses – literally – and videoing Greeves's beheading while he and Sannie sat on the beach like a couple of lovers out for a bit of midnight nookie. He checked his watch. It was two minutes to four. Super soldier Fraser and his men were in the water now, according to the sergeant back at Hoedspruit, and should be hitting the beach any minute. Under the plan, Tom and Sannie were to guide the SAS troopers up the trail to the house once they arrived.

A kilometre north of them, out of range of the shooting, was Sarel's old four-by-four, parked on the edge of the water, its headlights on full beam pointing out to sea. Bernard was in the vehicle, under Sarel's watchful eye. The lights served two purposes. One, in case Fraser's GPS coordinates were out, the twin beams would give him a visual fix on the approximate location of the target – though he would know to land a kilometre to the left of them; and two, the headlights were aimed at an angle, pointing towards a gap in the reef that protected Paradise Cove's beach from the ocean's swell. The tide was still fairly high, though it had started to turn. Low tide was not until six fifty-five in the morning, but there was still a risk that one of Fraser's rubber boats could be holed if it skimmed the top of the rocky reef.

Tom felt sorry for Bernard. He knew the ex-submariner wanted to get into the fight, but Tom had to agree with Fraser's assessment that with his injuries he would be more of a liability than an asset. Bernard had pleaded with Fraser over the sat phone that he alone knew the layout of the farmhouse, but Fraser had shot that argument down in flames by pointing to the extremely detailed floor plan Bernard had already provided. Tom, too, had seen the house for himself, so Bernard could not even claim to be the only one who knew its exact location. Sarel had sealed Bernard's fate by mentioning that he even had a GPS setting for the house as he had once led a four-wheel-drive rally through the dunes for a bunch of South African off-road enthusiasts. To make him feel better, Sarel had given Bernard his nine-millimetre pistol and would drive Bernard to the house once it was secured. There was merit, Tom supposed, in as many of them as possible being armed, just in case there was a terrorist sentry they hadn't accounted for who might spring out of the bush.

Tom shifted his pistol from his right hand to his left and wiped his palm on his shirt. Once again, he felt Sannie's touch on his arm. He wondered if she was just a touchy-feely sort of a person, or if she felt something of the attraction for him that he couldn't deny feeling for her. 'It'll be fine, man. Stay cool. Listen, I think I hear the boats.'

*

Chief Inspector Shuttleworth hung up on the Prime Minister of Great Britain and started to pace the concrete floor of the aircraft hangar, behind the SAS communications sergeant seated at a folding table littered with phones, laptops and radios.

He wiped his brow. How the hell could it be hot enough for him to be sweating at four in the morning anywhere in the world? He knew, though, that the heat was not the only cause of his perspiration. He had just had to reassure the Prime Minister that an operation he had no part in planning or executing was going according to plan.

The policy advisor from Number 10 was not going to be fobbed off to a signals corps sergeant when the Prime Minister wanted a first-hand update. She demanded to be put through to the senior man on the ground and the sergeant had gladly beckoned the police officer over. 'PM's office,' he said, but Shuttleworth wasn't to know that the policy advisor had already switched the phone through to the nation's leader. Shuttleworth had recognised the voice immediately and cobbled together an account of the operation's progress so far.

It was unfair, he thought, that he was now established in the PM's mind as responsible for this affair, when it was clearly a military operation. Surely the Prime Minister must understand the chain of command? *He*, after all, had authorised this action on foreign soil. Shuttleworth thought about Tom Furey. God help him. If Greeves was killed in the assault, the Hereford boys would break speed records in pointing the finger at the Met.

Shuttleworth stood by his earlier defence of Furey to Fraser. What worried him now was that his two best men – Tom and Nick Roberts – were both out of the game. According to Bernard, poor Nick was dead, and Shuttleworth wondered if he had been caught in the sort of honey trap that had clearly taken Tom's eye off the ball the night before Greeves was abducted. They *were* his best, but there was no doubt they had been found wanting. If it went well, if Greeves was brought out alive, then Tom might have a shot at keeping his job if not his rank.

There were lessons for all of them in this fiasco, but they were also lessons taught in basic training.

The SAS signalman raised a hand in the air, his other pressed to his headset. 'They're feet dry,' he said, indicating the assault force had landed on the beach, 'in case you want to ring the PM back.'

Shuttleworth grimaced. Perhaps he should call the sergeant's bluff and call Number 10 back. What harm would there be in the Prime Minister's office thinking he had a key role in the rescue? In for a penny, in for a pound. He picked up the laminated sheet of paper with all the key phone numbers on it, snatched up the satellite phone he had just been using and rang the number.

'Downing Street situation room,' a woman said.

'Get me the Prime Minister. It's Chief Inspector Shuttleworth, Metropolitan Police.'

Jonathan Fraser was in the lead boat and the first of the raiders to touch the sands of Mozambique as the

Zodiac shushed its way up the sandy shore. It was a small detail, but one he hoped might be remembered.

He had his MP-5 out and pointed ahead of him as he ran, bent double, towards the dune line. Off to his right the South African had extinguished the lights of his four-wheel drive. There was not another soul to be seen on the beach.

Ahead of him he saw a small light. Furey was using his cigarette lighter. It was like something out of a World War Two movie, but the prearranged signal was effective enough. With Chalky behind him and the rest of the assault force now dragging their boats into the moon shadows in the lee of the dunes, he strode towards the two police officers.

'Jonathan Fraser. Nice to meet you in person,' he said, shaking Tom's hand, though the greeting was hollow. Something else for the record. He smiled at van Rensburg as he shook her hand and she introduced herself. Very nice to put a face to that voice, which sounded sexy even over the sat phone. Fraser hoped she would be around for a debriefing in South Africa. 'Any noise from the house?'

'No, we're too bloody far away,' Furey pointed out. If he was one of his men, Fraser would have dressed him down for his insubordinate tone. The copper had made it plain that he wanted to keep his eyes on the target house. Fuck him, Fraser thought. This was his show and the plods were baggage now that they'd pointed to a pathway through the dunes.

Fraser keyed his personal radio. He had already made contact with Forsythe, the captain heading the blocking force. 'Dagger one, this is Dagger niner.'

'Dagger one.' Forsythe sounded calm in his earpiece.

'We're at the base of the dunes. Moving to the FUP now.'

'Roger,' Forsythe said. 'We're in position, boss.' Fraser knew Forsythe would be passing the information on to the sniper teams now, letting them know that their own men would be moving into the hollow in the dunes to the south of the farmhouse – the forming-up point – in the next few minutes.

Fraser turned to Tom. 'You two stay here and watch our backs. We shan't be long and I'll call you up once it's done. All right?'

'No, it bloody well isn't all right,' Tom whispered. Van Rensburg shook her head in support of him.

'We've got more than enough firepower to do the job,' Fraser persisted. This wasn't about politics. He simply didn't want two extra bodies wandering about the dunes while he had men in motion and sniper teams in overwatch.

'No deal, Fraser. I told you on the phone that Sannie and I are in on this thing until the end. Greeves's safety is my responsibility until I'm relieved.'

Sooner rather than later, Fraser thought. Still, he had neither the time nor the inclination to dally on this beach when there was a job to be done. 'Very well. S'arnt Major?'

White moved to Fraser's side. 'Sir?'

Fraser knew that his use of White's formal rank would alert his friend and chief head-kicker to the fact he was not happy about the orders he was about to issue, but he also knew Chalky would jump off a cliff if he told him to. 'As well as your other duties in this op, I'd like you to escort Detective Sergeant Furey and Inspector Van Rensburg.'

'Pleasure, sir,' White said, and there was no mistaking how he felt about his new job. 'Stay close to me and we'll all be going home with ten fingers, ten toes and two eyes.'

Sannie thought Fraser was a *windgat*, a windbag. No matter what Tom may have done wrong, he didn't deserve the treatment he was getting at the hands of the army guys, and neither did she. She had hated the way the smarmy major had looked her up and down. The man should have been thinking about his job, not getting into her pants. White, however, seemed like a decent *oke*, even though it was clear he resented having to shepherd her and Tom.

Sannie was excited. She couldn't deny it. Despite the jealousy and penis-fighting that often occurred whenever two armed organisations got together to do a job, she was genuinely looking forward to seeing the much-vaunted SAS in action. How many people, she wondered, could say they had seen a terrorist stronghold taken down?

The tactics interested her: the placement of snipers, the methods of entry they would use. She wondered how much experience the individual soldiers had. She imagined they had fought in one or more wars – probably Afghanistan or Iraq – but she privately doubted that any of them would have entered as many buildings in pursuit of armed offenders as she had in her ten years on the job.

As a uniformed policewoman she had fired her weapon three times, wounding offenders twice. She had very nearly been killed in one of her first raids. They had been following up a tip-off about a drug dealer whose neighbours had complained about him after he killed a local boy in an argument over a lost heroin delivery. Sannie had been the junior member on the team of uniforms backing up the detectives. She had actually been outside the block of flats where the man lived, standing by the police *bakkie* when the raid went in. The man was living in a first-floor apartment and when the sledgehammer took his door off its hinges, the man ran through to the back bedroom and jumped over the balcony railing, landing hard on the ground not ten metres from where she was standing. The man was holding an American forty-five automatic, a canon of a gun, and he aimed it right at her chest as he dragged himself to his feet. Sannie fumbled for her own pistol, which was still holstered, and the man pulled the trigger.

Nothing.

Her partner, a sergeant approaching retirement who had been assigned to look after the new girl, was faster than she on the draw and put the dealer down with two bullets in the chest.

Sannie remembered the shock of the incident, of how she had fought off the tears all day until she had gone home and crumbled in Christo's arms. She had thought about giving up her job, but her husband, then also still in uniform, had told her she must be blessed. She didn't think of herself as bulletproof, but the gangster's misfire had taught her always to be ready. She and Tom trudged up the dune behind the sergeant major.

'Please, God,' she said to herself, 'let this work out okay for Tom and for Robert Greeves. Tom deserves this. He's a good man.'

Fraser knelt in the shadows, in a depression between two dunes, and pulled his gasmask from its pouch. Around him, the other members of the main assault team were doing the same.

He did a quick communications check to make sure he could send and receive with the mask on. They would hit the house with flash-bangs – stun grenades that produced a non-lethal but sense-shattering explosion of noise and smoke – and CS, or tear gas, grenades as soon as the entrances were breached. Greeves would suffer as much as the terrorists from the shock and the chemicals but, unlike his captors, he would live.

'All teams, this is Dagger niner, confirm you are in position.'

'Dagger one, roger, over.' The blocking force and snipers were ready.

'Dagger two, roger, over,' said the commander of the second assault team, which would enter the house through the back door. Fraser was leading the assault team that would blast its way in through the front door of the house, on the beach side, and smash the window of the room where Greeves was being held.

'Dagger niner, this is one, over.'

Fraser tensed. He had been just about to give the order to move. 'Dagger one, this is niner. What is it, over?'

'We've got movement at the second window from the right at the rear. Shadows on the curtain, over. One X-ray. Looks like he was taking a peek, over.'

Fraser frowned. 'Roger, one. You know the drill when the assault goes in. If you see movement and you're not going to hit one of the assault team, then take him out. Do you understand, over?'

This was Forsythe's first real operation, even though he had practised his role in dozens of training exercises. Fraser knew he had failed to mask the irritation in his voice, but they all knew the rules of engagement and what was expected of them.

'Roger, niner. Dagger one, out,' the chastised captain replied.

'All teams, this is Dagger niner. This is it. Stand by, stand by . . .'

Sannie heard the scream and Tom looked at her, confirming he'd also heard the inhuman sound.

'Bastards,' White muttered under his breath.

There was the noise again. A high-pitched yelp followed by grunting. Surely, she thought, it couldn't be. She shook her head. No, she was right. She'd heard that sound a thousand times before – from as far back as she could remember, growing up on the banana farm.

'Sergeant Major,' Sannie said, tugging on the sleeve of his black jumpsuit.

'Not now, ma'am.' He turned to her, his annoyance plain. 'OC's just about to give the word to go in.'

'No, wait, that noise, it was . . .'

'Stand by, stand by. Go!'

At Fraser's command two men from each of the assault teams broke cover and ran, bent at the waist, to the front and rear doors. Each carried a small charge of plastic explosives covered with strong double-sided tape. They slapped the devices on the doors near the locks and activated the detonators. The method-of-entry men flattened themselves on either side of each door, and Fraser and his men, and the members of Dagger three, were on their feet and moving as the explosions shattered the balmy calm of the humid night.

Birds squawked and took to the air, but their screeches were drowned out by commands and the sound of shattering glass, closely followed by the boom of exploding stun grenades. Each bang was accompanied by a flash of blinding white light that lit the surrounding dunes. Fraser and his men had tinted lenses on their gasmasks and radio earpieces and ear defenders to protect them from the horrific sound and light show.

As they had rehearsed on the quick dry-run before they left Hoedspruit, one of Fraser's men was kneeling with a cut-down aluminium ladder by the window to Greeves's room. Smoke from the entry blast billowed from the opening and one of the men tossed a stun grenade inside. Fraser put a foot on the middle rung and hurled himself in as the grenade detonated.

Fraser landed, catlike, on his feet in the smoke-filled room and heard the terrible, wailing sound again. It disorientated him as he lifted his MP-5 and scanned the room with the aid of the torch fixed to the stubby barrel. 'Robert Greeves! We are British forces come to rescue you!' Fraser heard the rest of the team coming through behind him and the gut-thumping boom of another flash-bang going off somewhere else in the house.

Two shots were fired and someone swore from the corridor.

Fraser saw the bed through the smoke and something was writhing on it, screaming its head off.

'Jesus fucking Christ,' Fraser swore, and his mother would have slapped him if she'd heard him, but that was the least of his worries right now. 'It's a bloody . . .'

'Monkey. I'm telling you, that noise we heard was a monkey,' Sannie said as she and Tom ran, side by side, towards the gutted, smoking house, hard on the heels of the burly Warrant Officer White.

'Bloody cock-up,' she heard White muttering as he listened in to the radio transmissions. 'Stay here, ma'am, Mr Furey.'

'Bollocks,' Tom said, brushing past him ignoring the man's outstretched hand.

Sannie followed Tom, leaving White standing there in the open, shaking his head as he spoke into his radio.

Troopers were emerging from the house now,

removing their gasmasks. One started to laugh out loud, but White barked at him to shut his gob. The man complied immediately.

Sannie and Tom walked through the splintered, smoking remains of what had been the front door. The lounge area, furnished only with a couple of upturned wooden chairs, was empty, but the smell of cordite and smoke was strong in the air. Along with something else.

'Monkey *kak*,' Sannie said as Tom wrinkled his nose.

'How? It can't be.'

'I'm telling you.'

They turned right into the hallway and Sannie waved her hand in front of her face to clear the air. From the room where Greeves had supposedly been held, the shrieking and screaming continued.

When they walked in, Jonathan Fraser was standing at the foot of the bed, gasmask off and sub-machine gun hanging limply from his right hand. One of his men had lit a cigarette and the other was standing there looking down at the pathetic little creature writhing in fear.

'Told you,' Sannie said, though without a trace of triumph in her voice.

Strapped to the bed with plastic cable ties was a grey and white vervet monkey. The little primate was fully grown, though still only about a metre long when fully stretched out, as it was. It bared its sharp pointy fangs at them from its dark face and continued to screech.

'Just fucking shoot it, boss,' one of the men said to Fraser.

Fraser seemed completely dumbstruck.

'You'll do no such thing,' Sannie said. 'Give me your knife, soldier, and stand well back. All of you. Shame, this poor little thing is half out of its mind.' The big, tough military men all heeded her advice and took a pace back.

Sannie reached down and deftly sliced through the ties securing the monkey's feet. It flipped itself over backwards and tried to use its tiny humanoid feet alternately to scratch at her and gain purchase on the bare bed springs. Sannie grabbed its tail and hoisted it up off the bed, quickly slicing one of the two hand restraints. 'Make room for it. Clear the doorway and the windows. This'll be very quick.'

Sannie was right, and even she gave a little yelp and jumped back as she cut the final restraint. She just managed to get her wrist out of the way of the monkey's mouth, though she was right in thinking that its main priority was to flee rather than fight. With a speed that left all of them surprised, the vervet went flying out the broken window and into the night. 'How many others?' she asked.

The man who had suggested killing the vervet answered. Fraser still seemed in a state of semi-shock. 'Three. They were roaming around the house. One of the boys put a bullet in one of them – in its arm, he reckoned – but the other two were too quick. They scarpered right past us.'

Sannie shook her head. 'Poor little thing. He'll probably live, though. I've seen vervets getting around with only one leg and one arm after they've been caught on electric fences and –'

306

'For Christ's sake, woman,' Fraser said, 'I don't give a flying fuck about the bloody monkeys!'

'Cool it,' Tom said.

Fraser turned on him. 'Don't you tell me to fucking cool it. This is all your fault. Hear me? This was a fuck-up from the beginning and you're the one who caused it.' Fraser's face was reddening, his eyes bulging. He pointed at Tom's chest, but Tom stood his ground and said nothing.

Fraser took a deep breath and pinched the bridge of his nose with his fingers.

Tom looked at Sannie. 'We need to get word to Alfredo. Tell him to get his roadblocks set up early. It's almost first light.'

She nodded, but she could see Tom was just going through the motions. 'I'll go find Sarel and get him to take us to our car in his four-wheel drive. There's not much we can do here now.'

'Thanks,' Tom said. 'Major, if you'll excuse us. It's not over for us just yet.'

'Oh, yes it bloody well is,' Fraser said.

20

The detective in Tom wouldn't let him wallow in self-pity at the outcome of the raid – he would leave that to Fraser. He almost felt sorry for the SAS major. A mission that might have written him into the history books would now be remembered as a tragic farce.

Tom was beyond considering his or anyone else's reputation or career. He had already resigned himself that he would be out of a job by the time he returned to England but that couldn't shake him from his one remaining task – to find Robert Greeves, dead or alive. It had grown even firmer in his mind while he waited at the foot of the dunes for the assault boats to arrive. He had sinned and he would not be forgiven – by himself as much as anyone else – until he found Greeves. The set-up by Carla, the chase, and now the cunningly cruel decoy that had thrown them off the terrorists' trail, had become personal. He had been made to look a fool from start to finish. It was as if the terrorists were baiting him and rubbing his succession of failures in his face.

It was going to stop. Although he wouldn't admit it aloud, and quickly suppressed the errant thought before it even fully formed, it didn't really matter if Greeves was dead or alive. The men who had done this would pay.

He walked down the corridor to the bathroom. In a corner he saw a piece of crumpled newspaper with what looked like human hair on it. Other strands of grey and black were scattered about the floor. He recalled that Greeves's head had been shaved for the video. Tom had brought half-a-dozen zip-lock plastic bags with him from their hire car. Sannie had bought them at a service station in Mozambique to store any leftover food from their meals. He turned a bag inside out and grabbed a handful of hair. It might not prove anything other than that Robert Greeves had indeed been in the house, but everything counted in an investigation. He recalled the crime scene investigator's mantra – details, details, details.

He saw the bloody footprints on the polished concrete floor, in the bathroom and leading down the hallway. He supposed they were Bernard's, but there was only one set. Bernard had said that when he had spoken to Greeves in his room, the minister's feet had been bloodied, like his own. Had the terrorists put shoes on Greeves to walk him to the bathroom, or had they cleaned up after they had shaved him? If so, why had they left the newspaper with his hair on it sitting on the floor? He mentally filed away his observation and wished he had brought his notebook with him. He'd write down these thoughts later.

The stink of the place assaulted his nostrils. As a uniformed bobby he'd once been called to a bedsit in Islington where an old lady had died in her sleep but hadn't been missed for days. It was summer and when they'd opened the door he'd had his first whiff of a decomposing human body. The monkey smell wasn't nearly as bad but it was rank all the same.

How long had the animals been in there? he wondered. It was four hours, give or take, since Bernard had made his escape. The terrorists had worked quickly to capture the primates and ensconce them in the house before escaping. They must have known that the rescue team would have heat-sensing equipment. It was a brilliant ploy. The monkeys would show up as human-like on the infra-red radar, but only a very skilled interpreter might have noticed that the creatures were too small to be men.

He had been duped, and he felt stupid about it. If he had let Sannie come with him on his first recce she would have recognised the monkeys' screams, which he had thought was Greeves being tortured, immediately. If he and Sannie had been allowed to bring the target under surveillance while they waited for the assault troops, she could have called off the raid sooner and they could have been back on the terrorists' trail. If, if, if. They might have bought themselves another hour, but would that have been enough? Probably not.

Alfredo had no roadblocks operating after dark, so the terrorists were at least three hours ahead of them.

On reasonable roads, that could be three hundred kilometres by now. The next move, unfortunately, was up to them.

'Blood!' Tom heard the voice from the room next to the one in which Greeves and the hapless monkey had been imprisoned. 'Buckets of it.'

Tom walked into the room. Two black-suited troopers were shining a torch on the floor, illuminating a large bloodstain. 'Can you move away, please.' Tom dropped to one knee. The blood had pooled and then, judging by the adjoining smear, the body had been dragged a short distance. Using his Surefire torch, Tom focused on an imprinted pattern in the dried blood near the end of the drag mark. He guessed something fibrous – a blanket, perhaps – had been laid down, and the body rolled into it.

The trooper was wrong about the amount of blood. Not buckets – not even half a pail, in fact. Tom reckoned it was more like a pint, half a litre, give or take. It always looked like there was more of it than there was. He looked up from the floor to the walls. Nothing – no blood spattering.

'You thinking what I'm thinking?' one of the soldiers asked his mate.

Tom stood and swallowed hard. Although the soldier's estimate was way out, there was too much blood for it to be from a monkey's arm wound.

'Sir!' another voice called out.

'What now?' Fraser asked. He walked past the open door to the room in which Tom and the others stood.

Tom followed the major out into the hallway and to the kitchen. On a scratched laminate benchtop was a small grey-coloured box. 'What's that?' he asked no one in particular.

'It's a portable video playback monitor. I've got one at home for my digital camera,' the soldier who had found the device said. 'Do you think it might be booby-trapped, boss?'

Fraser strode across the kitchen and grabbed the box. The young soldier took an involuntary pace backwards, but nothing happened.

Tom thought the trooper was right to be concerned and he was worried by the wild look in Fraser's eyes. Was the man so incensed by their failure that he had given up caring about the possibility of injury to himself and his men – as well as ignoring all protocols about fingerprints and evidence?

Fraser flipped open the player's screen, placed it back on the counter and pushed play.

Nick Roberts's tortured face appeared on the camera. Tom screwed his eyes shut for a second, then forced himself to watch. Bernard had talked him through the scene he had witnessed on the tape, but nothing could have prepared Tom for the actual moving images of his former colleague's execution.

'Fucking animals,' the young soldier said, staring morbidly at the little screen.

'Who's that?' Fraser asked.

Tom explained and the major said, 'Sorry.' It sounded like he meant it. Ego and bullshit aside, Tom guessed the prickly officer had himself probably lost friends and comrades. It came as a shock to him, despite Bernard's warning, to see the blood streaming down Nick's face from the empty sockets where his eyes had been. He saw the pistol – small calibre, and silenced, maybe a two-two – brought close to Nick's temple and not a man in the room didn't flinch when the *pfft* sound of the muffled shot escaped from the video player's tiny speaker.

'Bastards,' another of the soldiers said.

Tom felt unsteady on his feet as another face flickered onto the screen. The video, like that of Nick's killing, was grainy and jumpy, but there was no mistaking the identity of the man who was taped as the hand of an unknown assailant – his face out of camera shot – forced him to his knees. It was Robert Greeves.

'This is what comes of stupid attempts at escape,' a voice said in the background.

Tom, like Fraser, craned closer to the small screen, straining to hear every word, but there was no talking. Tom heard footsteps in the corridor behind him, but was too engrossed in the image of Greeves's face to turn around.

Greeves stared at the camera, and his look was one of despair tinged with resignation and the last flushes perhaps of an angry response made before the camera started rolling.

As with Nick, a hand holding a small-calibre silenced pistol appeared, near Greeves's left temple. There was no statement; no threat, no warning. Just a solitary gunshot. Unlike the tape of Nick's execution, which had ended at this point, the camera kept rolling as Greeves's head flicked to one side. Blood pumped from the small entry wound and Tom caught a glimpse of the bulk of a man behind Greeves, and of gloved hands under the minister's armpits. The man was holding him up for the camera as the life force poured from him. The screen went blue.

Tom forced himself to analyse what he saw, even as bile rose in the back of his throat. He swallowed hard. It would have been a two-two hollow point. The narrowed lead walls of the bullet would have split apart on impact with the skull bone. The shock wave from the blast had turned the minister's brains to mush, and as the projectile opened up inside Greeves's head, the fragments would have bounced around inside, ricocheting off the insides of his skull but not exiting.

That was one reason why the assassins had chosen a small-calibre round. There would be no slug to dig out of a wall, and they would have picked up the ejected cartridge case. Professionals. Cut-down AK 47s for gunfights, and the two-two for the execution. Had the killing been planned all along? The man standing behind the seated politician had been there to hold him up for the camera – to give the world's media the shot they wanted, if they were sick enough to use it. Tom knew that once the bullet had done its work Greeves would have fallen like a puppet whose strings had been severed. There was no slow, rolling, theatrical fall to the floor like in the movies. Death was instantaneous.

'Replay it,' Fraser said.

Tom forced himself to watch it again. As Greeves again died on camera, Tom heard a sharp intake of air behind him.

'Bernard!' It was Sannie's voice and Tom spun around to see Bernard disappearing out of the room into the corridor. It had been he and Sannie who had entered while he was watching the video.

'He saw it?'

Sannie simply nodded. They both had the same thought, rushing from the room together with Tom narrowly beating Sannie through the doorway.

'Bernard!' Tom called as he ran through the house towards the smoking back door frame.

'There he is, heading for the dunes!' Sannie called.

Tom realised it must have been the same route Bernard had taken on his escape, running from the room where he had tried in vain to free Greeves through the house and towards the sounds and scents of the ocean. Tom caught sight of his moonlit silhouette as Bernard crested a large dune at a run.

He and Sannie chased him, but their feet were slowed by the deep, warm sand that made every step an effort. Tom had had dreams like this in which he was trying to escape from some unseen, unknown evil, but his progress was hampered by mud or sand. He wasn't running from evil now – just trying to avert its consequences.

Sannie caught up with Tom as he reached the top of the last dune. Spread out before them was the endless sea, its rippling surface flecked white-gold by the dying moon. Out on the horizon the sky was pinking as the sun waited to make another entrance.

Below them they saw the solitary figure slow as he reached the foot of the sandhill and walk out towards the water. The tide was turning, the patch of dark, wet sand widening with every small wave's gentle lap and retreat.

Tom ploughed on down the hill, Sannie by his side. She called Bernard's name again, but he ignored them.

'Slowly,' Tom whispered, placing a gently restraining hand on Sannie's arm as they reached the flat sands.

Bernard was walking into the water. The foam was at his knees when he stopped.

'There's nothing you could have done,' Tom said, his voice just loud enough to cover the distance between them. The water broke over his shoes and Sannie stood with a hand at her mouth.

'I know, Tom,' Bernard called, though still looking away from them, out to the first tiny fingernail of morning light.

'We'll get them, Bernard,' Tom said.

Bernard shrugged, then finally turned and faced them. 'Yes, I do believe you will, some day, but that's not the point, is it?'

'You did the right thing by going for help,' Sannie said.

'Yes, I know,' he said to her. He looked at her for a couple of seconds and slowly nodded his head. 'Yes, the *right* thing. I followed orders. His orders.'

'That's right,' Tom confirmed. 'I would have told you to do the same thing – you would have told him to do it if the positions were reversed.'

'Yes.'

'Come back, Bernard. We'll go down to Sarel's and get a cup of coffee, or something stronger,' Sannie suggested.

'A wake?'

She shrugged.

Bernard turned his gaze on Tom, who looked down at the automatic pistol hanging loosely by the other man's side. 'We let him down, Tom. You and me both.'

'I know I did, but you didn't. You were his best shot at freedom, Bernard.'

'No, I let him down by doing the right thing. The right thing by the book. That was always me in the navy, you know. Plenty of them used to joke about it. They said I crapped by the manual. They were right. I always had to do it better than any other man, because of . . . because of who I am, what I am.'

'Come on. Let's go get a drink, Bernard.'

Bernard looked back out to sea, towards the molten ball rising from the waters.

'Beautiful, isn't it?'

'Yes,' said Sannie.

'I need to talk to you again, Bernard. I need you to take me through every hour, every minute, every second from the time they took you and Robert until the time you escaped.' Tom stayed still as he spoke.

'I've told you everything I know.'

'There's always something else. Trust me, I know. There'll be some small detail that you'll remember – something someone said or did, or didn't say or do – that will nail them, Bernard.'

Bernard turned back to him and smiled.

'No, I've done quite enough already, Tom. Or, more to the point, I've done not quite enough. I shouldn't have left him.'

'No.'

'Yes, Tom. You know it and I know it. I ran.'

'He told you to.'

'I told Helen his last words. You know, he was think-ing of his family, and spitting bloody murder at those bastards as I left him.'

Tom nodded.

'He was a brave man.'

'He was,' Sannie said.

'I let him down.'

'You didn't, Bernard,' Tom insisted.

'I called you, you know?'

Tom was confused. 'On the phone?'

'No. When it happened. When they dragged me out of my bed, at the lodge, I called your name. I didn't know who else to yell for.'

Tom felt the sickness rising from his stomach again, the blood draining from his face. Bernard had said nothing of this before.

'I called for you, but you didn't answer, Tom. I sup-pose you were asleep. Can't expect you to be on the job twenty-four hours a day, though, can we?'

'Bernard, toss the gun over here.' Sannie sounded forceful, and took a step towards him, but Bernard started to raise the weapon and she checked her pace.

'We let him down. You and me.'

Tom was speechless, his mind still trying to process this new information. He had just about convinced himself that except for sleeping late – and possibly losing five or ten minutes of chase time – there was nothing more he could have done to prevent the abductions. He'd reasoned that there would have been no way he could have known what was going on, as he'd been in a separate suite both to Bernard and Greeves. This new revelation hit him like a blow in the solar plexus and threatened to drop him to his knees in the surf.

'Sometimes the right thing, being in the right place at the right time, doing the right thing by the book, just isn't good enough. I should have stayed with him, or taken on the single guard while he was fighting the fire before the others came back.'

'You would probably have been killed, Bernard,' Sannie said, filling the void left by Tom's ominous silence.

'I cared about him, you know,' Bernard said, looking back out over the water.

Tom started to move, his fists clenched by his sides.

'Tom,' Sannie whispered, but he ignored her.

'He was a good man, who could have gone on to do great things for his country. Too good a man for politics. I used to tell myself that I would lay down my life for him.'

Tom began to run, his feet raising geysers of water as he closed on Bernard.

The other man turned, so that one side of his face was bathed red-gold by the sun as it breached the waters.

Bernard raised his hand, placed the barrel of the pistol in his mouth, and pulled the trigger.

21

Three weeks later

The phone rang, waking him. He looked at the red LED display of his clock radio and saw that it was nine in the morning. He coughed, and was punished by the smell of stale Scotch.

'Furey,' he said into the handset, after retrieving the phone from the floor. His voice was croaky, as he'd started smoking again.

'Tom, it's Sannie.'

He raised himself on one elbow, earning himself a giddying head spin. He coughed once more. 'Sannie, this is a surprise.'

'Are you okay? You sound like you're ill.'

'Got a cold coming on,' he lied. 'Bloody London weather. Where are you, at home? I can call you back if you like.' He remembered the references to her tight family budget, trying to raise her two kids on one income.

'No, Tom, I'm at work. This is semi-official so they don't mind me calling overseas.'

'Oh, right. Of course.' Not everyone had lost their job over the debacle in Mozambique. He chided himself for his oversight. 'So this is business?'

There was a pause on the other end of the line and he regretted his last words. Did he sound petulant, as though he had thought she might be calling for personal reasons?

'Yes, it is business, though I've been wanting to call you, to make sure you're okay. That everything's all right with you.'

All right? The man he'd been sent to Africa to protect was dead. Another had killed himself in shame, leaving Tom feeling like he should have done the same thing, and he was suspended from his job indefinitely, pending the outcome of an official government inquiry into Greeves's death. 'I'm fine. Enjoying the break.'

'Tom, I know how hard this must be for you, but you'll pull through.'

'Right. Um, what is this about, Sannie?'

'I'm coming to England.'

That made him sit up in bed. 'When? Why?'

'I've been called to give evidence at the inquiry and my police service – and our government – has agreed to release me. It should be for about a week, they say. I'm arriving tomorrow morning.'

'Oh,' he said. He, too, had been called. He figured it would be the last nail in the coffin of his career. It irked him that while details about his late arrival on the morning that Greeves and Joyce had gone missing – and speculation about his drinking on duty the night before – had already been leaked to the media, there was no mention of the nation's elite counter-terrorist unit storming a house full of primates. It was a good pointer to how and by whom the behind-the-scenes information battle was being waged.

Tom had been inundated with calls from journalists on his return home, and had even had to suffer the ignominy of a few of them being camped on his doorstep until his resolute silence had finally had an effect. He would answer for his sins at the public inquiry, but he wouldn't lower himself by trying to plead his case or slander anyone through the press. He would take his punishment and do the best he could to find a new way to live out his remaining years. And that was that.

The resolve he'd felt in the immediate wake of the failed rescue mission, to find the perpetrators and bring them to justice, had disappeared with the plume of blood that flowed away in the receding tide of the Indian Ocean on that beach in Mozambique. Bernard's revelation, that he had tried to raise the alarm and called Tom's name in the night as the abductors grabbed him, still haunted him. There was no escaping the fact that he had failed in his duty. Even though Greeves had told him to have a nightcap, he shouldn't have taken the beer Carla poured for him, or let her into his room.

'Tom? Are you still there?'

'What? Oh, yeah. Well, it'll be good to see you again, even if the circumstances are hardly ideal. Where will you be staying?'

Sannie gave him the name of a hotel near Waterloo. He said he knew it and waited for her to make the next move.

'Perhaps we could get together,' she said after a brief pause. 'To talk about things.'

'Get our stories straight?' He forced a laugh, but she didn't reciprocate.

'That's not what I meant.'

'Sightseeing, shopping?'

'I know it must bother you, Tom – what happened to them, where they went afterwards, why no one's heard from them since then.'

If there was anything left in the bottle lying on the floor beside the bed he would have taken a deep swig right there and then. He hadn't yet begun drinking before midday, but there was no time like the present.

'They' – the Islamic African Dawn or whoever the hell they were – had killed him, as surely as they had put bullets into Nick and Greeves, and as surely as their evil had driven Bernard Joyce to his death. The only difference was that Tom was doomed to a long, lingering death.

They'd taken Tom's gun from him when he'd returned home, but he had a shotgun in the house. It had belonged to his father, who'd been fond of grouse shooting. On the first night after his official suspension, Tom had swallowed half a bottle of single malt and loaded the gun. He'd taken off his right shoe and sock – to use his big toe to pull the trigger – and put his lips around the barrel, but he couldn't go through with it. Too much of a coward – unlike Bernard Joyce.

Of course what had happened fucking bothered him. It had eaten away at his soul, at his mind and body, over the past three weeks, like a high-speed version of the cancer that had devoured Alex. 'Yeah.'

'Tom? What's wrong. Are you drunk, man?'

'Wouldn't like to get in a car for another couple of hours.' He tried another laugh, but all his jokes were failing this morning, it seemed.

'Well, whatever. I just thought I'd let you know I'm coming over. If you want to talk, you have my cell number. Just SMS me, if you like. I should let you get back to sleeping it off, I suppose.'

He waited to see if there was anything else, but she didn't say goodbye or hang up.

'Tom?'

He sat there, not knowing what to say to her next.

'Well, okay. This is too weird. Goodbye and –'

'Wait. Sorry, Sannie. I'm not drunk. Tell me what time your flight arrives. I'll come get you from the airport.'

'You don't have to do that. They've booked a hire car for me.'

'I could come out on the tube and help you navigate your way to Victoria. On your own, and without a GPS, it could be more dangerous than the African bush.'

She laughed, and he flashed back to how pretty she looked when she smiled. He wouldn't find salvation with Sannie van Rensburg – her visit was merely confirmation that he would be dragged through everything once again in a few days' time – but it would be good to see her, whatever the circumstances. He didn't want her to hang up. He'd thought about her a lot lately, even through the bouts of drunkenness and sleepless hours. If . . . if he hadn't let Carla drug him. If he had caught up with the abductors sooner. If Willie hadn't been wounded. If it had all turned out differently, he might have retired with his dignity intact and maybe pursued Sannie. There'd been a connection between them that transcended the professional on that wild drive through Mozambique. When he closed his eyes, he saw hers.

'Okay then. Thanks. If it's not too much trouble, that would be *lekker*.'

'So, if you're calling from work, you obviously didn't get suspended?'

'I did,' she said, and he could hear her relief that the conversation was starting to move beyond one-sided-ness. 'But it was just for a week. My captain gave me an official reprimand for taking off with you across the border, but privately commended you for having the guts to do what you did. Hey, last night I left you a message on your phone. Didn't you get it?'

'Um, no, I got in pretty late.' He'd been at his local pub until closing time. 'Sorry. How are your kids?'

'They're fine, and thanks for asking. Christo asked me the other day if you and I would be working together again.'

He didn't know what to say.

'What do you think?' she asked.

'About what?'

'Are we still working together, Tom? I've been running some leads at this end. I'm on a small task force that is working with your people to try to pick up the trail of the terrorists. I've been checking national park entry permits from five days before the abductions happened. It's tedious work, but so far I haven't found a registration number that matches the Isuzu they used.'

He thought he knew what she meant. She wanted to know if he was working on anything privately, from his end, even though he'd been suspended. He felt almost ashamed that he hadn't been, that he'd followed Shuttleworth's orders and kept his head down. What had happened to that determination he'd had in Mozambique, when his blood had still been up? It had disappeared; ironically, by doing what Bernard would have termed 'the right thing'.

'I've been told to stay away.' This sounded even lamer than he thought it would.

'Of course,' she said. 'Anyway, perhaps I can run some ideas past you when I see you.'

'Sure.'

'Do you think you'll keep your job?'

'No chance. Besides, who'd have me as a protection officer, even if I did survive?'

'Someone with brains, Tom. Someone who'd look at the lengths you went to, the risks you took to try to get Greeves back. A good person, which I know is rare in our line of work. But we don't get to choose who we take care of, do we?'

He sat there, in his bed, and again looked down at the empty bottle on the floor, the dirty clothes strewn about the room.

'You remember what I said to you? When we crossed back into Kruger after it was all over?'

'Yeah.'

'Then don't forget it, Tom. I'll see you in a few days.'

*

Fraser and the SAS men had taken Bernard's body with them and departed in the Oryx helicopters. Tom was offered a ride but begged off, saying he had to stay with Sannie and wait for the Mozambican police to arrive.

The special forces guys had no wish to stay and share with a foreign police force their part in the disaster. 'Suit yourself,' Fraser said dismissively, then he ran for the helicopter.

Shuttleworth was furious with Tom when he called in. Tom reckoned his boss needed him by his side to act as a lightning rod when he returned to the UK. Tom liked the guy, but could see no point in hurrying back to England to meet his fate.

Bernard's death had sapped his will. He was like a man in limbo, merely existing in the hours following the failed rescue mission. Sannie had done her best to keep his spirits up during the drive back to South Africa through the bush, retracing their earlier route.

After they crossed the border, back into the park, Sannie slowed as they approached a trio of bull elephants. Tom had lost his taste for game viewing and was mildly annoyed when she stopped.

'Look at them, Tom. What do you see?'

'Apart from the obvious?' He'd had virtually no sleep in the previous forty-eight hours.

'Bodyguards. Protection officers.'

He was confused, his mind dulled. She pointed out the two smaller bulls flanking the largest one, whose long, curved tusks reached almost to the ground. 'Those two, the younger ones, are *askaris*.'

'What does that mean?'

It was a Swahili word, she explained, for sentry or guard, which had come into common use throughout the rest of Africa during colonial times. It had often been applied to native African troops employed by white armies and, in South Africa, to black agents working undercover for the white government in the days of apartheid.

'If you take the word's original meaning, the *askaris* look after the old one, the important one. They are his eyes and his ears as he gets older. Their job, like ours, is to protect.'

'So? What are you trying to say, Sannie?'

'I'm not a hundred per cent sure, but it works two ways for the elephants. The younger ones look out for the older one, but at the same time they learn from him, and they benefit from his patronage. They become a formidable team. When the old one eventually dies, the younger ones are stronger, wiser because of their time with him.'

'You're saying I'm a better person because Robert Greeves is dead?' He laughed out loud.

'Not better, but wiser. Tougher. Tom, everyone needs an *askari* watching out for them.'

Tom hung up the phone and rested his head against the bedroom wall. He wondered who his *askari* was, and who was looking after Sannie these days.

He got out of bed and went to the bathroom. As he rinsed his face and brushed the taste of Scotch and cigarettes from his mouth, he remembered what she'd said about leaving a message on his answering machine. He'd ignored the blinking red light as he'd stumbled through the door last night, thinking it was yet another reporter trying to get him to tell his side of the whole sorry story. That was journalist speak for giving him enough rope to hang himself.

In lieu of a comb he ran a hand through his hair and walked downstairs to the kitchen. Checking his messages was the closest thing he had to a chore today.

He delayed the inevitable by taking a half-empty carton of orange juice from the fridge and draining it. It was days old and bitter. He coughed as he pushed the play button.

'Tom, it's Sannie. I'm calling from South Africa – well, I guess you know that – but I'm coming to England for . . .' Tom let the message play, simply because he liked hearing the sound of her voice again.

The next message started. 'Hello, Detective Sergeant Furey, it's Mary Whitbread from Channel Four again and I'd just like to –'

'Sod off,' Tom said to the machine and stabbed the erase button.

The next message was from another woman and Tom was about to get rid of it before realising the person's accent was so thick it was doubtful she was a British reporter. 'Mr Furey, if that's what I call policeman in this country, it is Olga Kamorov here.'

Olga? Russian, maybe? He didn't know an Olga, but her voice did sound familiar.

'We met in club, in Soho, few weeks ago. Oh, sorry, you know me as –'

'Ivana,' Tom said aloud. The stripper he had

interviewed when he'd been looking for Nick Roberts. Tom strained to hear the woman's voice as there was music playing in the background; perhaps she was calling from the club where she danced.

'I suppose you heard about Ebony – you are policeman, after all – but I wanted to talk to you about the man who used to come and see her dance all the time. Other police are not interested in talking to him, but I not so sure. Call me.'

Ivana – or Olga – left a mobile phone number and that was the end of his messages. Tom replayed the message and wrote down Olga's details.

He sat on a stool at the stainless-steel topped breakfast bar and tapped his front teeth with the end of the pen as he thought. When he and Shuttleworth had discussed it on his return to England, they had assumed Nick had been set up by the black stripper, Ebony, and that it was she who had lured him into the terrorists' clutches. Subsequent inquiries had showed that she never returned to work or her flat. She had simply disappeared.

Tom knew from Carla of Nick's predilections for African women. Carla had presumably also passed this on to her comrades and they had used Ebony as bait to capture Nick.

Why, he wondered, was a black South African table dancer in league with Islamic fundamentalist terrorists? There hardly seemed a less likely fit, and the same went for the promiscuous Carla. Money would surely have been a more likely motivator for both women.

Tom tore off the page with Olga's number and started making notes on a fresh sheet. He wrote

Money at the top, then underlined it. Next he wrote the following:

> *Kidnap/ransom.*
> *Why Bernard?*
> *Why the Iraq angle?*
> *A cover?*

It didn't make sense to him, and he scored a line through all of the points. He had talked himself out of the idea that Greeves had been abducted for money, though he was still unsure about the women's roles.

He played Olga's message back once more. '*I suppose you heard about Ebony.*'

He hadn't heard a thing about the dancer. What did she mean by that? Tom walked back upstairs, his stomach protesting all the way at its lack of food and coffee, and grabbed his cell phone off the bedside table. As he walked down again, he scrolled through the saved numbers until he came to the one he was looking for.

'Morris,' the voice on the other end of the phone said.

'Dan, it's Tom Furey. All right, mate?' Detective Constable Dan Morris was another protection officer. He'd been one of the officers who was following up leads on Nick's disappearance when Tom had left for Africa.

'Oh, Tom. Hi. Hang on, I'm driving. Let me pull over.'

Tom waited, taking his seat at the breakfast bar again. He flipped the pad over to a new page and kept the pen in his free hand.

'Sorry, mate. How's life, anyway? Keeping your chin up?'

'Just about. It's no barrel of laughs, Dan, but I'll know more after the inquiry.'

'Well, you know all the lads are on your side.'

It was a statement rather than a question, but Tom thought it sounded like Morris was just going through the motions. 'Dan, are you still following up this end on what happened to Nick?'

'Um, you know Shuttleworth told everyone that you were no longer working the case or any part of it?'

'Yeah. Look, this might help you, Dan. Don't mess me about and I won't mess you about.'

'All right. Yeah, we're trying to find out more of what he was up to, but, I'll tell you the truth, all we're getting is dead ends.'

'You mean literally or figuratively,' Tom said, writing the word dead on the notepad.

'Do what?'

Dan was a plodder. A good copper, but not the sharpest knife in the drawer. 'You mean dead as in bodies?'

There was a pause on the other end of the line. 'Maybe,' Morris said.

'The strip club you and Chris visited – remember it?'

'How could I forget it? Wish every job was like that one.'

Tom thought the laugh was forced. He knew he was getting close.

'She's dead. The stripper I told Shuttleworth about.

Ebony, the black girl Nick had been seen talking to a couple of times. The one who did a bunk from work.'

'Tom, that information hasn't been reported to the media. In fact, it's subject to a D-notice. How did you know about it? If Shuttleworth finds out you've been poking your nose into the Minx club he'll have your guts for garters.'

Tom wrote Ebony's name on the piece of paper, followed by *D-notice?*

'Tom? You still there?'

'Got to go, Dan. Thanks, mate.'

'Thanks? What for? You said you had something that might help us.'

'Bad line. You're dropping out, Dan.' Tom pressed the end button.

He shuffled the pieces of paper in front of him and dialled Olga Kamorov's cell phone number. As it rang he checked his watch. He wondered if she would be sleeping in, if she'd been working late at Club Minx the previous evening. Too bad if she was.

When she answered, it was in a whisper. 'Hang on,' she urged him.

Tom tapped the pen on the benchtop while he waited. 'Sorry, I was in class.'

'Class?'

'I am student.'

Student as well as stripper. She wouldn't be the first to pay for her studies by working in the sex industry. 'Olga, we need to talk about Ebony's death.'

'Good,' she said. 'Other policemen don't want anyone to talk about it. They tell all girls at club no one is to talk to friends or journalists about Ebony. But that is problem, and I try to tell them that but they don't listen to me.'

He wasn't sure what she meant by that last rambling remark, and was about to tell her to slow down and explain when she cut him off before he had a chance.

'I must get back inside for lecture. I meet you at lunchtime, yes? One o'clock?'

She was setting the ground rules and he didn't like being in that position, but he had little option save to play along. Besides, he had nothing else in his diary for the day. 'Okay, where?'

'There is a Burger King in Euston Road, opposite St Pancras, near Kings Cross. You know it?'

'I'll find it.' He hung up and walked over to the refrigerator. Inside was a single egg in a soggy carton and a half-pack of bacon. He put the frying pan on the gas hob and dropped in some oil. His stomach rumbled, so he put all the bacon in and cracked the egg. In the pantry was half a loaf of stale bread. He selected the least mouldy piece and chucked the rest in the bin, along with an assortment of pizza boxes and takeaway curry containers from the benchtop.

He continued to clean up while breakfast sizzled mouth-wateringly nearby. Working back from one o'clock he mentally planned his day. It would take him the best part of an hour to eat and get clean and dressed. He'd booked the Jag in for a service on his first day of suspension. He'd discounted the idea of going away anywhere and figured – correctly, so far – he would spend most of his time either drunk in a pub or drunk at home. He hadn't been wrong until now. He would have to take the tube to meet Olga.

He scooped the bacon and egg from the frypan, added another half-inch of oil and dropped in the slice of bread. He devoured the lot in seconds. Cooked breakfasts always seemed like a lot of effort for little return. He hoped that wasn't an omen for the rest of the day.

Upstairs he showered and scraped three days' worth of growth from his face, put on his charcoal-grey suit pants, black brogues and socks, and took a clean white shirt downstairs to the laundry to iron. Olga wouldn't know he was suspended – unless, of course, she had read a newspaper in the last week. Tom figured that if she had, she wouldn't have called him. He mightn't be on duty officially, but he wanted her to think he was. He wondered if the dancer would give him anything that might help Sannie's investigations back in Africa. He doubted it, but perhaps the South African police could run a check on Precious Mary Tambo.

Before leaving the house, he stopped to straighten his tie in the hall mirror and pull on his suit jacket. It felt good to have a sense of purpose again. It might come to nothing, but would keep his mind off Greeves, Joyce and the impending inquiry for a few hours.

Outside it was a perfect autumn day. The chill in the air helped clear his head, and he felt virtuous walking off some of his breakfast down Southwood Lane towards Highgate tube station.

Two young mums pushed their children in prams, chatting and laughing at something. It was a reminder that life went on, even though his world had been turned upside down. He wondered how Greeves's wife and children were faring, and if Bernard Joyce had family.

There were already Christmas decorations in some of the shop windows. He wondered what it was like for Sannie's kids at this time of year, without their father.

Tom entered Highgate Underground station and descended the long escalator to the platforms, his nostrils filling with the unnaturally warm, humid air. A Euston-bound tube train arrived within minutes and he nipped through the sliding doors into the hot, stuffy carriage. Only the drivers got airconditioning.

On the seat beside him was a copy of the *Metro*, the free newspaper handed out to commuters. He opened it and on page five found the news Sannie had already told him.

SOUTH AFRICAN BODYGUARD TO GIVE EVI-DENCE AT GREEVES INQUIRY
A South African police officer is being flown to the UK to testify at the inquiry into the abduction and killing of the former Minister for Defence Procurement, Robert Greeves.

Inspector Susan van Rensburg was assigned as the protection officer for Mr Greeves's South African government counterpart during two days of meetings between the two politicians.

Tom skimmed the recapping of the events, and looked for the 'why' in the story.

Mr Greeves's former spokesperson said the government had decided to invite Inspector Van Rensburg to appear at the inquiry in order to better understand security arrangements which had been put in place prior to Mr Greeves's visit, and to outline the events leading up to the minister's abduction.

'Shit,' Tom said aloud. An old lady sitting opposite in a plastic mackintosh looked up from her magazine and raised her eyebrows at him. Sannie's appearance was part of the government's efforts to set him up as the patsy for Greeves's death. He could have guessed it. He wondered what she would make of the story and if it would affect her evidence. All she could do was tell the truth – and that would be enough to have him dismissed.

He felt the fog of depression start to settle on him again, almost wilting the creases in his freshly ironed shirt.

'Only ever bad news in those things.' The old lady was looking at him, smiling as she nodded to the newspapers beside him. 'Stick with *OK!*, that's my philosophy.'

He laughed and nodded as she held up the glossy celebrity gossip magazine.

At the end of the noisy, jolting journey, he gratefully slid onto the crowded tube platform at Euston. Making his way out of this subterranean world, Tom surfaced in the brightly lit main-line station.

He left the bustling terminus, turning left into Euston Road and passing the gothic splendour of the recently restored and enlarged St Pancras International station. Just before King's Cross station, Tom weaved across the busy road to the Burger King.

He was half an hour early. He felt like buying a packet of cigarettes, but knew he shouldn't. His brain hadn't been at full speed when he'd spoken to Sannie on the phone, but he remembered now there was something he wanted to ask her.

There was an internet cafe a few doors down and Tom went in thinking he might find his answer there. A long-haired man looked up from his screen and directed him to a machine. Tom took out his notebook and typed 'primates of southern Africa' into the browser. He filled two pages and left the cafe at five minutes to one.

There were a dozen people inside the Burger King when he arrived but none he could recognise as the alluring young exotic dancer. He walked back outside onto the footpath. Perhaps she was late.

'Hey, Mr Policeman.'

He turned around and looked down. The girl who was talking to him had Ivana's – Olga's – voice, but he could have been looking at a different person.

She stood about five feet tall, much shorter than he'd remembered. Her hair was pulled back in a pony-tail and her lack of makeup revealed traces of acne scarring. She wore a baggy grey sports top with a hood attached, faded jeans and old trainers.

'You didn't recognise me.' Olga craned her neck back and peered up at him through rimless Coke-bottle glasses. 'You walked right past me.'

'Sorry.'

She shrugged. 'Not surprising. I have clothes on now and no five-inch stiletto heels.'

He smiled. 'And the glasses?'

'It should have been me not recognising you, instead of other way around. In club I can barely see the men who come in. All my time there is like in a – what do you say . . . haze.'

'Probably better that way.'

She nodded. 'We eat?'

They stood side by side in the queue, making small talk about the weather while they waited to be served.

'What are you studying?'

'Medicine at UCL,' she said. 'No jokes about anatomy or biology, though, please. I get enough of that from fellow students.'

The University College London campus at Bloomsbury was nearby. Tom was a little surprised she told her peers about her job.

'Is legal and is not money for sex, like some people think. You would be surprised what some students do. Not all of it is legal, either.'

He muttered an apology and said nothing more until they were served and took their food to a red laminate-topped table.

'Why you come alone? You not have partner, like TV policeman? Even in Russia, where government has no money, militia detectives have partner.'

Tom didn't want to lose the initiative before the interview began. He wanted to remind her, as much as himself, who was who in this exchange.

'What have you got to tell me, Olga, that you didn't tell the investigating officers?'

'So you talked to them?'

'Why wouldn't I?'

'I thought that since you were suspended from duty over African business that other police would not cooperate with you.'

'So you know why I don't have a partner.' As a medical student her IQ was no doubt higher than his. Still, he had a lot more experience in asking questions than she did. He placed his burger back in the paper bag and started to stand. 'I'm wasting my time here.'

'No, wait!'

He saw the panic in her eyes. 'Don't mess me about, Olga. I haven't come here to hear conspiracy theories or to indulge your fantasies of being an amateur detective.'

'Look, I know about you but I also remember that you came to club by yourself. This is personal for you. Something is going on here that is not right.'

Tom folded his arms, ignoring his food, and said nothing.

'Other detectives say not to talk to media about Ebony's death, right?'

He nodded.

'But journalist is the one who did it, even though police say they have questioned him.'

Tom took the hamburger back out of its wrapper and took a bite. He washed it down with a mouthful of cola. He knew that if he stayed quiet Olga would keep talking, and he was right.

'You remember when you come to club that I tell you about geeky-looking man with red hair who used to come often to see Ebony dance – in private shows.'

Tom nodded again.

'Well, he come back night after you were there. He was asking for her, but boss told him Ebony not show up for work. He start coming on to all other girls, including me, asking where she is. I say she is not here and he starts to get angry – what you say . . . agitated. He even offer me fifty quid to give him Ebony's home address, but I say no way.'

'Doesn't sound like he's the killer, then, if he's drawing attention to himself,' Tom said, wiping his mouth and feigning a lack of interest.

'Aha. That is what other policemen said. But can't you see that it was act? He was doing this deliberately to look like he didn't know where she was, but he was stalking her for two weeks before she disappear!'

Tom took another drink. 'Stalking? I thought you said he was a regular customer. Presumably you have men who come to see you dance more than once.'

Olga nodded and finally started to eat her food. She pinched small chunks from the burger bun and chewed each one methodically, over and over, while she thought about her next response. 'Yes, but Ebony met this guy outside of work.'

Tom sat back in his plastic chair. 'You didn't tell me this when I came to the club.'

'You were asking about Ebony and other man – the policeman you were looking for – not Ebony's stalker man.'

Tom nodded. At that stage he had been working on a theory that Nick and Ebony might have done a bunk together, not that she had been murdered by a nutter. 'How do you know this, did she tell you?'

Olga shook her head, and seemed to hesitate,

picking again at her burger bun, but leaving the meat untouched.

'Well?'

She looked up at him. 'Geeky guy left his card when he couldn't find Ebony and when no one would give him her address. His name was Fisher, Michael Fisher. He is –'

'He's a journalist, from the *World*.'

Now it was Olga's turn to lean back, arms folded, in a parody of Tom. 'Aha! So you know this man.'

Tom shook his head. He recalled the somewhat obnoxious, persistent reporter from the media conference Greeves had given at the defence contractor's offices prior to their flight to South Africa. Fisher was the one who was pursuing the line of questioning about Greeves's frequent visits to Africa.

Olga gave up trying to outwait Tom and resumed her confession. 'Ebony had a diary in her locker.'

'You broke into her locker?' Tom wiped his hands on a paper serviette.

'Lock was broken. I started to worry about Ebony after your visit and that night I opened locker to see if she had left suicide note or something.'

'Suicide?'

'Not unknown in my line of work. Yours too, if anything like Russia.'

Tom let that pass unanswered.

'Anyway, I look in Ebony's diary and last entry is note to *ring Michael*. She wrote cell phone number down. I check with Fisher's card and is same Michael.'

'So, she was talking to him, outside of work.'

'Yes.'

'And when she didn't call him, presumably because she'd been killed, Fisher came to the club and was "agitated" that he couldn't find her and hadn't heard from her.'

'Exactly!' Olga slapped the tabletop, causing another couple of diners next to them to look over. 'Perfect cover.'

It would be easy, Tom reasoned, to get Ebony's mobile phone records and find out if she had been called. He presumed Morris and Burnett would have done this as a matter of course, so he wasn't as convinced by this theory as Olga was.

'But what makes you so sure that Fisher had anything to do with her death?'

She shrugged. 'Is hard to tell you – to explain. I see lots of men in that place, and I know the looks in their eyes. There are the drunk ones, out looking for fun; there are the desperate ones who could never get look at naked girl any other way; there are the chauvinist ones who like the power of having girl do what they tell them . . . and there are the scary ones.'

'Scary ones? The stalkers, you mean?'

She nodded. 'The ones who are there with something else on their mind. You can see it in their eyes. Fisher was one of these. He was man on mission, and I think that mission was Ebony.'

Tom regarded Olga. She was bright – she had to be in order even to be admitted to study medicine – and she knew men. He thought she was being a little paranoid, but there was obviously something going on between Fisher and Ebony – aka Precious – that transcended the normal ogler–stripper dynamic. It was worth a closer look. He pulled his notebook out of his suit pocket.

'Presumably you told Detective Morris all this?'

She nodded. 'Morris – he is your friend?'

'None of your business. He is a colleague, though.'

'He is ignoramus.'

Tom kept the smile at bay. 'What did he say?'

'He said he would call Fisher, but his eyes told me that he thought I was crackpot.'

Tom let the next smile through.

'Don't mock me. You are smarter than Morris.'

Flattery would get her nowhere. He said nothing.

'Morris and other policeman came back to club yesterday and tell all girls and management that no one is to talk to media. I tell them, again, that media is where they should be looking and that Fisher came back to club again asking about Ebony and police investigation. Morris says to me, "You let me worry about Mr Fisher, darling." Pah! I give him, "darling". Creep.'

Tom held up a hand. 'Sounds like they've checked him out at least.'

'What happened to your policeman friend, the one you were looking for in first place.'

'He's dead.'

Olga placed a hand on the table and for a second Tom thought she might be about to reach out and touch him, in the same way Sannie had done on a couple of occasions. Perhaps there was something about him that inspired pity. 'How did he die?'

'He was tortured to death by terrorists. The same people who abducted Robert Greeves, the defence procurement minister, in Africa.'

344

Olga frowned, and Tom could see she was processing the information he'd just given her. She shook her
head. 'Ebony not working for Islamic terrorists. You
were looking at wrong girl for that if you think she
was involved in kidnap plot.'

'Why's that?'

'She was devout Christian.'

'Christian stripper?'

Olga looked offended again and folded her arms
with an 'harrumph'. 'I am trainee doctor exotic dancer.
Why not Christian stripper?'

Tom was stumped. Olga resumed her defence of
the dead girl. 'She was more Christian than any other
person I know. Church every Sunday and sent money
home to Africa to mission where she was educated.
Of course, she don't tell missionaries what she was
doing in England. She tell people in Africa she was
working as nurse's aide. I was trying to help her get
job like this in hospital.'

Tom's gut feeling was still that Ebony, having
played her part in luring Nick Roberts to a location where he could be abducted, had been killed
by the people who had used her. 'Perhaps she did it
for money.'

Olga shook her head vigorously. Most of her
burger was untouched and she wrapped it up in the
paper bag it had come in. Tom looked down at her
hands. He figured he didn't have to give a medical
student a lecture about eating disorders. It did make
him wonder, however, if Olga had some psycho-
logical problems.

'Ebony was good person,' she continued. 'Fisher

was up to something with her, though, and that's where you should be looking.'

'I'll talk to Morris again,' Tom said, pushing back his chair. 'Did you find anything else in her diary?'

'Not much. It looked new – like she had only been keeping it for last two weeks.' Olga pulled a scrap of paper out of her handbag. 'I found one other name, on same page as number for "Michael". Other name was D Carney.'

She passed the paper over, and Tom copied the name and cell phone number into his phone book. He'd seen the name Carney before, but couldn't quite remember where. He knew that once he had a few moments to himself it would come to him.

'Thanks for your time, Olga. Do you know who this Carney is?' Even as he asked the question he remembered where he had seen the name and number before.

She shook her head. 'Talk to Fisher. He is one you need to put this puzzle together, Mr Policeman.'

Tom stood. 'You probably know enough about my situation and police procedure to understand that Fisher has already been questioned and that it would be highly inappropriate for me to go harassing him when I'm suspended.'

She nodded. 'But I know you will anyway. You are good person. Morris, Fisher, they are creeps.' Olga tucked the remains of the burger in her day pack, shook Tom's hand and started to walk out the door. She looked back over her shoulder. 'Maybe I see you in club again some time?'

Tom shook his head. 'Maybe I'll see you in a hospital one day.'

She laughed. 'Maybe my turn to see you naked.'

What Tom couldn't tell Olga, of course, was that there was a definite link between Nick and Ebony in the form of the message the dancer had left on Nick's answering machine. Somehow he doubted that Nick had been planning to go to the club to hand over a donation to a Christian mission in South Africa.

After Olga left the restaurant, Tom stayed at the table and took out his notebook and pen. He wrote the name *Ebony* in the centre of a page and circled it. He drew a line off to the left to *Nick* and then extended out further to another circle containing *Greeves*. Off to the right of the stripper's stage name he wrote *Fisher*. He tapped his chin with the pen and then returned to the page and linked the journalist and the politician with a stroke of his pen. A circle. But was it mere coincidence that the dancer had something going on with the reporter as well as with the minister's protection officer?

There was only one way for Tom to find out – two, if he went through official channels but he doubted the latter would work. Dan Morris would be suspicious now, and Tom wouldn't put it past him to grass on him to Shuttleworth. Either way, he was unlikely to cough up the notes of his interview with Fisher.

As the train clattered back towards the city, Tom took out his mobile phone and notebook. He called the number for D Carney, though he recalled now that it was a man and his name was Daniel. A recorded voice answered the phone, though it wasn't Carney: it was a message telling him the phone was switched off or out of range.

Next he dialled directory assistance. 'Could I have the number for the *World* newspaper, editorial department, please?'

22

Tom tuned out from the image of the British Prime Minister on the widescreen plasma television monitor in the *World*'s foyer, which was broadcasting a satellite news channel owned by the same man who controlled the newspaper in whose offices he was waiting. The receptionist looked up from her computer and nodded to him. 'Michael's off the phone now, Mr Carney. He'll be down in a mo.'

Tom thanked her. He'd taken the Northern Line from King's Cross to Bank and then switched to the Docklands Light Rail to get to the newspaper's offices. Out of the window he saw a jumbled landscape. Shiny new offices and apartments jostled with face-lifted brick warehouses that had been reinvented as fashionable homes for wealthy incomers. Yet, sporadic remnants of the old Isle of Dogs held on. The last of its undeveloped, soot-blackened buildings waited, destined either for demolition or to be reborn out of the ashes of their grimy past. The planners might have breathed new life into the area, but they had stolen its soul.

The news crawler at the bottom of the television screen was repeating the only part of the PM's press conference that Tom had paid attention to: *PM confirms at least one of Robert Greeves's abductors, killed in South Africa, was Muslim.* Tom heard footsteps and looked over his shoulder. He recognised the thin, pasty-faced, red-haired reporter immediately.

'Daniel Carney?' asked Michael Fisher.

Tom nodded and held out his hand, but Fisher kept his by his sides. He looked Tom up and down, and Tom prayed that Fisher had never met the real Carney. He also hoped Fisher wouldn't recognise him from the press conference he had attended with Greeves.

So far, there had been no photographs of Tom published in the newspapers, as his identity was being protected by a Defence Advisory notice, more commonly known as a D-notice, on the grounds that the terrorist gang which had abducted Greeves was still at large and Tom had been involved in the killing of some of their number. The restrictions were voluntarily complied with by the media, but Tom knew his name and identity would not be kept quiet for long, especially if, as he assumed, things went badly for him at the inquiry. The journalists knew his name, which was why he'd been pestered continually for an exclusive. The fact he hadn't given one meant the media would show him no mercy when his name was released.

Tom had called Fisher from the train and their conversation had been brief. He'd already gathered from Fisher's tone that he wouldn't exactly be welcomed with open arms.

'I know who you are, Carney,' Fisher had said when Tom had called, masquerading as the freelance journalist. 'You're the bastard who did me out of a cracking story. Well, you won't get much from the stripper now, will you?' Tom had simply said he needed to talk to him about Precious Tambo's death. He had offered to come to the *World*'s offices and Fisher had agreed. Tom had no idea what he would find out, but it seemed that so far he was pulling off the charade.

'Is there somewhere we can talk in private?' he said.

'There's an interview room down the corridor. Is room one free, Sally?' Fisher asked the receptionist.

She checked her computer screen and said, 'All yours, Michael. For the next twenty minutes at least.'

'We won't be longer than that.'

Fisher led Tom down a hallway off the main reception area. They stopped at a garishly painted red door and Tom followed the shorter man in. He took the new spiral-bound shorthand notebook out of his right suit pocket. From his left, Tom pulled the cheap audio cassette recorder he had bought in an electronics shop on the way. He hoped the props would back up his impersonation of a reporter. He knew Daniel Carney was a journalist because he had seen the man's business card under Nick Roberts's refrigerator. He recalled thinking that the card looked low-budget. It was the kind you could make up on an instant printing machine, the sort often found at major railway stations. Whoever Carney was, he probably wasn't at the top of his game. Tom had wondered if Nick had been handed the card at a function Greeves had attended, or if he

351

knew the reporter socially. Given that his name was in Precious's diary, though, it was possible Nick had crossed paths with him at Club Minx.

'You can put that away and all,' Fisher said. 'I don't want anyone taping me.'

Tom nodded and slipped the cassette recorder back in his pocket. He left the notebook closed, on the table, sat down and leaned back in his chair, folding his arms.

Fisher looked at his watch. 'Well? What have you got to say that's so important?'

From Fisher's comments over the phone, Tom realised that Precious had something to tell the media, and that a bidding war had been going on. 'I've been told by the Old Bill that I can't write anything about Ebony's death.'

Fisher shrugged. 'No shit, Sherlock. They've done the same to us, by slapping a D-notice on the story. Makes you wonder what else she was up to with Greeves, doesn't it?'

Fisher was living up to his name, Tom thought, angling for information that he might have missed out on.

'It's why I'm here,' Tom said, keeping his arms folded.

'Well, I've got nothing to tell you, sunshine,' Fisher said, leaning back and mirroring Tom's body language. 'So if you've got nothing else to say, you'd best be on your bike.'

'I never got the whole story out of her,' Tom said.

Fisher raised his eyebrows, then broke into a grin. 'Do what? You outbid me by ten thousand quid and you didn't get the bloody story? You're fucking joking? Whose money was it?' Fisher reeled off the names of a few newspapers, but Tom didn't nod or shake his head to any of them.

'All I got out of her was the same as what she gave you – enough to get us interested,' Tom said.

'What, that she'd been rogered by Greeves?'

Tom nodded.

'Not bad in itself, but it wasn't much good to us if she wasn't going to let us publish her name and picture. She was a babe in the woods, thinking she'd get us to pay fifteen grand for an anonymous tip-off. I'm assuming you *did* get an agreement from her to go public with all the lurid details.'

'Of course. The extra cash did the trick.'

Fisher nodded. 'My editor wouldn't risk it. Bleedin' management's watching the pennies these days. So, who bankrolled you?'

'Can't say until it gets a run, but at least we didn't hand over the money before she disappeared. The coppers have been looking around the club, you know.'

'Tell me something I don't know. They were breathing down my neck at one point.'

'Me too.' Tom felt the barrier between them crumbling a little. Perhaps Fisher had finally accepted that the competition for Ebony's story was over and neither man had won. 'Funny about Greeves, though.' Tom unfolded his arms and leaned forward a little, as if he was about to share something with Fisher. 'Such a bloody ramrod-straight type, good family man and all.'

Fisher laughed out loud. 'What do you mean?

They're always the worst offenders! Think about it. The straighter the public profile, the kinkier they are behind the scenes.'

Tom smiled and nodded. 'True. Is that why your rag has been hounding him about Africa so much? Were you trying to shake him up, see if he'd been making a habit of bonking black women on his jaunts?'

Fisher relaxed a little as well, nodding as Tom spoke. 'Yeah, well, once I got an inkling that you were going to outbid us with the slag, I thought I'd try and shake his tree, see what other rotten apples fell out. Oi, and watch what you're calling a rag, sunshine. That's offensive.'

As opposed to slag, Tom thought, but said nothing. 'The other strippers at the club reckon you killed her.'

'Silly bitches.' Fisher shook his head. 'Look, when I found out you'd scooped us I went down there and I was pretty angry. I tried splashing a few tenners around to see if some of the others would talk – or if they'd give me Ebony's home number. I might have come across like your garden variety stalker, but the cops know I'm clean.'

'Oh yeah?'

'Yeah. I was in Africa when she was murdered, wasn't I.'

'You went for the Greeves thing?'

'Yeah. What a fucking shambles that was. I've got a snout whose given me some good stuff about the bodyguard copper who went over with Greeves.'

Tom swallowed, but hoped he'd hidden his flush of alarm. 'Such as?'

Fisher laughed. 'You think I'd tell you? Let's just say the boys from Hereford aren't as secretive as they like to make out when they've got some dirt to sling at the coppers.'

That bastard Fraser, Tom thought. 'So who do you reckon killed her?'

Fisher shrugged. 'Who knows? Probably was some stalker. She was raped, from what I've heard. If I was really into conspiracy theories I'd say MI5 or Greeves's bodyguard killed her to stop her from blabbing about the big man knobbing her, but Greeves's first bodyguard was tortured and killed by the terrorists, wasn't he?'

Tom nodded, though he didn't know how Fisher knew about Nick, as the circumstances of his death hadn't been publicly released. He started to worry that the reporter knew a lot more than he was letting on.

Fisher leaned forward until his palms were resting on the table, and stared into Tom's eyes. 'And his replacement protection officer, Detective Sergeant Tom Furey, currently on suspension pending an appearance at a parliamentary inquiry into the abduction and deaths of Robert Greeves and Bernard Joyce, is sitting in this room opposite me, isn't he?'

Tom slumped back in his seat. 'What gave it away? My picture hasn't been in the press so far.'

Fisher smiled. 'I paid that freelance photographer in South Africa to follow Greeves. The snapper said this prick of a security guard kept getting in his way. He emailed through the pictures of Greeves – nothing worthwhile – and pointed out the man who ruined the job for him.'

'Me.'

'You.'

Tom shrugged. He knew this could go very badly for him, impersonating Carney, but he sensed that the journalist wasn't about to go running to Scotland Yard just yet. 'What do you know about Carney?'

'Nothing.' Fisher held his hands out, palms up. 'I've never seen or heard of him before, and no one here or anyone else I know has either.'

'Unusual?'

'Yes and no. You get a lot of people who wake up one morning and decide that as part of their midlife crisis they want to become journalists. There are plenty of dodgy correspondence schools advertising courses in travel writing and freelance journalism, no shortage of gullible punters who think it's an easy ticket to fame and fortune.'

'But he outbid you by offering Precious Tambo what . . . twenty-five thousand pounds?'

Fisher leaned back again. 'Yeah. I wish I knew who he was stringing for. Not that any of the other news-papers would tell me. Maybe you could get a court order or something – force them to cough it up?'

'Not me,' Tom said.

'Yeah, not you. What about those other jokers who questioned me – Morris and what's his name?'

'Burnett. Maybe. Did you tell them anything about the bidding war?'

Fisher shook his head. 'None of their business.'

'This Daniel Carney's a suspect now. He could have been the last one to see Precious alive. It's possible he was masquerading as a journalist – he might have found out what you were up to in the club.'

'Not my job to catch killers, is it?'

Tom disliked Fisher, but he was right. It would be up to the police to find out who Daniel Carney was and who, if anyone, was bankrolling him. 'Who told you Nick Roberts was dead?'

'No way. I don't reveal my sources,' Fisher replied.

'Your friends at Hereford?'

Fisher shook his head. 'You won't get that out of me. However, you might want to start thinking about what you can tell me that will make you look less like the sacrificial lamb you are most definitely going to be at the inquiry, Thomas.'

'I found Carney's card in Nick Roberts's house, the night after he disappeared.'

Fisher bit his lower lip and refolded his arms. 'You think this Carney might be one of the terrorists? Think he might have tailed your man Roberts to the club so they could ambush him there?'

Tom didn't know. He felt as though he was running around in circles at the moment. 'From what I've heard about Precious Tambo, she didn't sound like the kind to keep company with Islamic jihadists.'

'She was a stripper. Not many girls are in that line of work because of the job satisfaction. She needed money – and maybe the terrorists had plenty to spare. Also, she had dirt on Greeves, which could have brought his bodyguard into the trap. It wouldn't have been kosher, but maybe she or the real Carney got in touch with Greeves's people and the minister sent his henchman to suss her out.'

Tom was thinking along the same lines, but something didn't add up. 'Did you ever contact Greeves or his press secretary to put Precious's allegations to him?'

Fisher shook his head. 'No way. I was keeping this one close to my chest. Once I had the stripper signed up I was going to go to him at the last minute for comment – late in the afternoon of the day before we went to press.'

Tom shook his head at the tactic. It was gutter journalism – have a two-page spread of lurid allegations ready to go, and give the target no time to formulate a response. The last thing a tabloid such as the *World* wanted was a rational explanation for Greeves's relationship with another woman or, worse, concrete evidence that the stripper was lying.

Fisher elaborated. 'If I'd gone to him with what I had he could have come out with all guns firing, given something to everyone. You know, "Forgive me, people of Britain, I sinned once, but now my wife and family have forgiven me and are behind me." That sort of crap.'

'It's a tough game,' Tom said.

'Yeah. You're about to find that out the hard way. Give me something from the inside on this thing and I'll go easy on you at the inquiry. I can make you look like a hero if I try hard enough.'

Tom pushed his seat back and stood up. He didn't want to be in the same room as Fisher for a second longer, and he didn't believe a word of what the man had just said.

'I'll call your superiors, tell them you were here under false pretences.'

Tom looked over his shoulder as he opened the

door of the interview room. 'Go ahead. I don't think it's going to make any difference to my future.'

Tom found a cafe near the newpaper's offices and ordered a tea. He took out his notebook and pen and cell phone. He dialled Dan Morris's number and the detective groaned when Tom told him who it was.

'I need a favour,' Tom said.

'Well, you're in no position to ask for one. I'm not going to let you drag me down with you. I'm hanging up now, Tom.'

'Daniel Carney?'

'What about him?'

Tom moved his tea away from his notebook and waited in silence.

'I'm hanging up.'

Tom blew on the hot liquid and sipped it.

'How do you know about him?' Morris relented.

Tom smiled to himself. Fisher's threat to tell his superiors about his unauthorised – illegal – investigation hadn't fazed him at all. He'd meant what he'd said: nothing he did from here on in would make things worse. He had resigned himself to the fact that he would not survive the inquiry with his career intact. It was liberating, in a way, to be free of the rules and regulations that had for twenty-one years governed his life as a policeman. All that mattered now, all that might, possibly, keep him in the job was if he could find something the others had missed.

'Tom? Answer me?'

'Carney's card was under Nick's fridge – probably slipped off the door.'

'Oh, right,' Morris said.

Tom could almost hear the squeaky wheels turning in his colleague's mind.

'Well, you're wasting your time there. I don't think he exists,' Morris said.

'Really?' Tom had already come to the same conclusion. It was hard to believe a freelancer who could command a budget of twenty-five thousand pounds from a newspaper would be unknown to other reporters in the industry. Also, the instant cards giving nothing but a cell number were a flimsy prop. Tom suspected the number was probably from a pre-paid SIM card.

'The phone number was a pre-paid,' Morris said. The confirmation brought no solace to Tom.

'There are a load of Daniel Carneys in the phone book and we've just about got to the end of them, but nothing so far.'

'Precious Tambo was raped, wasn't she?'

'Who told you that? I'm really going to hang up now, Tom. All the details of her death are being kept quiet.'

'A reporter.'

Morris groaned again. 'Bleeding hell. Goodbye, Tom.'

The phone went dead in his ear and Tom sipped some more of his tea.

Names. That was all he had. One didn't exist, and the others, Nick Roberts, Precious Tambo and Robert Greeves – the ones who could give him the answers he needed – were all dead.

On the table was a copy of the *Sun*, which the last customer had spilled a latte on. Tom flipped through it as he thought about his next move. On page five he saw a headline that galvanised him into action.

SLAIN MINISTER'S FRIENDS TELL OF JANET'S GRIEF. GREEVES'S WIDOW PLANS TO SET UP CHARITY IN ROBERT'S HONOUR.

In his wallet was a laminated card with the phone numbers for Robert Greeves, his key staff members, and Greeves's wife, Janet. There were numbers for the family homes in London, and in Bledlow Ridge, a village near West Wycombe in Buckinghamshire. The newspaper story said Janet Greeves was at the family's 'secluded, upmarket rural retreat'. Tom thought she would have the answering machine on for the landline but would have her cell phone turned on.

'Hello?' said the female voice.

'Mrs Greeves?'

'Who's calling, please.'

Tom thought she was right to be cautious. She would have been hounded by hundreds of reporters so far.

'Detective Sergeant Tom Furey, ma'am. I was with Mr Greeves, when . . .'

'Oh.'

'I'm very sorry for your loss, ma'am.'

'I've read about you in the papers, Sergeant, though not by name. Is this an official call?'

She was frosty, dismissive. It was to be expected.

'If you've seen the press reports, then you'll know I've been suspended.'

'Well, if you're calling to apologise, it's really not

necessary. I'm sure you did everything you could have done.'

He'd expected more emotion. Perhaps anger, or if she was forgiving, empathy or pity for him at failing in the line of duty.

'I'm sorry about the way things turned out, but I also have some questions for you which might help the investigation into your husband's abduction and death.'

'Yes, but you're suspended, as you've just pointed out. I've told the investigating officers about Robert's movements on the last few days before he left for Africa. There was nothing unusual. I understand if you're trying to clear your name, but –'

'It's not that. There are some sensitive matters that have come up, which I wanted to talk to you about in private. Perhaps it's better if they're not made part of the official record of investigation being undertaken by detectives Morris and Burnett.'

There was a pause on the end of the line.

'I really should be going. I'm late for an appointment. Perhaps if you give me your number, I could –'

'It's about the affair.'

Silence.

Tom waited. It always worked.

'I meant what I said about being late. I'm going to be with my children this afternoon and this evening. I can see you at eleven, tomorrow, at the Bledlow Ridge house.'

Tom was wired. He felt truly alive for the first time since Bernard's death. He'd pushed a button and Janet

Greeves had responded. She knew about her husband's infidelity – perhaps there had been more than one affair.

He hated having to wait until the next morning to see her.

Ideally, he would have played his trump card face to face. Now she'd have time to prepare herself for his questions, but he couldn't do anything about that. He finished his tea, walked to the DLR station and made his way back to Highgate.

Once inside, in the warmth of his home, he went to the study at the top of the stairs and turned on his computer. He typed *Robert Greeves* and *Africa* in the internet search engine's subject field. There were scores of hits, so he tried again, limiting it to news coverage and added *Michael Fisher* to the search words. This limited the hits to less than a page.

He clicked on Fisher's last story for the *World* before Greeves's ill-fated trip to meet with the South African defence minister. This was a critical piece about the 'globe-trotting junior minister's love affair with the dark continent and taxpayers' money'. It showed a full-length photo of Greeves, manipulated so that he was wearing a pith helmet and Bombay bloomers, with a pair of oversize binoculars around his neck and a gin and tonic in one hand. The story listed the minister's trips to Africa over the past three years.

As well as South Africa, the countries he had visited included Kenya, Tanzania, Namibia, Mozambique, Botswana and Malawi. The last, Tom noted, Greeves was also reported to have visited four times on holiday, as well as the two 'official' visits listed in the chronology.

With its crystal-clear waters and colourful tropical fish, fresh-water Lake Malawi has proved far more attractive than Bognor Regis for Greeves during the past three parliamentary recesses, Fisher had written.

Tom made a note of the country on his pad and spent twenty minutes looking for information about it on the internet. He found a map and saw that the landlocked country was east of Zambia and north-west of Mozambique. It seemed to be largely made up of the lake which Fisher had referred to in the story.

He decided that when he picked Sannie up in the morning he'd ask her what she knew about Malawi.

23

The pilot's British-accented voice came over the intercom, interrupting the movie that Sannie was watching without really paying attention to while she ate a breakfast of scrambled eggs, pork sausage and chips.

'Ladies and gentleman, just an update on our arrival. We've made up time and expect to have you on the ground at five-fifteen this morning and arrive at the gate on schedule at five-twenty. The weather in London is quite warm – it's fifteen degrees at the moment . . .'

Sannie washed some greasy sausage down with her orange juice. There wasn't a trace of irony in the man's voice. Fifteen degrees? Warm? That was less than half the temperature in Johannesburg when she'd left.

She checked her makeup in a hand mirror as they taxied, reapplying a little lip gloss. There was nothing she could do about the bags under her eyes. Even though the British government had paid for her to fly business class she had found it hard to sleep.

Outside it was still pitch black. In Africa the sun was rising at four-thirty by this time of year and it would be quite hot by now.

Sannie peered out the window and put the back of her hand against the Perspex; it felt cold. She shivered, wondering not for the first time if the clothes she'd brought with her would be warm enough. She was wearing jeans and high-heel boots for the trip, with a short-sleeve T-shirt over a long-sleeve one, and a cropped black leather jacket. It was very casual, but she planned to change into her black business suit as soon as she arrived at her hotel. Her first meeting, with Chief Inspector Shuttleworth, wasn't until two in the afternoon. She'd probably have time to sleep a bit beforehand.

It was nice of Tom to meet her at the airport, and while technically it was totally unnecessary, she was secretly grateful that he would be riding with her in the rental car, as she was a little nervous about navigating her way around London.

Sannie had never been to England before, and it was sad to be here under these circumstances. She knew the inquiry would go badly for Tom and she was determined that, while she would answer every question truthfully, she would also use every opportunity to praise his quick reactions and dogged pursuit of the terrorists once they found out Greeves was missing. She was also looking forward to seeing him.

The brief time they'd shared had been a roller-coast of emotions for both of them – from incredible lows when it seemed they would never find the missing men or the terrorists, to the high of finding Bernard alive and planning the raid, to the crushing defeat they'd suffered on the beach in Mozambique. She wondered if Tom had considered doing what Bernard had done.

He'd sounded in the depths when she had spoken to him on the telephone and she was worried about him. With his wife gone, and the possibility of his suspension becoming permanent, she knew he was facing a very uncertain future.

She looked out the window again.

The only thing she saw were the blinking lights of another aeroplane and it surprised her how close it looked. The furthest she'd ever flown was Mauritius, on holiday. That trip – her and Christo's first wedding anniversary – seemed like a lifetime ago, and it was. She thought of Christo as she always did, wearing the same clothes and smiling as he left to go pick up their son. She bit her lower lip as she gazed out into the impenetrable gloom. She'd allowed herself to get close to Tom. It hadn't been in a sexual way, but she had followed her heart and not her head when she had joined him on his mad dash across the border. It wasn't just because she wanted to help him find the men, it was because there was an energy or emotion that seemed to draw her to him. He understood the pain she had gone through in a way that few people could. It had hurt her to watch his zeal disappear after Bernard's death.

Sannie had tried to buck up his spirits on the drive back into South Africa, but the crushing depression had overtaken him. The attraction she had felt for him during the chase wore off then, though she still felt for him. She couldn't tie herself – for her sake, or her children's – to a man who couldn't cope with adversity. She wondered how he would be this morning.

She retrieved her carry-on wheelie bag from the overhead locker and joined the procession into the terminal. Sannie swallowed hard and felt her stomach churn. It was fear of the unexpected – of what would happen with the inquiry, and with Tom Furey.

Sannie turned her cell phone on as she walked up the air bridge, dragging her bag behind her. She sent a quick SMS to her mother as she walked, letting her know she had arrived. She'd been a saint, as usual, to agree to look after the kids for the week. Sannie was already missing them, though she smiled at the memory of Christo asking, 'Will you see your friend Tom, the Englishman?'

'Yes, my boy,' she'd replied, 'I will.'

Tom was waiting for her when she finally cleared customs and immigration. She spotted him immediately. He seemed a few inches taller than the throng of people around him.

The last time she'd seen him, when she'd dropped him at the Garden Court Hotel near Johannesburg airport, he'd been unshaven. His eyes were bloodshot and puffy from a lack of sleep, and his shoulders bowed with the weight of defeat.

Now, it was just after six in the morning and, even though he was on suspension, he was freshly shaved and wearing a smart business suit with what looked like a newly pressed white shirt and a maroon tie. His dark wavy hair was combed and he was smiling as he strode through the crowd. In his hand was something small and slender, wrapped in colourful paper.

'Sannie! Howzit!'

She laughed at his use of the typical South African greeting. '*Lekker*, man. And you?'

'Fine.' He held out his hand and she shook it. It was an awkward moment. They'd shared so much she almost felt like she should lean in close to him so he could kiss her on the cheek. He smiled into her eyes. 'Here, this is for you.'

He handed over the parcel and she let go of her wheelie bag to open it. 'Here, let me get that for you,' he said, grabbing the handle. She started to protest, but returned her attention to the gift.

'You shouldn't have, Tom,' she said as she peeled off the paper, then laughed again at the compact folding umbrella.

'Your British survival kit.'

She touched him on the arm, leaned close and kissed him on the cheek. 'Thanks.'

She saw the colour rise in his cheeks as he said, 'Not at all. You'll need it. Now, let's get your hire car sorted out for you.'

She smiled behind his back as he strode off, clearing a path for her through the crowd. She'd kissed him on impulse and, while it was still a bit awkward, she didn't regret the brief show of intimacy. He was a friend, that was all. And he'd need all the help he could get in the days to come.

He asked her about the flight and her mother and her kids while they waited in the queue for her to pick up her car. It was small talk and she could sense from the way he shifted his weight from foot to foot while he spoke that there was much more on his mind. Of course there would be. Sannie really hoped he hadn't come out to meet her so they could talk about her testimony at the inquiry. She felt sure he wasn't that sort of cop, but one never knew.

'What time's your first meeting?' he asked after she had signed the papers and collected the key. They walked to a shuttle bus stop outside the terminal and were waiting to be taken to the car park where the rentals were stored.

'Not until two, why?'

The shuttle bus arrived, stalling the conversation, and they got on, Tom easily hefting her bag, which looked very small when he held it. She really hadn't brought enough warm clothes. Perhaps she could go shopping for an overcoat before the meeting. 'What's on your mind, Tom?'

He shifted across the seat in the bus to make room for her. 'Well, as I told you in the email, my car's in the garage being fixed.'

'Yes. Just as well, as I was a bit unsure about navigating my way through London.'

'I was wondering if you'd like to take a little trip in the country with me, before your meeting?'

She leaned away from him and looked at him, as though reappraising him. 'Whatever for, Detective Sergeant?' she asked in a mock English accent.

He smiled. 'Nothing improper, of course, ma'am.' The humour vanished. 'I'm going to talk to Robert Greeves's widow this morning. I can take a train – she lives about an hour out of London – but I was wondering if –'

Sannie held up a hand. 'Tom, no. Really.'

'I thought that . . .'

'You thought wrong. You *know* I'm here strictly for the inquiry. I don't have to tell you what kind of problems it'd stir up if I started taking part in an investigation over here!'

'It's not an investigation. I've been suspended. It's just me paying my respects to Greeves's widow.'

She shook her head. 'No way. Look at you this morning. You're up to something, aren't you?'

He shrugged. They sat in silence as the bus passed long-term car parks and airport hotels whose neon signs were diffused by halos in the cold morning rain.

Sannie's curiosity started to get the better of her. She had half expected to see an unshaven, unwashed wreck waiting for her. A man wallowing in self-pity, looking for a shoulder to cry on. She'd been pleasantly surprised to see the handsome, upright detective she'd first met and, seeing his apparent change of mood, was glad for him. If she helped crack the case and find the men who had killed Greeves, her star would be on the rise back home; if the terrorists were still hiding in Africa, and Tom was able to uncover new information which helped lead the authorities to them, the Brits would need a liaison officer in South Africa.

'What can Greeves's widow tell you that you don't already know about the abductions?'

'Nothing.'

The shuttle bus stopped and they got off and walked along a covered walkway to another office. 'I'll drive, if you like,' Tom said after they collected the keys and directions to the car.

She shook her head and pressed the electronic lock of the Ford Focus, and hurriedly climbed inside to get out of the rain. She popped the boot, and Tom stowed her bag and then got in beside her, brushing droplets of rain off the shoulders of his suit jacket.

'So if she can't tell you anything about Greeves's disappearance, what can she tell you about?'

'Greeves.'

'What about him?'

'He was having an affair with a black South African stripper.'

Sannie's mouth opened. It took her a moment to realise this, then she closed her jaw and started the car. She navigated her way out of the car park in silence and Tom started directing her towards the M25. The windscreen wipers slapped from side to side and the only noise inside the car was the rush of the heater fan, which she had set to high.

'Who else knows this? Presumably the investigating police?'

He explained that there were, in fact, two parallel investigations going on. Tom had led the first, into the disappearance of Nick Roberts, to the strip club in Soho and the missing dancer, Ebony, aka Precious Tambo. It was only yesterday, however, that his talk with the reporter, Michael Fisher, had revealed a link between Ebony and Robert Greeves, which Nick may or may not have been aware of. 'The detectives looking into Nick's death, and the murder of Ebony, still – as far as I know – don't know about the Greeves connection.'

'Surely you're going to tell them?' Sannie asked.

Tom nodded. 'Left here, onto the motorway. The M25's like a giant ring-road that goes all the way around London. Of course I'll tell them. But I want to know more about what Greeves was up to. At the moment I'm working on the word of a dead exotic dancer, as relayed by a very dodgy tabloid journalist, who freely admits he didn't have enough to go public with. It pushed a button with Janet Greeves, though, when I told her I wanted to talk to her about the "affair".'

Sannie took the information in as she navigated her way through the thick morning traffic. The tiredness she'd felt on the aircraft had disappeared and she had to consciously tell herself to relax her grip on the steering wheel. She was getting the same feeling that she knew was driving Tom right now. He was on to a new lead in the investigation; it might, of course, come to nothing, but she wanted very much to be a part of what happened next.

Tom told her about the mysterious reporter, Daniel Carney, and his failed efforts to find any trace of him.

'Perhaps he's a South African, working in London. If the girl was South African, as you say, perhaps she knew a freelancer in the expat community.'

'I hadn't thought of that,' Tom admitted, frowning. 'See, I'm already glad you're here. At least you can get your people to check out Carney.'

She was trapped already, and she knew it. Damn it, she thought. 'Tom, when you pass on what you know to the investigating officers, I'm sure I'll be able to check out anyone they want me to.'

'You could be back in London by one, at the latest.

Plenty of time to change for your meeting. Did I tell you that you look great in jeans, by the way?'

Sannie snorted. Flattery would not get him very far at all. She checked her watch. It was still very early. They could stop at the hotel first and she could shower and put her suit on.

They slowed with the traffic, which eventually ground to a halt. Somewhere up ahead, through the rain and the enveloping fog, she could make out flashing orange lights. 'Tom, I went out on a limb for you before, but . . .' She knew her resolve was weakening.

'It'll be easier for Janet Greeves if there's another woman in the room. You know that, don't you?'

Sannie nodded.

'This is nice. More what I expected England to be like – rolling green hills and little villages with thatch-roofed houses,' Sannie said.

Tom looked across at her and smiled. He noticed she was drumming her hand on the car door. He was driving as they travelled through the biscuit-tin countryside of Buckinghamshire.

Tom knew the road well, as the Prime Minister's country residence, Chequers, was a little further along from where they would turn off. He'd been there on many occasions, protecting various politicians and dignitaries who attended meetings there or wanted to be seen at church with the PM on Sundays in the village of Little Kimble.

He knew she was nervous, but having her here was important to him. Not only, as he'd said, because he thought having a woman present might put Janet Greeves at ease, but also because it gave him a sense that he was helping move the official side of the investigation – albeit the South African side – further along. It was better than sitting around waiting for the axe blow which would end his career. Also, he liked being with Sannie. At a time when he had no one in his own country, professionally or personally, it was good to have her by his side again. She'd been his partner in Africa and he could trust her implicitly. She was also beautiful, and her perfume set his senses on edge.

'Here we go.' He turned left into Haw Lane, just after they passed Saunderton railway station. The road snaked upwards, bare winter trees flanking the approach to the upmarket village of Bledlow Ridge.

At the top of the hill Tom turned right and slowed until he found the name of the Greeves country estate – *Ingonyama* – in a cast iron sign on a gatepost. The wooden gate was open.

'That's Zulu for lion.' Sannie folded down the sun visor on her side and checked her hair and makeup. Tom thought she needn't have bothered. She looked cool, professional and sexy as hell in her black pants suit, boots and simple white blouse, open at the neck and showing a tantalising V of skin in spite of the cold. She'd checked into the Thistle Hotel near Waterloo, where overseas and out-of-town visitors to Tom's branch often stayed, and quickly showered and changed while he'd waited in the lobby. She wore a gold necklace made of many tiny links, but from a distance it looked solid. It followed the curves of her collarbone, caressing her tanned skin.

Tom drove up a long gravel road flanked by autumn-bare poplars. The rain had stopped, but the sky above was the colour of cold gunmetal.

'Kites.' Sannie pointed up at the three birds of prey wheeling above them. 'They look a lot like the yellow-bills we get at home.'

'Is that a good omen or a bad one?'

She shrugged. 'Bad if you're a snake.'

'Well, we don't have too many of those here in England. Let's enter the lion's den, shall we?'

Sannie frowned, opened her car door, then shivered. 'Lions don't have dens. Let's get this over with.'

Tom followed her along the flagstones. He was no historian or architect, but the house symbolised history and money: old red brick, bare wooden beams and well-kept thatch. The winter garden was drab but manicured.

The door opened before they could knock. Janet Greeves – Tom recognised her from pictures in the newspapers – stood waiting for them, unsmiling.

She was dressed for a walk, in jeans and green Wellington boots, and a dark olive Barbour jacket.

'Detective Sergeant Furey?'

Tom nodded. 'Morning, ma'am. This is Inspector Susan van Rensburg of the South African Police. She's involved in the African end of the investigation.'

Surprise and unease were plain on Janet Greeves's face, though she shook hands with both of them. 'So this is now an *official* visit?'

'All we want, Mrs Greeves, is to find out who abducted your husband and Bernard Joyce and where they might be now. Anything you can tell us that will help the authorities here and abroad to meet those aims will be appreciated.' She nodded and Tom thought he'd done a pretty good job of not answering her question. The woman was clearly off balance, though, and that wasn't a bad thing from his point of view.

'Very well. I thought we'd walk, if you don't mind. My daughter's inside, staying with me, and from our earlier conversation,' she looked at Tom, 'there might be some matters that she's better off not hearing about.'

Tom wasn't happy. Interviewees had no home-ground advantage when you questioned them in their own surroundings. What was on the walls, on the mantelpieces and stuck to refrigerators with magnets was often as interesting as a person's words.

'Um, if you don't mind, Mrs Greeves, I need to use your bathroom, please.'

Janet sighed. 'Of course.'

Good girl, Tom thought. Sannie was thinking the same way as he, and had found an excuse to get past Janet and into her inner sanctum.

'I'd better show you the way. It's a bit of a rabbit warren, this old pile.'

Tom hovered in the entryway as Janet led Sannie through the living room and pointed down a corridor towards the rear of the house. Tom noted the way Sannie's eyes scanned the walls, the coffee table, the piano, the fireplace. Tom heard a dull bass beat from upstairs. The gothic daughter, he presumed.

Janet walked back to where Tom stood, effectively quarantining him just inside the door. 'I wasn't expecting this,' she said in a low voice.

'Inspector Van Rensburg is making good headway in tracking down the suspects, ma'am.'

'Stop talking like a politician, Mr Furey. You gave me a clear indication that we would be talking off the record. I don't want anything I say to reflect badly on my husband's name – for the sake of the government, our children, and for *my* sake.' She folded her arms. 'Perhaps you should just leave.'

She was an attractive woman. Blue eyes and auburn hair, held back in a simple ponytail. She was slender – about five-six, he reckoned – with flawless English rose skin but the wrinkled upper lip of a heavy smoker. He smelled tobacco on her as well. She was in her midforties, he thought. Greeves had chosen well. Looks, breeding, and money – and a few years younger than himself.

'Like me, ma'am, Inspector Van Rensburg has no official jurisdiction here in England.'

'That's a very frank admission. I definitely think you should leave as soon as she's finished.'

'What it means,' Tom held out his open hands, 'is that we're not here to record what you say or take down a statement. I'll be honest. We – that is, the detectives involved in the case – are running into dead ends both here and in Africa.'

'All very well but, as I told you on the phone, I've told the investigating officers everything I can remember about Robert's movements leading up to his last trip.'

Janet turned at the sounds of Sannie's footsteps behind her. 'You have a lovely house, Mrs Greeves.'

She nodded. 'Shall we walk?'

Sannie nodded too and winked at Tom behind

Janet's back as she led them down the flagstones towards a converted barn which, judging by the lace curtains in the window, didn't house animals any more. Sannie lengthened her stride until she was walking beside the other woman.

'Your husband really loved Africa,' Sannie said. 'Did you travel with him often?'

'Once, on an official visit – for a conference to which spouses were invited – and once on a holiday, with the children.'

Tom had the same thought as Sannie, evidently, because she said, 'But he went several more times for pleasure, didn't he? By himself?'

'It wasn't always convenient for us to take holidays at the same time, and you're not quite right. Sometimes he tacked on a few days of recreation at the end of his official trips. That ghastly newspaper the *World* tried to make out he took holiday trips at the taxpayers' expense, but they were wrong.'

Sannie murmured that she understood. 'Did you ever consider investing, buying property in Africa?'

'He spoke about it every now and then.'

'Where was Mr Greeves's favourite place in Africa?'

'Lake Malawi. Look, what's all this got to do with his death?' Janet slowed her stride to make eye contact with Sannie.

'Mrs Greeves, it's important that we know as much as possible about your husband – not only his movements, but everything about his personal and private life – if we are to find out how and why he, and those around him, were targeted.'

379

Janet spoke slowly, as though trying to communicate with a foreigner. 'I – told – the – police – everything.'

Sannie nodded. 'Yes, except about the affair. Who was it with?'

Tom was half a pace behind them. He'd sensed that it was important for Sannie to try to build a rapport with Janet, and the simple act of her taking charge of the conversation and walking in step seemed to be working.

'Off the record?'

'For now,' Sannie said. 'You know I can't be more definite than that. However, you have my word that nothing of what you say will be communicated to the media by myself or Detective Sergeant Furey, and no other police officers here or in South Africa will need to know unless it is undeniably linked to future enquiries.'

'At least you're honest.' Janet drew a deep breath and slowed her pace. 'Nick Roberts.'

Tom's eyes widened, and he was pleased Janet couldn't see his face.

'Your husband's bodyguard?' Sannie, Tom thought, did a better job than he of masking her surprise. He was momentarily confused. Were Nick and Robert Greeves bisexual?

'Yes,' Janet said. Having breached some invisible barrier, the words started to tumble out. 'He was around the house all the time, and we often found our-selves together, in public and in private, while Robert was making a speech or holding private meetings. He was a good-looking man – attentive, and interested in me as a person, not just as Robert's political accessory.

380

I can't tell you how hard it's been grieving for two men – one in private and one in public. Not revealing my true feelings. There, I've said it.'

'Your husband didn't know?' Sannie managed to make the question sound empathetic rather than accusatory.

Janet shook her head. 'I doubt he would have cared. Probably would have been mad that it was Nick, but no, the fact that I was sleeping with another man wouldn't have unduly concerned him. We had what you might call an unspoken arrangement.'

'So if he was having an affair . . . ?'

Janet looked at Sannie and stopped. Tom stayed a pace behind them. 'I've told you, as I've told the others, everything I know about my husband's movements, publicly and privately for, oh, two weeks prior to his departure for Africa. In answer to your question, though, his schedule would not have allowed him fifteen minutes with anyone I was unaware of for at least a month prior to his death.'

'But he'd slept with at least one other woman,' Tom said. Sannie and Janet turned to face him, as if only now aware of his presence. 'Have you ever heard of an African woman named Precious Tambo, who also went by the name of Ebony?'

A laugh escaped Janet's mouth, then she seemed to make an effort to compose herself. 'My husband would never have slept with a woman.'

'You're saying he was gay?' Sannie asked.

Janet took a pace away from both of them and looked at Tom, then Sannie, spending a couple of seconds simply gazing at each of the detectives. Tom saw the faraway look in her eyes, as though her mind was processing some new information, and the hint of a smile flash across her face then disappear just as quickly.

'You came here thinking *he* was having an affair, with a woman, didn't you?'

Tom and Sannie glanced at each other, but said nothing.

'What a stupid bloody berk I've just been! I've spilled my guts to you about Nick and me, thinking that somehow my being with him might have compromised him, might have kept him from doing his duty sometime, or distracted him from the job of looking after Robert. But that wasn't it at all, was it? You came here to drag Robert's name through the mud. Bloody hell.'

'Mrs Greeves –' Tom held up a hand, but she cut him short.

'Get out. Get off my property right now.'

'Janet . . .'

'I'm calling my lawyer. I'd leave if I were you.'

'How bad was it, Janet?' Tom asked.

She paused, holding the phone up, showing him she was searching for the lawyer's name in the memory. 'What?'

'How bad was what he did to you, to your family?'

'Robert's dead. It doesn't matter.' Janet sounded bitter rather than relieved. She let her hand drop, the phone hanging limp by her side as her anger abated. She looked away from them, back towards her home. 'We have a fine son and a daughter who is finding her way. Robert never hurt either of them and they'll have a hard enough time in life without a father. They need never know. It's best for the Party and the government as well that Robert died a hero.'

'Tell us, please,' Sannie said. 'They need never know what? It might be crucial to finding his killers.'

'No, Inspector, it won't make a jot of difference, and I have nothing more to say to either of you. Please go and leave me, my children and my late husband in peace. Believe me, it's better this way.'

'And if his killers go free?' Sannie, Tom saw, was having a hard time maintaining her cool exterior.

Janet shrugged, lifted the phone and started to dial.

'Come on,' Tom whispered. 'Let's go.'

In the car, Sannie checked her watch for the third time in ten minutes as Tom hurtled back down the M40 towards London. 'Relax, I'll have you there in plenty of time.'

'I'm regretting going to see that woman already.'

Tom shrugged. 'Nothing we can do about it now. And it definitely helped, having you there. I don't think she would have opened up quite as much to me if I was alone.'

'So, was Greeves bisexual, or a closet gay? Was that his big secret?'

Tom indicated and overtook a lorry, turning on the windscreen wipers to clear the sooty, exhaust-coloured sleet from the hire car's windscreen. 'Well, he slept with a stripper, we know that much. It was odd, though, that Janet seemed so incredulous that he was having an affair with a woman.'

'Does any of this – their personal life – have a connection to the abductions or the terrorists?'

Tom thought about the question. There were surprises at every turn in this investigation, not the least of which was the revelation that Nick Roberts had been having an affair with the wife of the man he was supposed to be protecting. 'Nick was privy to all the family's secrets, by the look of it. I reckon that as well as going to the newspapers, Precious Tambo probably contacted Greeves direct. Greeves might have sent Nick to negotiate with her, and maybe make her an offer bigger than anything Fisher or Carney could match.'

'Well, they don't look like they're short of money.'

Tom nodded. 'Interesting that she didn't share her husband's passion for Africa.'

'Hmm. You picked up on that "*he*" spoke about buying property rather than "*we*".'

'Sounds like they would have been spending their retirements on different continents,' Tom said.

Another thought came to the forefront of his mind. It was something he had been mulling over for the past two days. 'Have your people done an analysis of the video tapes of Nick and Greeves being executed?'

'No,' Sannie said. 'We've asked to see them, but so far your government won't even send us a copy. We've seen tapes of Greeves's appearance on the television, but that's all. We've been told we'll get the results once your security service people have gone over them.'

That in itself was interesting. The video stored on the hard drive of the portable playback unit hadn't gone into police custody. Tom imagined that the SAS had handed it over to the Secret Intelligence Service, which would have had a representative present at the operations base in South Africa.

The traffic became thicker and slower as they closed in on London, joining the A40 when the M40 ended, stop-starting their way through the western outskirts of the capital. 'Shepherd's Bush – you'll be right at home here. This is where all the *japies* hang out.'

She looked out the window at the rows of shops, terraces and tenement blocks. 'I don't know how so many people can cram into one city. I'm claustrophobic already.'

Tom gave a sparse sightseeing commentary as they crawled along. When she saw a sign telling them they were in Notting Hill, Sannie said, 'I remember the movie. With Hugh Grant and Julia Roberts. Lovely.'

'I remember the race riots here, in 1976. I was just a kid, but it was ugly.'

'Same year as Soweto. I hope we're learning, Tom.'

Talking of Africa, there was something else he remembered that he wanted to ask Sannie. 'What do you know about monkeys?'

She looked at him askance. 'A little. I grew up with them all around me on the farm, and I see them in the bush sometimes. Why?'

'How would the terrorists have captured them?'

'It wouldn't be hard. If you park a car with some food in it – bananas, bread, marshmallows; anything, really – they'll get into it. All you'd have to do is put some bait in the back of a *bakkie* and be quick enough to lock them in. You could dart them, too, I suppose.'

'What about the one that was tied down to the bed? Are they easy to hold down?'

'No ways, man,' Sannie said, shaking her head vigorously. 'They'd bite and scratch you nearly to death. That one would have been darted or doped somehow. What are you thinking, Tom?'

He ignored her question, pointing out Hyde Park on their right as they cruised past. They crossed the Thames on Vauxhall Bridge, and when they turned left onto the Albert Embankment, Tom pointed out the office block where SO1 Specialist Protection was housed, Tintagel House, and landmarks between it and the hotel where Sannie was staying, a short walk away.

'Here we are,' he said, stopping the car outside the Thistle. 'Let's meet up after you've finished with Shuttleworth, but I don't want to be seen too close to work, given that I'm not supposed to be working the case.'

'What about near the Houses of Parliament somewhere – I'd like to take a look at the Palace of Westminster from the outside, before the inquiry, get my bearings,' Sannie said.

'Perfect,' Tom said. 'When you're finished, walk back across the river on Lambeth Bridge. There's a pub across the road from the palace, called St Stephen's Tavern. I'll be there in two hours, by which time you'll hopefully be finished. I'm going to find an internet cafe in the meantime.'

Sannie paused before opening the car door. 'Do you think Janet Greeves will have called your Chief Inspector Shuttleworth?'

'I'm afraid so. Good luck.'

24

Back in her hotel room, Sannie brushed her hair, fixed her makeup and walked back out into the bitter London cold. She found her way to Waterloo station and bought a British Rail ticket for the one-stop ride to Vauxhall. Already she was confused. As well as the London Underground – the tube, which she had heard about – apparently there were other trains.

The station was overwhelming, with its throngs of people rushing past her. Everyone seemed to know where they were going. She stopped a young man to ask directions, but he only spoke Spanish. An elderly English woman was more helpful. The train was warm but crowded.

By the time she alighted at Vauxhall's mainline station she wondered whether it would have been easier, in fact, to walk. Using the A-Z Tom had loaned her, Sannie found her way back to the Thames and the Albert Embankment.

She recognised the distinctive architecture of

Vauxhall Cross, the home of Britain's overseas intelligence organisation, the Secret Intelligence Service – SIS or MI6 – from a James Bond film she'd seen.

It had to be the most ostentatious secret building in the world. It looked like some futuristic temple, inspired, though, by the ancient Mayan or Mesopotamian stepped pyramids. Deep green shoots of glass, which looked to be thick enough to stop a rocket, sprouted from its angular beige terraces. Security men dressed all in black added to the Hollywood image of the spies' nest, which was topped off by a pair of bizarre giant white springs, festooned in turn with satellite dishes and radio antennae.

If Vauxhall Cross was like something from a George Lucas movie, the Metropolitan Police's old office building further down the Albert Embankment was straight out of the days of black and white television. It was an office block in the truest sense. No funky futuristic lines here – just an uninspiring, faintly depressing, sixties monolith of pale concrete and red brick that was grubby with age.

A bored-looking civilian security guard asked for her identity and pointed the way across the marbled floor, the only concession to flamboyance in the building, to the lift lobby. When she got out of the lift the stone was gone, replaced by dirty grey carpet tiles. She came to a wooden door with a glass panel and pushed a buzzer. It seemed she was expected, because when she said her name to a woman squirrelled away somewhere inside, the electronic lock clicked and Sannie pushed open the door.

Before her was mostly empty office space which

could have been populated by any bunch of bureau-crats anywhere in the world. It was fitted out with computer workstations. Two men and a woman in plain clothes were tapping away on keyboards. A mousy woman with horn-rimmed glasses looked up and said, 'Inspector Rensburg, is it?' The woman spoke loud and slowly, in the way that ignorant tourists do when they think slowing their delivery and increas-ing their volume will somehow make a non-English speaker pick up a few words.

'Van Rensburg.'

'Chief Inspector Shuttleworth's waiting for you. Corner office.'

'*Baie dankie.*' Sannie smiled to herself as she headed for the office, and casually wiped her right hand on the side of her black pants. With her other she brushed an imaginary stray hair from her forehead.

A man in his early fifties, with a thinning pate and the deep-etched lines of stress defining his gaunt face, opened the door before she reached it and said, 'Hello, I'm David Shuttleworth. You must be Susan?'

It started cordially, with the pair of them making tea in the office kitchen before getting down to busi-ness. Outside, the sky was still a uniform grey and it seemed to match the skin tone of most of the people she'd so far seen in this cold, crowded city. She knew the politeness would soon disappear. Shuttleworth ushered her into his office, which was a fishbowl on one side of the floor. He lowered slimline blinds to stop the other detectives from peering in.

'I've had a call from Robert Greeves's widow,' Shuttleworth began.

Sannie sighed. It had been too much to hope that the woman's fear of some defamatory news about her husband leaking out might have led her to keep quiet about their unauthorised visit.

'Inspector Van Rensburg.' All trace of civility had fallen with the blinds. 'I have no authority over you, but let me assure you that you most certainly do not have any jurisdiction here to be interviewing relatives of a deceased British politician.'

'Of course not, Chief Inspector, and I'm –'

'If it were up to me I'd have you on the next plane back to South Africa. Do you not think that we've looked into Robert Greeves's home life already?'

Sannie knew that any response from her at this point would be the wrong one, so she kept her silence.

'I know Furey's looking for someone else to put the blame on, some slip-up by Greeves or Roberts that might have made it inevitable that the terrorists would kill them, and that there was nothing Tom could have done to prevent it. But that is not the case.'

Sannie wasn't so sure about that, but again she held her tongue.

'From what I heard about you while I was in South Africa you're lucky to be still on the job. You let him lead you off on a wild-goose chase that –'

'That very nearly caught the people responsible and freed the hostages.'

Shuttleworth was having none of it. He stood and put his hands on his desktop, then leaned forward, closing the distance between them. 'Very nearly is not good enough. You two were playing catch-up all the time, and the villains outran you. Simple as that.'

'Tom Furey was the only one on the trail of those men and it wasn't his fault that they got away. Those are the facts of this case, and that's what I'll be telling your parliamentary inquiry, Chief Inspector.'

Shuttleworth sat down again and smoothed his tie. He looked, Sannie thought, like a man who did not raise his voice very often, especially not to women. She saw him struggling to retrieve his dour, unflustered demeanour. She also saw it as her opportunity to start questioning him. 'When will the South African Police Service be given copies of the execution tapes?'

Shuttleworth frowned. 'They'll get our analysis of the tapes when I do.'

'So you don't have them?'

He sighed. 'The SAS handed them over to the security service. They have their own state-of-the-art video analysis and forensics people. They'll do as thorough a job as anyone else.'

Sannie could sense the man's annoyance, not at her but, as she had guessed, at the fact that a government agency other than the police had grabbed such important evidence and was not sharing it; he had given her the company line and wasn't happy about it. The police were spinning their wheels in this investigation, and it clearly rankled the Scotsman.

Shuttleworth lifted his chin. 'How are your people doing with the burned-out vehicle and lists of people who entered the Kruger Park in the days before the abductions?'

Sannie explained that the licence plates on the torched Isuzu belonged to another vehicle. 'It was a BMW sedan which was car-jacked two days before the abductions. However, the registration number didn't show up on the lists of vehicles entering the park, which means the gang must have switched plates after entering. The chassis number was traced to the current owner, a Pakistani surgeon living in Pretoria.'

Shuttleworth's eyes widened at her mention of the doctor's heritage.

'Doctor Pervez Khan hasn't fit the profile of a terrorist suspect so far, though,' she admitted. 'We've checked him out. Wealthy, single – divorced, actually. A drinker and a bit of a midlife-crisis party boy, from what the detectives investigating him so far have learned.'

'They've questioned him, then?'

'No. He didn't show up at his practice two days before Greeves and Joyce were taken. Our missing persons unit already had a file open on him. His business partner reported him gone. Best guess so far is that he was car-jacked and killed. We've circulated his photo and a description of the destroyed vehicle to the media, but had no witnesses come forward.'

'Why would a doctor be driving an old pick-up truck?'

Sannie nodded. She had asked the investigating officers the same thing. Doctor Khan, she explained to Shuttleworth, owned a small holding in the Timbavati private nature reserve, on the border of Kruger, and used the four-wheel drive as a second vehicle for going to his bush retreat. 'His late-model Mercedes was in for a service at the time he went missing, so he was using his *bakkie* as a temporary replacement.'

Shuttleworth asked if the police had checked out

the doctor's lodge for signs of recent occupation. 'The detectives who visited his lodge said there was no sign of any recent vehicle movements, and the caretaker, an elderly African man who lived there with his wife, said the "boss" had not visited for weeks.'

'Hmm. So we can add the good doctor to our list of victims, then?'

'I suppose so. Even if he was involved with the gang, he'd be pretty stupid to use his own vehicle, changed plates or not. Also, his name doesn't show up on the national park's entry register. In fact, on that day there were no names recorded of people riding in or driving Isuzus that sounded remotely Pakistani.'

'Are you ready to face the inquiry tomorrow?' he asked her, changing the subject.

Sannie didn't know if one could ever truly be ready to go under the spotlight in a parliamentary inquiry, but she had resolved that all she could do was truthfully answer any question put to her, and she told Shuttleworth as much.

'You spent quite a bit of time with Tom Furey in Africa.'

'What's that got to do with me giving evidence?'

'It's not looking good for him, you know.'

She'd gathered as much from the newspaper reports, and from what Tom had told her himself. 'I won't be lying or omitting evidence, if that's what you're suggesting.' She had had enough of the glum-faced, bloodless creature across the desk from her. Tom would be well rid of him.

*

Outside, the gloomy weather matched her mood as she walked alongside the drab choppy waters of the Thames. It might have been beautiful on a sunny day, but even though it was only early afternoon the sky was the colour of elephant hide.

Crossing the river on Lambeth Bridge she had a good view of the Palace of Westminster, the seat of the British parliament, and the tower of Big Ben, which stood like a burly guardsman on sentry duty over the historic building.

When she crossed the bridge she saw two policemen standing on the corner of Horseferry Road. One had a Glock, with spare magazines in pouches wrapped around his thigh, while the other carried a Heckler & Koch MP-5, nine-millimetre submachine gun. Coming from Johannesburg, she was used to seeing police with guns – even security guards in her country carried semiautomatic assault rifles – but she knew that in England it was a fairly recent phenomenon. She wondered if the pale-faced, bundled-up people who strode determinedly past her were reassured or concerned by the presence of the armed officer.

She made her way, by dead reckoning, through the back streets of Westminster, out of sight of the river, towards Parliament. In a lane called Strutton Ground she stumbled on a small street market, the wares encased in clear plastic sheeting. Behind the rain-beaded covers, one stall appeared before her, like an oasis in the desert. Overcoats!

'Hello, my love, can I help you?' a middle-aged man wearing two fleeces and a windcheater asked her, rubbing his gloved hands together in anticipation.

The coats were not great quality but looked deliciously warm. Sannie tried on a couple before settling on a mock-tweed garment that was nipped fashionably at the waist and came to her knees. The cardboard sign on the rack said thirty pounds. She did a quick mental calculation and decided it was not a good idea to convert British prices into South African rand. Thirty sounded much better than three hundred and thirty and, besides, now that she felt a glimmer of warmth returning to her body, there was no way she was going to take the jacket off.

As she walked, the one hundred per cent artificial fibres started doing their job and she even managed to smile, unlike most of the grim-faced Londoners who motored on through the rain around her.

On the Broadway, where Tom said it would be, was New Scotland Yard. The revolving sign in front of the police building – which, again, she recognised from movies and TV programs – was smaller than she expected. Armed police guarded the entrance, behind crash barriers which she presumed were designed to stop car bombers.

Sannie continued on and the Houses of Parliament appeared in front of her as she rounded a corner, looming large like a fairytale palace, some gold trimming breaking the monotone. She would see the inside of the workings of British democracy soon enough, and for now she veered off to the left of the buildings, following the directions Tom had given her to St Stephen's Tavern.

He was waiting for her at a small booth in the far corner, and stood and waved to her when she walked in. The warmth was welcoming after her chilly walk, even if the place did smell of stale beer, wet clothes and musty body odour. Tom offered to buy her a drink and she asked for a gin and tonic.

'A reminder of Africa,' he said, placing the tall dewy glass in front of her.

'Cheers. After meeting your boss I wish I'd never left. When did they exhume him?'

Tom laughed. 'Shuttleworth's not a bad guy when you get to know him. He's a pragmatist, though, and he knows a scalp's needed in order for the government to get past all this. Unfortunately, it has to be mine.'

She stirred her drink and looked around her. With its high ceiling and stained-glass windows, the pub could have been part of a palace as well. 'You're sounding remarkably upbeat, all things considered.'

He shrugged and sipped his lager. 'I cocked up, Sannie, there's no two ways about it.'

She was curious as to why he no longer seemed to care about his career but was also showing no sign of letting the investigation rest. 'So, what were you doing while I was getting the Scottish inquisition?'

Tom told her he'd been to an internet cafe and had found more reports about Greeves, his career and his frequent trips to Africa. 'Have you ever been to Malawi?'

Sannie shook her head. 'It's somewhere we – I – always wanted to go. Funny, it's still hard for me to think of myself as a singular rather than a plural.'

'I know how you feel – although Mr and Mrs Greeves certainly didn't have that problem.'

'I'd like to take my kids to Malawi as well. They say

the lake is gorgeous and it'd be a fun trip up through Botswana and Zambia.'

'Yes, I was checking the route on the internet.'

'What are you thinking, Tom?'

She was starting to wonder if he actually was as fine as he made out. Certainly, it was good that he had a positive attitude rather than wallowing in depression. There was something else going on in his mind, though. Had he come up with a new lead while she was being grilled by his superior? She asked him the question.

'No, I don't think the kidnappers would have taken Greeves to Malawi if he was still alive,' he said. 'But I'd like to go there.'

'Why?'

'I liked what I saw of Africa – given the circumstances – and I think I'll soon have a bit of time on my hands. I was thinking of hiring a car and driving from South Africa up to Malawi.'

Sannie was suspicious, but played along. 'That would be expensive. I've got a Land Rover. It was Christo's pride and joy, but I hardly ever drive it any more. We only use it when the kids and I go to the bush. You could borrow it.'

'I'd pay you,' he said.

She shrugged. 'Give it a service and a good run and you'll be doing me a favour.'

They finished their drinks and Sannie went to the bar to buy a second round. While she waited for the barman – a young white South African guy with dreadlocks who, when he heard her accent, told her he was from Durban – she thought about what Tom had just said. Was he hoping to stay with her, perhaps travel with her?

'You look like the weight of the world's on your shoulders,' the barman said, sliding the pint of lager and another gin and tonic across to her.

'I'm afraid it is.' Sannie carried the drinks back and appraised Tom as she walked. He would forever carry the stigma of implied failure if the inquiry went the way everyone expected. Even abroad he might find it hard to get gainful work. Did she really want to have anything to do with someone without prospects? She had her children to think about. However, he was very handsome and she knew he was a good man. She felt comfortable around him – safe, which was ironic considering that he was always getting her into trouble. And when he smiled, as he did when she set down the drinks, she felt her heart beat a little faster.

'Well, let's drink to your next trip to Africa,' Sannie said, raising her glass. 'It can't be any worse than your last!'

Tom laughed. 'To Africa.'

They left the pub after their second drink. Tom said he would drive Sannie back to her hotel and he didn't want to be over the legal limit. He'd asked her if she had any plans for dinner and, as she didn't, she agreed to let him choose a restaurant.

Once he parked the car, Tom suggested that as it was still early they have another drink, in the hotel bar, before dinner. The first two had made her feel mellow and she agreed, although she switched to white wine as too many gins sometimes made her feel maudlin. 'Let me put it on my room,' she said as Tom went to pull out his wallet. 'The British government can pick up the tab.'

'Might be the closest I get to a retirement present,' he said, raising his lager.

'Stop talking like that, Tom.'

He raised his eyebrows at her stern tone.

'I mean it. Stop being so damned resigned to your fate.' She could feel her cheeks reddening, a combination of the alcohol and her sudden growing anger. 'You can't go down without a fight, man.'

He set his drink down. 'I'm just being realistic, Sannie, but I never said I'd stop fighting.'

'Tell me what you've got cooking. Why this sudden desire to go back to Africa?'

He nodded, as though it was a fair question. 'I'll need a fresh start. No one will give me a job here – not even as a night watchman at Tesco. In a sense, I've got nowhere else to go, so I may as well try Africa.'

She shook her head. 'I don't believe you. What else? There must be another reason.'

He swivelled on his stool at the bar, so that his body was facing her. He looked as though he was about to say something, but then thought better of it. 'Nothing,' he said. 'Let's go get dinner.'

'All right.' She felt disappointed, as if he'd been about to say something that would affect her. 'Okay, but I want to get changed.'

'I'll wait down here.'

'You'll be legless by the time I get back. Come up to my room and you can watch TV while I get ready.'

Why, Sannie wondered, as they walked across to the lifts, had she made such a suggestion? She could feel his eyes on her as she stood looking up at the illuminated floor numbers, waiting for the lift to arrive. It was too late now.

Once in her room she handed him the television remote. 'Make yourself at home. I'm going to shower as well.' Though she didn't want to say it in front of Tom in case he was offended, there was something about London that made her feel grimy. Between the overly heated indoor areas, which made her perspire, and the drizzle mixed with exhaust fumes and grit, she felt as though her skin was coated with a greasy layer of muck. Her fingernails, too, were filthy. She already missed the sun, even though she knew she'd be complaining about the heat in a month's time.

Sannie grabbed her toiletry bag, closed the bathroom door, slipped out of her shoes and stripped off her business suit. The high pressure blast of hot water invigorated her and she decided to wash her hair as well. She could hear the TV in the room, so she knew Tom would be fine.

It was odd, she thought, being naked in the bathroom, reapplying her makeup and knowing that Tom was just on the other side of the door. It wasn't until she went to hang up her towel on the hook that she realised she hadn't brought her clean clothes in with her. Her bag was still on the bed. She blamed the extra drink.

Sannie finished her makeup and wrapped the towel around her, knotting it between her breasts. The hotel was nice and clean, but was not the sort of place that offered fluffy white bathrobes.

'Excuse me,' she said, emerging.

Tom stood and looked at her. She felt his gaze on her, saw the way he tried to keep his eyes on hers. She was painfully conscious of the skin she was showing. Her legs, which she was proud of; and her arms, which could have used another day a week in the gym to keep them toned. She darted across the room and grabbed her bag. As she lifted it the flap fell open – she'd forgotten that she had opened it to get out her cosmetic bag.

'Oh, *fok*!'

'Here, let me help.'

Tom dropped to one knee, as did she, but Sannie had to use one hand to keep her towel held together. With the other, she scooped up bras and pants, shoes and strewn clothing. It was very embarrassing, but he started to laugh.

'Here, give me that.' She reached out and grabbed the white silk blouse he held.

They were close, kneeling on the floor, their faces less than a metre apart.

'Thank you,' Tom said, still holding onto the garment.

When she pulled it she felt his fingers through the sheath of silky material. 'For what?'

'For agreeing to come with me today, for everything you did in South Africa, for . . .'

'It's nothing.' Sannie still held the blouse and he wasn't surrendering it. She continued to feel the heat of his skin through her fingers as she wrapped the fabric around her hand. It wasn't nothing, though. She'd risked her career, her future – again – for this dark-haired handsome man kneeling next to her in a hotel room in a foreign land.

She was acutely aware of her own nakedness under the towel, and the growing feeling of warmth radiating from her core. It was him, the excitement, the recklessness, the remoteness of all this from her normal life. It was why she'd invited him into her hotel room.

Tom leaned closer and kissed her.

Time seemed to stand still then, and the kiss went on forever. They were two starving souls and they consumed each other, first kneeling on the floor, then sitting. She was aware of the towel falling away from her body. The feeling of his body against hers, the brush of her erect nipples against the cotton of his shirt, was electrifying. Her skin suddenly felt hypersensitive, tingling. When he moved his lips to the side of her neck and down her collarbone to the point where it joined her shoulder she thought she might faint in his arms. God, it had been so long since she'd felt this.

Sannie held it all together, every minute of every day. The demands of a job in a male-dominated profession in which she had to do it tougher, harder and better than any of them; the constant struggle to spend enough time with her kids and avoid the guilt of not being a stay-at-home mom; the moments of grief that still brought her to tears – sometimes it was all too much. But here, now, so far from home, she wanted nothing more than for him to take her away. Physically. Mentally. Sexually. She melted into him, but at the same time felt her body stiffening with spasms of pure pleasure with each touch of his lips to a new part of her.

He lifted her, as if he sensed that was exactly what she wanted, onto the bed, then shrugged off his jacket. He looked down at her and she opened herself to his gaze, revelling in the lasciviousness of it. He started to undo his tie and slip off one of his shoes. 'Don't bother,' she breathed.

His feet were still on the floor, his hands either side of her, as he leaned down over her. She reached for him, taking a few moments to trace the outline through his trousers, before slowly unzipping and dis-covering him.

He moved his hand between them, parting her, then finding her clitoris. She moaned and arched her back to push against his touch. She guided him to her as she felt his fingers, first one, then a second, enter her. She was more than ready for him, and when he withdrew she moved the head of his cock between her swollen lips.

'Sannie . . .'

'Yes, Tom. Oh, please . . .'

He entered her, like that, and she locked her hands around his neck and her legs around his waist. She lifted her hips to meet his thrust and he drove harder into her, so that her bottom was raised off the bed-spread at the end of the first long, slow stroke. Her eyes were locked on his as he paused there, and she felt weightless, balanced on him. A part of him.

Tom started moving and she almost didn't want to let him go from that place, until the friction started to work its magic, again and again. Holding her in his strong arms, he lowered his face to kiss alternately her lips, her cheek, the side of her neck, her collarbone again, on the spot that still burned from his first touch.

Sannie kept her eyes open as long as she could, imprinting every ridge and furrow of his face into her memory. If she didn't see him again after she left London, she wanted never to forget the man who had made her whole again. His every thrust sent another wave of pleasure through her.

And he, feeling her body grip, tighten and ripple over his cock, hearing her start to cry out, took up the pace, driving harder, yet still controlled, into her. She closed her eyes and drew her body up to his, moulding perfectly to him as she held him tight and cried again. As he joined her.

The guilt came, as Sannie knew it would, as Tom lay, naked, beside her an hour later. 'Room service will be here soon, I should get my clothes back on,' he said.

'I'll get dressed.'

'No, stay there.' He stood and pulled on his trousers and sat beside her on the bed as he buttoned his shirt. 'You're thinking about Christo, aren't you?'

She nodded, biting her lower lip.

'Me too – thinking about Alex, that is. I know I shouldn't be feeling guilty, it's not like you and I are having an affair . . .'

'I know, but . . .'

'But it's all right,' he said and by his tone she knew that he was reading her mind. Nothing that felt this good, this right, could be wrong. Christo would never leave her heart or her thoughts – and she realised Tom would cherish his wife forever, but he had made her complete again. She wanted to be back in his arms, to feel the safety of his embrace.

She reached out and grabbed his hand as he started to move. 'Yes, it is. All right, I mean.'

There was a knock at the door, followed by, 'Room service.'

Sannie made Tom take off his clothes again to eat dinner, despite his protesting that it was embarrassing. They sat opposite each other on the bed, eating cheeseburgers topped with bacon and egg, and a side order of fat greasy chips. If she was going to throw caution to the wind she might as well go all the way. Tom poured her champagne and they clinked glasses.

She told him more about growing up on the farm, and the first boy she'd ever kissed. When she admitted that Christo was the first man she'd ever slept with she saw realisation slowly spread across his face. To his credit, he said nothing after learning that he was the only man other than her husband whom she'd had sex with. He simply leaned forward, wiped some ketchup from the corner of her mouth with his finger, then kissed her.

They made love again after dinner and washed each other in a long, soapy bubble bath.

Later, with the lights off, he lay staring at the ceiling, one arm crooked behind his head, the other around her as she snuggled into him.

She ran her fingertips through the wiry hair on his chest. 'Are you thinking about the inquiry?'

'No,' he said. 'Africa.'

25

Tom weighed the folded pair of jeans in his hand then tossed them aside. His bag was nearly full, in any case, and he already had a pair of lightweight tan trousers in there.

The clock radio on his bedside table was tuned to an FM music station and the news came on at the top of the hour. He stopped his packing to listen. The second item was a direct lift from the morning's papers. The inquiry had ended the previous day and it was likely that Robert Greeves's bodyguard would not face charges over the Minister for Defence Procurement's abduction, but would 'remain on suspension pending the outcome of a departmental disciplinary hearing'. The bastard DJ that followed the newsreader had even made a joke about it. Tom snorted. None of it mattered.

The result was predictable, but Tom had been more interested in some of the evidence that had been presented than in the outcome. The inquiry had been held in the Boothroyd Room, one of the committee rooms in Portcullis House, the modern administrative neighbour and handmaiden to the grand old Palace of Westminster.

The room was named after Betty Boothroyd, a former speaker of the House of Commons. There had been a bronze bust of the formidable-looking woman on Tom's left as he had entered that first day. In front of him, through thick, bulletproof windows, was a view of the Thames that took in some office buildings, a quadrant of the London Eye and St Thomas' hospital.

The committee members, drawn from both the major parties and the Liberal Democrats, sat at beech-coloured desks formed into a large U-shaped arrangement. The chairman sat at the bottom of the U, resting a folder of notes on a thick glass lectern. Behind him was a tapestry of country fields, though for some reason it was all in shades of blue. Tom took one of the few vacant seats in the front of several rows of cloth-covered seats reserved for members of the public. In this case, that obviously meant the press, as he noticed a flurry of note-taking as he entered.

Inside the U was a small table with a man and woman sitting at it. There were notebooks in front of them. They were the recorders, and their position was lowered so that their heads were barely at the same level as the desktops at which the committee members sat. A bizarre little piece of subservience, Tom thought.

Looking around, he saw four television cameras mounted on the walls. Even though the media's cameras weren't invited, the proceedings were being recorded. Edited excerpts would be released to the media at the end of each day's session.

Over the first four days, before he had a chance to speak, Tom sat through the testimony of a string of police, forensic scientists, military people and 'foreign office' staffers whose names were suppressed from the public record. Spies, in other words. Tom had assumed that MI6 people would have accompanied the SAS task force, and he knew from what Shuttleworth had told Sannie that the SAS was playing a lead role in the ongoing hunt for the terrorists. There was nothing, however – perhaps deliberately, perhaps not – to indicate they were any closer to catching them.

Of particular interest to Tom was the senior civilian crime-scene investigator's testimony. Her name was Rachel Rubens. She told the inquiry she and a male colleague had been flown to the old farmhouse in Mozambique on an Oryx helicopter – back-loaded on the same aircraft which had brought Major Fraser, the first of his men and the body of Bernard Joyce to Hoedspruit air force base.

The public inquiry was being presided over by a government member of parliament, Miles Jensen. He was young for a politician, in his late thirties, and ambitious. Tom assumed he saw the high-profile chairmanship as a chance to make his mark with the media. He was persistent to the point of rudeness in his questioning, but Tom had been done over by professionals – lawyers – in his days as a uniformed constable appearing in court cases.

Jensen had asked Rachel to tell them about the

physical evidence in the villa relating to Robert Greeves and his tragic death.

'There was a quantity of hair found in the bathroom, mostly on the floor, and some strands on a sheet of newspaper. It was black and grey in colour and subsequently matched positively to a DNA sample obtained from Mr Greeves's home.'

'And the sample was obtained how?' Jensen queried.

'From one of Mr Greeves's hairbrushes in his London home. There was also blood and CSF in the bedroom where Mr Greeves was held captive, and four severed plastic cable ties.'

'CSF?'

'Sorry,' Rachel said. 'Cerebral spinal fluid. It's what surrounds the brain, in the skull. There was CSF mixed in with the blood, which is typical for this type of wound.'

'And these fluids, the plastic ties, were all subsequently matched to Mr Greeves?'

'Yes. The blood and CSF were a positive match and there were skin cells and some blood on the plastic ties, which we surmised had been used to bind his wrists and ankles to the bed on which he lay. There were also strands of Mr Greeves's hair in some of the bed springs, near where his head would have been.'

'And the pattern of the bloodstains? What can you tell us about that?'

Rachel took a sip from a glass of water on the table in front of her. Tom noticed that she glanced quickly around the room, though by the time he turned his head to see if he could spot who she was looking for, or at, she was already looking back at Jensen. 'It was consistent with the pattern resulting from a small-calibre gunshot to the head at close range – that is, where the blood has poured from the entry wound rather than been expelled via an exit wound.'

Jensen prompted her with a couple of other questions in answer to which she elaborated on the pattern on the floor of the room. It was gory stuff and Tom noticed a couple of pale, shocked faces among some of the politicians present. He wrote a word down on his notebook. *Consistent*.

'Thank you, Ms Rubens. Unless there is anything else you think might be of interest to the inquiry, I would like to thank you for your presence and your testimony.'

'There is one more thing,' she said. From the way he looked up from his notes at her, Tom guessed that Jensen had not been expecting any additions. He had, however, invited her to elaborate. 'The floor had been wiped.'

'Wiped?'

'Yes. The perpetrators had partially smeared the blood on the floor, wiping it with what we guessed was a rag, perhaps the size of a tea towel. Detective Sergeant Furey's initial report concluded that Mr Greeves's body had been dragged a short distance – about a metre – from where it fell, and was then wrapped in some sort of fabric. From fibres gathered at the scene we can say this was a wool and nylon mix blanket. While this is true, we also found evidence through a smearing pattern and other fibres – possibly from a tea towel – that the perpetrators had made some attempt to clean up the bloodstain, but perhaps gave up.'

'You found no such "tea towel", though?' Jensen asked.

'No. It was . . . well, we thought it was a bit odd.'

'How so?'

'Well, it wasn't like a sponge or a wet towel or anything. If they were trying to clean it off the wall they couldn't have done a worse job. All it did was spread it around, sort of smear the bloodstains.'

'I see,' Jensen said, in that way, Tom thought, that people do when they want to sound learned but really have no idea what to make of what they have just heard. 'Perhaps our terrorists weren't as professional as they seemed?'

'I don't know, Mr Chairman,' Rachel shrugged.

Having been suspended and therefore not included in the follow-up investigations, this was all new to Tom. It seemed, on the face of it, that all the correct boxes had been checked. The villa had been sealed off and gone over with a fine toothcomb; plaster casts had been made of footprints and tyre tracks where possible – not easy in the sand – and fingerprints lifted and cross-checked. The only prints that had been identified were Greeves's and Bernard's. The terrorists had apparently worn gloves the whole time, or wiped the place clean before they left.

Tom closed his suitcase and looked around the bedroom, making sure he hadn't forgotten anything. He patted the breast pocket of the single blazer he was taking – the navy blue one – and felt the passport and ticket folder. He had the case in one hand and a day pack with his carry-on stuff in the other. He kicked the bedroom door closed and walked down the stairs. Halfway down his cell phone started to ring, but as his hands were full he couldn't reach it.

Downstairs, in the hallway, he took out the phone and it beeped, telling him he had a message. 'Hi, it's me,' Sannie said on the recording. 'I'm about ten minutes away. I still don't know if this is such a good idea. Call me if you want me to keep driving.'

He thought about her, about the nights they had spent together. He'd invited her to stay at his place after the first day of the inquiry, but thankfully she'd gone back to her hotel first, to get some things. He'd arrived home to find Southwood Lane almost blocked by TV vans and unmarked newspaper cars. He'd slowed as he approached his home, then rammed his foot down on the accelerator as a couple of the vultures recognised him. Rather than give them the satisfaction of a car chase, he'd stopped at the tube station and made it onto a train before the first of the paparazzi had even found his car. He'd taken refuge, hating that he'd run from his own home, in Sannie's hotel room. He couldn't have risked going out again later in the evening in case they trailed him to Sannie, and he couldn't not see her again.

She was what had kept him going as the case mounted against him, and he loved her for the way she was sticking by him. Even when she was giving the evidence that sealed his fate, he'd known by the

412

quick glances she'd given him as he spoke that she would see him through this.

'Inspector Van Rensburg.' Jensen had paused to clear his voice. 'Tell the inquiry, if you will, what Bernard Joyce said to you and Detective Sergeant Thomas Furey on the beach in Mozambique just before he took his own life.'

Sannie gave a précis of the statement that Tom had typed up from his notes, which had already been tendered to the inquiry as written evidence. Having it in writing wasn't enough. Jensen was an astute enough media player to know that the press needed someone saying all this. Without Sannie's account the words might not be available in the public domain until the full transcripts were released with the inquiry findings. That could be weeks away. The reporters who crammed the room had been biding their time, and not at all patiently, for this moment. Jensen, Tom reckoned, had probably tipped off a few, because it seemed there were more journalists in there at that moment than there had been since the opening session.

'Yes, that was Mr Joyce reflecting on his own actions – his belief, which most of us would disagree with – that he could have done more to save Mr Greeves. But there was more, wasn't there, Inspector?'

Tom saw her eyes shift to him and he prayed none of the reporters had been sharp enough to catch and understand it. 'Yes,' she said.

Jensen drew out, word by painful word, Bernard's assertion that during his abduction he had cried out to Tom for help.

And, as Jensen had pointed out in his summation

after Sannie had stood down, the record of evidence had already shown that Detective Sergeant Furey had slept soundly – after consuming alcohol, and entertaining the female manager of the luxury safari lodge in which he was quartered – and had apparently not heard Bernard Joyce's call for help.

Tom was finished even before he took the stand, as he'd known he would be all along. It didn't hurt any less, though, knowing the outcome. He reckoned he'd put on a brave face. He'd answered every question put to him fully and honestly, even as the words chipped away at any vestige of residual professional respect he might have held onto.

'Did you take any illegal drugs that night, Detective Sergeant?'

'I did not.'

It seemed to be the only positive thing he'd said during the preceding fifty minutes of his testimony.

'I remind you, you are under oath, Detective Sergeant Furey.'

'You don't need to remind me of that.' It was the closest he'd allowed himself to sarcasm or resentment of Jensen. He didn't like the man – the way he fawned on the press, or the way he treated the SAS major, Fraser, like a little tin god to be bowed and scraped to – but Jensen was simply doing his job. His mission was to find a scapegoat and it had been all but done before the inquiry had opened.

Jensen had let the words slide. The media had already been leaked reports of the cocaine found in Tom's room, and official statements from Pretoria and Scotland Yard had confirmed that no charges had been laid against him. Other evidence, including some of Sannie's, had already established that Carla was crooked, and the media had come around to the idea that the drugs were part of a set-up. Not that it helped Tom, of course, who was being painted as at best gullible; at worst negligent in his duty to the point of criminality.

The truth, Tom thought, as he moved his bags to the doorstep and locked the front door, was where it usually sat – somewhere in between the best and worst of what people believed. He'd done a good job tracking and almost catching the terrorists – and Shuttleworth assured him this would come out in the findings, as the government needed something remotely positive to highlight – but he had been seduced, morally if not physically, by Carla. Whether or not she had drugged him, he had to admit he'd drunk alcohol, and this was against regulations – no matter what the quantity. And, although he had made it plain in his evidence that he did not have sex with her – the inference being he was too sedated to fuck her – he had let her into his room, with some intent to bed her.

Two men died as a result of his actions. He would have to live with the guilt he felt over Bernard's death for the rest of his life; Bernard had made sure of that.

This was a good time for him to be leaving – late in the evening. The newspapers had passed their deadlines for the next morning, so there was little point in staking out his home at this time of day. There would be no fresh angles until the release of the inquiry's final report and recommendations. This morning's papers had summed up the highlights of the last day. *DRUGGED, DRUNK BODYGUARD SLEPT THROUGH AIDE'S CRIES FOR HELP*, read the headline above the fold on the newspaper that Tom tossed into the bin outside his house. He'd forwarded the mail to his cousin's place in Kent and cancelled the papers. He didn't know when he'd be back in England. Technically, he supposed he shouldn't be leaving the country without telling Shuttleworth. His absence would be noted when the inquiry reconvened to hand down its judgement.

'Fuck 'em,' Tom said to himself. He saw the little red Ford Focus come round the corner and slow to a crawl as Sannie checked the house numbers. She'd never seen his home, but that didn't matter now.

Sannie saw him, flashed her lights and waved through the arc of the slashing wiper blade. Tom ignored the drizzle and waved back. When she stopped he looked up and down the darkened street again, making sure there were no photographers lurking. Sannie said that her bags were in the boot, so he slung his on the back seat and got into the passenger's seat. She leaned across and kissed him. She tasted like a promise of sunshine.

'I was wondering if you'd be here. Did you get my message?'

He nodded. 'I was still packing. Did you really think I wouldn't want to leave?'

'I don't know. I think it's the best thing for you.'

'You don't sound convinced.'

'It's because I'm not. It's okay if you want some time out, to wait until the media storm blows over, but if

416

you're running away you might never be able to run far enough.'

'I'm not running away.' He buckled his seatbelt and stared straight out the windscreen.

'I know.' She changed gear and pulled away from the kerb, then let her hand rest on his knee. 'And that worries me too. I think you might be chasing something.'

He raised his eyebrows.

'I think you might be chasing a phantom.'

Tom's airline seat was in economy, while Sannie's return ticket was business class. She tried to get him upgraded at the check-in at Heathrow, but her section was full. 'We can swap halfway through, if you like,' she'd offered.

'I'd better get used to economy from now on. No more business and first on the job for me.' He'd paid for the ticket out of his savings and while he wasn't short of money – he had enough to travel for six months if he wanted – there would be no more where that came from unless he eventually found a job of some sort. The pension he'd worked more than twenty years for was just a dream now.

While he couldn't get an upgrade, Sannie was able to get him into the BA lounge, and Tom downed three beers to Sannie's single gin and tonic. 'It'll get me through cattle class,' he explained.

They sat together on a two-seater lounge and held hands in between sipping their drinks. 'Tom, we haven't even discussed where you'll be staying.'

She'd offered to lend him a vehicle for his

travels – the Land Rover Defender had sat virtually unused in her garage since Christo's death – but they hadn't had time to discuss any further details of his visit.

'I was planning on getting a hotel room near the airport and coming out to see you the day after we arrive – to check out this vehicle of yours, if it's still on offer,' he said.

'Of course you can still have the bloody truck, Tom. But I want you to come stay with me. For as long as you want. I've been thinking about it over the last twenty-four hours.'

'What about your kids?'

'That's mostly what I've been thinking about. I wouldn't do anything to hurt them, but they liked you the last time and at least they've met you once. I've got a small guest flat at the back of the garage. It's yours if you want it.'

He leaned over and kissed her on the cheek. 'Of course I want it. I don't know where I'll end up, Sannie, but it's nice to know I've got somewhere to start.'

'Have you got any idea where you'll go?'

He shrugged and picked up his beer, taking a long swig. He was, she thought, either avoiding answering the question or really had no idea where he was going. She thought the first of these was correct. He was still holding something important back from her. This whole running away to Africa idea didn't ring true; it didn't make sense that he would find solace or escape in a continent where his career had come to a shuddering, bloody halt. He was after something – someone. If he was going after the terrorists alone, he was mad. Dangerously mad. While she'd broken the rules on his account several times, she was not going to drive off into the wilds of Africa with Tom, toting her nine-millimetre in her handbag to back him up. Of that she was certain. The combined resources of the South African, British and American governments were looking for those men. Tom Furey couldn't achieve what police, spies and satellites had failed to. Could he?

Their flight was called and they parted in the queue to board. He kissed her and told her he would see her at the other end.

Yes, she thought, but for how long?

26

'*Wat doen jy?*' Tom, lying on his back under the Land Rover, turned his head at the sound of the voice and saw a pair of small bare feet and skinny golden-brown legs.

Tom's hand was drenched with hot black oil as he unscrewed the plug in the engine sump and let it flow into the tin bowl. His own legs, in shorts, were already starting to turn pink, he noticed as he used his elbows and feet to slide himself fully into the open. He recognised the young voice and the boy standing there, but had no idea what he was saying.

He held up a hand to shield his eyes from the sun's bright glare. 'Hello, Christo. Remember me? I'm Tom.' The boy's face was haloed by the afternoon sun. Tom wiped his brow with the back of his clean arm. The heat was a shock all over again after London.

The boy nodded. 'What you doing?' he asked again, in English.

Tom sat up, grabbed a rag he'd found in the garage, and wiped his hand as best as he could. The sump hadn't been drained since the boy's father's death, and who knew how long before that. It stained his hand black. 'I'm changing the oil. Have a look underneath. You can see it draining out.'

Christo shook his head. 'This is my dad's *bakkie*.'

Tom saw the boy's frown and his little brow furrow in concentration as he tried to work out what was going on. Good luck, matey, Tom thought. 'I know. Your mum's letting me borrow it for a little while.'

'Where are you going?'

'On a bit of a holiday.'

The boy nodded. 'Mom's taking us to the Kruger Park for the weekend. Ouma's coming as well.'

'That's nice.' Tom guessed Ouma was Sannie's mother, Elise, who had collected them from the airport, shortly after she had dropped Christo and his little sister, Ilana, at school. Elise had smiled when Sannie introduced Tom to her, but he detected no warmth in her eyes. It would take time – if he had it. He didn't tell Christo that he was planning on accompanying them to the national park and setting off on the rest of his journey from there. He'd let Sannie break the news.

'Are you coming to live with us after your holiday?'

How the hell should I know? Tom thought. 'I don't know, Christo. Hey, I've got something for you.'

The youngster's eyes lit up. Tom left the sump draining and walked into the comparative cool of the converted granny flat in which he was staying. He'd left the airconditioner running, but it seemed to be struggling in the heat. As a last-minute thought he'd stopped in a souvenir shop at Heathrow and bought a football with Manchester United's logo emblazoned on it.

'Cool!' Christo bounced it straightaway and kicked it, hard enough to reach the brick security wall. It bounced back at him and he dived across the grass to catch it, like a goalie.

Tom laughed as he pulled on a T-shirt. 'Good work.' He saw Elise watching them through the kitchen windows. A black maid was standing next to her, and Sannie's mother was saying something to the woman but keeping her eyes on Tom. He smiled at her but she did not return the gesture. He mentally shrugged it off.

'Mom will be home soon and then we can use the swimming pool, but not before,' Christo informed him. 'Ouma can't swim,' he whispered. Tom nodded, sharing the confidence.

Elise came to the back door. 'Christo! Come in here and have some milk. I have baked some treats as well.' She held a plate of biscuits, which Tom could smell from the other side of the swimming pool.

'Yay!' Christo forgot his questioning and his soccer ball and scampered for the house. Elise ruffled his hair as she steered him towards the house. She disappeared inside the kitchen again, but returned with a bottle of Castle Lager.

'Here, Tom. It looks like you could use a beer after your work,' she said. The corners of her mouth were curling upwards slightly. She walked towards him. 'Come, let us sit in the shade.'

'I'm not finished yet, not by half, but a beer would be lovely, thanks.' He hoped this signalled a defrosting, but he wasn't banking on it. Elise led him to a wrought-iron outdoor table and chairs, underneath a shady tree with red flowers.

'Sannie's husband loved that truck.'

Tom opened the beer and took a long, grateful sip. 'It's kind of Sannie to lend it to me. I'll bring it back in one piece.'

'It's not the Land Rover I'm worried about getting broken, Tom.'

Well, he thought, at least she didn't waste time coming to the point. 'I'm not here to hurt anyone.'

She waved her hand, possibly shooing a fly away, but it also had the effect of brushing his words aside. 'My daughter was just coming right after the death of her husband. I know what she did with you – for you – in Mozambique. I can't forgive her for that, but it's in the past. She knows she shouldn't have taken such risks, with her life and her job, but she did it because of you.'

It was as much an accusation as a statement of fact, he thought. There was no way he could argue with the woman, though.

'Don't lead this family into more danger, Tom.'

He took another drink. 'I won't. Where I'm going, what I'm doing . . . I'll be on my own.'

Elise nodded. 'Good. That's her car now.'

Sannie had gone into the office midmorning to report in to Wessels on the inquiry and her trip. She told Tom she had no plans to mention the Englishman staying in her flat, and he had agreed that was a good idea. She'd been released from work early, though, to spend some more time with her kids. Christo came running from the house, a biscuit in his hands. Ilana, who had avoided Tom so far, stuck her head out the back door and peered down the driveway. The electric gate rolled open and Sannie drove in.

She scooped up both the kids in her arms and plastered them with kisses, before setting them down and waving to Tom. Elise stood, nodded to Tom to ensure her warning had been received and understood, then waved to Sannie and retreated indoors.

'Put your cozzie on and join us in the pool,' Sannie called to Tom as she walked towards the house, a child clinging to each of her legs.

'Let me finish with the truck first.'

Sannie waved and disappeared inside, while Tom crawled back under the Land Rover and replaced the sump plug. As he lifted the spanner to tighten it he realised the last person to have touched the tool before him was dead. It was odd, being among another man's possessions. With his family. He couldn't blame Elise for her suspicion or for her silent resentment of him.

He refilled the engine with oil from an unopened container he'd found in the garage. He'd do the filters, too, before dinner as Christo had laid in a good store of spares and consumables.

The Land Rover was fully kitted out for camping in the African bush and Tom could tell that Sannie's late husband had been passionate about his vehicle. It was immaculate, inside and out, save for a layer of dust which had settled since it had last been driven. To Tom's surprise it had started, albeit slowly, and he had left the engine idling for half an hour to warm the old oil and restore some more life to the twin-battery system he'd discovered under the bonnet.

On top was an aluminium roof-rack with custom-ised fittings for two gas bottles, which Tom found under a tarpaulin with some other camping gear, and a pair of jerry cans. There was also a big rectangular thing on the roof, which he thought at first was a storage box, covered with a waterproof canvas cover. How-ever, when he undid it, he discovered it was a fold-out rooftop tent. Inside, in the back, was a compressor-driven fridge-freezer which ran off the dual battery system. The fridge lid had been chocked open with a piece of wood to stop mould from forming, and when he worked out how to turn it on while the engine was running, it hummed to life and soon started getting cold. In the garage were plastic boxes filled with neatly packed camping essentials, including cutlery, plates, cups and pots in one box; non-perishable cooking basics in another; and a third crammed with portable lights, an air compressor and various electrical adapt-ers. He'd expected that he would have to fit out the vehicle himself, but Sannie had already told him he was welcome to whatever he could find in Christo's well-ordered trove of gear, tools and equipment.

Tom replaced the oil filler cap, lowered the bonnet and looked up as the back door opened again. Little Christo and Ilana, in their swimsuits, charged for the in-ground swimming pool and Sannie walked behind them, smiling and laughing. She carried a green-coloured rum cooler drink in a bottle and another beer, which she held up to him. She looked good enough to drink herself. She had changed out of her

425

suit into a yellow bikini top and a pair of short-cut blue board shorts with an Australian surf brand running down the side. He'd seen her naked, and in her bra and pants, but now, if it were possible, she looked even sexier. She was a promise of long, carefree summer holidays and endless sunshine. A world without murder and terrorism and politics. She threw back her head and laughed at something her mother had said from the kitchen, and swayed her hips as she swung the bottles by her side and walked towards him. This was a Sannie he hadn't seen before. At home with her children, safe from the outside world and free to be a kid again herself. She looked like a flirty teenager as she came to him and leaned a hip against the warm aluminium fender of the truck.

'*Jissus*, but I missed the sun.' She upended the cooler and used the serrations of its cap to lever off the top of the beer bottle, then unscrewed the twist top on her drink. Tom drained the dregs of the one Elise had brought him. The leftovers had already been warmed by the afternoon sun, but the lager Sannie handed him was cold and dewy. He wanted her, right then, and allowed himself the brief fantasy of life forever after by the beach with this sun-kissed girl. 'You're *filthy*, man,' she said, looking at his hands. 'Did the truck start okay?'

'First time.'

She sipped her drink, then, in reply to a demand from Christo, called out that she'd be in the pool soon. 'Come join us for a swim,' she said to Tom.

'I'm nearly finished here.' He gestured to the truck. 'Go play with your kids. I'll watch you from here.'

Sannie pouted. 'Was my mom horrid to you?'

He smiled. 'Not in so many words, but you could say that the riot act has been read and understood. She's only trying to look after you.'

Sannie nodded, then looked over her shoulder. Her mother was watching them from the kitchen. 'Mom! Get in the pool!' Ilana yelled.

'Duty calls,' she said, setting her drink down on the Land Rover's fender. Tom watched as she turned and ran, full pelt, to the edge of the pool and executed a running dive that barely raised a splash. She surfaced and lunged at the two children. 'Here comes the *krokodil*!' The children squealed with delight.

Elise had cooked a roast chicken dinner, though she barely acknowledged Tom's compliments on it.

Christo had lost his initial reservations about the near stranger in the house, and pestered Tom with questions about English football teams and the country's rugby side. Despite Sannie telling the boy to be quiet and eat his greens, Tom was happy to chat to him. Little Ilana was still quiet and shy, though a couple of times she smiled at him, then giggled, before hiding her face behind her hand. They were lovely kids, he thought. A credit to their mum and their prickly ouma. He could understand the older woman's protectiveness.

Sannie had showered and changed into a simple slip-on sundress with a bright sunflower print. It showed off her tan and barely came halfway down her slim, athletic thighs. Like her kids she was barefoot at the dinner table, and Tom was perspiring freely, despite the fan that blew across them from a kitchen benchtop.

'Is David Beckham the best football player in the world?' Christo asked.

'Carrots, Christo,' Sannie said, in between chewing on a wing.

'He gets his photo in the newspapers more than any other player,' Tom said. Christo nodded as if this settled the argument and Tom felt toes running up his shin.

He glanced across at Sannie sitting opposite – her mother was at the head of the table – but she ignored him. She asked her mother to pass the salt, running her foot higher and higher until it rested in Tom's crotch. He coughed, and Sannie asked him if he wanted more water, or another beer. 'Oh, I'm fine just as I am,' he said. She smiled and he thought he caught the hint of a wink. She wriggled her toes and he felt himself starting to harden. Tom concentrated on his chicken.

After the meal Elise boiled the kettle for coffee, telling Tom to stay seated. He was extremely grateful. Sannie grinned behind her mother's back.

'What's funny, Mom?' Christo asked.

'Nothing, my boy. Just something funny Mommy heard at work today. You and Ilana can go and watch TV for an hour, if you want.'

'Yay!' The children left the room.

'I'm going to turn in early,' Elise said. 'I've got my book to read. Goodnight.'

Tom wished her a goodnight, then breathed an audible sigh of relief when it was just the two of them left in the kitchen–dining room. 'Is it safe for you to stand?' she giggled.

'Barely. You're incorrigible. What were you thinking, with your mother right there?' He smiled.

'It's like being fifteen again. It adds a delicious element of risk, don't you think?'

Tom shook his head.

'Let's take our coffee outside.'

They sat beside each other in a swinging chair by the pool, and Tom loved the feeling of her bare leg pressed close against his. They chatted for a while, avoiding talking about the case or Tom's imminent trip. Sannie explained, though he didn't need her to, that her mother had loved Christo and was concerned that Sannie would never find a man as good as him to be a father to her kids. 'Not that I'm laying that on you, of course.'

'I never thought I'd have a family,' he said. 'Your kids are great, though.'

She blew on her coffee and sipped it. 'They can be monsters at times, believe me. But I do want the best for them.'

'Does that exclude me?'

She looked at him. 'Of course not. Is that what you want, though?'

'I don't know what I want, and that's the truth. But I love being here, in this house, with you, and your kids . . .'

'And my mom?'

'Well, let's not push it.' They both laughed.

Later, after she had put the children to bed and made sure her mother was safely ensconced in her

429

room, Sannie came back outside with two open bottles of beer. 'You never got in the pool this afternoon. Can't you swim?'

'Of course I can,' he said, accepting the beer and taking a large swallow.

'Then come in now, with me,' Sannie said, sitting her untouched drink down on the grass. She stood and held out a hand.

'I don't have my swimming trunks on,' he said.

She looked over her shoulder, back at the darkened house, then grabbed the hem of her dress and lifted it over her head. 'Neither do I, lover.' The white skin where her pants and bikini top had been shone invitingly. She turned and walked away from him, not looking back, and slid silently into the water.

Tom kicked off his docksiders, shrugged out of his T-shirt and unbuttoned his shorts as he followed her. At the edge, he stripped off his underpants and lowered himself into the water. Sannie swam underwater from the other side, and emerged in his arms. She kissed him, long and deep, her tongue darting inside his mouth. He started to say something, but she put a finger to his lips. The pool water was salty, as was she. It was like kissing a mermaid.

She led him, half wading, half swimming, to one side of the pool where a bougainvillea tree in the yard blocked the view from the kitchen, just in case anyone came to the window for a peek. When she stood on the bottom, the water reached halfway up her breasts, her nipples just breaking the surface. He placed one hand under her bottom, his other arm around her, and drew her to him, lifting her easily in the water. She encircled

430

him with her legs and moved her hand between them. She parted herself for him and he lowered her.

He'd never made love in the water before, but the moment she slid to the base of his shaft he remembered that instant on the hotel bed, when time had stood still, as he had rested, briefly, as deep inside another being as it was possible to be.

'Mmm, I could stay here all night,' he said.

'Forever,' she whispered in his ear.

With their bodies held by water, however, there was scope for long strokes, deep and satisfying. Using her thighs as a pivot she rode him high, taking him right out to the thick end of him and holding him tight there until his grip on her waist forced her back down to the base. He snaked an arm between them and rubbed her clitoris with his thumb. Her pace quickened and she worked him harder with her muscles. Her grip as she rode up sealed them tightly together, then she relaxed to be merely firm on the way down.

With his thumb rolling over her clit, she peaked hard – an orgasm that detonated through her body and sent a blast of heat over his cock and into the water around them. She wrapped her arms around his neck, and he freed his hand to smooth the wet blonde strands of hair from her face so he could look into her liquid blue eyes.

She moaned as he started to move inside her again, and it almost felt like she was flying. As he drove up into her with renewed urgency he lifted her breasts clear of the water, taking first one, then the other of her nipples in his mouth, trapping them between his teeth and tongue, sucking greedily.

When he felt the now familiar sensations of her mounting second orgasm, he looked up at her. 'Leave your pretty blue eyes open this time. I want to see them when you come.' As he felt her again, he joined her, filling her completely.

Afterwards, they showered together in the flat at the rear of the garage and she slept with him, pressed close in the single bed. They left the sheet off, and let the ceiling fan cool them and blow the mosquitos away. Sannie slept, her head pillowed on his chest hair, but Tom lay awake for most of the night, one hand crooked under his head.

She woke in the pre-dawn and stretched like a contented cat. He smiled at and kissed her. Her hand moved, seemingly by its own accord, to his rising erection.

'Do you really have to go off on this trip by yourself?'

'Yes, baby.'

Elise's attitude towards him softened slowly over the following three days. Perhaps, Tom thought as he stacked the camping fridge–freezer in the back of the Land Rover with frozen steak, *boerewors* and a six-pack of Castle, it was because Sannie's mother knew he would soon be out of their lives.

Still, she'd been helpful, taking him to the local supermarket and butcher, and pointing out an auto spares shop where he'd bought extra oil, filters, a fan belt and radiator hoses. He got the gas bottles filled, and made the bed in the rooftop tent with clean linen and a blanket. He sorted his clothes, leaving some behind at Sannie's, and bought an extra pair of shorts and a khaki bush shirt for the road. It was Friday afternoon and he was ready to go. When Elise returned home after picking up Christo and Ilana from school, Tom started packing her ageing Toyota Condor people-mover for the weekend trip to Kruger.

'I can help,' Christo said, standing beside him in his school shirt and shorts, minus shoes.

'Good man.' Tom could have packed the wagon more quickly by himself, but he sorted small boxes and cooler bags for the boy to carry and let him pack things where he wanted to in the boot. He would have to learn some day, Tom thought. They chatted about soccer and television shows as they worked, and Tom, to his surprise, found himself laughing at a couple of jokes the boy made and generally enjoying his company.

'Are you coming back here after your holiday, Tom?' Christo asked as he hefted his own small backpack full of clothes into the Condor.

'Yes, I have to bring your dad's truck back.'

'No, are you coming to stay with us?' At that moment Elise appeared from the back door, a picnic basket in one hand. She stopped to listen.

Tom sighed. What to say? He pushed the cold box to the back of the cargo area and wiped his hands on his shorts. He looked down at the boy. 'Would you like me to come and stay?'

It was Christo's turn to ponder his answer for a moment. He nodded his head.

'I forgot something,' Elise said, and turned back to the kitchen.

Before Tom could speak to Elise, Sannie arrived, honking the horn of her Mercedes as the electric gate rolled open. 'Hey, man! I thought you guys would be packed already,' she chided. She kissed Christo and smiled at Tom, then ran inside, pausing only to kick off her high heels. 'I'll be changed in ten minutes, and you'd better be ready!'

Sannie had finished work early, at one o'clock, but even so they had to drive hard to get to the park before the entrance gates closed at six. The Land Rover blew blue smoke for the first half-hour, but eventually the long-dormant engine warmed up and Tom found he could coax it up to a hundred and ten. Sannie had suggested that Elise could drive the children in the Condor and that she would ride with Tom, in case he needed directions. 'The kids have hardly seen you for a week, Sannie,' Elise reminded her.

Tom thought her mother had made a good call. Besides, he needed to get used to navigating himself around Africa. Sannie soon outstripped him on the motorway, easily sitting on a hundred and twenty. Via her cell phone, she told him that they would go on ahead and start setting up at Pretoriuskop camp. Tom assured her that he could read a map well enough to find her.

It was the same road he and Sannie had driven together from Johannesburg to Tinga Legends, on the recce trip before Greeves's abduction. It seemed like a lifetime ago and, in a sense, it was. Tom's old life was over. No job, no future – at least not in England. He considered this. No, he told himself, it wasn't quite over yet.

When he passed the hijacking hotspot warning signs near Witbank he felt a pang of concern for Sannie and her family. However, Sannie had her Z88 service pistol with her, and she had given Tom her private firearm, a nine-millimetre South African-made RAP 401, a compact semiautomatic. Its short barrel made it easy to conceal, but the eight-round magazine was less than half the capacity of the Glock he would have been carrying if he was still on the job. Tom had hoped that she would offer him a firearm. One of the reasons he wanted to drive to Malawi, rather than fly, was so he could carry a weapon. He hadn't told Sannie of his ulterior motive.

He broke his first law of the trip when he arrived at the Numbi Gate entrance. He should have declared the pistol, but did not. He had it stashed in the toolbox under a mountain of gear in the back of the Land Rover. Over the next two days he would find a better hiding spot for it for when he had to start crossing borders. Sannie had gone through the motions of asking him why he thought he needed to take a gun with him out of South Africa, but had given up in the face of his silence. She'd given him two spare magazines and a box of bullets as well.

On the short drive to Pretoriuskop camp from the gate he slowed and stopped to watch a white rhino grazing by the side of the road. It ignored him, contentedly munching away on the short green grass that had sprung up in a burnt patch of bush with the first rains of the season. On its back was a tiny bird with a red bill. An oxpecker. The animal's *askari*, as Sannie had called it. Tom had no one to guard any more, and the feeling was liberating in a way. He was here for himself and no one else. Ironically, his very next thought was of Sannie and her kids. He checked the time on his watch and made it in through the wooden gates of the rest camp with only minutes to spare before the curfew kicked in.

The rest camp consisted of a camping area and rows of bungalows, ranging from small rondavels, as Sannie called them, to larger, self-contained houses which would sleep a family of six. There were plenty of mature trees and the lawns were green and well kept, with some help, no doubt, from the trio of warthog that darted across the road in front of Tom's Land Rover, their tails pointing straight up like antennae.

He found Sannie, Elise and the children at the top end of the camping ground, which occupied a series of terraces down one side of the complex. An electric fence, reinforced with thick metal cables to keep elephant at bay, surrounded the encampment.

'Did you see the rhino?' Ilana asked him.

He bent over and assured her that he had. The little girl had been warming to him over the past couple of days and he felt bad that he would soon disappear, as had the last man in her life. Sannie finished hammering in a tent peg, and stood and wiped her brow. She had made short work of setting up the nylon dome tent in which she, Elise and the kids would all sleep. She wore camouflage shorts, and a stretchy orange tank top that revealed her flat belly when she stretched and yawned.

With some direction from Sannie and the kids, Tom soon had his fold-out rooftop tent erected for the first time. It looked cosy, and he thought it would be even cosier if during the night Sannie climbed up the ladder to join him.

Tom engaged Elise while Sannie took the kids to shower, asking her to instruct him on the finer points of barbecuing – or *braaiing,* as the South Africans called it. He'd made a few attempts in his tiny back yard in London and on holidays in Spain, but none that could be classed as overwhelmingly successful, he told her. Elise laughed and talked him through the basics of lighting the fire, waiting for it to die down to glowing coals and then adjusting the circular grid which moved up and down on a metal pole attached to the wok-like fire tray. It seemed simple enough.

He cooked, with gentle encouragement and advice from Sannie and Christo, and the steaks weren't nearly as burned as they might have been. It had been a long day for all of them, especially Sannie, and they were all in their tents by nine.

Tom lay in his rooftop bed and listened to the noises of the bush – the squeak of bats, the screech of an owl, the comfortingly familiar croak of frogs in the nearby dam. Far off, he heard the low groans of a lion calling to his pride. Sleep came slowly.

Sannie woke him at four, and chivvied him out of bed and into the Condor. At this time of year the camp gates opened at four-thirty. Elise was staying in camp, but Sannie and the kids were determined to go out and try to find the lion who had been calling again in the pre-dawn dark, closer to camp. They found him, no more than a kilometre away, lying on the bitumen road, still calling. He lowered his head and thrust out his snout, as if to squeeze every last little note out of his huge lungs. It felt to Tom like the metal panels on the Toyota's sides were vibrating.

They drove to Skukuza, where Sannie had introduced him to Isaac Tshabalala. It brought back bad memories for Tom, but galvanised him for the long journey ahead. Sannie bought the kids burgers and ice cream for lunch and they all swam in a pool in a picnic site, located down the road from the camp on the banks of the Sabie River. It was, Tom noted, the same river that Tinga Lodge overlooked. As much as he enjoyed pretending he was part of Sannie's happy family life, he found that he was itching to get on his way.

'You're distant,' she said to him as they sat alone by the evening campfire. On Saturday night there was a wildlife documentary video screening at Pretoriuskop camp's open-air cinema, and Elise had taken the kids so Sannie could have some private time with Tom. Hyenas whooped and cackled in the distance, but the noise was on the big screen.

He nodded.

'Are you going to tell me or not?'

He looked at her. Every new angle, every nuance of the day's lighting, seemed to reveal more of her beauty to him. Bathed in the orange glow of the fire it seemed as if the warmth he felt radiated from within her rather than from the smouldering coals. Part of him wanted just to hold her and let his body dissolve into hers.

She persisted through his silence, her exasperation rising. 'Look, think of me. I'm still on the fringes of the investigation. If you've got a new lead, then tell me! I'll give you a head start on this wild-goose chase you're on, but if you find them you'll need back-up. I can't get a team of recce commandos to you with fifteen minutes' notice, you know. What do you know about these terrorists that we don't, Tom, that the British government doesn't?'

'If I find out anything new, I'll call you,' was all he said. He didn't want her with him. He didn't want to get her excited. He didn't want her actions, no matter how well intentioned, to tip off his prey. For all those reasons, and for her protection and the future of her kids, he couldn't tell her anything.

'There's no point risking your life on a private vendetta, Tom. The man you were sent to protect is buried in some unmarked grave in Mozambique. Even if you find the killers, it won't bring Greeves back, or even resurrect your career. You must know that! Get it through your head, Tom – the man is dead!'

Tom's face betrayed nothing – certainly not the one thing he was completely and utterly sure of.

Robert Greeves was still alive.

27

Tom eased his way into Africa.

Kruger was a National Geographic channel idyll of wildlife and scenery. He travelled north, leaving Sannie and her family behind to pack up and head back to Johannesburg. His mood altered with the changing landscape.

The south of the park was characterised by thick, dense bush, and plenty of humans on the road, in private cars and open-top safari vehicles. He was irritable as he inched around a traffic jam parked beside a rhino, but he realised part of the source of his frustration was leaving Sannie behind. Also, little Christo and Ilana had plainly been disappointed at his departure. He felt bad about having raised their expectations that there would be a new man around the house. He'd wondered what it would be like becoming a stepfather. It might have scared him if the kids hadn't been so much fun and so well behaved – they were a credit to Sannie and the father they'd known so briefly. He pushed the thoughts of parenthood from his mind.

As he moved north, both the bush and the crowds thinned. Open grasslands replaced the long grass and thornbushes of the southern part of the park. He was gradually leaving what passed for civilisation, with all its attendant responsibilities, rules and commitments. For the first time in twenty years he was accountable to no one except himself. He missed Sannie, but he was free, too, to concentrate on the mission ahead.

He stopped at Satara camp, in the middle of the park, and camped near the perimeter fence. A trio of old male buffalos settled down to sleep just on the other side of the wire. Tom wondered if they thought they would be safer there, close to the camp. In the distance a lion lullabied him to sleep. He was getting more used to Africa by the day.

The next morning he rose early, but not to go in search of wild animals. He took the sealed road west from Satara to another of Kruger's gates, Orpen. He checked his map of the park, which also included the private game reserves adjoining the national park. Wealthy South Africans had bought up land on the border of the public park during the apartheid years and developed a network of private reserves, run along similar lines to the national park but for personal gain. In the past, a fence had separated public from private land, but this had come down in recent years, allowing animals to migrate freely from Kruger into these adjoining lands. Some of the properties had been developed commercially, with lodges charging premium rates for foreign visitors to experience a luxury safari, while other tracts were held by individuals for their private use at weekends and holidays.

He passed a township called Acornhoek, then turned on to a dirt road which took him deeper into the private reserves. Eventually, he came to the entrance to the Timbavati private game reserve, which resembled one of the gates into Kruger. Timbavati had its own rangers, turned out in smart, pressed uniforms; its own rules; and its own entry fees. He paid his money, explaining that he was heading for Doctor Khan's property, and that he was an invited guest. This was a lie, but the security guard didn't question him. He also asked for directions to the late doctor's property – which still didn't arouse the man's suspicion – saying that while he had permission to visit he had never been there before.

Tom passed an open-top Land Rover game viewer and waved to the driver and his tourists. He followed signs on stone cairns and turned off the main road through the reserve, to the left. According to the guard, Doctor Khan's place was six and a half kilometres further along.

He set the trip meter and came to an unmarked turn-off guarded by a lone bull elephant who was using his broad forehead to push over a stout-looking tree. Sannie had told Tom that elephants did that to feed on the roots and, sometimes, just to get at some leaves that would otherwise have been out of reach. He had no time to watch the mighty creature, so he geared down and continued along the deteriorating track. He put the Land Rover into low-range four-wheel drive to negotiate a dried-out sandy river crossing and planted the accelerator to climb up the steep opposing bank.

The lodge, when at last it came into view, was simple but stylish. Thatch roof, single storey, with whitewashed walls, rendered and painted a tan brown. There was also a thatched outdoor dining and bar area, with no walls on three sides, overlooking a small pumped waterhole on the other side of the river – presumably the same one he had just crossed. A sole buffalo was drinking from the concrete pond. Tom stopped the Land Rover and got out, grateful for the chance to stretch his legs and feel a cool breeze on the damp back of his shirt. The airconditioning in the Land Rover either hadn't been gassed for years or wasn't working.

'Hello?' He walked to the shady lounge area and looked around. There was no dust on the two tables or the wooden bar top. A glass-door fridge, secured with a chain and padlock, held a wide selection of beers and wine. Behind metal grilles in a cupboard over the bar was an equally impressive selection of spirits, including some expensive single malt Scotches. On the wall on either side of the drinks cabinets were photos set in tasteful, though rustic, wooden frames. There were shots of all of the big five – lion, elephant, rhino, leopard and buffalo; a picture of a swarthy but dapper-looking man Tom took to be Doctor Khan kneeling beside a dead buffalo and resting on a hunting rifle; and another of the sun setting over a glassy body of water. The sunset was framed by a latticed arch, dripping with bougainvillea, which led the way to a narrow strip of white sand.

'Morning, sir, can I help you?' An elderly black man appeared from behind the house. He wore blue overalls and wiped his hands on them as he walked over.

Tom turned from the photographs and pulled his wallet out of his shorts. 'I'm Detective Sergeant Tom Furey, from the London Metropolitan Police. I'm here in relation to the disappearance of Doctor Khan.'

'You are from East London?' the man asked.

Tom had heard of the town on South Africa's coast. 'No, from England.'

'Police have been here already, sir.' The caretaker looked Tom up and down.

Dressed in shorts and a T-shirt and driving a camping vehicle with a tent on the roof, he hardly looked like an investigating detective. Tom decided to keep talking and bluffing. 'I'm working with the South African police on this case and they have asked me to check your records and guest book to see who's been staying here recently.'

'The doctor, he kept all the books at his house, in Jo'burg, sir. Police would have seen all of those?'

'Of course.' Tom strode across to the bar. 'But the guest book . . . where is it?'

'Doctor Khan, he always said not to talk to anyone about his friends – his guests, sir.'

Tom turned on the man. 'What's your name?' He took his notebook and pen from the pocket of his shorts.

'Amos, sir.'

Tom pretended to write. 'You're coming with me, to the police station in Acornhoek, and you're going to explain to the headman there why you're not cooperating with this important investigation.' The man looked worried and Tom felt sorry for him. He had no right – legal or otherwise – to threaten the caretaker. 'Unless, of course, you just give me the bloody guest book. Now!'

Amos seemed to cringe at the barked command. He ducked behind the bar and withdrew a large leather-bound volume. Tom simply nodded as the older man slid the document across the bar. He stood there, though, watching Tom as he opened the book.

Tom started at the front, which dated back three years. Only about a third of the book was full, he noted. Obviously the doctor didn't entertain too many guests. On the fourth page he found the two names he was looking for. One above the other. His face showed no recognition, but in his mind he was punching the air. He felt his heart beat faster as he moved through the following pages. Three more entries – the same two names on each occasion. It was all he needed, though he also committed three other regularly appearing names to memory. Two listed Pretoria as their home address, while the third was from Russia, which was interesting. He would have to check them all out. There were no entries for the past four weeks.

'When was the doctor here last, Amos?' Tom closed the book.

Amos retrieved the book and placed it carefully under the bar. 'Other police asked that, sir.'

Tom knew he was on shaky ground. The longer he lingered, the more suspicious the old caretaker would become. 'I know you told them, Amos, but we're cross-checking his last movements. It's important that you tell me.'

Amos looked skywards, as though he was calculating the date. 'One month ago, sir.'

'And he came in his Isuzu. His *bakkie*?'

'Yes, sir. I still have the telephone number of the police who came, sir. Can we call them now?'

Tom ignored him and pointed to the beachside sunset picture. 'Where was that taken?'

Amos was surprised by the question, the reaction Tom had hoped for. He wanted to get the old man's mind off calling the police. 'Malawi, sir.'

'The doctor's beach house?'

Amos nodded.

'At Cape Maclear, right?'

'Yes, sir.'

'The other police didn't ask about Malawi, did they?'

'No, sir. Perhaps we call them now.'

Tom put his notebook and pen away, and turned and walked back into the sunshine. 'That won't be necessary. Thanks for your help, Amos,' he said, as he strode across to the Land Rover. He was in business.

Back inside the Kruger National Park, Tom made it as far north as Shingwedzi camp just before the gates closed at six-thirty. The sun melted behind the thorny bushveld outside the perimeter fence as he unfolded the tent and lit a fire. He turned on his mobile phone and called Sannie at home.

'Tom! Where are you?'

He told her, then started recounting the morning's

trip out to Doctor Khan's private game lodge in the Timbavati.

Sannie cut him off. 'Tom, you're crazy. If the local cops find out what you're up to, you'll be arrested. You didn't tell me you were sticking your nose into our investigations over here. When I told you about Khan being the owner of the *bakkie* the terrorists used, I didn't expect you to go investigating him!'

'Sannie, listen to me. Robert Greeves, with Nick Roberts as his protection officer, visited Khan's lodge on at least three occasions in the last two years.'

There was silence on the other end of the phone.

'Sannie? Presumably you guys ran a criminal check on Khan.' It was all too much of a coincidence – Khan having a property on the border of Kruger, not far from Tinga, and disappearing just before the abduction. He wanted to check out the doctor's life for himself, and his first cursory look had revealed a solid connection to Greeves that the South African police had missed. That was sloppy detective work, if not something worse, on their part.

'Of course. It came up clean – I double-checked.'

'What about ongoing criminal investigations?'

Sannie paused again. 'I don't know. I'll check tomorrow, but what am I to tell my people – that you're freelancing on this?'

'No. Tell them you're acting on a hunch. Ask the detectives who went out to Khan's place if they checked his guest book. They obviously didn't. They were probably looking for bomb-making kits or AK 47s, but Khan was no terrorist.'

'Then what do you suspect them of, Tom?'

'Try your sex crimes unit. We know Khan was a bachelor who liked to party – but how and with whom? You've got to dig deep on this guy. He's got a connection with Greeves and I don't believe in coincidences.'

'No cop does. Are you all right, Tom?'

'Yeah, I'm fine. You?'

'I miss you.'

'Me too.'

'Are you coming back?'

It was his turn to pause. 'Once all this is finished. I've got to bring your truck back, remember?'

'Don't joke. What is "all this"?'

'I'll let you know when I find out, Sannie. I promise. I'll call you back when I can.'

He hung up and put some lamb chops on the *braai*. He ate and drank alone, save for a hyena which paused outside the camp fence and looked at him with mournful eyes. It was amazing, Tom thought, how quickly he'd become used to the presence of predators around him. He spoke to the hyena as though it was a pet, gently telling it he had no food to spare. There were plenty of signs on the fence and in the toilet blocks warning campers of the perils of feeding wildlife.

Tom opened another beer and thought about the road ahead of him.

Africa continued to reveal herself to him, at her own languid, alluring pace.

He packed in the pre-dawn cool and left for the Pafuri Gate in the far north. He stopped on the bridge over the Luvuvhu River to take in the view. Below him, browsing in some bushes on the bank of the fast-flowing river, were some antelope he hadn't so far encountered. The map book Sannie had given him had pictures of animals as well. The chocolate brown creature with fine white stripes and dots and a long shaggy beardlike mane was a nyala. If the animal knew he was there, it ignored him. He envied its peaceful, simple existence. It still had to beware of lurking predators, though. In Africa, death could be as close as the next tree. He got back in the Land Rover and drove off.

Tom left behind the increasingly empty and restful national park, and was thrust back into the conflicts of modern-day Africa as he drove through the lands of the Venda people. Here, traditional reed and mud huts with bright geometric designs painted on the walls and pointed roofs stood side by side with new, utilitarian brick houses, funded by government construction programs. It looked to Tom as though the authorities were trying to skip the twentieth century altogether, to catapult people whose living standards had not changed much since the nineteenth into the twenty-first century. There was still a long way to go, from what he could see.

The Land Rover's windscreen wipers worked overtime, trying to give him enough visibility to see through a sudden downpour, which drummed hard and loud on the vehicle's aluminium roof. A trickle of water ran down the inside of the windscreen and door pillar, behind the dashboard, down the accelerator and over his sandalled foot. Some things were common to Land Rovers around the world, no matter the model or age.

He stopped in the hot, sticky border town of Musina, where the sun broke through the clouds and sucked the moisture back into the heavens, to top up on food and fuel, and headed west for another ninety-odd kilometres. There he drove across the dry bed of the Limpopo River, which marked the border between South Africa and Botswana at an out-of-the-way crossing called Pont Drift.

It would have been quicker for him to reach his destination by driving through Zimbabwe, but Sannie had warned him that the country's perennial fuel shortages were a problem. Botswana, he soon discovered, consisted of miles and miles of empty countryside. He crossed more sandy riverbeds and skirted a herd of skittish elephants while driving through the Mashatu Game Reserve, where the land had been picked clean of vegetation and resembled, in places, the surface of a hot, dusty, red moon.

Once back on the tar road he made good time, heading ever north. The monotony of the black ribbon flanked by thick thorny bush would have put him to sleep if it weren't for the deep rumble of the diesel and the heat of the engine pulsing through the firewall. Slowing only for towns, most of which seemed to be guarded by a police car and a radar speed trap, he kept the Land Rover above a hundred kilometres an hour for most of the rest of the day.

Hot and tired, he followed the signs to the Marang Hotel in the bustling regional city of Francistown. It was another of Sannie's recommendations. She and

Christo had stopped there on their honeymoon, on their way to the Okavango Delta. It was strange to think of her with another man, now that he knew every inch of her slim, golden body. Past the hotel itself and its shaded green lawns and swimming pool was a dusty camp ground. He said a polite good evening to an elderly South African couple in a Land Cruiser, but avoided a conversation by heading to the pool. The cold water sluiced the grit from his skin, and he ordered a beer from the poolside bar's waiter while he lay on a canvas-covered sun bed and let the fast-closing gloom cool his body.

The next day was more of the same, the monotony of the empty bush broken only by the sight of two elephants. The first was dead, its carcass swarming with the giant flapping wings and pecking hooked beaks of vultures. He dropped his speed to eighty and a gust of wind brought the unmistakable stench of death into the cab. The second animal gave him a fright when it charged across the road in front of him. He braked hard, missing it by a couple of metres, and tried not to think about the damage he would have caused to the truck and himself if he'd hit it. Sannie had advised him not to drive at night, and he could now see why. With not a streetlight for hundreds of kilometres, and the thorn-studded trees growing thick right up to the sides of the road, a collision with an animal would spell disaster.

He stopped to refuel in the middle-of-nowhere outpost of Nata, a crossroads settlement where one route ran north, towards Zambia, and another took travellers west, to the lush inland paradise of the Okavango

Delta. Nata itself, however, was a strain on the eyes. The rains were hard-pressed reaching here, and a cloud of glary white dust hovered over two filling stations, a cheap hotel, a post office, a general store, a shebeen and a butcher's shop. A small man with the fine, almost oriental features, of the San – once known as the Bushmen – came up to Tom while a chatty attendant filled his tank with diesel, and asked for money, cigarettes and beer. The whites of the San's eyes were a rheumy yellow and he smelled of booze. Tom shook his head, both at the man and the effects of so-called civilisation on an ancient people.

It was hot. It was dry. He found himself drinking water by the litre. When he went to the bathroom at the service station he noticed the skin of his right arm and the right side of his face – the parts of him most exposed while driving – were brick red. He put on extra sunscreen when he got back in the truck, but it seemed little could protect him against the elements. He ran a hand through his damp hair and felt grit. The distances he was travelling staggered him when he overlaid them on England, Scotland and Wales. Sannie had warned him he would see 'MMBA – miles and miles of bloody Africa', and she was right.

The humidity climbed as he neared the Zambian border. Here the land started to dip into the Zambezi River valley. He crossed the frontier on a ferry at Kazungula, and a rare breeze off the water cooled him momentarily as he leaned on a safety railing and watched a pied kingfisher hover above the surface before plunging in for the kill. The bird emerged and flew off, its beak empty. Would his hunting trip be equally fruitless?

He reckoned there was a fifty-fifty chance that the theory coalescing in his mind was right. He wouldn't know for sure until he made it to Malawi, and there was still another whole country to cross first.

Zambia was poorer, edgier and more run-down than the pleasantly prosperous backwater of Botswana or busy, flashy, manic-depressive South Africa. Here and there were signs of development, either through foreign aid or an influx of tourist dollars, but elsewhere the country had the feel of an old elephant down on its knees, struggling to stand upright again. On the Land Rover's radio was news in English about Zambia's recent election. The opposition had been defeated and was claiming corruption on the government's part. A spokesman warned of protests on the street and the announcer mentioned an increased police presence was planned to counter the demonstrations. Tom got the feeling that democracy was still more of an ideal than a reality in many parts of Africa.

On the way into Livingstone, the closest town on the Zambian side of the mighty Victoria Falls, he passed signs to a new five-star hotel and a shopping centre complex under construction, but in the town itself he watched a security guard beat a street urchin with a wooden baton. The boy, dressed in ragged shorts and a too-big T-shirt, ran off, blood running through the fingers pressed to his scalp.

Tom had no time or inclination to visit the Victoria Falls, though in his mind he briefly played out a scene in which he and Sannie and her kids returned to go sightseeing. On the road out of Livingstone he watched a pair of young boys riding towards him in a cart constructed from the rear tray of an old pick-up, pulled by a pair of battered, scarred donkeys. They whipped the animals in a cruel frenzy to get out of the way of a shiny new Mercedes-Benz which roared past them and swerved to avoid a head-on with Tom at the last second. Tom leaned on the Land Rover's horn, but the gesture was wasted. The Merc had probably been travelling at close to two hundred, he thought. This stretch of road was good, courtesy of the Danish government, according to a road sign, but half an hour later Tom was dodging potholes as deep as his forearm.

It seemed the roads in Zambia were as much a footpath as a vehicular route. As he drove he passed a constant procession of people walking to or from school or work, or from one poverty-afflicted village to another. A young man with legs and arms like twigs and dressed in a hessian sack, a look of madness in his eyes, was followed by a man in a suit and tie, riding a pushbike. Women in brightly printed wraps with babies on their backs walked on the roadside, ignoring him and other traffic, carrying themselves with the aloofness and grace of giraffes, while children in starched uniforms yelled and waved frantically as the Land Rover rumbled past them.

Tom lost count of the number of police checkpoints he passed through. Sannie had warned him that, apart from border crossings, these would be his biggest inconvenience. She was right, and he tried to remember to be patient and friendly. He stopped for the night in a camping ground situated on a farm near a small town called Choma, on the Livingstone to Lusaka road. As he was the only camper, he used the opportunity to take Sannie's nine-millimetre from the toolbox and strip it and clean it.

Tom rose at four-fifteen and pulled on nylon running shorts, a T-shirt and his trainers. He figured it was safe to leave the vehicle where it was, so he did twenty minutes of stretching, then set off for a run. He followed the dirt track, which led from the farm to the main road, keeping a careful eye on the uneven ground. He didn't want to twist an ankle. Once on the main tar road he settled into a rhythm, breathing deep and slow. At this hour there were few cars and for long stretches it seemed like he was the only person in Africa. The sun peaked above the flat horizon after about half an hour, turning the open grasslands on either side of him the colour of molten gold. He checked his watch, turned and headed back. A gaggle of children in pressed maroon and white uniforms, presumably from families employed on the commercial farm, giggled and pointed at him as he passed. He waved and smiled. It felt good to be exercising again. In the coming days he needed to be sharper than he ever had in his career – both mentally and physically. Back at his campsite he finished off with fifty push-ups and a hundred sit-ups. In the shower he enjoyed the feel of the strong spray pummelling his invigorated muscles. When he dried himself he caught sight of his face in the mirror. He nodded and said out loud, 'Ready.'

28

Immigration officer Goodenough Khumalo put a hand over his mouth to stifle a yawn and said, 'Next.'

The man at the head of the non-residents' queue was tall and white, with jet black hair and a moustache. Goodenough watched him as he walked, noting his smile and the way he looked him in the eye. Nothing to hide? We'll see, thought Goodenough. The ones to pay close attention to, he had learned, were those who fidgeted nervously and looked every which way and those who seemed too full of confidence. Behind the man were at least another forty or so people from the South African Airways flight from London. Goodenough was in no particular hurry – he had nowhere else to go.

'Good morning, how are you?' the man said as he stepped up to the high counter. He wore a blue cotton shirt, navy blazer and tan trousers.

'Fine, and you?' Goodenough said, taking the British passport and sliding it towards himself.

He looked at the photo and glanced up at the man. A match. He even had the same moustache. Goodenough checked the issue date. The passport was only a month old. He flicked through the pages. The man had been to South Africa once already since the new document was issued, only a few weeks ago. He used his barcode scanner and the man's details flashed up on the screen in front of him. The green sticker in the passport was a three-month visa. It was still well in date, so the holder could pass in and out of South Africa as often as he or she wished during that period. Each time, the sticker would be scanned and the entry/exit date electronically registered on a computer.

'Mr Daniel Carney, your visa is still valid.'

'Yes,' the man said, smiling.

'How long do you stay in South Africa this time?'

'Just three days.'

Goodenough looked at the white immigration arrival form which Carney had completed. 'I see you are a freelance journalist. Are you here on business or pleasure?'

'Mostly pleasure. In fact, I'm in transit. Though I might write a story on your country's preparations for the soccer World Cup. I think it's fantastic that Africa's finally getting to host it, don't you?'

Goodenough thought the man was trying to distract him. He nodded, and tapped the keyboard in front of him. He was actually doing nothing, but he wanted the man to think he was further checking him out. He glanced over at Mr Daniel Carney, who simply smiled again.

'Where are you going to after South Africa?'

'Mozambique.'

'Do you have your onward air ticket?'

'Um, no. I'll be driving a rental car.'

Goodenough looked up and, for the first time, thought he saw a crack in the man's facade. Carney scratched the back of his head. Most people experienced a degree of nervousness, no matter how mild, when dealing with people in authority. This he knew well. He'd had to deal with hysterical women, angry men, and crying children in his time. However, there was no reason for him to detain this man, even though his gut instinct told him that there was something not quite right about him.

He stamped the man's passport and slid it back across the counter. 'Enjoy your short stay in South Africa.'

'Oh, I'm sure I will.'

Sannie arrived at the headquarters of the South African Police Service Protection and Security Services at 218 Visagie Street, Pretoria, at seven-fifty in the morning and took the lift to her floor.

The General Piet Joubert building was not much to look at from the outside, or the inside. Its concrete facade was studded with panels of tiny blue tiles, which did little to enliven its drabness.

She greeted Lizzy, the receptionist, and grabbed a copy of the *Citizen*, one of the daily tabloids, as she usually did. On the way to the coffee machine she read the front-page story, which was about an operation by the Family Violence, Child Protection and

Sexual Offences Unit to break a people-smuggling racket. *SEX SLAVE TRADERS BUSTED*, screamed the headline.

Sannie whistled softly as she took her coffee to her workstation. It had been a big effort, run in conjunction with police in England, Germany, Italy and Mozambique.

She sat down, sipped her coffee, and laid the paper down in front of her and continued to read.

Police spokesperson Inspector Martha Nel said the highly organised gang moved illegal immigrants from Mozambique into and out of South Africa by road in concealed compartments in shipping containers on long-distance freight vehicles.

Inspector Nel said: 'Boys and girls, mostly orphans, as young as eight and nine years old, were transported illegally. Some of them were smuggled by ship from Mozambique to Europe.

Sannie shuddered. As if she couldn't imagine the fate of the youngsters, the article went on to say that the victims, lured with promises of work and accommodation abroad, were sold into illegal brothels. Most of those transported, however, were young women in their late teens and early twenties.

From the article, Sannie gathered that the operation had gone down a few weeks ago, but details had only now been released to the press. She imagined it was because the investigating officers hoped to net more of those responsible after the initial bust, which had involved the interception of a container load of young people at the Komatipoort border post. The driver would have talked to minimise his sentence, giving detectives the name of the next person up the chain, and so on.

Sannie knew the woman quoted in the story. She and Martha Nel had completed their training together and had both been posted to the rough Johannesburg flatland suburb of Hillbrow, patrolling the mean streets and seedy hotels in the shadow of the landmark JG Strijdom telecommunications tower on their first assignment. They had followed separate career paths, though, when Sannie met Christo and applied for training as a close protection officer. Sannie opened her contact book and dialled the number for the child protection unit's offices in the Southern Life building in Pretorius Street. She waited for a couple of minutes while the receptionist on the other end transferred her to Martha.

'Sannie, howzit? It's been what, five years? How are your kids?'

They exchanged pleasantries and Sannie accepted Martha's condolences over Christo's death. 'Shame. I remember reading about it. He was such a good man.'

'Martha, I'm sure you're very busy today, but I was wondering if I could ask you a few questions about the people-smuggling operation.'

'*Ja*, you're right about being busy. I've done five radio interviews already this morning. The boss is holding a press conference at ten, so I don't have long, Sannie, but I'm happy to help if I can.'

'What's the South African angle, Martha? They

were bringing people into here, according to the article.'

'Most of them were being sent abroad, but there were some Mozambicans brought into South Africa.'

'I don't mean to demean your operation, but that's hardly big news, is it? I mean, we've got Mozambicans crossing every day.'

'You're right, Sannie, but it was just kids coming into South Africa with this gang. We think they were being brought to individuals, to paedophiles, rather than to brothels, as was the case in Italy and Germany. This was almost like people getting cars stolen to order. We think the offenders here would ask for a boy or girl of a particular age, and pay big money for them.'

'So we're not talking about guys who would go to the local brothel or try to entice kids into their car?'

'You got it. Wealthy people. Businessmen, professionals, that sort of thing. Very discreet. The kind of pigs who would have a respectable image to protect.'

'Have you made any arrests in that group?'

'Not yet. The guys we've picked up in South Africa so far aren't talking. The money and the power of their clients has got them scared. We had better luck with the Germans and the Italians. The middlemen squealed and the police over there have raided half-a-dozen brothels in both countries.'

'And in England?'

'Good and bad luck. We got the names of two Pakistani gentlemen and passed them on to the English. It turned out they were already under surveillance for people smuggling, though the pommies were more interested in them for moving possible terrorist suspects. The sex trade victims were a bonus.'

'So what went wrong?'

'The surveillance team was caught out when they entered the men's home to download files off their computer. The suspects returned and set off a remote-controlled bomb that destroyed the computer, killed the IT guy downloading the files and burned the house down.'

'*Jeez*,' Sannie said. 'Sounds more sophisticated than just people smuggling.'

'The English were probably right about some terrorist link, but any information that might have been on that computer was fried. We held off releasing any information while the British tried to find another link to the people smuggling, but they eventually came up with nothing, so we went public today. Sannie – sorry, hey, but I've really got to run . . .'

'Oh, that's fine. Thanks so much, Martha. Sorry, one more question.'

'Okay.' Sannie heard the impatience now in Martha's tone.

'The people you've picked up here in South Africa . . . do you think they'll talk eventually – give up the names of the paedophiles they were supplying?'

'You can bet on it. We'll break them down, one way or another. Even if we have to give the bastards witness protection and exemption, we'll get the main men.'

'I'm sure you will. Before I go, can I give you a name? Doctor Pervez Khan.' Sannie gave Martha the doctor's home address. 'He's listed as a missing person, but you might want to mention his name in your questioning of the subjects.' She said goodbye and hung up.

Sannie had come into work early to ensure she could get onto one of the few computers in the office. She turned on one of the terminals, finished her coffee and skimmed the rest of the newspaper while she waited for the ageing thing to boot up. When it finally came to life she logged in and checked her emails. There were two belated replies to the enquiries she had started in relation to Daniel Carney. Sannie had followed up her theory that Carney might be a South African expat living in London.

The first message was from the South African embassy in London. The senior press officer there replied that she had no knowledge of a South African journalist named Daniel Carney. A search of their log of media calls over the past year had turned up no mention of anyone named Carney. 'Damn,' Sannie said as she closed the message.

The next was from the South African Union of Journalists. Again, it contained no news. There was no record of a Daniel Carney ever registering as a freelancer, or joining the union. She had already received replies from all of the major newspapers in South Africa saying they had never heard of the man.

So apparently he wasn't an accredited reporter. Who was he, then?

Sannie decided she would check with the Department of Home Affairs whether anyone by the name of Daniel Carney had entered or exited South Africa in the last few months. She checked her contact book again and called a man who had helped her with such queries in the past. It was a long shot, but she could think of no other avenue at the moment.

Her contact was out of the office, so she asked for and was given his email address by the operator. Sannie typed a brief message and sent it off.

Elise pressed the button on the remote control and the security gate rolled open. 'Christo, stop it. Don't pull your little sister's hair!'

'But she bit me, Ouma!'

'Don't tell tales. You're bigger than her, my boy. You must look after her.'

'And she must not bite me!'

The kids, normally so well behaved, had been being a handful this afternoon since she'd picked them up from school. Perhaps it was the heat, or maybe they were unsettled because of the disruptions to their routine. Elise believed the latter was more likely.

Sannie's trip to England, the coming of the Englishman to stay with them, and then his departure just as the children were warming to him, was all too much for them, Elise thought. Although she wouldn't admit it to Sannie she, too, had felt her initial dislike of the foreigner weaken a little as she got to know him better. He was a good man, she supposed – otherwise, why else would Sannie have taken to him? Yet he was obviously not the sort who could commit to family life. Why, she wondered, would he up and take off into the bush by himself? From what she had gathered, the man was still on the trail of the bloody terrorists who had killed his boss. That was fine, if you wanted to act like some action movie star, but she was worried that he might try to drag Sannie along with him, as he had done in Mozambique.

Elise was not sure Sannie was smart enough not to be enticed on some foolish adventure again. For all her academic ability at school and dedication at work, Sannie had always had a wild side. She'd grown up like an African kid on the farm, despite Elise's best efforts to civilise her. Pierre, Sannie's father, had been too soft on the girl. She hadn't been promiscuous as a teenager – at least, not as far as Elise knew – but she was concerned that she had obviously been having sex with the Englishman. Elise was not happy about any sex out of wedlock, though she knew standards were different these days. In any case, it came down to whether the man was right for her daughter, and her grandchildren. The Englishman could be charming, but he wasn't the kind to stick around, as he had just proved.

'Ouma, please, please, please, can I go in the swimming pool?'

Elise felt sorry for Christo but, while his swimming was quite good, it was a firm rule in the household that the children could only use the pool if their mother was present. 'No. You must wait until your mother comes home.'

Christo grizzled and Ilana yelped again. Elise parked the car and turned the engine off. 'Help me take the shopping inside,' she said to Christo, who frowned but obeyed, and went to the car boot. The phone started ringing. 'Grab two bags and bring them,' she said, rushing to the house and fumbling with her keys.

'Hello?'

'Mrs Van Rensburg?'

'Mrs De Winter, actually,' Elise said to the English-speaking man on the line. It sounded like he was on a cell phone. 'Who's calling?'

'Mrs De Winter, my name is Daniel Carney, I'm a journalist, from England – a friend of Tom Furey. I wonder if I might have a word with Tom, please? I understand he's staying with you.'

Elise frowned. She was naturally suspicious of any strangers – one had to be, with the crime rate the way it was in Johannesburg these days. But the man was English, and he knew Tom had been staying with them. She relaxed a little. 'He's not here.'

'Oh, I'm sorry to hear that. Has he left on his trip already?'

So, Elise thought, the man at least knew of Tom's movements. '*Ja*. A few days ago.'

'Again, I'm sorry to hear that. I'm only in Johannesburg for a couple of days and I wanted to catch up with him. I've got some information – some documents – that I brought with me from England. They'll be of great help to Tom, but it seems I've got no way of getting the information to him.'

'Well,' Elise paused. She could tell the man to drop the papers at the house. Sannie would know what to do with them.

'Perhaps I could just drop the documents with you. Sannie would be interested in them, as well.'

'Where are you, Mr . . . ?'

'Carney. As a matter of fact, I'm just up the road from your house, driving towards it now. I rang the

466

bell before, but there was no one home, so I waited until I saw your car come in.'

Elise licked her lips and ran a hand through her grey hair. 'Um, my daughter will be home from work in a couple of hours. Perhaps you can . . .'

'I'm on a flight in two hours' time, Mrs De Winter. How about I just drop the papers off with you, and I'll call Sannie later tonight?'

'Ouma! There's a car at the gate,' Christo sang out.

She supposed it would be all right. The man obviously knew Tom, as well as having mentioned Sannie's name. Elise picked up the remote control for the gate from where she'd dropped it on the kitchen counter, and pressed the button.

Sannie had gone out late for lunch and when she returned, there was a yellow Post-it note with a phone message on it. Jay Suresh, her contact at Home Affairs, had returned her call and said to call him urgently. If it was urgent, why couldn't the receptionist have called her on her cell phone? Sannie sighed. She dialled Suresh and, while she waited on hold, logged in again to the shared computer and brought up her emails.

There was also a message from Jay, which she opened while still waiting to talk to him in person. *Hi, Sannie. You must be psychic! Daniel John Carney, British Citizen, dob 21/7/64 arrived OR Tambo International Airport on the BA flight from London this morning at zero-eight-hundred. He had an existing visa and this was his second entry.* Suresh also gave the date of Carney's first arrival. She checked her calendar.

It was four days before Greeves and Joyce had been abducted from Tinga.

'Sannie, hi. Sorry, I was on another call,' Suresh said. 'Sannie? Are you there?'

'Hi, Jay. Sorry, I just read your email.'

'Hey, did you know this guy was going to arrive today?'

'No. No, I didn't.'

'Weird, hey?'

'Terrifying, more like it. Flag this guy, Jay. It's important. We can't let him leave South Africa without talking to him.'

Sannie thanked him for his help and strode into Wessels's office. The captain, who was also eating a late lunch, at his desk, motioned for her to sit down. She hadn't told him anything about Daniel Carney or Precious Tambo and her affair with Robert Greeves, so it took a few minutes to explain.

'It's the closest thing to a new lead we've had in the Greeves case,' Wessels said when she finished. 'Get on to it. We need to check hotels and guesthouses, car rental places – the lot. I'm afraid it's going to be a late finish for you today.'

'That's fine. My mom's with the kids. I'll call her.'

Sannie went back to her workstation and called home. The phone rang and rang until finally she heard her own voice on the answering machine. 'Mom? Mom, if you're there, pick up. Mom?'

There was no answer and the machine timed out. She dialled again and called down the line once more. She wondered if her mother had taken the kids out somewhere. She tried her cell phone but that, too, went through to voicemail. Sannie chewed her lower lip. Her mother had lost two cell phones already, so it wasn't beyond the bounds of possibility that she and the kids were out getting ice cream and she'd left her phone in the car.

Sannie busied herself calling the major hotels in Johannesburg, starting with those closest to the airport. After calling six, with no luck, she tried her home and her mother's phone numbers again. Nothing. She started to worry.

Wessels walked out of his office and stopped by her desk. 'You look anxious.'

'I can't get in touch with my mom or the kids.'

'Sannie, I've just told Erasmus and Ndlovu they're working late to help track down this Carney fellow. It won't look good if you clock off now.'

'I know that,' she said, more quickly and harshly than she'd intended. 'But I'm worried about them.'

Wessels sighed. 'Gee, I'm an old softy. Go, quickly. Make sure you keep calling hotels on your cell phone all the way home and back. I'll tell the others you're going to Home Affairs or something.'

'You're a star,' she told him, and he blushed and turned away, heading briskly to the coffee machine.

Sannie was halfway home in her car and talking to the reception at the Holiday Inn, Sandton, when her phone beeped, signalling she'd received a message. When the desk clerk told her there was no Daniel Carney staying at the hotel she ended the call and checked the message. When she played it back there was nothing. Silence, except for the low hum of a car engine. She'd hoped it would be her mother. Perhaps it was, and she had accidentally dialled her number without knowing it. Sannie checked the caller ID, but the number was blocked so it wasn't her mother.

She drove one-handed, holding the phone in her other hand. It started to vibrate and ring.

'Van Rensburg,' she said.

'Inspector, pull over if you are driving. I wouldn't want you to have an accident.'

'Who *is* this?' The man's voice was altered, as though it was coming through an electronic synthe-siser. A chill ran down her body.

'That doesn't matter for now. What is important, however, is that I have your children.'

29

Tom had tried to call Sannie from the Zambian town of Chipata, but hadn't been able to get reception for his mobile. In the morning he had crossed the border from Zambia into Malawi, a frustrating process of queuing and to-ing and fro-ing that took the best part of two hours.

It was a relief to be on the last leg towards Lake Malawi, even if it was on the poorest excuse for a road he had come across in his life. To call it surfaced was a gross exaggeration, as there seemed to be more holes than tar, and in some sections a new route had been carved out on either side by drivers taking to the verges.

If Zambia was a poor country, Malawi was destitute, but the people seemed friendly enough. He got smiles and waves from children and polite nods from adults as he bounced and cursed his way towards the lake that took up most of the small country.

He checked his phone regularly, but still had no reception. However, in a few places he noticed roadside phone kiosks. If he couldn't get a signal at Salima, the next major town, he would use one of them, or look for a hotel on the lake shore from which he could pay to make a call.

As in Zambia and Botswana, Malawi's roads were lined with signs advertising tombstones, coffins and funeral services. Twice he passed open-top *bakkies* carrying coffins flanked by mourners in their best shabby clothes. He imagined this was what it must have been like to live through Europe's Black Plague: the slow but inevitable whittling away of whole households, villages and communities until the survivors dispersed, perhaps taking the sickness further afield. At the border post he'd noticed young girls with braided hair and wearing tight, sequin-covered jeans climbing into the cabs of long-distance lorries which queued while awaiting customs clearance. Africa's roads had replaced its rivers as ribbons of life – and death.

Salima might have been a pretty town once, but it seemed as chipped and holed and crumbling as its main road. He parked outside a bank and changed some pounds into kwacha, to have cash for his coming nights' accommodation and food and fuel for the Land Rover. He hoped to be in Malawi no more than a couple of days, but was prepared to stay until he had answers to the questions that drove him onwards.

While the town looked as though it was on the lake shore on his map, the reality was different. The water was a further twenty kilometres, on the shores of Senga Bay. The road now ran atop a raised embankment over flat land that he guessed must flood when the rains came. There was even less room to manoeuvre around potholes now, so he spent much of the drive in second gear, climbing into and out of the eroded basins.

Instead of being greeted by a panorama of the massive inland waterway, he found the beach at Senga Bay guarded by walled villas, guesthouses, and a white concrete hotel, whose gate he drove through. In a yard behind the main building, still with no view of the water, was a small but shady camp ground. There were two other South African-registered vehicles, a jeep and a Land Cruiser, parked under a tree. They had rooftop tents like his and a washing line was strung between the two roof carriers.

Tom went to the hotel's reception and asked if there was a phone he could use. He checked his watch. Five pm. Sannie might not be home, but Elise and the kids would be. He would try Sannie's cell and then her home landline.

He signed in and paid for his campsite, and dialled Sannie's cell phone. It was busy but, unlike his phone, didn't go through to voicemail when it was engaged. The home phone rang until the answering machine kicked in, and he left a message.

Tom tried Sannie's mobile again, but it was still busy, so he went in search of the hotel bar. At least he'd been able to leave a message at Sannie's house, and she'd get it eventually.

Sannie had stopped her car on the side of the highway. Cars whizzed by her.

Ordinarily, stopping was the last thing she would have done – even to talk on her cell phone. To stop or, worse, break down on a main road in Johannesburg was to invite the attention of car-jackers. However, it was impossible to listen to the inhuman, distorted voice on the other end of the phone and concentrate on the road at the same time.

'I told you, I have no idea where Tom Furey is!' She knew she should keep her cool and not antagonise the caller, but he had her children. She wanted to scratch his eyeballs out – to kill him.

'You will soon enough. There's a message for you on your home answering machine. He is at Salima, on the shore of Lake Malawi. If he gets to Cape Maclear, where he is heading, you will never see your children again.'

'Are you in my bloody home? I'm going to –'

'Shut the fuck up, you stupid bitch. You will never see your children again if Furey does not turn around and return to England via South Africa. Do you understand what I am telling you, Inspector? Your children will not die, not immediately at least, but you will never see them again. The same goes if you tell your police superiors or anyone else what I've just said.'

Sannie started to cry, the fat tears rolling down her face. She thought of the paedophile ring that the police had just busted.

'Listen to me, Inspector. Contact Furey – I don't care how you do it – and call him off. If he gets to Cape Maclear we will know first. He will die and your children will disappear – forever. Your children are already out of South Africa. When Furey is in London they will be released and you'll be told where to find them.'

'No, please . . . let me talk to them and I'll –'

'You can stop this, Inspector. Tell Furey that Robert Greeves is dead and there is no way he will ever find the men who abducted him. He can, however, save your children.'

'Wait . . .'

The phone line went dead. Sannie wiped the tears from her cheeks, smearing her makeup, and rammed the car into gear. She dropped the clutch and floored the accelerator. A car horn blared behind her as she barged her way back into the traffic, but she ignored it.

On the way home she called Wessels and, through her sobs, explained that her kids were gone. Despite the kidnapper's warning she blurted out what she knew of Tom's travels. This was no time to hold back information from her boss. Wessels told her he was on his way to her place and would dispatch some uniformed officers immediately.

Sannie stopped two hundred metres from her home, drew her pistol and cocked it. She walked the rest of the way to her gate and pressed the remote. She darted in as soon as the gap was wide enough and, weapon raised in front of her, kicked open the back door, which had been left ajar.

'Police! Mom? Where are you?' With her left hand Sannie cuffed away errant tears and steeled herself for what she might find.

She moved through the kitchen and checked the kids' rooms and hers. She saw Ilana's Barbie on the floor and two of Christo's toy cars. She choked back another sob and kicked open the bathroom door, bringing her pistol to bear.

Elise was sitting on the toilet, fully clothed, but her hands and ankles were bound with plastic cable ties and her mouth was gagged with masking tape. Sannie holstered her pistol and ripped off the gag.

'Oh, baby, I'm so, so sorry.' Her mother started to cry.

Sannie tried to calm her as she knocked makeup and pill bottles from the bathroom cupboard in search of a pair of nail scissors. By the paleness of her mother's face it looked like she was in shock. Sannie snipped through the ties and helped Elise stand. 'It was only one man, Sannie, but he had a gun and . . .'

Sannie ran a hand through her hair. Now was the time for her to bottle her own emotions and get a good description of the kidnapper. She had to calm her mother down and extract every scrap of information she could from her – as though she were any other witness.

'I'll put the kettle on, Mom. Get some paper and a pen and start writing down everything you can remember, right from the start. Especially what he looked like. Did you get a good look at him?'

'Sannie, I'm so, so sorry. If he hurts them I'll kill myself and . . .'

Her mother was becoming hysterical. 'Sit down! Write, Mom, and then I'll ask you some questions.'

Outside she heard the wail of a siren.

'He said he was a journalist, from England, and that he knew Tom. He said his name was Daniel . . . um, let me think of his surname. Daniel . . .'

Sannie turned from the stove and felt the blood

draining from her own face. She swallowed hard. 'Daniel Carney?'

'Yes, that's it. Daniel Carney.'

After having a couple of beers, Tom went to reception and picked up the telephone handset. Nothing.

'Ah, but it is broken,' the woman said.

'I don't suppose you have any idea when the line will be fixed?'

She shook her head.

Ah, Africa, he thought. He said goodbye to the receptionist and walked back out into the night. The sky was clear and the moon was on the rise. He walked around the hotel to a security fence which isolated a patch of beach for hotel guests only. A light breeze decorated the lake's surface with silvery ruffles. Tiny orange lights winked further out. Fishermen, he supposed. In other circumstances it might have been lovely. But not tonight.

When Tom returned to the Land Rover he slid out the toolbox and placed it on the front seat. He took out the nine-millimetre pistol and unwrapped it, and loaded the two spare magazines with eight bullets each from the box Sannie had given him and put them in the zippered internal pocket of his shorts, which he would wear again tomorrow. He carried the pistol up the ladder into his rooftop tent. He didn't think he would need the weapon tonight, but he might tomorrow.

*

Wessels was trying to be comforting and professional while at the same time struggling with his obvious anger at Sannie for not telling him earlier about Furey's safari to Malawi.

'Does the bloody fool think he can take on a gang of terrorists by himself?'

Sannie shrugged. 'I wonder if there are any terrorists at all.'

'What do you mean? Of course there are.' Wessels sat beside her on the couch in her lounge room. Elise had recovered enough to make tea for the uniformed officers, and a forensic team busied itself taking prints and looking for other evidence that Daniel Carney might have left behind. 'They killed Robert Greeves, Sannie.'

'I think Tom thinks that Greeves is still alive. The kidnapper told me to tell Tom that Greeves was dead, as though that would make him stop whatever he's been doing.'

Wessels sighed. 'But why would the terrorists keep him alive, and why fake his death? He's worth far more to them as a live hostage.'

'Greeves's wife told us her husband often talked about retiring to Malawi. That's why Tom's gone there, I think.'

'He didn't *retire*, he was executed. The English police have it on video.'

'They also have the death of another man on video, Nick Roberts, Greeves's first protection officer.'

'*Ja*, so what?'

'I've just been over and over the description of Daniel Carney that my mother gave, Henk.'

'And?'

'When we get the passport photo of Carney from the British Foreign Office, I'm pretty sure I'm going to know who he really is.'

Tom woke before dawn, folded the rooftop tent and secured it, and hid the pistol beneath the driver's seat of the Land Rover before locking the vehicle. He walked in bare feet through the hotel to the lake shore and, after a few minutes of stretching, started to run.

He ran harder and faster, alternating sprints with slow jogging. When the lake gave up the first shimmering sliver of the new day's light, he turned and ran into the clear water, striking out towards the unseen far shore, much to the amusement of two paddling fishermen. The water was cold, and it shocked his nerve endings to life. He knew that in a few hours he would be baking and sweating in the Land Rover, so he enjoyed the invigorating coolness while it lasted.

He jogged across the beach and back to the camping ground. There was no need to shower after his dip in the clear fresh water. Lake Malawi, like everything else he had encountered in Africa, was not as he had expected. He'd had visions of muddy, turgid water – perhaps a huge inland cesspit. However, he'd discovered it was more like the world's largest swimming pool, with a white sandy beach. A beautiful place. He watched the male and female eagles pass the red sun, and wished Sannie was here with him to share the moment.

*

Sannie had stayed awake all night, but there had been no more phone calls. Wessels dozed on her couch and the uniformed police had just left, replaced by two from the morning shift. Her mother was asleep in her room, thanks to a tranquilliser administered by a police doctor who had called in during the night.

She paced the linoleum tiles of her small kitchen, another cup of black coffee in her hand. Try as she might, Sannie couldn't stop herself from imagining the horrific things someone might be doing to Ilana and Christo. As a police officer she knew just how evil adults could be to children. Even though she wasn't patrolling the streets any more, hardly a day went by when the media wasn't reminding her by reporting the rape or murder of a child. Some people in South Africa still believed having sex with a virgin was a way to cure HIV-AIDS. Sannie sniffled back the tears before they came; she had to be strong. She'd asked herself, over and over, what she would say to Tom if he called. Part of her wanted to do exactly what the kidnapper said – to get him to drop his foolish quest. However, the very demands the man had made on the phone confirmed that Tom was on the right trail, and dangerously close to whoever was behind this bizarre plot. The other part of her – the veteran police officer who had faced bullets and death in the line of duty – wanted to find these men and arrest them.

No. Find them and kill them.

Sannie peeked through the door at Wessels, who was now snoring in front of the TV, which was tuned to the sports channel. A golf tournament had put him to sleep. She picked up her handbag, and took the cordless phone from its cradle and walked outside into the yard. It was just after eleven and she shielded her eyes with her free hand against the sun's glare.

'South African Airways, good day,' said the female operator.

'Hi. I need to make a booking, please. What time is your first flight to Lilongwe, Malawi?'

Inside the house again she went to her bedroom, stripped off the blouse, pants and boots she'd been wearing for nearly twenty-four hours, and stepped into the ensuite to shower. She took only a few minutes to wash and then dress. She selected a short-sleeve khaki bush shirt and matching trousers and hiking boots. From the closet she fetched her gym bag and packed it.

Wessels stirred as Sannie walked back out into the lounge room. He yawned. 'What are you up to?'

'I know it sounds crazy, but I'm going to the gym, Henk. I think some exercise might help me. I'll only be gone an hour and I've got my cell phone.'

He rubbed his stubbled chin and then stretched his arms. '*Ja,* a workout might help relieve the stress. I'll stay here until you get back and then I'll have to go into the office. A couple of detectives will be here soon to stay with you – in case he calls again.'

'Okay, see you.' She walked out quickly, before he twigged that hiking boots weren't the most normal thing to wear to the gym.

In the garage Sannie shifted some boxes – mostly Christo's old stuff – and found his diving gear in a tin trunk. She rummaged through the mask, fins and life vests until her hand closed around the solid length of the weapon. She lifted the diving knife free of the clutter and unsheathed it. The stainless-steel blade was nearly thirty centimetres long. Razor sharp on one side – she remembered how he used to test it by shaving the hairs on his forearms, which always made her shiver – and wickedly serrated on the other. It glittered in the pale dawn light coming through the window. There was no way she would get on to a commercial flight with her police-issue pistol unless she had the paperwork to prove she was on official business. But she wasn't going into their lair unarmed. She carefully replaced the knife in the stout plastic scabbard and buried it at the bottom of her bag, under the lift-out semi-rigid piece of vinyl covered card that kept the bag's shape. If her bag was inspected by customs when she got to Malawi, a woman carrying a diving knife but no scuba gear might provoke questions and she didn't want to be delayed. She zipped the bag shut and got in the car.

So far on his trip Tom had only called in the evenings and she knew he wouldn't bother trying again until tonight. He would be at Cape Maclear long before then. She only hoped she could beat him there. She started the car and opened the security gate.

30

The turquoise waters of the lake were fringed by a long white crescent of sand that stretched away as far as Tom could see. The beachfront here was not overdeveloped, as it had been at Senga Bay.

Instead of midrange concrete hotels, there were backpacker joints consisting of sandy camping sites and simple reed and thatch bungalows and, closer to the national park at Cape Maclear, at one end of the beach, were the holiday houses of Malawi's wealthy minority and expatriate investors.

He wore a cap pulled low down over his eyes, a pair of sunglasses and his board shorts. Despite the liberal smearing of sunscreen he'd applied, he could feel his back burning in the midday sun. If he looked like a silly white tourist, all the better, he thought. He strolled along the water's edge, politely but persistently waving away the diminishing gaggle of touts who trailed him down the beach.

'You want souvenir, Mr? Painting? Wood carving?'

'No thank you.'

'You want *dagga*, Mr? Malawi Gold?'

'Definitely not, thank you.'

'You want girl, Mr?'

And so it went on. Eventually, he hoped, they would tire of him.

The camping ground where he'd parked the Land Rover was typical of the others he'd passed. Each was separated from its neighbours by a flimsy U-shaped fence of woven reed, with the side facing the beach left open, to allow the guests to enjoy the view and, presumably, the touts to ply their trade uninterrupted.

A pair of bronzed girls with Australian accents sat together on sarongs smoking and chatting as an African girl threaded beads into their hair and braided it. It was a good look on black women, Tom thought, but he wasn't sure how it would go down in Sydney.

Further along the beach, half-a-dozen tourists in wetsuits and masks waded into the clear water and squatted to put on their fins. The South African dive master went from person to person, helping them through the ungainly manoeuvre.

Out on the water a fibreglass speedboat sent up a fantail of spray in a tight turn which the water-skier behind couldn't handle. With a squeal she went skidding off, hitting the surface with a painful-sounding slap. Tom shook his head.

Beyond the ski boat, which was returning to pick up the now-laughing girl, was an island that looked like a clump of granite boulders, topped with tall trees. A pair of fish eagles, their distinctive white heads and red-brown bodies standing out plainly from the dark foliage, watched the waters for their next meal.

From what he'd seen on posters in the campsites and hotels, and learned from the touts who persisted with him, the lake was home to myriad brightly hued tropical fish called cichlids. If he'd been here on holiday he would have gone snorkelling or diving, but he was searching for something else – a house with a bougainvillea-covered archway leading to the beach and lake.

As Tom neared Cape Maclear itself he noticed that the houses became larger, grander and better kept. Most, he guessed, dated back to the sixties and the height of British colonialism in what was then known as Nyasaland. As such, they tended to be single-storey villas, with whitewashed rendered facades. The current owners, whoever they were, had maintained neatly trimmed lawns and gardens. It was, he supposed, what passed for millionaire's row in a dirt-poor country. He also noticed fewer touts – even his own entourage had dwindled to one persistent teenager. When a blue-uniformed security guard stepped from a lawn onto the white sand, the boy turned quietly and walked back along the beach.

Ahead of him he could see a fence and sign marking the end of the public beach and the beginning of Cape Maclear National Park. From his enquiries at the campsite he had learned that to enter the national park one had to go inland a little way to the road that led to the point. Beyond the fence the shoreline was pristine bush and boulders, the latter perfect for diving off and snorkelling amid. A pair of guards sauntered onto the beach from another villa and Tom slowed his step. He yawned and stretched, and then turned and waded into the water. Leaving his cap and sunglasses on, he started breaststroking out towards the middle of the lake. When he had covered about fifty metres he turned and floated on his back. Looking towards the shoreline, he now had a better view of the fronts of the line of villas leading to the park boundary.

Near the end of the row Tom saw a trimmed hedge, about the height of an average-sized man, which obscured the view of a house. Above the hedge was a glittering coil of razor wire, which meant that behind the shrubbery there was a security fence, perhaps electrified. What interested him most, however, was the gate in the centre of the hedge, in which a security guard stood. Framing the man was a lattice covered with red bougainvillea. Slowly he turned on his side and started swimming back the way he'd come.

On the beach, a hundred metres further down, he emerged from the water to be greeted by the dogged young man who had tried to sell him Malawi Gold – marijuana. For the first time that day, Tom wasn't displeased to see him.

'Boss, would you like some . . .'

'What I want, my friend,' Tom ran his hand through his hair, slicking away the cool, fresh water, 'is some information.'

'Me, bwana, I know everything about Cape Maclear. You want it, Solomon can find it.' He beamed with the friendliness of a salesman close to clinching a deal.

Tom walked back towards the camping ground and the boy fell into step beside him, striding out to meet Tom's pace. 'Who lives in the house with the big hedge?'

'Ah, bwana, I am hungry.'

'My money's in my vehicle.'

'Then shall we go, boss?'

Tom shook his head. When they reached the camping ground he told the youth to wait on the beach, and he went to the Land Rover and fetched his wallet. He opened it and peeled off some notes. Back at the water he palmed the tout ten dollars. 'He is an Indian man.'

'From Malawi?' Tom asked.

The boy shook his head. 'No, South Africa.'

'What's his name?'

'This man, he likes his privacy, bwana. A friend of mine was ... visiting that house one night, and the security guards caught him. They beat him very bad, bwana.'

By visiting, Tom assumed the boy's comrade was trying to burgle the place.

'I should not be talking about that place. Bad things have happened there.'

'Such as?'

The boy shook his dreadlocks. Tom peeled off another green note.

'The women in the village – my mother, also – tell us never to go near that man. He has been coming for many years and the women say to all the children you must never talk to that man or go in his car.'

'Name?' Tom asked again.

The boy glanced over his shoulder, nervously, as if the occupant of the house might be following them. 'Khan,' he whispered.

Tom nodded. He felt his mouth start to dry and his pulse quicken. 'Is he there now?'

Solomon shook his head. 'He is on his island, I think. I saw his boat some days ago.'

'His island?'

'Yes, he is a rich man, bwana. The island is far, about five kilometres, but I can organise a boat for you.'

Tom nodded. 'Okay. For tonight.'

'A speedboat, bwana, or a kayak for you?'

Tom rubbed his jaw. He didn't want to telegraph his approach. 'This is what I want, for this afternoon . . .'

Captain Henk Wessels poured himself a cup of coffee from the percolator pot in Sannie's kitchen and picked up her cordless phone. He pressed the redial button and gulped the lukewarm brew while he waited for the phone to answer.

'South African Airways, good day,' the female voice said.

Wessels hung up the phone without speaking and slammed the cup down on the counter. He reached in his trouser pocket for his car keys.

'Bloody woman. I should have known.'

Sannie parked her car at OR Tambo International Airport, grabbed her sports bag, locked the car and jogged across to the terminal. She took the lift to level two, cursing its slowness, and stepped out into the departures hall.

She scanned the check-in counters until she found

an SAA desk with the flight to Lilongwe, Malawi illuminated on the sign board behind. She glanced at her watch. Less than half an hour to boarding – she had only just made it.

Shifting her weight from foot to foot like a boxer eager to land the first blow, she tried to breathe deeply as the rotund African businessman in front of her badgered the woman behind the desk for an upgrade. Her cell phone rang and she forgot her impatience.

'Van Rensburg.'

'Sannie, it's Henk. Where the bloody hell are you?'

'Umm . . .'

'Bloody hell, woman, it doesn't matter. We've found your kids!'

Sannie squealed with delight, causing the businessman and the check-in clerk to stare at her. She didn't care. 'Where? How, Henk? How are they? Please god, tell me they're safe. If anyone's touched them I'll . . . Where are you . . . are you on your cell phone?'

'Slow down, Sannie. Yes, I'm in the car on my cell. Two uniforms have the kids. There was a complaint of some excessive noise in a house in Boksburg. The officers went to visit and there was a shoot-out. There was a man guarding Christo and Ilana. He was killed, but your kids are fine, Sannie. The police with them say they appear to be unhurt.'

Sannie started to cry, cuffing the tears away. 'Oh, Henk. I have to get to them.'

'Okay, okay. Where are you? I've been to the gym and it's clear you're not there.'

She felt guilty and embarrassed about her impetuous actions, and thought about Tom. She had to get some word to him, but for now he was on his own. 'I'm at the airport, Henk. International terminal.'

He was silent for a few seconds. 'On any other day I'd throw the bloody book at you, Inspector. Stay right where you are and I'll come to you. I'll lead you to the house.'

'Just give me the address, man. I'll drive there myself.'

'Sannie, I want to be there with you. You've been through a hell of a lot. Also, who knows . . . there might be accomplices on their way back to the house. I need to take charge of the scene and then we'll move your kids out. I couldn't let the uniforms take them away just yet. I want to catch these bastards, Sannie.'

'Me too.' She knew he was right, and not just about the operational aspects. She needed a friend to lean on now as well. 'Hurry, Henk.'

She rushed outside and across the road, causing a BMW driver to slam on his brakes. Sannie ignored his insults and ran through the car park, clutching her bag. 'Oh, no, man!'

The front tyre on the driver's side was flat. How the hell did that happen? She felt like screaming. She unlocked the car and was lifting the carpet in the boot to get the jack out when her cell phone rang again. She swore, then answered it.

'It's Henk. I'm just pulling into the airport car park. Where are you?'

'You're here already?'

'I was already on my way to Boksburg, and travelling fast,' Henk said.

She gave him directions to the bay where she was parked and he pulled up thirty seconds later.

Henk pushed a button and his electric window slid down. 'Ag, just get in, Sannie.' He leaned across and opened the passenger door of his Ford Falcon. 'We can come back for it later.'

Sannie nodded. He was right and she couldn't wait a minute more to see Christo and Ilana. 'Okay. Just let me lock it.' Her gym bag was on the rear seats, where she had just tossed it. She reached in and grabbed it. A car with a flat tyre was like an open cold box to a monkey when it came to thieves. She locked her vehicle with the remote, threw her bag in Henk's car and jumped in. 'Okay, man. Let's go!'

The muscles in the fisherman's back rippled as he propelled the dugout effortlessly across the lake's surface. In contrast, Tom was sweating profusely, even though he was doing nothing – other than bailing with the cut-off, capped remains of a plastic Coca-Cola bottle.

The water glittered like a massive silver satin sheet littered with gold coins. Behind them, Lake Malawi was devouring the sun once more.

'Crocodile Island,' said the fisherman, lifting one hand from the paddle and pointing to the green speck ahead of them. Tom heard a fish eagle cry, another indicator they were nearing land.

Solomon had told Tom that the island was no more than a kilometre in diameter. It had been developed as a small, exclusive tourist resort and could cater for a dozen people. Khan had bought it as a going concern, but Solomon had said that, as far as he knew, it was not operating commercially any more. 'He has friends coming to stay.'

'Staff?' Tom had asked.

Solomon had shrugged. 'Not from around here. No one local. Sometimes, the fishermen say, boats go there in the night-time.'

Tom wore his black swimming shorts and a brown long-sleeve T-shirt which clung sweatily to his skin. It had protected him from the afternoon sun and would conceal his still-pale skin once he was on the island. His trainers were slung around his neck, the laces knotted together. He had borrowed a water-proof rubber bag from the diving and snorkelling supplies at the campsite. In it was Sannie's pistol and the spare magazines, along with a telescoping club, similar to his Asp, and a pair of handcuffs that Tom had brought with him from Christo's garage. He'd found a whole trunk of equipment that Sannie later told him her husband had used when working private security jobs, which he sometimes did after hours to supplement his police income. As well as the cuffs and cosh he'd found radios, slimline body armour – for wearing under a suit – and a can of pepper spray.

The fisherman stopped paddling. 'No further,' he said.

Tom nodded. The man had already told him he would not risk landing on the island. His English was not good enough for him to explain why. 'Trouble,' was all he could say. 'Okay. Sunrise.' Tom pointed at the pink sky where the sun had just disappeared and raised his arm into the air. The fisherman nodded. He would return to the same spot at dawn.

As plans went, Tom's were virtually nonexistent. He had not been able to find a phone that worked in Monkey Bay, so he couldn't have told Sannie what he was up to even if he'd wanted to. Not that he would get much support from the South African Police Service where he was now. He'd wanted to pass on the rumours he'd heard about Pervez Khan, although the information from Solomon would hardly be enough for the South Africans to extradite him.

Tom swung his legs over the side of the dugout and slid silently into the water. The bag floated and he held it out in front of him as he swam towards the island, about a hundred metres distant. Despite the name, Solomon had assured him there were no crocodiles in the water. Tom wasn't sure he could believe the boy, so he breaststroked as fast as he could with one arm.

Solomon had explained that there was a wide, sandy beach on one side of the island, and a rocky shoreline of boulders on the other. With Solomon translating, he'd asked the fisherman to drop him near the rocks. The chalets and bar of the old resort overlooked the sand, Solomon had said.

His feet found slippery purchase on a submerged boulder and he carefully stood upright. He placed the waterproof bag on another smooth, round rock, still warm from the vanished sun, and boosted himself up out of the water. He sat and pulled on his trainers, and took the pistol and spare magazine from the bag. The latter he slipped into the pockets of his board shorts. He had a total of twenty-four rounds with him. He hoped he wouldn't need all of them – any of them. He stashed the bag in the cleft of two rocks, the blue plastic just visible, at the base of the tallest tree on this side of the island. With the richly purpled sky behind him he headed roughly eastwards, towards the inhabited side of the island.

The bush was dense, almost tropical, unlike the countryside he'd seen in the rest of Africa so far. He was a world away from London, out of his depth, but driven on with every step. Small things scurried through the sparse undergrowth as he moved. He did his best to ignore them and pressed on. Something screeched in the trees above him, perhaps a bat or an owl.

The vegetation thinned ahead of him, and Tom could see the outline of buildings. He smelled wood smoke and noticed an African-style water boiler, an old fuel drum cemented above a bricked fireplace, with a chimney behind it. There were four simple masonry buildings with sloping roofs made of corrugated asbestos sheet. Staff quarters, he thought. No lights shone.

He moved to the nearest building and flattened himself against its back wall. Peering around, he saw a much more substantial building, whitewashed and thatch-roofed. Either the main lodge or a larger bungalow, he assumed. He continued moving. When he came to the building, he saw now that it was one of a line of four which faced onto a well-kept lawn and, beyond that, a narrow, white sandy beach. Out on the inky waters of the lake he could see the bobbing lights of fishermen in their dugouts. A mild breeze off the water cooled his face but couldn't dry the sweat on his body.

A pale glow shone from one of the windows in the main lodge. The smoke from the boiler had told him someone was in residence. He moved from cover to cover, from tree to hedge, to the shade cast by an outdoor umbrella structure made of reed, sheltering a table and chairs.

The lodge had a verandah, set about a metre above the grass with an extension of the roof overhanging it. Tom saw flickering shadows, cast by a candle the flame of which was gently being swayed by the breeze off the lake.

Holding Sannie's pistol out in front of him, he moved to the side of the lodge building. With his back pressed against the whitewashed walls he edged closer to the verandah. When he came to the corner that marked the end of the built structure, he slowly craned his head around it so he could see out over the deck.

There, sitting in a wicker armchair, and very much alive, was Robert Greeves.

31

Sannie urged Henk Wessels to drive faster.

'Hey, I don't want us getting in a car accident. The house is just up the road.'

'I know you. You look worried,' she said. 'You run your finger around your collar when something's wrong.'

He looked at her. 'Of course I'm worried. The sooner we get you reunited with your kids the better. I want them out of that house in case the other kidnappers come back.'

She nodded. It was odd, though, that Henk hadn't called in more uniformed officers already, to move her children somewhere else. It's what she would have done, but then, she wasn't the captain.

'Here it is.' Wessels stopped the car.

There was nothing unusual about the modest single-storey home except for the two uniformed police outside, and, additionally, the fact that both the officers were white. There were still plenty of whites in uniform, but it was a little odd to see

496

a pair of them together. Most of the junior ranks these days were black Africans, unlike when Sannie had joined the police service. Sannie nodded to the officers, who smiled back at her, as she followed Wessels up the garden path, impatient to get to her children.

Wessels pulled out a key and unlocked the front door.

Sannie brushed past him as he opened it. 'Christo? Ilana?'

She entered the shabbily furnished lounge room, and smelled stale cigarette smoke and old cooking oil. 'Christo? Ilana?'

'Mom?' Christo called from the kitchen. He ran out, his sister hanging on to his shirt tail.

Sannie put her hand to her mouth and rushed to them. She dropped to her knees, flung her arms wide and drew them to her, and buried her head in Christo's shirt, letting the fabric soak her flood of pent-up tears. She was too overcome to speak.

'Where have you been, Mom?' Ilana asked.

'This man who knew Tom came and collected us, Mom. Is Tom okay?'

Sannie sobbed, deep and hard, and stepped back from Christo so she could wipe her eyes with the back of her hand. 'Christo, listen to me. Are you all right, my boy? Are you hurt? Did that man ... hurt you? Did he hurt your sister?'

'No, Mom.'

Ilana looked up at her, and when Sannie saw her blinking back the tears, she started to cry again herself.

'Mom, are you okay?' Christo asked.

'Yes, my boy, I'm fine. Let's go. I'm taking you home.'

Tom was looking at Greeves and didn't see the broken beer bottle in the grass. The glass shattered and crunched when he moved his feet.

'Who's there?'

Tom made no move to hide. He was more than ready for this confrontation. He stepped into the light.

'Detective Sergeant Furey,' Greeves lowered himself slowly back into his chair. 'Take a seat.'

'I'll stand.' Tom kept looking around him, his pistol hand following his gaze as he swept the verandah, watching the flanks, and the door that led back inside the lodge.

'I expect you've got some questions. Scotch?'

Tom shook his head.

'Well, don't mind me if I have another.'

Tom detected a slight slurring of the minister's words. From what he could see, Greeves looked in fine shape. His face and arms were golden and healthy looking in the reflected light. His hair was brushed and he wore a crisp white cotton shirt, open at the neck, with navy chinos.

'On your feet. Let's go.'

'Oh, not so fast, Tom. You made it this far. At least tell me how you knew it was all a fake, that I was never truly abducted.'

'You first. Why?'

'Why what?'

498

'Why did you fake your kidnapping? What kind of a scandal made you do it?'

Greeves said nothing. He refilled his glass from the decanter on the table and took a long sip.

'It was Ebony, the stripper, wasn't it?' Tom listened hard for any sound of movement in the house, and checked each side of the verandah again while he waited for the reply.

'Yes.'

'When did you sleep with her?'

'You tell me.'

Tom looked down into those cold grey eyes. 'How old was she? Ten? Eleven?'

Greeves exhaled and raised his glass, waving it casually. 'If you must know, she was twelve. I didn't know it at the time, I thought she was older.'

'And you think that makes it all right?'

'All right?' Greeves stared back at him, defiant. 'No. And that's the truth. I know it's not all right, but I can't change it. It's just the way I am – the way I'm wired. I like young girls. I'd forgotten all about her. It happened in South Africa, years ago. She came to England as an illegal, saw my picture in the newspaper one day, and contacted me. She bloody well made an appointment at my constituency surgery.'

'And you had her killed.' Tom felt the anger rising in him and tried his best to control it, to stay calm.

'No! I've never killed anyone in my life.'

'You lying bastard.' Tom took a deep breath of his own. He needed to keep it together. 'You sent Nick to get her . . . to kill her.'

'No. I swear it. I swear on the life of my children. I

told her it wasn't me . . .'

'But you recognised her.'

Another sigh. 'Yes, I knew it was her, but I tried to convince her she was wrong.'

'And so you sent Nick to do your dirty work.'

'No, nothing happened. Not for a few weeks. She called my office and left me another message, saying, cryptically, that she'd been talking to the media and only I could do the right thing. Helen, my press secretary, told me, although she thought it was a prank call.'

'Was that when you sent Nick to negotiate with her, after she contacted you?'

'Nick's dead, Tom.'

'Bullshit. He's masquerading as a journalist called Daniel Carney. It took me a while to put it together, but as soon as I realised you'd faked your death, it was obvious Nick was still alive as well.'

Greeves looked to one side of the verandah, and Tom followed his gaze. Greeves turned his eyes back to Tom. The defiance had gone from his face. 'What gave it away? I'm curious.'

'The monkeys.'

'How?'

Tom recalled his internet research, about African primates. 'Vervet monkeys are only active in daylight hours. They sleep in trees overnight.'

'So?'

'So, you and your band of merry men would have had to capture them during the day. Bernard's stage-managed escape didn't happen until well after dark. Your people lured the monkeys into cages during the day and kept them somewhere nearby. As soon as Bernard made it away safely you had the monkeys brought in and positioned in the house. You all had plenty of time to get away. It was proof the whole set-up had been planned well in advance.'

Tom waited for a reaction, but got none, so he continued. 'Someone drew half a litre of blood from you at some stage – not a difficult operation for your friend Doctor Khan – and spread it around the room where you'd been held, to make it look like you'd been shot. Khan even drew some cerebral spinal fluid and mixed it with the blood. Nice touch, that, though the spinal tap mustn't have been pleasant. The hair was a giveaway, though. You made a mistake there.'

'Really? Do tell.'

'The "abductors" left your hair on the bathroom floor, after they'd shaved your head, for us to find. However, there was no blood in the hallway from the supposed wounds on the soles of your feet, which Bernard had seen as "evidence" of your torture.'

'And you figured this out all by yourself?'

'The clues, the evidence, were all there. All it needed was motive. That was the hard part. You wanted to drop out . . . to get out of the public eye without shaming your Party, but you couldn't just quit. There was more to it, even after you had Nick kill the African girl.'

'You think you know it all.'

'Most of it. You can fill in the blanks when I get you back to London. Your mate Khan was the nail in the coffin, wasn't he?'

Greeves shrugged. 'You tell me.'

501

'I heard on the car radio that the South Africans recently busted an international people-smuggling racket, whose main purpose was to supply the sex trade – including underage boys and girls for sick perverts like you. Khan needed to disappear too – I'm betting he knew the trail would lead to him. I'm also betting that the UK link was those two blokes in Enfield who blew up their own house. Was that Nick who topped them in the street? Had you sent him there as well, to get rid of some connection, or record they had of you?'

'So, what are you going to do with all this information, Tom? The world thinks I'm dead. The British government is happy – there were rumours of my imminent demise already circulating. The press has swallowed the story. What would it take for you to turn your back?'

Tom shook his head. The bastard was trying to buy him. 'A decent, honourable man took his life because of you, and you took my life away from me. I want it back.'

'Well, that's not going to happen. Who else have you told your little tale to?'

'I was wondering when you'd ask. I've sent a letter to a friend of mine who's a crime-scene investigator. She'll know the right questions to ask the right people. I've also told her that if anything happens to me, and she gets stonewalled by MI6 or the government, to pass on everything to Michael Fisher at the *World*.'

'I wish you hadn't done that.'

Tom looked up towards the lodge's front door, from where the cultured female voice had come.

Janet Greeves emerged from the shadows. She held a two-two calibre semiautomatic pistol, fitted with a silencer, in her right hand. 'Drop your gun, Detective Sergeant Furey.'

'Do as she says,' said another voice from behind Tom.

He turned and saw a swarthy man holding a short-barrel AK 47 assault rifle emerge from the line of trees that shielded the main lodge from the first guest bungalow. He was trapped.

'Doctor Khan, I presume?'

The man smiled and shrugged. 'It doesn't matter who I am. Drop your gun now, Furey, or I'll shoot.'

Tom noted the man had a large mobile phone hanging heavily from a clip on his belt. A satellite phone, he guessed. Tom considered his options. He could take one of them out, but not both of them. What he needed to do now was stay alive, for as long as possible. Not that he fancied his chances. He crouched, aware of the two weapons following his every move, and placed Sannie's pistol on the tiled verandah floor.

Greeves started to get up from his chair, but his wife took a step towards him, out of the shadows, and swung her pistol towards the politician's head. 'Stay where you are, Robert.'

'What?' Greeves looked back at his wife, the puzzlement plain in his face.

'Cover him, Pervez.' Janet Greeves closed the gap between her and Tom, but stopped out of arm's reach of him.

'Pervez?' Greeves looked imploringly at the

Pakistani-South African, but the man just shook his head. 'What the bloody hell's going on?'

'Furey knows too much,' Janet said to her husband.

'I can get away, get a new identity. Why are you betraying me?'

Janet laughed. 'Betraying *you*? Don't be pathetic, Robert. It was worth the gamble, but our bodyguard friend here was too clever. For his own good, and for yours.'

'You bitch.'

Tom looked from husband to wife, and back again. 'What did he do, Janet? Did he touch your children just like he touched the African kids when he was over here for work and play?'

'Very perceptive. I knew early on in our marriage that Robert wasn't particularly interested in me, save from using me to breed a couple of children, which were part of his political career. The overseas trips started early on, and I had my suspicions. When our daughter was ten, I caught him sitting on her bed, looking at her body, lifting her nightie, while she was asleep.'

'Janet, please . . . he doesn't need to know . . .'

'Shut up, you miserable piece of shit.'

Greeves looked as taken aback as Tom was by the vehemence. It was as though he was seeing these feelings released for the first time. Janet looked back at Tom. 'I told him then that if he ever touched the children I would have him killed. Arrest and a trial would hurt the kids more, I thought, not to mention the damage it would do the Party.'

'So, the agreement was that he'd indulge his sexual desires overseas – with other people's children.'

'Don't judge me, Mr Furey. I did what I did to protect my family. Honestly, I wish the events that led us to being here now had happened a decade ago.'

'Janet, this is ridiculous . . .'

'I said, shut up.'

Tom kept his eyes on the woman. 'I suspected you knew what was going on, with the fake abduction, but I didn't realise you were the mastermind. What forced you to act – the stripper threatening to go public, or the breaking up of the sex-slave smuggling ring in South Africa?'

'Both, in fact. Pervez here convinced Robert that he could safely, discreetly, bring . . . God, I hate saying it . . . a child into the UK. An African child, for that's my husband's sick little fantasy. Robert had . . . ordered an eleven-year-old girl for himself. If Pervez had been caught there would have been a trail leading to Robert. Nick found out about the impending operation through his contacts in the South African police, and tipped me off.'

Tom looked at Greeves. The man had been going to *buy* a child. He returned his focus to the wife. 'So you and Nick were having an affair – that wasn't just a red herring?'

She shook her head. '"Affair" might be too strong a word, as it implies some romantic involvement. I have needs, and Nick was more than happy to satisfy them – physical needs and business needs. I sent him to the girl, Ebony, and told him to pose as a journalist and offer more money than the *World*. I would have been happy for her to leave England with a bag of money, but she changed her mind. She told Nick she'd prayed about what she was doing, and that even if she gave the money to her church, back in Africa, God wouldn't be happy. She told Nick she was going to go public, whatever happened.'

'So you had her killed?'

'I said before, Nick helped me with a number of personal and business needs. If it had just been the woman, that would have been the end of it, but the South Africans were on to this other sordid little business.'

'I'd hardly call the international trafficking of children for sex a sordid little business,' Tom said.

'Don't try my patience, Furey.' She straightened her arm, raising the pistol to his eyes.

Tom thought she looked like a leopardess sizing up her prey. Like the silent predator, she had been waiting in the background, watching for her moment to strike. He glanced at Greeves again and saw his face was white with fear. Greeves had good reason to worry – Tom sensed his wife had been waiting, perhaps hoping, for this opportunity. This man who had travelled to the world's war zones in defence of British foreign policy, stared down the media and the opposition in parliament, was cowering in the face of the woman who had held his destiny in her hands for so many years.

'Why go through the whole charade of the abductions, the tapes to the media?'

'I owe nothing to my husband, Sergeant Furey. I did not, however, want my children to suffer more than they had. Also, I am a staunch believer in our government, but the Party wouldn't survive yet another sex scandal, especially one of this magnitude. Having Robert and Nick die at the hands of terrorists would only strengthen the resolve of the great unwashed British public to support their leaders in their fight against evil.'

Tom was tempted to throw the last word back at her, but he held his tongue. The woman was a zealot and he knew there was nothing more dangerous in creation. He turned to face the man with the assault rifle.

'What happened to Carla Sykes? She was part of the kidnap plot.'

Janet shrugged. 'She had a past history of involvement with drugs – as I believe you found out. There was some cocaine waiting for her in a hotel room in Mozambique – a bonus arranged by Nick as a replacement for the quantity she planted in your room. I doubt we'll hear from her again.'

Tom tried not to let the shiver show. 'And you, Doctor? When did you change sides from husband to wife?'

'Me? I never had a side. Mrs Greeves offered me money to organise the abduction of her husband. I paid for the mercenaries and sent them on their way after Mozambique. If they are caught, or ever decide to go public, all they will do is recount how their "terrorist" paymasters let them go, just before they killed their hostage. Now Mrs Greeves has offered me more money to . . .'

'To do as I say.'

'Where's Nick?' Tom asked.

'On his way here,' Janet said. 'I flew here when he told me you were closing on Robert and Pervez. I needed to get a feel for things first-hand, to see if the situation could be saved. Clearly, it cannot. I'm assuming that since you told Robert you'd sent a file to your crime-scene investigator that your South African partner knows everything as well?'

Tom shook his head. 'No. Absolutely not. All she knows is that I was on my way here, to Malawi. She has no idea about any of this . . . about you.'

'That's not true, I'm afraid,' Janet replied.

He felt his fear for Sannie and her children rising, burning, inside him.

'You *must* believe me. I didn't tell her all my suspicions, just in case something like this happened. I knew the odds were against me. She can't prove anything. You'll get away with it. Kill me and no one will know. I'll just disappear. Please believe me, Janet. I was bluffing, you know, about the letter to the investigator and the press.'

Janet shrugged. 'I thought you might be. She was given a warning, Tom, which she has failed to heed. She knows, all right.'

Tom shook his head. They had an insider. He felt a fool now, even as he learned he'd been right. He'd exposed Sannie and her family. 'Sannie has two small children. Don't leave them without a mother.' He thought he saw a moment of doubt cross her face, a slight softening. He was wrong.

'They're all together right now. You're right about not leaving the children without a mother.'

'We'll wait for Nick to get here.'

'Janet,' Greeves said. 'Tell Pervez to back off. I'm no threat to you.'

'Oh, yes you are,' she said. 'You're a threat to everything I have. But it'll be quite interesting, letting your bodyguard decide whether you should live or not. Pervez?'

The Pakistani shifted his gaze, from down the rifle's short barrel at Greeves, across to Janet. 'Yes?'

'I'll cover these two. Get Wessels on the phone.'

32

Sannie ushered the children into the hallway of the house in Boksburg. 'Henk?' She heard the captain's mobile phone ring, then his muted voice as he answered it.

She paused in the doorway of the kitchen. Wessels had his back turned to her and was nodding as he spoke. '*Ja*, I understand.' He ended the call.

'Henk, we're going. Do you want to take us, or can the uniformed guys give us a lift?'

'Sannie, it's not safe for you to go. I've just had a call from the team watching your home. There's a car that's cruised past three times. The guys on duty are lying low inside and have called for back-up. We should wait here, just until it's safe. This *skurk* is still on the loose.'

'Then we'll go to headquarters – anywhere but here. I don't want to stay here.'

'I'm going to send the guys from outside – they'll get to your place quicker than the nearest patrol car. I want you here, with me, where I can keep an eye on you and the kids.'

'Come on, man. This doesn't make sense.' Ilana tugged on her pants leg. 'Wait a minute, baby. We'll find a hotel, Henk. I'm not staying in this bloody dump.'

Wessels held up his hands, palms out. 'Sannie, please. I know this is a difficult time for you, but why don't you just go into the kitchen and make a cup of tea or something? We're stretched thin and there's a kidnapper on the loose. I can't chauffeur you and the kids around just now. And, like I said, I want to make sure you're safe.'

'Well . . .'

'That's better. I'll just go and tell the uniformed guys.'

'Come on,' Sannie said to Ilana and Christo. 'Let's see if there's any food in this place.'

'I'm pleased you're here, Mom,' Christo said, opening the refrigerator in the kitchen.

Through the window in the front lounge room Sannie could see Henk talking to the uniformed policeman. The man glanced inside, shrugged and then walked off, down the garden path, to where his comrade was getting into the white police *bakkie*.

Sannie thought the kids were holding up remarkably well, given that they'd been abducted – it seemed they hadn't initially thought Carney was a bad person, despite all she'd drummed into their heads about not going anywhere with strangers. But, according to Henk, there had been a shoot-out and the man guarding them had been killed. 'Did the gunshots scare you, my boy?'

Christo looked up at her, his faced screwed up

511

in puzzlement. 'What gunshots, Mom? I didn't hear any.'

Tom looked around the verandah. Greeves was sitting on the edge of his chair, nervously looking at Janet. Every time he tried to speak she cut him off midsentence.

Janet looked calm and resolved. Khan had just told Wessels that the Englishman knew everything, so they could not afford to leave any witnesses, anywhere. Tom hadn't met Sannie's boss in person, but he could only presume that if this was an order to get rid of her – and her children – then the Wessels in question was her superior. Khan was right-handed, and had slung his AK 47 over his right shoulder, with his hand on the pistol grip. He had worked the buttons of the cell phone with his left hand and Tom had noted the difficulty of the manoeuvre. As Tom expected, when it came time to finish the call, Khan had to look down at the satellite phone and search for the end-call button.

Khan was off to his left, about four paces away and behind him, and Greeves was in front of him, also slightly to his left. Janet was to their right, perhaps six metres distant.

Janet looked at Khan and said, 'Well?'

Both were distracted. Tom knew he had only one chance, and that Khan, armed with the rapid-firing military weapon, posed the greatest danger. He turned and ran at a crouch, bounding across the short distance between him and the Pakistani. As he drew alongside the wide-eyed Greeves he flung out his right hand. The flames on the two candles on the low coffee table, the only artificial light on the verandah, were already flickering with the sudden displacement of air, and they flew into Greeves's lap as Tom knocked the table over. Greeves yelped like a frightened child as the hot wax spattered through his trousers.

Tom heard Janet's silenced pistol cough twice as he hit Khan in a rugby tackle. He grabbed the startled man around the midriff and turned him as his charge pitched both of them over, so that the other man fell on top of him. He felt the doctor's body flinch and stiffen as a two-two slug entered him somewhere. Tom had gambled that the small-calibre bullet wouldn't penetrate through to him, and he must have been right because he felt no pain.

Khan was still alive, though, and he thrashed in pain and rage, landing a hard blow in Tom's ribs with his elbow.

Tom had studied videos of street fights, caught on security cameras, mostly in the States, and he knew that the only way to survive in a brawl like this was to unleash uncontrolled aggression. He reached around with one hand and gouged his fingers into Khan's eyeballs. He balled the other into a fist and slammed it twice, hard, into the man's kidneys. Khan relinquished control of the rifle's pistol grip to try to tear Tom's hand from his eyes. Tom seized his chance, grabbing it himself, even though the weapon was still hanging from Khan's shoulder.

In his peripheral vision he saw Greeves scuttling away, like a crab, crawling on all fours, but stopping to pick up Tom's discarded pistol. Janet was firing now, and Tom heard a bullet ricochet off the tiles, close enough to his head for a chip of stone to slice into his cheek.

Tom pulled the trigger, hoping Khan would have been undisciplined enough to have the safety set to fire. He was right. The selector was on full automatic and the long burst of eight or more rounds punched holes in the roof and shattered one of the front windows. Janet Greeves turned and ran back into the house.

Khan's breathing was ragged, and Tom could feel the strength oozing from the wounded man. Mercilessly, he punched him hard again in the stomach and rolled out from under him, unhooking the rifle in the process. Khan reached up a hand, but Tom ignored him. In the split seconds before the rage in him subsided, Tom hovered the end of the barrel near the doctor's head and curled his finger around the trigger.

No. The man was evil, a trader in human misery who had turned his back on a noble profession, but it wasn't in Tom's nature or training to execute a man in cold blood.

Tom snatched the phone from Khan's belt and slid off the deck onto the grass, about a metre below the surrounding railing. As he started to circle the lodge he looked across and saw Robert Greeves lying on the stone tiles, a pool of blood slowly ebbing from him. As Tom drew alongside the prone form, he saw the lifeless eyes staring out across the darkened lake. There was no faking this time.

Greeves had taken a bullet to the head, from his own wife's hand. The woman who had gone to such elaborate lengths to protect her family, the political party to whom she owed her allegiance, and even the man who had betrayed her, had eliminated the cause of her woes.

Tom prised Sannie's pistol from Greeves's lifeless hand and stuffed it in the waistband of his shorts.

He sat on the grass, resting the AK on the edge of the verandah, and pointed towards the entrance to the lodge through which Janet had disappeared. He turned on the satellite phone and closed his eyes for a second, trying to visualise Sannie's mobile phone number. He had called it enough times and he forced himself to remember the digits.

The phone started ringing.

'Mom, your phone's ringing!' Christo called from the kitchen. Sannie had moved to the lounge room to try to hear what Wessels was saying to the departing policemen. She looked over at her son and saw that Christo had traced the ring tone to her sports bag, which she had dumped on the floor.

'I'm coming.'

Christo hoisted the bag up onto a bar stool, behind the breakfast bar, and unzipped it. He was rummaging among her clothes. 'Here, my boy. Let me find it.'

The front door of the house opened behind her and she heard Wessels's footsteps on the polished concrete floor.

She found the phone just as it beeped, signalling she had a message.

'Sannie?' Wessels said.

She ignored him for the moment, as the voicemail service told her she had one message.

'*Sannie, it's Tom. Listen to me, this is very, very important. Wessels, your boss, is working with them . . . with the gang. You have to stay away from him. Take the kids somewhere safe and wait for me to get back from Malawi. I'm going to get on the first plane out of here and fly back, and . . .*'

'Sannie, I need to talk to you, in private,' Wessels said from behind her.

She smelled him. The cheap aftershave she'd once been prepared to overlook. She let her free hand casually fall into the sports bag. Slowly, she sifted through the clothes.

'Put the phone down, Sannie, this can't wait.'

As she turned her head, lowering the phone, she saw him casually brush his jacket to one side. She saw how the weight of the spare magazine in his coat pocket aided the movement, how it started to swing open. She glimpsed the black metal of his pistol, and saw where his fingers were heading.

Sannie's hand closed around the hilt of her dead husband's diving knife. She drew back her other hand and threw her mobile phone at Henk's head. It bounced off him, barely causing him to check his pace.

'Run!' she screamed at her kids as she pulled the knife from the bag. With her now free hand she ripped off the plastic sheath and discarded it. She lunged at Wessels and felt the blade's movement slow as it ran along the side of his belly, under his open suit jacket. 'Get out!' she said to Christo again, who was transfixed.

Wessels grunted and looked down as the red smear stained his white business shirt. There was a rent in the fabric, but Sannie thought she had only cut him, not penetrated any vital organs. She snatched back her hand to stab again, but Wessels bellowed with rage and lashed out with the back of his hand, the blow catching Sannie across the side of the head. She staggered back against the breakfast bar, clutching for support with her free hand.

Christo grabbed Ilana by the forearm and ran out the back door of the house, from the kitchen. Sannie righted herself and lunged again at Wessels, her primal protective instincts seeking to keep herself between danger and her children.

'Bitch,' he hissed, this time drawing his pistol.

She threw herself on him as he paused to rack the weapon, grabbing the slide with his left hand and pulling it back to chamber a round. Sannie stabbed blindly and felt the knife sink into flesh. Wessels toppled backwards onto the floor.

Sannie pulled on the hilt to free the blade, but the pressure inside Wessels' stomach was sucking at the steel, holding it in. She grunted with the effort, but Wessels recovered his wits. He was at least twenty kilograms heavier than she, and, even wounded, far stronger. He flung her off him with his free hand, and lashed out with his foot, kicking her in the ribs and sending her sliding another metre from him.

Wessels stood and grabbed the knife handle. He bellowed, a low, animalistic groan as he wrenched it free. A spurt of bright blood followed the terrible sucking noise and Wessels staggered, the colour draining from his face as he fought the pain. He dropped the knife, but raised his pistol at the same time. He fired once, the noise like a small explosion in the confines of the house.

Sannie's first instinct was to run out the back, but she knew that would draw the killer after her, and he would have a clear shot at either her or her kids. Instead, she stood and ran towards him, weaving as he fired another erratic shot. She hit him hard in the chest with all her weight, and pushed him onto his back again. She clawed at his eyes and grabbed his pistol hand with one of hers, trying to wrest the gun from him.

Wessels wrenched his gun hand from her clutch, drew it back and with the butt of the weapon landed a vicious blow on Sannie's temple. The force stunned her, and she slumped against him.

'Now you fucking die,' he said, wheezing with pain and the shortness of breath from her charge, which had winded him. He turned the gun so that the barrel was against her head.

'Why, Henk . . . ?' Sannie blinked to try to focus on his face. 'Why my children?'

'Khan's caretaker in the Timbavati called them, in Malawi, and told them Furey was on their tail. I tracked his border crossings through Interpol. It was only a matter of time before he found Greeves. Furey's a nobody, but if he told you, and you got the authorities here involved, then it would have all gone to shit for them. They wanted me to buy your silence, but I told them you were too *high-minded* to take a bribe. I told them the only thing that would keep you quiet was your kids' safety. Roberts *told* you not to tell me what he wanted you to do, Sannie, but you did. What kind of a fucking mother are you?'

She stared into his eyes. 'I hope hell exists.'

Christo had run outside and led his screaming little sister to a backyard shed, where he had ordered her to wait. Hearing the gunshots inside, he knew his mother was in mortal danger. He thought of his father, and the terrible, terrible memories of the funeral. He had only been little then, but he hoped he would never again have to see someone laid out in a box and then buried in the ground. He ran down the side of the house, back to the front door. It was still open. He paused. In the distance he heard police sirens. Help was coming, but how long would it take for the police to arrive? He heard a crash inside, and the sound of something or someone falling over. His mom needed him.

He crept inside and saw the pair of them, Captain Wessels and his mother, lying on the floor. His mother's boss had his gun at her head. Christo saw the bloodied knife on the floor, just behind them.

Christo hesitated. This couldn't be right. Captain Wessels was a good man. He'd heard his mother say so. Then the captain said something bad – called his mother a bad name.

Christo ran forward and scooped up the knife.

Wessels turned his head at the sound behind him and looked up into the grim-set face of the small boy.

*

Sannie watched Wessels's hand move, the squat black barrel of the pistol travelling towards her son's face.

'No!' she screamed. Half rolling, she sank her teeth into his wrist and bit down as hard as she could. The gun discharged again, nearly deafening her, but she clamped her jaws tighter, not stopping even when she felt the first spurts of blood in her mouth.

She was aware of movement above her, and a momentary reflection of light on polished stainless steel as the knife came down in an arc, and into Henk Wessels's right eye.

Tom heard a moan from inside the lodge.

He wiped the sweat from his brow with the back of his hand. Khan had stopped his crying – for good, he thought. Tom looked up over the raised deck of the verandah and heard the groaning again.

He'd tried three times to get a number for the Malawian police, first at Cape Maclear, and then at headquarters in Lilongwe, but each time he'd got one – from UK directory assistance who put him through to Malawi – the number was either wrong or simply rang off.

Janet Greeves had shown she was ready to kill, and he didn't fancy going into a darkened building to flush her out. His strategy was to sit tight until daylight and try either to negotiate with her, then take her into custody, or keep trying until he made contact with the local police. The other unknown was Nick Roberts. He was supposedly en route, and Tom tightened his hand on the pistol grip of Khan's AK 47 in anticipation of that showdown.

The satellite phone rang.

Tom looked at the screen and saw the caller identification had been blocked.

'Hello,' he said into the handset.

'Khan?'

There was a noise behind the voice, like the whining of a motor. Tom turned the phone away from him slightly, to muffle his voice. 'Yes.'

'The sun will shine on those who stand.'

Shit, Tom thought. It was obviously a coded challenge, and Tom had no idea of what the reply was. 'What did you say?'

'Is that you, Furey?'

Tom said nothing.

Nick laughed on the other end of the crackly satellite connection. 'I heard the gunfire. I wondered if it had all gone pear-shaped. If you've got Khan's phone, then he's dead. Have you met our Janet yet?'

'It's over, Nick.'

'Yes, right, Mr Bruce Willis, sir. Next you'll be telling me you've got me surrounded and a crack Malawian police weapons team are on their way.' Nick laughed again.

Tom heard the motor die, then held the handset away from him. He was getting the noise in stereo. 'You're close, aren't you,' he said. 'I can hear you.'

'Well, if you've got the phone, you've probably got Khan's AK as well, so I ain't coming ashore. Is Janet still alive?'

Tom said nothing. He raised his head to look out

over the lake and saw a darkened boat, betrayed by the glimmer of its wake, which hadn't yet settled. It shone like a pathway leading back to the mainland. Tom moved at a crouch, to the trees between the lodge and the first bungalow, and followed the cover down towards the water.

'If she isn't dead, you should kill her. That way, those spoiled brats of hers will inherit their millions and think both their dear old mum and their sick-fuck old man were killed by the big bad terrorists. Everyone will be happy.'

Tom was near the shoreline. He could see Nick now, silhouetted against the sky, talking on his phone.

'Where are you, Tom? She's paying me a lot of money, matey. I could give you a share if you keep quiet. You want to know the rest of that password "the sun will shine on those who stand"? The rest of it is: "before it shines on those who kneel under them". I'm still standing, Tom, and you're still fucking kneeling. Come stand with me.'

Tom wanted to keep Nick standing, talking in the boat. 'Why, Nick? Was it just the money? Was it Janet?'

'Hah! Nice try. It was both – and neither.'

Tom paused. The way Nick had tailed off into silence made him think the man wanted to talk, to unburden himself.

'The wife was desperate – horny as a fucking rabbit – and also determined to keep Greeves in politics. I didn't say no to the sex, and I needed the money after my missus split. But there was more to it.

Crossing the line. Knowing I could now get away with whatever the fuck I wanted to when on tour – booze, coke, women. More. And no one could hold me accountable. If Khan's dead – or Greeves, or Janet, or all of them – then you know what I'm talking about when I say it's a rush. It's the fucking ultimate, isn't it? The power to take life. I'll tell you what, Tom . . . if you keep quiet about me I'll give you a hundred grand. Pounds, not dollars.'

Tom stayed silent.

'Of course, Thomas, if you shop me, I'll find you. I'll fucking do you, and I'll rape that stuck-up cunt Van Rensburg in front of her children before I cut her throat. What'll it be?'

'Come into shore. Let's talk about it,' Tom said. He understood now – Nick was mad.

There was silence for a few seconds. 'Nah. Tommy's a good boy, aren't you, Tommy? Wouldn't be here otherwise. The others would have offered you money, too. You're the white knight, aren't you, Tommy? Nope. I'm going to have to go to South Africa now and finish that bitch off myself.'

Tom heard the engine start. Nick would get back to the mainland before he could. If the Malawian police didn't catch him, it was feasible that he could get back to South Africa – to Sannie and her children – before Tom could reach them.

Tom placed the phone down beside him and raised the assault rifle to his shoulder. He looked down the open sights and took a breath. It was a long shot, but not impossible. About two hundred metres, he reckoned. He'd put a bullet into the centre mass of a target at longer ranges. He took a breath and curled his finger around the trigger. Nick bent to reach for something, and Tom heard the boat's engine roar to life.

As Nick stood straight again, Tom started to squeeze. Before he could fire the shot he was knocked forwards, as if a prize fighter had come up behind him and punched him square between the shoulderblades.

Janet Greeves shuffled along the verandah of Pervez Khan's luxury lodge, the two-two silenced pistol hanging limply by her side. 'Nick . . .' she croaked.

The nose of the speedboat lifted and the pitch of the engine escalated to a whine as it left a fantail of spray behind it.

Tom gasped for air, trying to refill his winded lungs. Each gulp brought a new stab of pain. He tried to reach up his back with his hand, to feel for blood. His fingertips touched a piece of still-hot metal, but there was no wetness.

From Christo van Rensburg Snr's stash of security gear in the garage, Tom had also borrowed a slimline body armour vest, which he'd donned under his long-sleeve T-shirt. It couldn't have stopped a shot from an AK 47, but the two-two round had done little more than wind and bruise him. Tom rolled painfully over onto his side and picked up his AK 47.

'Put down your weapon, Janet,' he called to her, the words causing him more pain.

She looked at him. 'He's gone.' She coughed, and blood oozed from her mouth, down her chin.

Tom saw the soaking red stain on the right side of

her blouse. He must have hit her with his first spray of fire from the AK, while he was wrestling with Khan. 'Let me get you to a doctor, Janet. Put the gun down.'

She turned to him and dropped the pistol. Tom stood, his strength returning, and jogged across to her. When he was three steps short, she collapsed to her knees. She had an arm outstretched, towards the lake, and the disappearing boat.

'I lied,' she croaked, as Tom took her in his arms.

'Hush.'

'I loved him. Not Robert . . .'

Tom held her as she died.

Epilogue

'Farming life agrees with you,' Sannie said as she ran a hand over his bare tanned bicep.

Dressed in a short-sleeve blue and tan bush shirt and khaki shorts, Tom was at least starting to look the part of a lowveld farmer. 'It certainly agrees with you,' he said, dropping a hand to her firm bottom, caressing it through the thin cotton of her sundress. She giggled and slapped his hand away, then turned her face to his so he could kiss her.

They resumed trudging up the hill, the rich red earth clinging to Tom's boots and squelching through Sannie's toes. Since he'd seen his first cobra he always wore hiking boots on the farm, but no amount of persuasion could get Sannie or the kids to follow suit.

It had been two months since the shoot-out in Malawi and Sannie's harrowing fight with Wessels. Christo had been to see a child psychologist a few times but, apart from an occasional nightmare, he seemed to be coping. Both Tom and Sannie had told him over and over that he had saved his mother's and sister's lives, and that his father would have been proud of him.

Still, Tom knew the boy would wrestle with his demons for some time, perhaps for the rest of his life in some form or another.

Tom had returned to England as soon as he knew Sannie, Elise and the kids were safely ensconced on the banana farm they had bought outside Hazyview, not far from the one Sannie had grown up on. Even so, he had spent the bare minimum amount of time in London, where the first snows had fallen more as grey, gritty sleet.

Shuttleworth had escorted him to a meeting with the Prime Minister in which he had been assured that, subject to signing a confidentiality agreement in which he promised not to mention any of the circumstances of Greeves's death, he would be reinstated in his old job and considered favourably for promotion.

Tom had declined, settling instead for early retirement. When his home in Highgate was sold they would be able to pay off the bridging loan on the farm and live very comfortably for many years to come. Tom bagged his cold-weather clothes for charity and packed the album of pictures of him and Alexandra, which Sannie had said she wanted to see. He'd kissed the silver-framed photo of her taken on their wedding day and said, 'You'd like her, Alex.' He'd boarded the evening BA flight to Johannesburg with no regrets.

He knew nothing about banana farming, but Sannie and Elise were teaching him what they knew, and their neighbours were filling in the gaps. He'd thought they would eventually move to the coast – perhaps

Durban or Cape Town – but Sannie had rejected both of those options. The longer he stayed, however, the more he thought of the farm as somewhere he could live, rather than just hide out.

'When are you going to stop wearing this?' Sannie asked, lifting the tail of his shirt which he habitually wore hanging out to hide the Glock in its holster.

'You know when,' he said.

Tom slept fitfully.

The electricity was out – again. Whether it was load-shedding or the failure of an ageing substation, he wouldn't know until the morning, but either way it annoyed him. He had no regrets about moving to Africa, but it was sometimes not easy learning to live without things he took for granted in England.

A mosquito buzzed around his ears. No matter how often he slapped himself, he never hit it.

Sannie lay on her back, her chest rising and falling rhythmically. Her golden hair was in disarray, one bare leg sticking out from under the sheet. They had made love when they'd gone to bed. If she'd said she wanted to move to a malarial swamp in the upper reaches of the Amazon, he would have gone with her. He loved her.

He smacked his cheek again, swore quietly, then got up.

He padded on bare feet to the farmhouse's kitchen. Instinctively he flicked the light switch, but nothing happened. He turned on the rechargeable battery-powered camping lantern on the bench. Inside the fridge was a bottle of water that was still cold. He poured a glass and moved to the window to drink it. He looked out over the seemingly endless rows of banana trees and marvelled at how his life had changed. For the better.

Roxy's basket was empty. He wondered if she was off chasing a bush baby – one of the small, bushy-tailed primates that lived in the native trees near the house and cried like human babies most nights. But all was quiet.

Normally the big Rhodesian ridgeback was good at sensing movement, and would have been at the kitchen door, tail wagging, hoping for a midnight snack. She only barked at black people – a legacy of the former white owners of the farm who had trained her – but she was usually alert to anyone who was up and about after hours.

Tom took the keys from their hook inside the pantry and unlocked the door. He reached for a mosquito that had hitched a ride on his shoulder blade, missed and scratched. 'Roxy?' he called softly.

He walked along the verandah that surrounded the nineteen-fifties whitewashed house. He loved sitting out here with Sannie in the afternoons, watching over the rim of his beer glass the sun go down. He didn't want to wake the children, but he was sure Roxy would find him by the time he reached Ilana's bedroom.

He was about to turn back towards the kitchen, giving up on the stupid dog, when he saw the curtain.

Ilana's window was open.

He lengthened his stride. The fabric hung limply out of the window. The sliding flyscreen should have been down, and the strut that held the window open latched firmly in place. Sannie checked it every night. She was more careful about protecting her children than her husband-to-be from insects.

Tom felt his heart beat faster. He held the curtain to one side and looked in.

'Ilana!'

He retraced his steps and ran inside. Sannie already had her shorts on and was sitting on the bed pulling a T-shirt over her head when he entered the room. 'What's wrong, Tom? Did you call me?'

Tom moved to his side and pulled the Glock from under his pillow. As always, it was already racked. He took a breath. 'Ilana's gone.'

Sannie put a hand to her mouth. 'My baby! Christo?'

'He's . . .'

'Mommy? Where's Ilana?' Christo walked into their room. 'She's not in her bed.'

Tom saw the dawning fear and realisation on the little boy's face. 'Is it that man?'

Tom had his mobile phone out and was dialling a number. He held it up to his ear as Sannie opened her wardrobe and reached under a pile of winter jerseys. She slapped a magazine into the butt of her RAP 401 and cocked it.

'Mommy?'

'Mommy and Tom are going to look for Ilana, Christo. I want you to . . .'

Elise walked into the bedroom, tying a robe in front.

Tom had the phone to his ear and was waiting for

an answer. 'Sannie, you're not thinking straight. You stay here and look after Christo. I'll get . . .' He held up a hand to silence her protest. 'Hello, Duncan? You're awake already?'

Duncan Nyari had left his job as a guide at Tinga and was helping Tom and Sannie out on the farm, and running a small freelance tour business from the old manager's house, where he now lived. 'Birds making too much noise down the fence, Tom. Thought it might be that leopard that killed the dog on old Du Toit's farm.'

Tom told him Ilana was gone and ordered him to come to the house to help him look for spoor.

'*Yebo*,' Duncan replied. 'I've got the shotgun.'

Sannie took Christo's hand. 'Come, put some clothes on, my boy.'

'I have to get you to safety,' Tom said. He dialled the emergency number for the police.

Sannie looked up at him. 'I'll take Mom and Christo to the Du Toits next door. Then I'm coming back to help you.'

Tom nodded. He didn't want any of them out of his sight, but he and Duncan had to pick up the trail of whoever had taken Ilana. She was a happy little girl and he was under no illusions that she might simply have run away from home and would come back when she was hungry. Tom got through to the police and told them what had happened.

He walked outside with Sannie, Elise and Christo, and put them into the Land Rover. When he looked at the terror on the little boy's face, he hated himself for bringing more misery to this family. No, his family. They were his responsibility now.

'Call me when you get to the Du Toit farm and stay there, Sannie.'

The four-by-four blew diesel smoke as she started the engine and revved it. 'Don't tell me what to do. Once I've dropped Mom and Christo, I'm coming . . .'

Two shots from the darkness made Elise scream. Christo started to cry. The noise came from down the hill, away from the track that led to the main gate.

'Go!'

The wheels spun for a second until the chunky tyres dug into the mud, and the Land Rover hurtled away from the house.

Tom had seen the footprints in the mud, but had not pointed them out to Sannie, in case she decided to send her mother off with Christo and join him on the hunt. He needed to know that they, at least, would live, even if he couldn't save Ilana. Sannie wouldn't think that way, though.

Tom raised his weapon and moved towards the noise, staying in the first few rows of banana trees rather than using the pathway. It didn't take him long to find Roxy's body. She lay on the path, her throat cut. The kidnapper must have lured her close – perhaps with food – and been ruffling her head, keeping her silent, when he cut her throat. Tom knew it was a white man. An Englishman.

Further along, he heard groaning from the grove on the other side of the path. 'Duncan?'

'Tom . . . I've been hit.'

'Stay quiet; save your strength,' Tom whispered.

He peered out from the banana trees and looked down the track. It seemed clear, and he sprinted from cover and slid in the mud to Duncan's side. Duncan winced as Tom opened his bloodstained shirt. 'Shoulder and gut.' He pulled off his T-shirt and pressed it to Duncan's stomach wound, which was the more serious of the injuries. 'Hold this. I'll call an ambulance.'

'He . . . he has Ilana . . . He is a white man.'

'I know. I'm going to get him.'

'Tom . . . she was not moving. He was carrying her over his shoulder. I couldn't get a clean shot.'

Tom nodded. He called the ambulance service and spoke quickly, quietly, to the operator, then hung up.

'That way,' Duncan croaked and raised a hand to point. 'He is running.'

Leaves slapped Tom's face as he ran parallel to the track, following the lengthened stride of his quarry's footprints in the mud beside him.

Sannie stopped the Land Rover outside the front gate, got out, and told her mother to get behind the wheel.

'But Tom said . . .'

'Just do it, Mom! Take Christo next door and stay there.' Sannie shut the door and walked down the fence line, her body hunched like that of a stalking lioness tensed for the kill. Her mother drove off into the night, in the opposite direction from where the gunfire had come.

The man, or men, must have climbed or cut the fence, as there were no fresh footprints on the driveway, and the gate had been locked. If Sannie found the person who had taken Ilana, she would kill him.

Off to her right, the farmhouse, visible on the hill,

was still in darkness. Good old Eskom, she thought. If the power came on now, the security lights placed at intervals along the fence might illuminate her. She prayed, for the first time ever, for the darkness to continue.

Sannie saw the break in the wire mesh and stopped to listen.

Footsteps.

She heard rustling in the banana trees and dropped to one knee. Steadying her shooting hand by cupping it in her left, she aimed through the gap in the fence at the noise.

Was he carrying Ilana in his arms or over his shoulder? Sannie would have little time to decide whether to aim for the head or the centre body mass. She was a good shot. She would not miss.

Sannie could hear the man's laboured breathing now. She saw the hand holding the pistol. She started to squeeze the trigger, taking up the slack.

'Tom!'

He broke from the cover of the banana trees and stopped in front of her, holding his weapon up. 'Jesus, you scared me.'

Sannie stood and fought to calm her breathing. She looked at the ground and cursed herself for not having done so before. 'He's already gone.'

They scanned the mud and flattened grass more closely, then walked across the tarred road. There were no corresponding footprints on the other side. 'He's headed up the road,' Tom said.

They started to jog, side by side, on opposite sides of the darkened country road, but slowed when they heard the revving of an engine, the grinding of gears.

A double-cab *bakkie* crested the rise in front of them. Its headlights were out and the driver was weaving, as if he wasn't concentrating fully.

Sannie held up her free hand, gesturing for the driver to stop, but the vehicle accelerated towards them, its engine whining. 'Tyres, Tom,' Sannie called. 'Ilana's somewhere inside.'

Tom nodded and stopped, feet apart, his right hand resting on his left. Sannie mirrored his stance and they opened fire as the vehicle bore down on them.

The *bakkie* jinked left and right, and when Tom saw Nick Roberts's wide-eyed face he wanted to put the next bullet through his head, but it wasn't worth the risk. If Nick lost control completely, Ilana might die. He fired twice more, and knew that either his or Sannie's shots had found their mark. Rubber screamed on bitumen, and the pick-up slid off the road, ploughing through mud and grass, and heading for the gum trees planted on the other side of the road from Tom and Sannie's bananas.

'No!' Sannie yelled, as she ran down the embankment after the vehicle.

The pick-up slammed into a tree trunk and the force of the impact activated the driver's side air bag. The vehicle's horn blared continuously and steam hissed from the ruptured radiator.

Tom was at the driver's side, pulling the door open with one hand and covering Roberts with the other. 'Out!'

'Ilana? Ilana?'

Tom glanced in the back as he dragged Nick out

of the car by his shirt collar, and saw that Sannie had found her daughter lying on the floor in the back of the truck.

Roberts knelt on the ground. When Tom had grabbed him he'd been dazed, but now he started to laugh.

'She's breathing. She's alive, Tom!' Sannie clutched the little girl, to her breast. She took her cell phone from her shorts and called her mother, telling her to bring the Land Rover.

Tom held his Glock under Nick's chin as he quickly searched him for weapons. 'What did you do to the girl, you bastard?'

Roberts shook his head, as if to clear it. 'Relax, relax. It's only chloroform. She'll wake up soon.'

'His pistol's in the cab, Sannie,' Tom said. Still holding her child, she retrieved Nick's weapon from the front-passenger-side floor.

'Why, Nick?' was all Tom could think to say as he stood and took a pace back.

Roberts smiled up at him, then shrugged. 'Man's got to eat, Tom. You fucked my life up, old mate. But I reckoned I could earn enough to live nicely from the sale of a little white girl.'

Tom closed the gap between them again and used the butt of his pistol to smack the side of the man's jaw.

Nick coughed blood. 'My, my. Gone native, have we? The old Tom Furey wouldn't have roughed up a prisoner. But he would have gone running to the guv'nor if he'd caught someone else teaching a protester some manners.'

Tom shook his head.

Sannie knelt in the grass behind Tom and lay Ilana down. She smoothed the fair hair from her eyes and leant over her, listening to her breathing. Satisfied the child was alive, she kissed her and stood.

'So, what happens now, Thomas?' Nick asked.

'We call the police, and you go to jail for the murder of Precious Tambo. There'll also be some questions about the death of Carla Sykes from an overdose of contaminated drugs.'

Nick started shaking his head, and his face broke into a broad grin. 'If that's the best you've got on me, I'll never do serious time. They'll have enough to do me on conspiracy charges, but that's assuming the UK government wants a public trial. I haven't read anything about old Greeves in the papers, Tom, since you got back to Africa. That means they're keeping it hush-hush. What did they do, buy you off with a pension? And no one here cares about that slag, Carla. Nah. You've got nothing on me in South Africa, except for maybe breaking and entering.'

'Kidnapping,' said Sannie.

He laughed again. 'Attempted kidnapping? Three to five years, tops.'

'Shut up, Nick, you're boring me.'

'He could be right, Tom,' Sannie whispered.

'Listen to the lady, Thomas, she's a smart one.' Nick shrugged. 'I don't care. I'll do my time, wherever or whatever it is. And then I'll come back and find you. And if your kids help put me in stir, Sannie, I'll track them down and kill them when I get out, and that's a promise.'

Sannie raised her pistol so that it, like Tom's weapon, was pointed at Nick's face. She looked at Tom. He glanced at her briefly, not wanting to take his eyes off Nick for too long, and nodded.

Captain Isaac Tshabalala scratched his bald head. He still hadn't forgiven Furey and van Rensburg for disobeying him and running off to Mozambique while he was trying to conduct an investigation into the British government minister's disappearance from Tinga.

He stood beside his patrol car, looking up the hill at the farmhouse where the former police officers both now lived, surrounded by neat rows of banana trees. It was ironic and mildly annoying that after being transferred from Skukuza to Hazyview, one of his first major cases was the investigation of a shooting outside this pair's property.

One man was dead and another was wounded, though the doctor in Nelspruit said Duncan Nyari would recover.

Furey and Sannie stood beside each other at the end of the deck, their bodies touching as they leaned on the railing and looked out over their farm. Furey waved at Isaac, who waved back. The Englishman then took his woman's hand in his. They had obviously had a harrowing night.

It was unusual that the villain in this crime was a white man. An armed offender had broken into the remote farm – there was clear evidence of where the man had cut the security fence and entered – and a gun battle had ensued after the owners surprised him attempting to abduct a child. Furey and van Rensburg had stopped the kidnapper's vehicle, and the man had allegedly fired at them and attempted to escape on foot with the child. The two ex-police officers had returned fire and killed him.

A niggling feeling told Isaac there was more to this crime than met the eye, but he was happy to see these two troubled souls at peace for the moment. The older woman, van Rensburg's mother, bustled noisily into the house and Sannie's two children ran past her.

Tom and Sannie turned and hugged the children.

Isaac put his cap back on, got into his car, and drove out the front gate.

Acknowledgements

A very good friend of mine, who wishes to remain anonymous, has worked for many years as a protection officer for the London Metropolitan Police. In the course of his career, he has provided close personal protection for politicians and other important persons who are household names.

Through the course of several conversations and emails, he explained to me the ins and outs of his job and answered dozens of questions. He checked the manuscript and, as well as correcting my many misinterpretations of what he's told me, proved to be a ruthlessly efficient apprentice copy editor. Thank you.

Tinga Legends Private Game Lodge, and its sister lodge, Tionga Narina, are real places. I was introduced to them by Robert and Lesley Engels, friends from Cape Town, who suggested I set the relevant scenes of this book in existing locations. Thanks to both of you for a wonderful stay and a very good idea.

I hope my descriptions of Tinga Legends Lodge do it credit, as it really is one of the most beautiful places it's ever been my pleasure to visit. Check it out at www.tinga.co.za

Fortunately (or unfortunately, depending on your point of view) no one I've met at either of the Tinga lodges remotely resembles the entirely fictitious and extremely bad

Carla Sykes.

Thanks, also, to Tinga's real-life marketing director, Ian Taylor.

Although I travelled to London to research the scenes set in the UK, my friend Ray Philpott helped me fill in the gaps in my failing memory and incomplete notes when it came to some of the places described in the book. Thanks, mate.

Hannelie Dargie, a friend and loyal reader, and Tracey Hawthorne, a friend and scathingly honest critic, both read the manuscript in search of Afrikaans and other South African-specific 'howlers'. Any that remain are Tracey's fault.

I have Dr Grahame Hammond to thank for medical information relating to head wounds, and for keeping me sane during the months we spent together in the army, in Afghanistan in 2002.

Thanks, too, to former crime scene investigator Brian Dargie, who helped me stage-manage some deaths and provided lots of gory details about bodily fluids.

My good friend John MacGregor and his brother, Rod, joined Nicola and me in Africa while I was writing *Silent Predator* and accompanied us on a drive to Mozambique. Although their car hire company might not wish to know the details, John and Rod proved it was possible to drive the Kruger-to-Xai Xai road in a small two-wheel-drive rental car.

I cannot do what I do without the love and support of my wife, Nicola, who has to suffer the long bouts of silence and brooding fits when things aren't going to plan. My aim in life is to be good to her as she is to me.

As always, my mother, Kathy, and mother-in-law, Sheila, proved to be excellent proofreaders and I thank them all for their help, and for having my wife and me.

It's true that writing is a lonely business, which is why it's nice to recieve a friendly email or call once in a while, or share a drink or three with other people who know what it's like. My friends Peter Watt, David Rollins and Di Blacklock are all wonderful people as well as brilliant writers, so go and buy their books.

Five books on, and it's still hard for me to believe how lucky I was not only to be published, but to end up working with such a professional, friendly bunch of people at Pan Macmillan.

Thanks to Jane Wood and everyone at Quercus. Great to be working with you. And thanks to Isobel Dixon, my agent at Blake Friedmann.

And, most of all, since you've made it this far, thank you.